I0772136

BATTLE
TIDES

Also by S. David Acuff

- Fiction novels -

Historian's Proper
High School Masquerade
Slay Bells Ring
The Wrestling Girl

- Nonfiction books -

Semi-Centurion:
What Doesn't Kill You Makes You Funnier

- Screenplays -

Masquerade
Moved
Psychedelic Foreclosure
Restoration
The Christian Zombie Movie

BATTLE TIDES

By S. David Acuff

BATTLE TIDES
v 1.0

© Copyright 2024 | S. David Acuff
All rights reserved.

No part of this book may be reproduced in any form or by any
electronic or mechanical means, including information storage and
retrieval systems, without prior written permission,
except in the case of brief quotations in critical
articles and reviews.

BRAVOBAY BOOKS
Los Angeles, California
bravobaybooks@gmail.com

ISBN: 979-8-9888293-2-4 (hardback)
979-8-9888293-3-1 (paperback)
IMPRINT: BravoBay Books

DEDICATION

First, to my three Jedi Princesses who
are, by far, my greatest legacy…

Caitlyn - a mama bear protector with a
righteous heart and a keen vision

Alexis - a lyrical poet with a full and
prophetic heart of worship

Raegan - the bravest explorer and the
wielder of truth and jokes

To my editor Bryan Thomas Schmidt
for holding my feet to the fire with his invaluable
industry knowledge and craftsmanship

To an unbelievable roster of SciFi mentors:
George Lucas, Philip K. Dick, Steven Spielberg,
Ridley Scott, Denis Villeneuve, John Kessel, Stan Lee,
Orson Scott Card, Michael Crichton, Andy Weir,
and Tolkien & Lewis…

…thank you for making the
future so real.

TABLE OF CONTENTS

*"What maketh a man, is it the mind,
the body, or the soul?
What maketh a man, is it not desire?"*

Tomos v. KACorps hearings
NeoTokyo | 2522

- Prologue -
TEST FLIGHT

Planet Earth, Miramar Settlement, 2415AD

Conditions were pretty damn perfect.

Above the salt line of the Miramar Settlement, it was 16 degrees Celsius. The Caribbean airstream pushed lazily across the inlet and swept long-tailed sea condors along its thermals. These nasty-spirited fire-birds were descended from the first batch imported after the original Outworld expeditions a hundred years ago. They'd been a menace to the aquatic life here since their early arrival, and today they returned to their favorite hunting ground using their favorite hunting technique.

That is to say, an alpha would swoop down, disappear below the salty brine, and resurface with a tuna or a dolphin squirming in its talons. Then, a protector condor would circle low, blowing a fiery ring to ward off the rest of the pack and isolate their mate, who would simultaneously feast and chum the waters. This, of course, brought the larger sharks to the surface, only to be snatched high into the air, and soon the entire pack was dining. Occasionally, the sharks would score a sea condor, but more often than not, the advantage was aerial; the evolved flight tactics favored the alien birds of prey.

High above, puffy cumulus clouds hung in the sky like one of those CiCi-D paintings from the Colonial Rise, just after the Third World War, circa 2264. But that was over 150 years ago. The difference being—unlike her brilliant and peaceful oil renderings eschewing man-made tech—this perfect vista was pockmarked with four menacing Ranger skiffs hovering in a delta formation just off-shore.

Their matte-black elongated fuselages and short, fat wings made it obvious from this distance how the elite group got their handle: the SkyCross squadron. Up close, their Tartan-Ballard engines hummed and whirred electronically as internal gyros fought the up-drafts and crosswinds to anchor them all securely in a precise 3D airspace.

Below the waterline, the ocean was calm. The crystal-blue waters created high visibility for fifty me-ters. Sea life swam in and around an active underwater city. This was Miramar, the top-secret test facility of the Kytos Alliance's Air Corps. But its formal military des-ignation had long since given way to the nickname giv-en by the handful of test jockeys that even knew it ex-isted: *Bravo Bay*.

A brand-new D/U/G was moored beyond the base, tracking sea life, area conditions, and a thousand-per-second ever-shifting variables. The *Defensive Underwater Guardian* was a scientist, gatekeeper, weatherman, and, in case of attack, first line of defense. Although the AI Mother Drone was anchored in place by a retractable leash, the forty-plus micro-drone swarm it housed was highly weaponized and coordinated efficiently, effectively, and autonomously by D/U/G.

In its signature deadpan style, D/U/G relayed a status report to Bravo Bay HQ: *'It's exactly twelve minutes before high tide and a statistically acceptable day to rattle death's door.'*

The AI's message pinged the Heads-Up Display (HUD) of the day's fresh meat—a 24-year-old captain named Michael "Dash" Strouthers. *'Roger that, DUG,'* he mentally relayed back as he squeezed his six-two frame into the cockpit of the H2X-Ø Mustang and latched an umbilical cord into the life support Relay at the base of his neck. Here in docking pod four, the vehicle looked to Dash like it was relaxing in a giant jacuzzi, like an athlete the morning before the big game. As the turbulent water levels outside the ship rapidly engulfed the wings, he cinched his five-point harness into place across his chest and lap. The final seats hadn't even surfaced from the design labs yet, so this retrofitted HX-45 chair had been jerry-rigged into place.

There was no rear seat for a RIO, either, just an empty hole. It was just as well because, per Bravo Bay protocol, the NAV for this inaugural sortie should be vacant. With the recent upheaval from the Draccario secession from KACorps, hot-shot pilots were even harder to come by. Every available driver wanted a piece of the new Mustang, but it was a finicky ride. Nobody but Dash came close to passing SIM quals.

From the thigh pocket of his flight suit, he pulled out a small, weathered flight log notebook. He kissed his ancient lucky charm and slid it into the scrum box. The little chamber was currently empty, but after an air-sub went active-duty, it would be outfitted with the standard emergency toolkit, some rations, a homing beacon, a weapon, etc.

Next, he triggered the canopy. The dual inter-locking halves slid forward and back into place and sealed with a small sucking *swish* sound. Now that the sea-foam smell was trapped outside the glass, Dash breathed in the slight tinge of a mechanical hydraulic mixture that was so familiar in these new rides hot off the factory floor.

The ComLink in Dash's HUD crackled to life again with a friendly female face. *'Captain Strouthers, radio check. Radio check one, check one,'* relayed Major Stephanie "Step" Phillips from her position up in Flight Control.

"Radio check: affirmative, Step. Readin' you loud and clear," Dash replied. "Though I won't be gettin' used to someone else's words rattlin' around in my head, that I won't."

'It's devilish,' he added over the HUD link.

"Roger that," Step said with a knowing chuckle. Dash watched her twist her dirty blond hair into a messy bun and pin it up with a five-inch prong. Knowing her, it was not just a fashion accessory but a makeshift weapon if needed. Step continued, "All the new toys…"

'*…and all the glitching bugs to work out,*' she added, saving her private commentary for their encrypted mind-link Relay.

* * *

In contrast to the bubble of silence inside the Mustang, Flight Control was an echo chamber abuzz with activity. A half-dozen international personnel monitored flight gear, network traffic, atmospheric and vehicular stats, and especially those damned pesky sea birds who had picked one helluva spot for their morning picnic. Step watched another bull shark get plucked clean out of the water. She sighed, annoyed. "Ranger Lead, who we got top-side today," she asked into her headset.

"It's Gigsby, ma'am," Ranger Traci "Gigsby" Riggins confirmed as her face popped up on Step's feed.

"Gigsby, keep an eye on the sky trash and barbecue their asses if they swarm any closer to our reef."

"With pleasure, Step," Gigsby flashed a thumbs up and a smile. That'd be a fun order to fulfill if it got the green light.

'*Major,*' D/U/G chimed in, '*I could swarm and reduce the flight hazards to negligible levels in 22.3 seconds if cleared for live ordinance, ma'am.*'

"Negative. Stand down, DUG." Step rubbed a bandaged thumbnail along her brow. "Last thing KA-Corps wants is for their trillion-dollar octo-brain to be used for a glorified duck hunt."

'*Heard,*' D/U/G said with an exaggerated sigh.

"Maybe," Step offered the temperamental AI, "we find you some other target practice later on if you're up for a training op?"

'*Absolutely,*' D/U/G perked up. '*That would really skimmel my wibblers, Major.*'

"Okay, that is not even a—never mind. Dash, you all zipped up?" She asked as her eyes flicked across his ship readouts for the twentieth time. They hadn't changed. All indicators showed the cockpit seal was solid, and all systems were optimal.

"Aye," Dash answered. "Snug as a bug."

"About damn time. All right, then, what say we light this tuna?" Step circled a finger in the air to her comms team. "Last looks everyone," she added, off mic, as they leaned into their monitors. "Go time."

* * *

"Aye," Dash said, punching a button labeled スタート, which he knew to translate "start" from the original Japanese manufacturers.

Start.

Humble beginnings to such an auspicious event along man's quest for air superiority. The Wright Brothers, Chuck Yeager, Alan Shepard, Quantile Fisk, Dav'n Jess, and now Dash Strouthers. Faster. Stronger. Farther. Longer. Pushing that envelope. Bleeding that edge.

Fwooooom.

Goosebumps formed on his arms as the whole cockpit shimmied and purred to life. Readouts, monitors, and heads-up displays cycled around Dash through startup sequences and settled one by one into ready status. "Not bad. Cold boot to systems ready in 3.4 seconds."

* * *

"That's almost 5 seconds faster than last week," Step tapped some info directly onto her screen, and maintenance logs popped up. "What did you do?"

"Talked with Gator, and we decided we'd bypass the Break Cycle all together since it's pullin' the same as the G12 adapters."

"Smart." Step called up the G12 specs on her monitor. *'You know, the brass at KACorps R&D will be thrilled to know you've outfoxed their brightest eggheads with a workaround,'* she relayed.

* * *

'They don't know the half of it.' Dash relayed back as he chuckled to himself, *'It'll be worth the demerits.'* He watched the Seabee performing his final launch tasks on his wing. The fresh-faced kid removed the final fuel hose and retracted the gangplank from the H2X. Stepping back through a porthole, he closed the hatch behind him, lifted off a safety latch, and punched a big red button. Yellow lights accompanied a warning buzzer. Two-minutes. Dash had watched this same process a hundred times during training.

"Flooding the tubes," the Seabee announced to everyone on comms. Dash could see he was a little nervous—hell, they all were—so when the kid looked up at him in the cockpit, he held a hand up and gestured for him to "calm down." The kid nodded and smiled. He was hitting all the right marks and doing a great job. They all knew details mattered. As did grace under pressure. It's what brought people home alive. Dash was thankful he had such a highly trained crew to have his six. Even the ones that looked like they hadn't hit puberty yet.

He checked at his foot pedals. Down below, he could see the walkway underneath that led to the ship's living quarters. Once fully operational, this long-range fighter would comfortably hold two crew members and four extra passengers. On long flights, he'd be able to lower his seat from the cockpit and access some fairly comfortable R&R space. Not luxurious like some of the executive yachts he'd seen. KACorps wouldn't allow for that. But they'd be adequate.

Looking out over the fuselage, Dash watched the floodgates open all the way and water levels rise even faster around the mid-sized fighter. It was odd to see a naked fighter jet, totally void of the standard marks or colors of any specific Ranger unit. This one was much larger than any of its predecessors because of the new triple-engine build.

It was the first time they'd all seen the new Cyrenium shell, too, which wrapped around the ship like a smooth and curvaceous protective skin. It was pliable enough to repulse space frag and small arms fire, yet durable enough to withstand the bottom of the ocean or the most ornery hyper-gate. Word on the street was it could punch through a mountain, but Dash didn't want to test that theory on its maiden voyage out.

"Damn, that bird's sexy, Dash. Bring her home in one piece, yeah?" The Seabee smiled through the portal to Dash, adding a hang-loose, all-ready signal. This was something the Bravo flights had adapted years ago, as opposed to the traditional thumbs up on the more regimented carriers.

"Y'ain't seen nothing yet, mate. Hold on to your knickers." Dash smiled back, returning the sign through his cockpit window just before it was engulfed under a swirling agitation of sea foam.

Dash turned his focus to his instruments, checking and double-checking them. Finally, he pulled a pair of olive-colored Nomex flight gloves from his other thigh pocket and wiggled his fingers into place, snug as a second skin. He slid his left hand over the throttle controls, and his right hand gripped the flight stick. If it weren't for the climate conditioning, his palms would have been a sweaty mess. While these controls, augmented by the mental Relay, had definitely improved since the first trials, for a while they were notoriously touchy. And buggy as hell. He remembered at least two SIM rides that he'd crashed and flooded because he was so acclimated to the sticky controls of the older HX-45, the fastest and most maneuverable ship in the Air Corps. Correction: *formerly* the fastest and most maneuverable ship in the Air Corps. But this new airsub would cut an entire barrel roll with the small flick of a wrist. It was like flying a hummingbird.

"Well, Dash," Step's voice cut through his headspace, "All systems are go. You ready to take her for a swim?"

"Aye," he exhaled slowly. "Light 'er up."

'First time outta the gate, Dash,' she cautioned him via Relay.

But Dash broke in, *'I got it, I got it, you break it you bought it. I'll be gentle with her, Step. Promise.'*

"Just looking for a nice, easy lap around the lunar dale and back," Step replied. "What's left of it, anyway."

When her mic was open, Dash could hear the nervous click of her pen. *'What the hell is she so nervous for?'* Dash thought. *'I'm the spam in a can strapped to the two-megaton space submarine.'*

'You know I can hear you until you close your mic,' Step chided.

Dash swore. "Sorry, Major, I'll never get used to this new tech." He shook his head to clear it up. He took a deep breath and exhaled through his pursed lips. There were three engine modules on the panel in front of him. He flicked the safety off the first, hesitated a second, and then punched it. The Hydros slowly began to whine as they spiraled up to speed. He wiped a dust fleck off of buttons two and three and then focused his attention up the tube as the bay doors opened. At the end of that track lay the open waters of the Caribbean. And D/U/G.

"SkySAT, this is Bravo Bay," Step called up, "requesting final clearance for that moon dance. Over."

"This is SkySAT. Roger that, Bravo Bay. Be advised that you have a 90-minute window before the entire Draccario fleet begins their mass exodus. And good riddance, if you ask me. Until then, the lanes are clear."

*'Well, sh*t on a sunstick. That's two days ahead of schedule,'* Step said privately to Dash. "Okay, 10-4, Sky-SAT. Alright, Dash, the waters are smooth, the sky is clear, and you've got the ball."

"Copy," Dash acknowledged. He slowly opened and closed his fingers on the controls a couple of times, making sure he was nice and limber. Feather's touch. It was important to be one with your bird. Loose. Just like the water all around him. Flowing. Responsive.

Dash relayed out, *'Open the gate, DUG, and count me down.'*

'Heard,' D/U/G replied as he lowered the shields. *'You're in the blue in ten, nine '*

Dash pressed a thumb against a MobileComm mounted to his left, and a 3D picture of a beautiful blue-haired Japanese woman rezzed up on-screen. He and Mizuke had met when he was stationed under Neo-Tokyo. They had fallen in love and been married almost five years ago. Usually, this picture of her was his other lucky charm. But she'd been missing since Colonel Wexell's attack on the *Bellevue*. He had to remind himself that everything would be okay. One thing at a time. He shoved his fears back into the basement and resolutely returned both hands to the controls.

"Bleed the edge," Dash said with a resigned confidence.

"Hooah. Bleed the edge," Step echoed the base credo back at him.

'Six. Five.' Track lights illuminated the submerged launch tube. *'Three. Two—'*

At zero, the sub restraints flicked open, Dash juiced the throttle, and the Hydros sucked in thousands of gallons of water per second in a frothing swell that catapulted the Mustang swiftly down the tunnel. Lights strobed overhead as he glided along. Half-way down, he felt the sonic safety pulse D/U/G emitted, which dispersed any unsuspecting sea life lingering near the mouth of the portal. Most of them would swim off after the first pulse, by the second, not even a sardine remained—the coast was completely clear.

The H2X-Ø super-sub shot out of the launch tube and into open water. Urging the Hydros faster, the Mustang jumped forward, leaving the Bravo Bay superstructure and D/U/G behind in a cloud of bubbles.

"Mustang clear," he notified the base.

"Mustang clear," Step confirmed. "And have you got a visual on your escort? Aft. 7 o'clock high."

Dash turned his head, and, sure enough, there was the chase sub, bearing down. HX-45f class. Old school. Inside would be his old buddy, Lt. Colonel Vincent "Gator" Gordon. They'd flown a hundred missions together, and it was an honor to have him along on this particular test flight as well. "Visual confirmed, haha. Better late than never, Gator."

"Wouldn't miss it, Junior," Gator replied. "Had to see this new toy causing all the freshmen to sh*t their diapers."

"Just try t' keep up, old timer," Dash threw a hang-loose sign to his wingman through the canopy.

Gator returned the signal. "Now, this is being recorded for posterity, so try not to puke up your toenails this time."

Dash winced and looked down at the 3D picture of his wife again. *'That's something Mizuke would have said,'* he thought to himself, forgetting again about the HUD-link.

'Stay with us, Dash!' Gator said privately back to him.

'I know. Don't worry, I got this.' Dash flexed his fingers once more and then nudged the throttle up to 18%. As the two subs cut across the ocean floor, they suddenly crossed over the lip of the Puerto Rico Trench, and a bottomless deep lay open beneath them. He rolled the Mustang over and dove into the abyss. Gator followed.

Inside the cockpit, the ambiance of the HUD changed seamlessly. With limited window visibility, the augmented reality maps provided eyes into this dark wonderland. Dash's eyes began to glow white. Moving from your physical eye to cybervision was strange the first few times because the ship around you just sort of disappeared, and it was almost as if you were free-floating through the water at break-neck speeds. Dash's shoulders sagged a little as he relaxed. This now felt like any of the hundred SIM rides he had performed.

The two ships darted in and out of huge underwater structures. Gator took a curve that thrust him forward into pole position. He and Dash had played this game many, many times. Dash snugged up tight on his contrails. Back during the topside racing days, this was known as "drafting." They had studied the technique at the Kytos Academy to glean any combat advantage it may have to offer. The two moved seamlessly in and around one murky structure after the next. Close enough to see that these underwater playgrounds of theirs used to be a thriving cityscape. Havana, from the looks of it.

They flew past a skyscraper, and Gator's slipstream knocked a spire loose from the balcony of what was left of an old hotel.

Dash swore and jerked the stick to the right, almost over-compensating himself right into the iron skeleton of an abandoned construction project. He deftly rolled out of the collision course and rejoined Gator on the building's far side.

"Good hands, Mustang," Gator said, checking his friend over his shoulder.

"Getting some proximity warnings up here," Step chimed in. "What's going on out there, boys? Thought we were taking things slow and easy."

D/U/G started to answer, '*The Mustang was almost*—'

'*Shut it, DUG!*' Dash relayed and then, breathing heavily, read from the displays, "Pressure's stable. HUD sync and visibility are excellent. Hydros maintaining 20%. Very responsive, ma'am."

"Roger that, Dash," Step confirmed. "You are clear to begin Level Two maneuvers. Let's get vertical."

Dash reached up to engine number two and engaged it. "Spinnin' up Atmospheric drive," he called back. "Increasing throttle to 25% and breaking for the surface."

The sunlight began to penetrate through the deep blue waters more and more with the shallower altitude. The Mustang cut through the Caribbean underwaters like a knife, leaving Gator's chase sub further and further in its wake. The HX-45 had the older Atmos drives, which required its pilot to breach, sit atop the water for a few seconds while they purged, and then it could take off into the sky.

The Mustang's newer tech was far superior. Dash was about to perform the first breach and burn. The stern of his ship creaked and groaned with the vastly changing hull pressures, but all the shielding seals held, and the ascent was a smooth ride.

"Ready to breach in 20 seconds," Dash said, his heart pounding in his chest.

The SkyCross Squadron hung there in place, ready to break anchor and pick up the air-to-air visual inspection whenever Gator's rig stopped for its mandatory purge. They'd be able to escort Dash the rest of the way into space and back.

"Ranger Force is in position," Gigsby reminded them.

"Fifteen seconds," Step informed them all, "til history is made."

"Come on, Dash!" Gator cheered him on from a good two hundred meters below.

Dash watched as the water line rushed toward him. "Come on, baby," he muttered under his breath.

The Mustang breached, spewing the ship high into the air like a baby humpback. Startled, the sea condors scattered in every direction, bellowing loudly. Back in the cockpit, there was a brief moment as the Hydros detected oxygen intake and switched over to the Atmospherics. Dash watched the engine lights blink from green Hydros, to yellow Hydros to green Atmos in a split second. And with a loud burst, the Atmospherics kicked in, and the burn began, pinning him to his seat. The Mustang launched successfully skyward.

"Atmos are go," he said, his white knuckles excitedly clutching the throttle, "I repeat, Atmos are a go."

There was a small celebration in the control room when Step broke in, "Roger that, Mustang. One for the record books. Confirm Ranger visual."

Dash rolled the ship, and, indeed, there was Ranger Gigsby and her four SkyCross fighters closing into escort position fast. "I got 'em, Step. Visual confirmed."

The Rangers assumed formation around the Mustang as they all climbed up through the stratosphere. The pattern, with an assist from their special NAV gear on board, would help scramble the Mustang's footprint in the sky. The last thing they wanted was to attract the wrong attention to their secret base and especially to this latest project, which would be a substantial military game changer.

Dash's eyes swept over the controls, and all the ship's vitals were green. "Bravo Bay, I am throttling up to forty-five percent," he informed them.

"Roger that, Dash," Step called out. "Shoot the stars."

As the Mustang increased its speed, the Rangers began to struggle to keep up. As the distance between them increased, Dash called out the speeds. "Mach 15… Mach 18… Mach 25… Mach 30…"

Dash reached down and engaged engine number three. "Ions coming online."

"Ions coming online," Step echoed to Base. "Ten seconds to sub-space."

"Ten seconds to sub-space," Dash confirmed, adding playfully, "To the moon, Alice."

Those would be the last words recorded by Captain Dash Strouthers. His only visible hint of a problem would be the split second when the yellow warning light flicked on over the supposedly inactive Hydros, just before the Ions kicked in. There was a massive explosion, which marked the end of that H2X-Ø prototype. And the end of Dash Strouthers.

- 1 -
THE HUNTED

Planet Da'karh, 2561 AD

A fuzzy, bright light cut through the sticky blackness, and with an abrupt and painful jerk, Jacques Bastille re-entered consciousness. His first thought was, *Who the hell is Dash Strouthers*? These military-grade Byno-Cores were supposed to be wiped clear of their previous seed-lines and inhabitants. He was going to need this meat-suit tuned up and scrubbed out once he figured out wherever the hell he was.

Bastille's eyelids flapped open, and he tried to make sense of the warm pillow his head rested upon. But it was no pillow. It was sand. Some sort of beach, perhaps? A vacation? As his hearing recalibrated and the ringing diminished, he could pick out the roar of the ocean's surf somewhere in the distance.

He quickly deduced that the planet's atmosphere was breathable since there was a gaping hole in his helmet and he was still alive. He struggled to his knees and hit the release lever around his neck. The helmet unlocked, and he peeled it off. He spit out sand and blood from his otherwise parched lips. A small tract down the left side of his face was tender, and he winced when his glove skimmed across it. It felt like it had been recently flame-broiled.

Bastille ran a quick internal system scan. In his retinal-HUD, there were a bevy of warning messages indicating internal damage to the cybernetics of his Byno-Core. His body-armor was charred and trashed, most likely the only thing that had kept him alive, absorbing the bulk of… well, whatever had happened. Swaths of his tattered desert cloak caught in the wind and swirled around him.

One of his arms felt like it was just shy of broken. And the other—

Wait, why can't I feel my right arm? Something caught his eye a few feet away from him. It was a hand buried in the sandy dunes. Still wobbly on his knees, he edged closer. He grabbed the hand whose tattered glove looked identical to his own and pulled. The arm came free from the sand; loose grains rushed in to fill the void as if nothing had ever been there. Was this his arm? Dumbstruck, he looked over at his right shoulder. Where an arm should have been, there was just a tangle of wires hanging out, sparking from time to time when the tips crossed.

What the hell...

Bastille forced himself vertical. And what were these small, black floating things drifting down from the sky? He grabbed at one passing by. It looked like burning fabric, and it turned to black powder in his fingers. Turning around slowly, his breath caught in his chest, and his mouth fell open. It was no ocean. The sound was the plume of fire from a gigantic, crash-landed C-Class freighter going up in smoke.

Is that my ship?

Another explosion sent more blackened debris and fireballs raining down all over the area. Bastille shielded his eyes with the loose arm. From the looks of it, the ship had skidded for a quarter klick, digging a channel into the soft ground before it nose-planted and settled where it was.

I don't remember being thrown clear. Or escaping. In fact, I don't remember—anything!

He studied the burning wreckage behind him for a clue. Any clue. The front half of the ship was destroyed, but the stern was still intact—for the moment. The entire shell was riddled with holes. Very recent battle damage. Very precise battle damage. He noted the massive Sig Cannons retrofitted to the hull. That meant this was no casual freighter. If it had artillery, then it would also have munitions aboard. Which meant there was a weapons hold, and even if it had only been partially stockpiled, between that and the fuel cells, this whole ship could atomize into stardust at any moment.

Bastille collected the arm and willed himself to his feet. Moving unsteadily away from the ship, his foot caught on a strap, and down he went again. Some sort of black duffel. Military grade. There was an electrolock whose PIN most likely floated around the foggy abyss of his fractured databanks, along with most every other lost bit of memory.

So, maybe he hadn't been so much thrown from the ship; rather, he had walked away, headed… somewhere. Nowhere.

A new sound pricked his ears, and he instinctively crouched low behind a smoldering section of fuselage. It was a small battle skiff like the Outworlders favored. The top of the ship was a hammer-head shape that swept back into a long and pointed tail. Attached below was a pod like a turret. It housed a variety of guns poking out in every direction. It rotated around as the three landing struts unfolded from the belly.

Bounty hunters.

That much was coming back to him now. The bounty hunters were still after him. They had shot him from the sky and were circling high above, there to finish the job. But why? Bastille checked his gun belt. The holster was empty.

The ship landed, sending a tornado of sand in his direction, handily erasing the last vestiges of footprints he'd left behind. Bastille ducked down, holding his desert cloak against his face to block the grainy assault.

An access ramp lowered, steam spraying from the exhaust seals, and a bounty hunter stood cautiously on the gangplank, assault blaster leveled. Powered up. The protocol was to perform a scan on the wreckage for survivors, but there'd be too much heat and smoke for the sensors to return any useful intel. He stood on a single leg the size of a small oak tree.

He wore no helmet. Probably couldn't fit one over that horned toad head of his. He had some armor on, but that scaly lizard skin made it redundant. A trade precaution. He slid the large rifle onto a back sling and latched it in place. Then he bent down slowly til those clawed hands touched the ground and he moved forward, dragging his leg appendage behind him, swishing it side to side like a tail.

The Snake moved into the wreckage area. Bastille watched him slither towards an open hatch, crawling his way quickly along the ground. He was either crazy or desperate. Neither would bode well for Bastille.

He waited for his enemy to disappear inside the smoking freighter, then sprang forward to follow. He faltered when a second bounty hunter dropped down from the battle skiff's hatchway.

Since when do Outworlders work in pairs!?

Well, it was too late now to duck for cover. Bastille was out there. Exposed. He veered left, using the skiff's landing strut to mask his line-of-sight approach. He gambled that the bounty hunter would be too fixated on the fantastic wreck before him.

The hunter stood on his gnarled, monopod of a leg, rifle drawn. He scanned the area, dangerously close to turning around, when a small explosion near the ship's bow—what was left of it—riveted his attention forward again.

Suddenly, Bastille was upon him, charging low and throwing his good shoulder right into the bounty hunter's back. It sent them both off balance and his rifle flew to the ground. The bounty hunter slammed into the side of some jagged metal and bellowed in pain.

Bastille, still at his back, clenched his fist and hammered down on the base of his skull again and again. The beast wheeled on him, and its armored elbow cracked into Bastille's forehead, severing a loose connection in his memory synapse that caused an excruciating short circuit.

Fzzzzzzzht.

* * *

Planet Earth, NeoTokyo

Dash Strouthers lay in a medical facility with Mizuke by his side. This was the same beautiful, blue-haired Japanese woman from the picture in the cockpit of his H2X-Ø Mustang. Dash was very confused. He looked around, getting his bearings. A doctor to his left had clearly just administered an anesthesia boost into the crook of his arm. There was a restraint on his head, holding him perfectly still. Not that he could move anyway. His whole body was strapped to this hospital bed.

"W-who the hell is Jacques Bastille?" Dash whispered hoarsely.

Mizuke leaned forward to trace her delicate fingers across Dash's furrowed brow. "Shhh shh, Dash. Easy. The procedure is going great. You're going to be okay. Even better than before, right, Doctor Morrisey?"

"Or your money back." Doctor Morrisey winked at them. Morrisey unwrapped a new sterile multitool onto the tray beside them. The cylinder had a bunch of surgical devices interlocked together, with a socket at one end. Then he unscrewed his left hand. He removed it altogether and set it aside, replacing it with the multitool. He snapped it into place with a final twist. The tools extended out like robotic fingers and lit up and whirred as the doctor tested them out.

"What's happening?" Dash asked both, but neither. "I had a dream. I was fighting a lizard man. A bounty hunter."

Off of Mizuke's questioning look, the doctor reassured her, "Slight disorientation at this stage is very normal."

Mizuke maneuvered her rolling chair closer to the bedside. She tucked a lock of her blue bangs behind her ear and leaned close to Dash whispering, "Listen up, Hotshot. With these new KACorps neural implants, you will have your pick of *any* ship in the Air Corps. It's what you've always wanted, Dash. Bravo Bay is *this* close."

To illustrate, she held up her thumb and forefinger an inch apart. Dash opened his mouth to talk, but no words would form. Mizuke smiled and kissed his cheek.

Dr. Morrisey motioned for Mizuke. "Mrs. Strouthers, if I could have you step back out into the theater, we are ready to continue with phase three."

Mizuke stood, wrinkled her nose at Dash, and then followed a Byno-Nurse escort out the door. She appeared again on the far side of a raised window and took a seat alongside some other mystery spectators. Dash's head was swimming now. He found it difficult to focus.

As the meds kicked in, the doctor settled back into place at the top of the bed, where Dash's scalp was lifted off and brain tissue and circuitry were exposed. A salve of NITs (Nanobot Integration Technology) worked away, fusing the metal mesh together. Extending a small pair of tweezers, the doctor placed a small titanium oxide chip onto the circuit-bed in Dash's brain. And as it snapped into place, it sparked.

Fzzzzzzzht.

* * *

Planet Da'karh

Jacques regained consciousness with another blow to the head from the savage bounty hunter, but he was still too stunned to deflect it. Unfortunately, there was no time to decipher whatever the hell this Dash and Mizuke mess was all about. He may have lost his mind, but he was determined not to lose his head. The lizard assassin seemed intent on it, though.

This close to him, Bastille could see the clan markings all over this guy's green-ish gray lizard skin. This was one of those extreme Outworlders. Human, but in the loosest sense of the word. So genetically modded up and mutated, there wasn't much of a person left. Quite literally, he was the perfect cold-blooded killer. Hence their derogatory name, Snakes.

The bounty hunter released Bastille, who fell back, grunting with pain as he crashed into the ground. The Snake was also wounded and bloodied. He crawled towards his rifle, but jerked to a dead stop about a foot away. When he turned around to see why, Bastille was standing on his tail, brandishing his own severed arm like a club. The arm swung down hard and connected with the bounty hunter's head. The impact of tungsten bone against the lizard's skull flattened the creature to the ground, senseless.

Bastille dropped the arm, picked up the large assault rifle, and, planting the barrel tip firmly against the bounty hunter's back, pulled the trigger. With a flash, the Snake's life was ended. Dusty contrails spread from beneath him as the desert absorbed the shockwave and viscera from the blast. Bastille turned to check for the other Snake, but he was still inside the burning ship. So he slid the gun strap over his shoulder. Then he set his severed arm atop the black cargo bag and stuffed them both behind the landing strut.

Wrapping his cloak around his mouth and nose, Bastille climbed up into the burning freighter and leaned into the smoking doorway. The second bounty hunter was nowhere to be seen. Bastille picked his way quickly through the hazy corridor. Emergency lights flashed as the last of the ship's power drained. A message repeated over and over through the comms overhead: "Hull breach imminent. Please make your way to the escape pods. Hull breach imminent."

He slowed down when he came to a cross-corridor. Peeking around the corner, he saw the Snake up ahead working on a dead crew member. The lizard brandished a curved blade, lifted the corpse up by his hair, and sliced off the Relay box at the base of his neck. Dropping it into a pouch around his waist, he let the body slump back to the floor. He was collecting evidence. No, more than evidence, he was collecting digital scalps.

Bastille backed up into a separate hallway. Though his mind was a dark abyss, he leaned into the small, vague familiarities he felt, almost a deja vu, as he maneuvered through the ship, relying on muscle memory. Left. Right. Right again, until he arrived at the captain's quarters. Power throughout the ship was waning, so he had to muscle the sliding door open manually.

The room was a disaster. Bastille entered and began to kick through the rubble on the floor, searching for any clues or anything helpful. He spotted his Mauzer pistol amid the debris. He grabbed the barrel, and the gun snagged on a hand that gripped it firmly. He twisted the pistol loose and tucked it into his holster. Then he threw a mattress and some broken shelves to the side to reveal a female form, crumpled beneath. Electric blue hair. The wall next to her showed the full impact of her body when the ship had crashed. Bastille bent down and checked for a pulse, but he could already tell from the strange angle of her neck, she was gone.

Who are you, blue-haired goddess?

He rolled her onto her side, took out his own knife, pried the Relay cartridge from the box at the base of her neck, and tucked it into a pocket. He studied her face again, but there was no mental information pulling up a match. On-screen in his retinal-HUD the facial recognition reported an "Error!" Just a software glitch and a mysterious ache in his heart.

He straightened up. Not much more he could do here. He headed back toward the door and, on muscle memory, pressed the wall to his right, and a panel opened with several armaments inside, including a belt of explosives, which he draped over his neck like a bandolier. The other stuff he couldn't really carry one-handed, so he'd just have to leave it behind.

Another explosion at the front of the ship rocked the whole structure and shifted everything at once. Bastille stepped out into the corridor, and there was the bounty hunter advancing in his direction, headlamp penetrating the smoke. Bastille slowly reached his left arm across to the Mauzer on his right hip. The Snake noticed him, too, and they both drew down and fired at each other, diving for cover. Bastille was the first to his feet, scrambling deeper into the ship to find an alternate exit.

A full minute later, he jerked open a large door to reveal the cargo bay, bent all to hell. The entire tail section was vertical, and the only exit portal was forty feet up. Bastille climbed up the boxes and debris and used the floor grates to scale his way toward the door.

Damn this one-arm business.

He was out of breath by the time he reached the escape latch and pulled the handle. The door blasted open. Looking outside, he could see the bounty hunter's ship, the dead Snake lying on the ground cooking in the sun, and the black duffel right where he'd left them thirty feet below in the sand.

Back in the cargo bay, the remaining bounty hunter slithered in just as Bastille hung a leg over the side to jump. They caught each other's eye, and Bastille smiled. The Snake raised his rifle and would have had a clean shot, but a high-pitched whine distracted him to his left. It was a magnetic detonator Bastille had left on the wall as a parting gift.

Bastille dropped down to the desert below as the cargo bay exploded high overhead. He scrambled for the bounty hunter's ship and pulled his black duffel onto the lift.

Once aboard, he dropped the bag and climbed into the pilot seat on the bridge of the battle skiff. He tossed his loose arm onto the console, and granules of sand splashed around it. The support Relay at the base of his neck glowed blue as it uplinked with the ship's systems. He half expected it not to work, but apparently he'd paired with this system before. So, with a thought, he lifted off, swinging the nose of the hammerhead skiff around toward the rear exit of the C-Class transport.

There, glaring back at him, was the bounty hunter just climbing into view. The Snake drew his rifle and sent some flak toward the departing ship. Bastille casually switched on the targeting system, and as he powered the skiff backwards and away from the transport, he swung the turrets around and let loose a barrage of missiles.

The bounty hunter attempted to jump free, but it was too late. A chain reaction of explosions blew a huge crater into the desert floor.

Bastille spun the skiff around and kicked the throttle wide open. Metal shards and debris rattled against the back of the ship as he cleared the blast plane. Barely. Bastille swore through gritted teeth as he evaded the gigantic mushroom cloud; the ship's digital instruments glitched in and out from electrical interference in the shockwave that overtook them.

Everything stabilized after that, and he pulled the nose up and accelerated toward open space. He was only too happy to leave the desert planet behind, which he now recognized as Da'karh. This memory thing was going to frustrate the hell out of him. Like finding all the right answers the day *after* a big test. As he climbed, he jacked the ship's umbilical cord into the Relay box at the base of his neck and snapped it into place. Suddenly, his Retinal Heads-Up Display synced with the ship's HUD. He checked over the monitors, and something caught his eye in the bottom corner of the display. It was that same 3D picture from Dash's H2X-Ø test flight.

Mizuke? What the hell is going on?

As the hijacked ship broke through the planetary exosphere, the Atmos drives kicked over into the Ion drives and Bastille instinctively flinched, but the ship pulsed safely forward.

\- 2 -

THE REBOOT

Deep Space

Having put significant distance between himself and the bounty hunter ambush on Da'karh, Jacques Bastille slowed the stolen vessel to a lazy drift and triggered the NAV computer, full screen.

This, of course, was complete gibberish. The Outlanders had evolved a language all their own. And not a Latin-based language, either, which so many of the inner colonies relied on. It was closest to Japanese kanji but had a decided braille influence as well on its characters. And to hear it spoken was more like a series of clicks and pops, almost like a bat.

Bastille sighed heavily as he detached the umbilical from his Relay box. He slouched back and stared absently up at the ceiling, which appeared to be a giant lighting fixture. He found a fader on the arm of the chair, and when he moved it up, the whole ceiling lit up until the bridge glowed orange, like he was inside a chicken roaster.

The temperature immediately began to spike. That explained the special non-metallic porous surfaces throughout the bridge, which could withstand high heat without affecting their own surface temperatures. It allowed you to be warm without the danger of scalding yourself trying to drive the ship.

Damn lizards.

He was happy to leave them both on the desert planet where they belonged. He shut the lights down and spun the chair toward his duffel bag. The lock caught his attention again. Up close, it appeared to be biometric. He figured there was a 50/50 chance of it being the thumb or index finger. He grabbed his arm from the dashboard and pressed his dominant thumb to the lock, and the magna-seal broke and the bag popped open with a hiss of depressurized air.

He tossed the arm aside again. Rifling through the bug-out bag, there were all the usual necessities: some food bars, Hydro packs, a shower kit, a change of clothes, a double-barrel blaster rifle and ammo, more magnetic detonators, and—*bingo*—a data jack. All of this was seated atop six rectangular packages wrapped mysteriously at the bottom. He lifted out the data jack.

These items were important clues to who he might have been before the accident, but none of them triggered the rush of memories he was hoping for. Even the humid, moldy smell of this ship was familiar somehow, but he couldn't prove it by summoning even a single memory as to why. The items in the emergency kit—especially the rifle—felt natural in his hand.

It felt like home. Like the way he had rushed that bounty hunter on Da'karh without hesitation and then dispatched him so casually. Home.

I was definitely a soldier of some sort, he thought. *Just, maybe not the most law-abiding sort. Mercenary, maybe.* He held up the black-market data jack, the rarest of the high-tech skeleton keys worth a fortune, but again, he had absolutely no clue as to why it was part of his bug-out bag. Well-used from the looks of it.

He decided he would use it to hack the battle skiff's mainframe and manually reboot it. Easier said than done. He powered down the ship, and when the last LED flickered off and the bridge fell silent, he jerked out the CORE cartridge and seated the jack in its place.

That was the easy part. Tracking down the Nav-COMM's junction box would take some digging to find. And then, rebooting everything all at the same time—that would be difficult with two hands. With one? Well, there was no sense in getting all fatalistic before it was absolutely necessary.

Damn, it's so warm.

Bastille awkwardly stripped off his soiled shirt and tossed it in the captain's chair. His skin was a relief map of war wounds and battle scars. Overlaying all of that was a particular pattern on his neck, back, and shoulder that could have been a tattoo but was certainly not manmade. It branched and flowed like the blood vessels of a lung or a complex lichen just below his skin's surface. This fierce scar was generally found only on dead bodies, the often fatal result of a lightning strike. But no matter who was trying to kill him—gods or men—it seemed like Bastille could never stay dead for long. A blessing and a curse.

Bastille started at the console to his left. He worked his knife up under the heat-shielded coverlets to pry them loose. Forty-five minutes later, a disemboweled computer trail led down the wall, through the torn-up flooring, and a few feet toward the door.

"Dammit," he swore, removing the last section. Sweat dripped from his brow. He sheathed the knife, reached his arm into the NavCOMM junction, and hovered over a breaker switch. Then, balancing on one knee, he raised his boot to the dash. Six inches short of the data jack.

Nope. No good.

He flopped back against the wall with a loud clang. His mind raced as he extrapolated a thousand scenarios; each ended with "fail" or "dead," and it left him exhausted. He would never be able to trigger both at the same time.

Temporarily, he gave up and reached into the duffel for a food bar. Ripping it open with his teeth, he took a bite. Tasted so good. The mouthful fizzled as he swallowed, like an old-fashioned seltzer. Immediately, the synthetic vita-boost hit his system, and he felt better as his energy surged. By the time he finished the last bite, he could barely sit still; he was buzzed.

He wiped his hand on his pants and felt the Relay cartridge in his pocket—the one he'd gotten off the naked, blue-haired goddess from his ship. He pulled it out and considered it for a moment.

He reached behind his neck and snapped the cover plate off of his own Relay box. Then he carefully nested hers on top and snapped it into place. There was an instant whiteout as his body synced to it, and when his vision returned, his HUD showed a freeze frame from a woman's point of view.

There was a brief pause before the Viddix began playback. She was in his captain's quarters, and the room was erupting violently. Loudly. She was clinging to a door frame to steady herself. Screaming the whole time. Suddenly, there was an explosion; the south wall rushed toward her, and there was a cracking sound. The Viddix signal blanked out.

Bastille's head twitched painfully, and it automatically threw him sideways. He banged his head on the floor as he fell.

Ouch! That was too close, he thought as he sucked air and pushed his way vertical again. Had the Relay been fully engaged, his own body could have co-experienced the on-screen trauma; his neck would not have necessarily broken, but his heart could have stopped beating the moment hers had. Amateur mistake. He climbed back into the pilot seat and tapped gently near a bump forming on his brow. He hissed in disapproval when his fingers found it.

So that scene was the last few grisly seconds of her life—almost his own. Bastille sat back up and scrolled carefully this time, back into the timeline, playing from a new data point. Here, he saw his own sweaty face, panting in pleasure. He was lying on the bed as she straddled atop him, breathing heavily as well.

Bastille couldn't help but grimace as he watched his on-screen lovemaking. He'd never seen himself mid-coitus before and made some mental performance notes for next time. *Gross*, he decided. *Never make that face again, old man!*

He watched himself grab the woman's perfect breasts and squeeze them. Watched her speed up her breathing and her pace as she rode him. Watched his face contort weirdly in ecstasy. Heard the ship's proximity alarm, interrupting. Then saw himself bolt from the bed as the wall monitor and helm announced an intruder. Another ship.

On the Viddix, Bastille dressed himself in record time.

"J'Annelie, my gun," he growled, casting about for the missing weapon.

J'Annelie shrugged back at him. "On the bridge?"

"Okay, hold tight. Probably raiders. We'll take care of it, and I'll radio back," he said, rushing from the room as he buttoned his shirt and pulled on a boot at the same time.

Still inside J'Annelie's Viddix point of view, they watched Bastille exit, and then she slid her hand up under the mattress and produced a gun from beneath it. His gun. The Mauzer.

"Hey!" Bastille pounded the console of the bounty hunter's ship with a steel fist. "Two-faced little rat."

Back on-screen, the woman rose from the bed and looked up into the mirror, and Bastille caught a good, long look at her. Stunning. Late 20s. And damn sexy standing there holding his gun. She had shoulder-length curly blue locks pulled back into a clip. Tall and athletic.

With practiced ease, she flipped the gun open, checked the stock, snapped it back closed, and knocked the heel of her hand against the side of it, throwing off the safety and powering it up in the same instance.

She touched a finger to the back of her earlobe and said, "Shleev'n griz'a d'ahn!" And then followed it with a bunch of clicking sounds. Then she aimed the gun at her reflection and mouthed the words, "Bang."

Bastille froze the picture. Leaning forward—he realized this was completely unnecessary within the virtual landscape of his mind—his eyes glowed white as the sync continued. He cropped and captured a pic of the gun-toting goddess on the HUD using the retinal cam. He'd save that one for later, uh, scrutiny. As his eyes scanned her slender form, something caught his attention on her shoulder.

What are those marks?

He zoomed to her left shoulder in a small area that would have been covered by a bikini line. There were three black lines. Short lines. Stacked up on top of each other. Squared off on one side, pointed at the other. Perhaps that tattoo would have meant something once upon a time, but right now it could have been a birthmark, for all he knew.

Focusing again, he took another HUD pic of it. He'd have to run it through the D/S next time he was in range to access StarNET.

Scanning the footage backwards once more, he let it skip to the beginning. It didn't get too far—maybe six months or so into the file—before an abstract logo encryption came on-screen and froze in place. Whatever was available prior to six months was classified. Or simply didn't exist. Bastille sat back in the chair.

"J'Annelie, you mysterious gun-stealing little minx—"

Suddenly, his HUD scrambled, and the Relay box beeped twice before it began smoking. "No, no, no," he said, ripping it quickly from his neck. But some fail safes had been triggered. The Relay cartridge in his hands had been completely wiped and sizzled into a blackened ooze in his hand.

"Dammit!" He threw it across the bridge, and it smacked the canopy, sticking to it like an amorphous blob of tar.

Up on the dashboard, a finger on his right hand twitched. Bastille stood, curiously. He checked the stub on his right shoulder, but there was no visible activity. The sparking had stopped as tiny NITs had begun auto-repair mode. That was another dead giveaway of a possible military background. Civilian tech didn't have high-level nanoid repair capabilities like this. It was too new and too expensive.

Still, a phantom link to his severed limb would be next-level. He grabbed the arm and held the hand up close to his face, inspecting it. Concentrating all of his focus, he stared at the index finger he had seen move. At first, there was nothing, but after a moment, the fingers began to twitch. And then move. Bastille relaxed and then tried it again. With a little practice, he was able to straighten and curl the finger. And then the whole hand.

Bastille smiled. Growing in confidence, he counted to five on his severed arm. It probably took a good ten minutes.

"One, two, three," he began, holding up the correct fingers for each, starting with the index finger. Three was a little more difficult. Took a little more concentration. "Fouuuuuuur…" Four took even longer to tuck the thumb and move those fingers into place simultaneously. "Five."

Five happened fairly easily.

"And what do we say to the bounty hounds?" The hand closed and raised one middle finger.

Bastille chuckled and sat back in the chair. Laying the arm up on the console, he rested the hand atop the data jack. Again, with some concentration, his thumb and index fingers were able to grab the switch. With a little bit more focus, the wrist moved, and the switch was now in the open position. The cockpit sprang to life.

"Okay. Alright," he said, shutting the system back down and resetting the hand position. "Okay."

Bastille quickly stepped back to the NavCOMM master panel. Reaching inside, he flipped and held the breaker module open while mentally willing his other hand to move. Up on the dash, the fingers slowly squeezed together. It took a couple of tries, but the switch was thrown, and the whole bridge came to life again. Bastille waited about seven seconds. A bead of sweat formed on his brow, but sure enough, all the power to the NavCOMM flickered, and he released the breaker.

"Hell yeah," Bastille celebrated, laying back on the floor.

One by one, all the systems powered up again. The light at the base of the data jack began to twinkle, and as the NAV computer came back online, all of the on-screen words shifted to something a lot more familiar: BaseZero. English.

Bastille synced his Relay with the comm monitor and searched back through the message archives until he got to one transmission that read:

> High Priority Bounty:
> Jacques Bastille >> Dead or Alive!

Bastille skimmed to the end and saw the name there. *Bender.*

Triggering the NAV device, he commanded, "Bender, VerDav'n."

The NAV system sprung to life, plotting courses, accessing available wormhole passages, and doing a myriad of calculations on-screen. Bastille continued reading the transmission until the NAV system beeped loudly. Then he slid back over to check the route alternates.

There were four or five different paths, but they all led to one dark spot at the edge of the known universe: the Outlands.

Bastille selected the four-day journey. Not too direct. Not too circuitous. He wanted some extra travel time to plan and prepare, but not to meander. No one meandered into the Outlands. That would be a huge security red flag. So, if he had to go there—and it was his only lead so far—he'd bang right on the front door.

So be it.

- 3 -

THE OUTLANDS

VerDav'n Colony in the Outlands

An older, salvaged Aurora band lined the edges of this outermost jump gate. It was Draccario space-tech forcibly appropriated by KACorps bureaucrats, in turn hijacked by the Outworlders. Working together with the fusion rigging eight hundred meters across, the ring-shaped gate capped the Krayt wormhole and stabilized it. While KACorps Code 13.248.243.5 made it illegal to tamper with or travel a jump gate, the Outworlders were beyond such jurisdiction. And being technologically unaccountable—some might even say reckless—they had painstakingly coaxed and moved the wormhole from the neighboring galaxy where it had been discovered to just off their VerDav'n colony, a process that had taken more than thirty Earth years.

Unlike the AlphaN1 wormhole in the Milky Way —a heavily guarded and fortified KACorps gateway— nobody tended this K-gate. They didn't need to. Nobody but the Outland Snakes roamed these parts, besides a few suicidal or enterprising refugees. Those were usually dispatched quickly. Except for one skeevy bastard who simply went by the handle Bender. And that's who Bastille was headed to see.

The dark pool of the wormhole began to crackle with energy, and four of the beacons on the Aurora ring lit up as the K-gate sprang to life. Just four active beacons were necessary to pass through a smaller vessel like this one. The battle skiff surfaced back into neutral space like an orca breaching the ocean to draw breath. Radiation from the hyperspace travel created banding light contrails around the ship. Its wake glowed green and purple as it lifted off the surface of the hyper-gate platform.

The long ride had given Bastille plenty of time to get cleaned up and rested. He had even managed to squeeze into one of the bounty hunter's spacesuits. Star charts around him shifted into new positions as the onboard computers recalculated and aligned with the current satellite beacons.

Looking out over VerDav'n, Bastille swore softly and thought, *This little backwater seed colony has grown into a huge spaceport.*

And that wasn't the biggest surprise. As he looked past the planet, he was just in time to see a massive spherical warship diving down into another jump gate.

Two jump gates? What in God's name have they been doing out here?

He magnified the star map, but the other wormhole wasn't even marked or identified. It was completely off-grid. As soon as the warship and its escorts had submerged into hyperspace, that wormhole went completely dark. You almost couldn't see it if you weren't looking directly at it. Even then, you would blink twice and think your eyes had played tricks on you.

Bastille punched the throttle and veered the hammerhead down toward the VerDav'n surface. The star map rendered up a trajectory flight path, and Bastille stuck close to it. He kept one eye on the security monitor, too, as his ship was scanned multiple times and received clearances along his route. At least the bounty hounds he stole this ship from had good credentials. He originally had laid odds that he'd be blasted out of the sky upon re-entry.

The battle skiff cut across the sky and headed south of the city. He spotted a bazaar of sea condors coasting along the VerDav'n thermals. This was their motherland. Their natural habitat. Dav'n Jess, the first explorer of this star system, would have bagged and tagged some firebirds and taken them home to Earth as specimens and trophies, as if Earth needed another variety of apex predator in the mix. And sometime during the Surface Wars, these firebirds would have liberated themselves in the confusion and migrated to their new home around Miramar's island settlement—a similar temperate climate to this area.

Bastille watched a familiar valley river far below. Though he couldn't recall having visited this place before, he felt that instinctual heart tug that bordered on déjà vu. So he guided the ship along the river toward the switchback in the canyon, and then he slowed his approach. Reaching back, he pulled the helmet on and sealed it into place.

It wasn't long before he was hailed. A crazy, towheaded, fat man appeared.

Bender.

"Welcome back, boys. Good hunting, I hope?" His large, sweaty face was way too close to the comm camera.

Bastille nodded.

"Haaahaaaa," Bender slapped the workbench beside himself, causing the tools to jump in place. "I can't believe you put that squiffing Ma'kobi in his place. You didn't bring him with you, did you?"

Bastille nodded again.

"Holy hog tits, the bounty on this—we're gonna be able to buy our own planet, raze it into a dustbowl, and rebuild it as New Thegas with money left over. You just made my day. Hey, where's Dak? He, uh, not make it?"

Bastille shook his head.

"Oh. Well, who needs that pignut anyway? Just leaves more bounty for us." Bender suddenly remembered, "How about the girl? The BLU unit."

Bastille shook his head again. Did Bender mean J'Annelie the rat?

"Ah, that's a crying shame." Bender made the sign of the cross on himself and kissed his fingertips at the end. "Worked so hard for that undercover gig. What a waste of a premium skinbag." He keyed some things into his keypad.

"Alright, well, Landing Pad III is all yours, Veegr. Slam it into auto, and I'll reel you in. Meet you in the shop, and bring that bastard, Bastille, with ya. Or what's left of him. Haaahaaaa."

The monitor blinked off, leaving an abstract logo encryption on screen. The same one from J'annelie's Relay cartridge. Huh. At least now he knew whom she'd been working for. She must have been the one who gave up their location to this man and his bounty hounds. Bastille flexed the fingers on his hand. The glove made creaking leathery sounds as he clenched it into a fist and then released it. In the HUD, he switched the helm to remote and immediately felt Bender take control and re-route the ship.

Landing Pad III was an extruded surface joined to the side of Bender's Canyon Compound by a walkway. The battle skiff touched down, and Bastille withdrew down the gangplank, duffel in tow. He banked on the fact that Bender would be so unsuspecting that he wouldn't check the security monitors and notice that his good pal Veegr was walking in and not slithering.

Eight hundred meters below were the teal blue waters of the Synad River, which curved around the switchback like a giant horseshoe. Some cattle-like creatures grazed along the fertile, marshy edge. Every now and then, they'd raise up on their hind legs and sniff the air for danger. Prairie lizards, most likely. Natural food source of the sea condor.

* * *

Bender sat at a workbench littered with robot innards and consoles from the past forty years. He looked like a mad scientist, which wasn't too far off the truth. Holding up some welding goggles, he made a final solder to a switchboard in front of him. On the opposite wall were five Cryo-tanks, two of which had a complete human form inside. The identical adult females rested in suspended animation awaiting a new host; their long blue hair halo'd creepily around the head and shoulders like water snakes. The other three were in various stages of construction. Long, sinewy strands mapped out the core of a body and bone structure. All along those strands, an army of NITs constructed cells, tendons, muscles and skin.

That was Bender's main commerce on VerDav'n: Re-cycling. That's what had won him entry with the Outworlders who spared his pitiful life—the fact that he was one of four Reeks (aka Re-cycle geeks) in the universe that could pull off a Re-cycle. And the fact that he had killed off the other three Reeks before making his way to the Outlands to hide out from the KACorps regulators—it made him a prestigious guild of one. Reeks were a much bigger deal before those Draccario scientists figured out the aging genome. Well, the assholes couldn't stop death, but they did find a way to extend the average lifespan by almost three hundred years. But before that, if a wealthy person wanted to cheat death, they would have their *tchula*—their mind and essence seedline—transplanted through the Re-cycle process into a younger body. A newer, homegrown version of meat-suits like Bender manufactured here. It was outlawed because too many criminals were using the experimental process to keep the slave trade alive. Others were using it as a sort of bootleg witness protection program. People like Jacques Bastille.

Blam.

Bender jumped as a cybernetic arm landed on the table in front of him, scattering various projects all over the place. An arm he picked up and recognized instantly as some of his own creation.

"Haaaahaaaaa. You mean to tell me that this is all that's left of—" Bender spun around in his seat to see the one-armed Ma'kobi behind him. "Bastille?"

He turned ghostly white. Bastille took a step forward and Bender took a step back, falling against his own table. He held the loose arm in front of him, defensively. Scrambling quickly, Bender drew a gun. "Stop, Bastille, I swear I will—"

Bastille cocked his head sideways, and the arm that Bender held bent at the elbow and grabbed his face in a vice grip. Bender fired a shot that went wild and dropped the pistol. He clawed at the hand, squishing his face, unable to wrest free of it as the force increased to excruciating levels.

"Ow, OW. AAAAhhhhhh!"

"Sit down and shut up." Bastille growled at him and kicked Bender in the gut. Bender fell into the closest chair, whimpering compliantly. Blood trickled down from his nose between the fingers.

"First, you're gonna put my arm back in the socket. And I'm talking better than new. Second, you're gonna tell me why you sent bounty hounds after me and my girl. Next, if I haven't killed you by then, you're going to explain who the hell Dash Strouthers is. Yes or yes?"

Bender nodded his head. Bastille pulled the hand off of his face and stood back. Bender rubbed his large jowls. "Jacques, my old friend, how long has it—"

—he darted for the door, but Bastille was ready with the old, outlawed Mauzer and blasted the living sh*t outta him.

A hundred years ago, Mauzer technology began as step one of a transporter experiment—the type you see in those ridiculous sci-fi classics. An oversimplified version of the theory was to separate a person's molecules, duplicate them, and then reanimate them on the other end of the line.

Their engineers never made it past the separation part. It was a messy failure. But the military was intrigued because, as a weapon, there was plenty of need to scatter an enemy's molecules into oblivion. Later, they found that the low-level tachyon pulse of the Mauzer would ever so briefly stretch the molecules, and then they'd snap back into place. The pain involved for the subject was beyond belief and threw their systems into shock. It was used for a while as a stunner, then later as an interrogation device before it was outlawed all together.

Bender hit the floor, unconscious. His body twitched at pain levels that his brain could not even hope to register.

Bastille holstered the weapon. He now had some time on his hands, so he looked over the lab. It seemed like a second-hand junk store. But a high-end junk store. In fact, Bastille was more convinced that this was the place where his data jack had originated. Bender would have certainly been able to acquire one of those, or perhaps he was the mastermind who had built and coded it in the first place.

His curious attention was drawn to the glowing blue Cryo-tanks. The two finished females floated in a bent pike position. They had on their shoulders that familiar tri-mark tattoo. He moved closer, pressing against the glass. Yes, it was the same mystery symbol as J'Annelie's back on Da'karh.

He looked up at their faces, which were by and large obscured by the wispy blue hair, but the last one had spun further around and was uncovered; he could clearly make out that face.

Mizuke.

Bastille could scarcely believe his own eyes. This was the woman from his Dash Strouthers visions, flashbacks, or whatever they were. Mizuke. Times two. The other three were still too early in the process to determine gender or type. They weren't full-on clones because, he knew, you had to grow those from a fetus. Took much longer and burned out quicker. These hybrid constructs were built full-sized and ready to go. Around age sixteen upon completion, by the looks of it.

One thing was for certain: if Bender's heart had in fact not burst from the Mauzer shot, he'd have a lot to answer for.

\- 4 -

BENDER'S CHOP SHOP

VerDav'n Colony in the Outworlds

To call this a laboratory would be a fanciful misnomer. Bender's workshop was a bloody chop shop—a hoarder's playground full of illegal experiments and banned tech. That was what made his loose working arrangement with the Outlanders so beneficial. To them, the more verboten and outrageous the technology, the more they had to have it. It kept the playing field lopsided and interesting. Bender would provide them with top-notch weaponry, Med-tech, and body mods found nowhere else in the universe, and, in turn, they would keep the KACorps probes off his back.

At the center of the clutter was a crude hospital setup, which had serviced thousands of modifications. On one table was a massive dead crocodile, flayed open for parts and study.

Bastille sat in a Med-chair right next to it, trying to tune out the horrific rotting smell as he monitored Bender's progress on his arm repair. Bender got a little too sloppy with some wiring and zapped Bastille unintentionally.

"Hey," Bastille growled. "Give me a reason to release this trigger and blow your fat head clean off!" Bastille held his thumb on a trigger remote in his good hand. That way, if he went unconscious or suspected any foul play, he just had to lift his finger off, and the slave collar around Bender's neck would detonate, blowing his head off.

"I am not fat, I'm harvesting skin cells for—never mind, look man, I'm still recovering from that squiffing Mauzer. I still can't feel my left foot, and you wanna cry about a little pinched nerve? Now, hold still. Most patients are usually *not conscious* during this part of the operation because it hurts like a corker. You want two arms again? I'm all ya got."

Bender leaned in and zapped him again. Bastille winced and held the trigger higher. Bender objected, "Seriously, not helping the cause. Why don't you take your damn mind off the pain and tell me about that skinsack, Dash Strouthers?"

Bastille relaxed a bit. Bender began again, more cautiously, stitching the cybernetic arm back into the socket. Bastille eyed him cautiously. He wasn't sure how much to reveal, but he had nothing else to go on, yet, so he decided to tell Bender the truth. Sometimes, to receive trust, you first have to extend trust. And, hell, he could always kill him later.

"After the crash on Da'karh—the attack—I dunno," Bastille searched the ceiling for the right words to explain, "I suddenly started having these… memories. An entire previous life randomly surfacing in my head."

"What do you mean surfacing?" Bender dropped one tool onto the tray beside him and picked up a small drill with an abrasive brush at the tip.

"It's like I've got two people living in my head now," was the best way Bastille could explain the feeling. "It's faint, but I can tell he's in there. Growing."

"That's not possible." Bender leaned back watching Bastille's face carefully. "It's just not," he shrugged, and then pulled a magnifier into place and began smoothing some edges with the drill bit.

"It's happening. Captain Michael Strouthers. Call sign, Dash. Kytos Alliance Corporation Air Corps Test Pilot in Miramar aka Bravo Bay. Serial Number 1-4-1-6-0-9-ZED-ALPHA. It's all there, Bender. And if I concentrate hard enough, I can smell her jasmine perfume."

"Who?" Bender lowered his goggles. He followed Bastille's gaze to the Cryo-tanks.

"M-Mizuke? That's. Not—No." Bender lowered his voice and glanced around nervously. "Look, we totally wiped everything clean from the Byno-Core during your Re-cycle. You are a hundred percent you, my friend. Look at that shiner on your melon. What—you hit your head too hard, and now you're talking like you've squiffin' seen a ghostline?"

Bender studied his face for a moment. Bastille had a look of desperation there. A brief vulnerability.

"Wait, how is the rest of the memory array holding up? Any recall problems, or—?"

Bastille's eyes flicked to Bender, whose own eyes widened as he realized, "Oh my goddess, you've lost some memory."

Bastille swiftly hooked his good arm around Bender's head and pulled him close, seething; any trace of vulnerability was gone. "I will end you this moment, I swear to you."

"Bastille, man, it's me, dude. No wonder you've been acting so weird, like you don't even recognize your best friend. Come on. You saved me when I was just a low-level company squat on the *Bellevue* galleon. Sound familiar? You took me in." Bender smiled weakly. "You made me, man."

"You tried to kill me," Bastille added.

"That's just good business, dude." Beads of sweat gathered on Bender's forehead. The Relay box at the base of his neck blinked furiously. "That bounty was too freaking ridiculous to pass up. You know how many people I could buy off with all those qubits? Governments? Militia? Make my own city. Whatever, man. Almost done with this arm, could we maybe—?"

Bastille shoved him back. Bender adjusted his goggles and then rolled the medical cart back and pulled a smelly goo container forward. Selecting a special applicator, he began to lift some white material from the goo and spread it over the torn flesh between the shoulder and arm. As the synthetics hit the flesh, it began to oxidize and smoke as it bonded together, forming new tissue.

"You remember nothing?" Bender probed further. "So, okay, then why even come here?"

"The manifest on the bounty skiff. One of the last ports on their ship log. I recognized the name as soon as I saw it. Things are familiar, but foggy. Some things I remember so clearly."

"Like…" Bender prompted him.

"Like wanting to kill your fat ass," Bastille said matter-of-factly. The fist closed on his new arm. Bastille slowly opened it again, closed it, flexed the fingers, and rolled the wrist around.

"There. You're welcome, asshole," Bender said, wiping his hands on a dirty rag. "Free of charge. Okay? That's what friends are for. Now, take it easy for a few minutes and let the new skin acclimate."

Bender engaged a machine that pulsed UV light into the new skin, cooking it and aging it so that it blended more seamlessly with the old.

"What about the ghostline?" Bastille asked.

This made Bender explode into a belly laugh. "What? It's just a memory malfunction, you feckless sack. A short circuit. When squiffin' voices start squiffin' *talking* to you, then come talk to me about squiffin' ghostline, ya pignut. Everybody knows KACorps just made that squat up so they could outlaw our big business," he laughed some more. "Pshht. Ghostline."

"Who put the hit out on me?" Bastille cut in. "Had your fingerprints all over it."

"You know—" Bender straightened, rubbing his palms down his lapels thoughtfully. "If you're wanting me to fix your memory, we're gonna have to cut into that huge noggin of yours. But to do that, I'm gonna have to knock you out," Bender explained matter-of-factly.

"*Who* put the hit out on me?" Bastille repeated this, unstrapping his arm from the surgical rack and climbing off the Med-chair.

"General Wexell, of course," was his answer. But it didn't matter. There was no memory attached to the name. "Really?" Bender cocked his head. "Nothing? You've really got no clue? *The* General Wexell?"

"Why would he want me dead?" Bastille pressed.

"Oh boy. Okay, first off, *she*. Ya sexist peen. General Wexell is all woman. Don't ask me how I know that. Now, what say we make a little trade, hm? I give you something you want. You give me something I want." Bender held his hands up to show he wasn't trying to pull anything.

Bastille held the trigger up as a reminder. Bender moved to a wall of storage boxes and dialed a code. Box number thirty-eight slid forward. He pulled it from its slot and held it up for Bastille to see. "More specifically, I give you your old life back and you give me," he indicated the trigger in Bastille's hand, "my life back."

"What's in the box?" Bastille furrowed his brow.

"For starters," Bender lifted the lid and pulled out a launch key. "How about your old ship back? It's still in the garage downstairs. Right where ya left it before you went underground."

He wiggled the key tantalizingly.

"Fine," Bastille reluctantly agreed. "But you still have to tell me about the girl in these Cryo-tanks. Who she is and what the significance of the—"

Bastille saw Bender's eyes flick left and automatically reacted. In a split second, he had dropped to a knee, cleared leather with the Mauzer, and atomized two Snake Soldiers approaching stealthily behind him. The rest of their unit scrambled for cover in the gigantic laboratory and just outside in the hall.

The Relay on Bastille's neck pulsed blue before he yanked Bender down to the floor with him. Grabbing the box and the launch key from Bender, he shoved them inside his bug-out duffel, and then Bastille moved low toward a back exit.

Bender pointed frantically to his explosive slave collar and said, "Hey. *HEY.* What about this thing?"

Bastille smiled and tossed him the trigger. Bender caught it and recoiled for a second. Nothing happened. No explosion. "You lying little—"

Piff piff piff. The Outlanders sent a few test rounds of gunfire to shake Bastille into the open.

"I wouldn't stick around here," Bastille called back to Bender. "It's about to get nasty."

"Wait, what—" At that moment, Bender heard the whining turbines of the bounty skiff that Bastille rode in on, settling into attack position right out the window. "Brilliant," he said, ducking low as the ship opened fire and the world around him exploded. He reached up to the wall and triggered a safety latch. A metal door sealed off the Cryo-tubes in a safe room.

Meanwhile, Bastille slung the duffel over his shoulder and exited as Snake soldiers were mowed down by the battle skiff's hell-fire cannons. Bender scamper-crawled into the hallway, where Bastille had waxed another Snake and was already turning the corner and gone.

Looking back into the room, he watched a couple of missiles streak inside. Bender barely lunged forward and slammed the button to close the blast doors before the whole lab shook on its foundations, buckling the walls and the doors. The force threw Bender back against the corridor. He clumsily recovered to his feet as smoke oozed out of every ruptured crevice, and then emergency foam shot from their ceiling mounts.

Bender could see through the gap in the walls that at least one of the Cryo-tanks had been destroyed. "No, no, nonononono, Mizuke. My baby, my darling," he pounded the door. "I'm gonna kill you, Jacques Bastille. You hear me?!"

General alarms sounded throughout the compound. Meanwhile, Bastille ducked into an alcove as a couple more soldiers crawled past, headed toward the lab, clicking and communicating with each other. When the coast was clear, he looked up both hallways unsure which way to go. In his HUD, one doorway up the hall blinked green. He didn't have time to decode what was happening, so he ran through it and hit a stairwell. The left stairs blinked green, so he ran down one flight. When he emerged, he was in the cavernous garage bay.

"This is nuts," he admitted. Inside the bay, he paused, wondering which ship was his. There was another battle skiff, a couple of hover cycles, and a little D-Class transport. Another blinking trail on the floor led him forward. He ran past the transport, and there it was. His ship. It was battle damaged and all modded up, but it was a Mustang. H2X-1 model, to be exact. Home.

Jumping into the cockpit, he slid the activation key into place, synced it with his Relay box, and the heads-up display activated. The ship sprang to life. Five point two seconds later, the Mustang lifted off the ground even before the canopy had fully closed and sealed.

Snake soldiers began to file into the back of the garage. Bastille paid them no mind; he just punched the throttle forward to maximum, and the ionic boom and resulting shock wave shattered everything in there, from metal to bone. It all blasted through the back wall and tumbled down towards the Synad river far below.

Bastille strained forward in his seat. On the outside, he fought the extreme G-forces against his body. That was the lesser of the two evils, though. Having retained the uplink with his stolen hammerhead skiff, the simultaneous H2 link was taxing his mental Relay.

Wasn't it Lieutenant Flint Malloy who fried his array and stroked out, attempting a bi-neural transport jack? Bastille thought it was fascinating that this specific memory would surface right at this moment, but he didn't have the bandwidth to give it any more consideration. Sweat from the strain formed on his forehead.

Bastille surprised his pursuers with a bombardment of missiles from the bounty skiff's arsenal, which doggedly trailed them. Most of them tore off to engage the skiff. Bastille pointed the H2 for the stars, quickly putting distance between the lagging enemy ships trying in vain to catch up. As the distance to the hammerhead increased, his strain increased, and his control over it weakened.

Ahead, between him and subspace, a three-ship formation bore down on him. They weren't going to pull any punches now that they knew who he was. They'd bounce him out of the sky the first chance they got. Bastille smiled and triggered the missile array on the H2, but warnings on the monitor instantly showed there were zero in stock.

He switched over to guns, and warning chimes rang again. Empty. No ordinance.

Shik'amooha, he swore in a language he could not recall having ever learned.

The battle skiffs ahead opened fire with a barrage of missiles, and Bastille rolled the Mustang wildly to avoid contact with the first wave. Meanwhile, the rear Coda Force blasted the bounty skiff into dust, painfully severing his bi-neural uplink. And then it happened again.

Fzzzzzzzht.

* * *

Planet Earth, Miami Bay

Sim Training. Young Dash Strouthers cut the virtual H2X-Ø Mustang hard left, just missing an on-coming pair of HX-45s in this intense virtual dogfight. The ships dodged in and around a long abandoned Miami sky-line—above water this time. Their only spectators were the cracked and charred cement gargoyles that retained their vigil atop the tallest buildings. As they rocketed past what was left of the historic Freedom Tower, loose mortar and debris scattered to the ground.

"Wooohooo, close, but no bingo," Gator said over the comm. "What, no more ammo, so you're gonna avalanche us to death? Give it up, Dash. I'm gonna wax your tail."

"Never," Dash said through gritted teeth as he pulled tightly to jockey into position behind Gator's ship. Overhead, the sky was dotted with other fighters engaged in aerial combat play. While maneuvering, Dash punched in a sequence and drove straight up in the sky toward the frenzy above.

"What the hell are you—" Gator stopped short as he saw a blue spark on the back of the H2. "You can't do that. That's cheating."

Dash slammed his power off, ignored the altitude buzzer, and hit the EMP button. A spherical pulse in all directions from his ship, short-circuiting everything in its path for miles around.

"Balls," Dash said, realizing his error as all the ships above began to drop downward. His own H2 was not one hundred percent fly-by-wire like the 45s and still retained the special aerodynamics it was required to have for flying beneath the ocean. So, he was able to barrel roll it and glide it to a certain extent. But none of that mattered when fifteen dead ships rained down like anchors from the sky above. Dash was about to reignite the H2 when a 45 ripped into the Mustang, blowing it to pieces.

Sim over.

Fzzzzzzzht.

* * *

VerDav'n Colony in the Outlands

Bastille could feel it immediately. The Dash Strouthers "residue" or "ghostline" had grown even more. Evolved. This thing inside him was clearly communicating through visions, flashbacks, and glimpses into a world Bastille had never known. He was probably the one in his retinal-HUD showing him the escape path from Bender's chop shop. Plugging into this Mustang's Relay and D/S might have strengthened him even more. Especially if this had been Dash's original ship, there was the possibility, however insane it sounded, that some backup files existed.

Kaboom.

The Mustang jerked to the right with a mind of its own as an explosion rocked dangerously close beside him. Bastille checked six again. The Snakes launched an array of missiles headed his way. Overhead, the Outlanders were closing fast.

I must be losing my mind.

Bastille took his hands off the throttle and nav stick as the Mustang continued to maneuver beneath him. He spoke into the air, "Alright, Dash. If you're there, bud, do your thing."

The Mustang rocked its wingtips in compliance, and then this new force took complete control. Bastille saw in the HUD the command for the EMP, which rose up on the spine of the ship. The H2's power cut off, and then a blue pulse shot through the air, immobilizing thirty other ships and missiles. The surrounding Coda

Force was nothing but sky trash now plummeting to the ground. Dash rolled the Mustang to clear the ships above. As he glided into a safe lane, he reignited the engines, which came online in an improved 3.4 seconds.

"Well, sh*t," Bastille said when he saw it. "Helluva reboot."

The Mustang creaked and groaned as Dash fired all thrusters at once and jumped toward the stratosphere. The tracer missiles, with their NavCOMMS fried, veered aimlessly, and then gravity took over as they ran out of steam.

Bastille checked over his shoulder. He was certain that Bender's outpost and all those poor prairie lizards far below would not survive the maelstrom headed their way.

As they cleared the exosphere into space, Bastille saw a warship and escorts on an intercept with him and the K-gate. He had to make it to subspace. It was his only chance to lose them. The EMP would take hours to fully recharge. It would be no help here. "What's the play, Dash?"

Generally speaking, a pilot slows down to a moderate drift into a hyperlane in order to increase one's chances of making it into and, subsequently, out of a dive into hyperspace in one piece. That's what the Coda Force on board the warship was counting on. That's what Bastille was counting on.

"Dash, you think maybe we should—"

Dash kept the throttle on a full burn and directed their ship right into the center of the gate. The warship realized, too late, what was happening and opened fire, but the Mustang plunged through the flak and dove straight into hyperspace.

Bastille's last thought before he passed out was that this was probably what it was like to be shot with that Mauzer. And then his entire being was ripped into the hyper-dive.

\- 5 -

THE SHADOW MOON

Triangulum Quadrant

When Bastille regained consciousness, he immediately grabbed for an emergency sick pouch and blew chunks into it. His head throbbed. His vision was blurred. A hyper-dive hangover was a thousand percent worse than any hangover he'd ever known. He remembered that the Coda Force was in pursuit and scanned the heavens quickly to gain his bearings. There were no pursuers. He relaxed a little. There was also no extensive damage he could see on the Mustang's scopes. According to the NavCOMM, he was somewhere adrift in the Triangulum Quadrant. Wherever the hell that was. There looked to be a giant ice planet right next door, but predictably, it showed no signs of civilization.

"Dash?" Bastille spoke softly, as if trying to wake someone. Nothing. No response. "Dash." He tapped the back of the Relay box to re-seat it in case it had popped loose. Still nothing.

"DAAAAASH!" He banged on his head and jiggled the controls of the ship. Silence. Bastille checked the ship's log. He had been out cold for four hours.

Systems at three percent. I need a refueling station. And possibly a lobotomy. Or an exorcism. But first, fuel. Where the hell am I?

Bastille called up the star charts and flipped through a bunch of star systems. While he looked those over, he reached into a pocket down to his left and grabbed a power bar, cracked open the shell, and took a bite of the chewy, sizzling sustenance. The headaches were the first thing to dissipate. Slowly, his vision racked into focus, and his entire belly warmed up—a warmth that spread to all of his extremities. This was a powerful and well-needed meta-chemical boost. All of his senses came alive as his blood sugar leveled out.

Scanning the star charts, Bastille found a few promising worlds. He would punch in the coordinates, but each time the computer would warn of "insufficient fuel" to reach them. This went on for about twenty minutes before he finally found a good candidate. He would just barely be able to make this small mining colony. If it still existed. He locked in the coordinates, fired up the Ion drive, and pushed the throttle forward. When he did, all the systems immediately died, and the entire cockpit went dark.

"Sh*t," Bastille said. He punched a few buttons. Nothing happened. He reached under the dash and fingered some connectors, but everything seemed tight.

Bastille laid his head back into the headrest and sighed. Then he took another huge bite of the power bar. At least if he was going to die, he wouldn't do it on an empty stomach.

He watched the stars slowly circle above him as the ship continued its lazy little drift. It was a mesmerizing and dazzling display. A million billion sparkling lights in every direction. So peaceful. One part of the sky contained cosmic dust and gases that formed gigantic fingers in the heavens. So beautiful. Two minutes later, Bastille noticed something and perked up.

"Wait a minute—" he said, squinting against the vast and starry void.

Two of those stars were moving. Growing larger. They were headed in his direction. After several minutes, he was able to recognize them as scientific vessels. Of the St. Croix variety.

The Mighty Draccarios, he thought, *what are those religious nuts doing way out here?*

The St. Croix people were deeply spiritual and, quixotically enough, the most technologically advanced humans that ever existed. In fact, among other things, their scientists had discovered hyper-diving and developed the Ion drives in the first place. Or so they'd claimed.

Years ago, the Kytos Alliance Corporation branded them an outlaw cult and annexed their science and some of their ships. They could have fought back— Lord knows they had the tech for it—but being a peaceful group, they enacted a mass exodus and disappeared among the stars. No one had heard from them in a century and a half, and it was assumed their fleet had been sucked into a black hole. Or that they had been raptured as their ancient texts had foretold. Or both. One thing was for certain: they had taken some of the brightest scientific minds with them when they left.

Rumor had it that their engineers had been working unsuccessfully on developing a new species—silly as it sounds—of megasaurs. That's right, dragons. They combined the fire-breathing sea condors and various lizard strains to create a war dragon. A real, live, armor-plated, sentient species of fire-breathing lizards. They were even supposed to fly. With their resistance to heat and radiation, these were to be the guardians of the NeoTokyo topside and protect it from marauders and malcontents.

But any Viddix footage that turned up on the StarNET looked like fake computer graphics. For one thing, the so-called dragons looked to be the size of kittens. Also, those dumb lizards were scared of their own shadows and wouldn't hurt a soul. Much like their creators. Hence, the entire laughingstock—humans and beasts—became known derisively as the Mighty Draccarios. It didn't help their cause that the lot of them had turned tail and run off into space.

Bastille watched the Draccario ships slow their course and navigate into the dark umber of the ice planet on the far side. There was no way they would see him, even if they were looking directly at him. He was a tiny silver speck in a sea of white dots. He squinted and could make out a Shadow Moon where the vessels descended until they were swallowed up in its darkness.

Then, just like that, his ship's functions returned.

"I see it, Dash." Bastille called up the star charts again, and there was no Shadow Moon reference, only the gigantic ice planet, ESB K-80.

"Whatever you are, you're completely off-grid," he said, scratching at his beard.

Clutching the joystick, Bastille bumped the thrusters, and the Mustang lurched toward the Shadow Moon. Not wanting anything to short out again, Bastille maintained this slow, gentle pace all the way there.

It took the better part of an hour before he circumnavigated the ice planet and arrived at the Shadow Moon—easily the size of the Earth's moon before it had been ravaged in the war. But up closer now, the whole thing looked like a giant water droplet.

The comms chimed when a message was transmitted from the planet. It was layered in a variety of languages, and his system separated out the BaseZero: "Unidentified craft, introducing Phaedra Planet Security. Please to state business."

"Phaedra? Great, hey, hi. This is Captain Jacques Bastille, haha, you are not gonna believe this, but I am on fumes here, outta gas. And my peaceful vessel—which is no threat whatsoever—is in need of some minor repairs and some fuel, and then I'll be on my way."

"Please to stand by while scanning of your ship of weapons," the metallic voice responded.

Good luck with that, Bastille smiled to himself and sat back with his hands behind his head, whistling. Waiting.

A minute later, the HUD beeped as the scan was initiated, and then the Phaedra security bot continued, "Confirmed, Mustang. Approved clearance with secure proceeding of coordinate uploads. Any deviant attempt follows entire deletion from atmosphere and life."

Deleted from atmosphere? And life? So much for the peaceful doormat people, he thought.

"Roger that, Phaedra, I come in peace. In fact, we should grab a Ghorkan Ale when I land for—"

"Connection terminated," the HUD interrupted.

Bastille shook his head. He wasn't trying to start an international incident, but he could tell this group were sticklers for protocol. Not grammar, obviously, but protocol. He sat back as the autopilot took control of his vessel.

He watched curiously as the drives were switched from Ion to Hydros, seconds before encountering a strange water barrier around the planet. Breaking through that thick exospheric vapor canopy, he was then switched from Hydros to the Atmos drives.

As the clouds cleared, a beautiful, lush green planet lay beneath him. Trees, fields, and rivers with exotic creatures flying above a forest canopy. Amazing. It always felt good to be back under gravity's pull. To be surrounded by good old-fashioned, breathable O2. He checked the monitor, and it showed conditions outside similar to Earth's own environment. This was apparently some sort of gigantic bio-dome.

The Mustang began to ventilate and recycle its oxygen systems to acclimate to the surface pressure. Bastille suppressed a yawn as his ears popped. Otherwise, this was his favorite part. He inhaled deeply, and his nostrils filled with a potpourri of smells. It was such a stark contrast to the bleak and sterile metallic odors he endured for weeks traveling through deep space.

Da'karh was a dustbowl, and Bender's place on VerDav'n smelled of swamp water. This scent was alive. It was grass and foliage and flower buds and dirt and home. The only thing that would have been more perfect was if it had the salty brine of the sea smell he loved. But that was just being nit-picky. This was heaven.

Bastille was soaking it all in when the comm broke in on him: "Mustang, first of last warning. Please resuming auto-pilot or face to deletion."

Bastille panicked. "Sh*t, I didn't touch anything." He looked over, and manual control had been engaged, and the ship barrel-rolled down to the planet's surface.

"Dash, what the hell—" he started to say when an electron beam from the planet's surface buzzed past, missing them by a fraction of a millimeter. Or did it? An aftershock jolted through the cockpit and all the electronics went batsh*t.

Fzzzzzzzht.

* * *

Planet Earth, NeoTokyo

Officer's quarters. Dash sat at the dinner table, staring off into the distance, while a room full of houseguests smiled expectantly at him. There were balloons and birthday streamers, and what appeared to be a small feast laid out before them. His wife, Mizuke, kneeled by his chair with a Med-gun against his wrist.

"Honey?" she said, nudging him. "I asked, 'How does it feel?' Did the Vancinex injection take effect?"

Dash noticed the small red spot on his arm where the shot must have entered. "Yeah, sorry, I—" he was about to mention the crazy Ma'kobi Captain and the shadow moon, but thought better of it. Hell, they would just figure that it was the drugs talking. And maybe it was. He was still a little loopy. He smiled instead and answered, "I feel… *great* all of a sudden. Hit me again, babe."

Everyone erupted with laughter. Mizuke stood and took her seat beside him at the table. "Now don't be greedy, Dash. That's a full dose. Heaven knows we don't want to get you hooked on this stuff. You'd end up some kind of Sonic Wafer addict, like my sister."

"Well, I can take it," said Colonel Jacobs, a large, red-bearded man. He pulled his own sleeve up. "It's the nectar of the gods. And the all-seeing eye. Hit me."

Mizuke hesitated a second, but Jacobs was not joking. So, she pressed the silver tip into his forearm and squeezed off a round.

A tiny puff of smoke signaled the transaction, and the Colonel sat back, staring at the chandelier. Everyone leaned forward expectantly. He held his breath as long as he could and then slowly exhaled a thin blue trail of smoke. "I can damn well see the future, kids. That stuff is intense. Freddy, you will need that heart murmur checked soon."

Freddy exchanged a knowing glance with Pamela, his wife. She tenderly squeezed his arm. Vancinex had long been abused in the civilian market by people wanting a cheap hallucinogen, but that's not why the Draccario chemists invented it. They had found that with certain test subjects, like Jacobs, it indeed gave a super-heightened awareness—some would say even a glimpse into the future. Dash wasn't on board for the last part of that religious mumbo-jumbo as much as his wife was. He just liked that it felt like a warm, soul-cleansing hug, which left you with a euphoric sense that all was right with the world and anything was possible.

The Colonel continued, "And someone in here is pregnant. I can feel the quickened heartbeat of a tiny life form."

Everyone looked around the room, searching for the guilty party.

"False prophet! Stone him!" Mizuke ribbed him as she stood and continued, "But close. Thanks for up-ending my surprise."

She lifted a small creature cage from a pile of wrapped presents "I was going to wait on this one, but thanks to Colonel All-Seeing-Eye over here—"

Everyone chuckled as she placed the container in front of Dash. Mizuke continued, "Honey, we've been instructed at the laboratory to take these runts home and work with them. Train them. Love and foster them. I thought… well, I thought it'd kinda be the perfect couple assignment for us."

Dash was intrigued as he looked over the domed container before him. "How mysterious."

Mizuke triggered the release of the base locks. "This one has not imprinted yet," she instructed. "Brand new batch. It is very important that, in the first few seconds, you look him directly in the eye. Don't look away. You'll feel a weird sensation—an uplink we call it—and you'll know it's done. Ready?"

Dash looked skeptical.

Mizuke reassured him, "Don't worry, Dash, this is just a simple role-based access control pattern. Like pairing your headphones with your computer. Just means you're the only one who can tell him what to do. Ready?"

"Ready? I'm scared to death." Dash patted Freddy's shoulder but kept his focus on the silver orb. "Freddy, did you bring Violet one of these... couple surprises?"

"Sure did," Freddy admitted. "They're beautiful and amazing creatures. Almost bit her hand off, but she loves it."

Violet punched his arm playfully and then demurred quickly. "That's not true." She tucked a strand of hair behind her ear adding, "Tr'm is a very sweet boy."

"Okay," Dash gulped down the last swallow from a wine glass, and, placing both hands on the table, he sat forward.

Mizuke twisted the handle, breaking the seal. Then slowly, she lifted the lid from the platter. There, curled up in a ball on the blanket, was a Mighty... small Draccario—laughable, really, because it did look like a hairless little kitten. It had two little nubs where the wings should have been. It looked more like a scaly pug with bat's ears than it did a lizard or even any sea condor that Dash had ever seen. It stirred, skittered around a bit, blinked a couple of times, and then nervously searched the faces around the table. Everyone else closed or covered their eyes. No one wanted to risk connecting. Then it found Dash. And it locked on. Unblinking.

Dash watched the little beast as its breathing returned to normal, as it calmed and settled into this little staring contest. His own breathing steadied to match the dragonling, so ugly, it was cute. Finally, it sneezed once and then blinked away a nictitating membrane—like a second inner eyelid—and Dash looked into those clear, steely gray eyes.

Maybe it was the Vancinex, but he could have sworn he heard a voice that said something like, "Ruhzaah," and then the uplink snapped hold as the creature launched at his face.

Fzzzzzzzht.

* * *

Phaedra the Shadow Moon

Bastille's eyes were open and lifeless. He lay there on the floor, staring into space. His hands were bound behind his back with some silk fabric. A young woman stood in the doorway. She wore the flowing, white robes of the St. Croix people. Her piercing green eyes studied the stranger in every detail. With the slightest tilt of her head, she stated simply, "He's back."

"Not the nose—" Bastille sucked air, blinked a couple of times, and looked frantically around to gather his bearings. These back-and-forth shifts were taking their toll. It wasn't like watching a movie of the past; he was reliving things. Experiencing things and feeling them deeply with every sense as if he had been there. It was wild. And he hated it.

He stopped wiggling when he spotted the girl; she couldn't be more than eighteen. There was something odd about her, he thought. For one, there wasn't an ounce of fear in her. And Bastille knew he looked chewed up and spit out. For two, her stance was not haphazard and slouched, but poised and, well, tactical, would be the word he'd use to describe it. Right down to her boots. Third, it had to be the way she wore that Mauzer around her hip—his Mauzer—with the safety off and ready. Barely hidden just inside the folds of her robes.

Bastille was mindful of the fact that this was his first contact with the long lost Draccario zealots. He'd have to choose his first words as diplomatically as possible. He mustered a grin and said hoarsely, "I gotta piss."

She just stared back.

"Hey, little dipper," Bastille said, extending the wrist binders awkwardly behind him. "Help a guy out?"

"Gen, what did you—" D'erik entered and stopped beside the girl. "Oh."

D'erik was a full-sized adult. Lithe and fit in a trim suit, he was clearly the girl's father. Or butler. He brushed past Gen and squatted down beside Bastille. "Phaedra's Sky Security is on its way here to pick you up, Captain. Two things have kept you alive so far: Well, to be perfectly frank, your flying skills were inspired. No one has ever penetrated our defenses like that before and lived," he said, honestly impressed.

"Maybe you cut me loose, and maybe I don't snap your spine in two," Bastille leered menacingly. "Maybe."

"Secondly," D'erik continued, unphased, "you didn't head for the technology sector or the weapons bunker or treasury at all. You flew straight here to our botanical gardens and smashed our dendrobiums."

This caught Bastille off guard. "Your what?"

"Orchids. Flowers. Lots of medicinal purposes. Was just about harvesting time, too, when your big ship just—pbbbbbt," he flattened one hand against the other to illustrate.

Gen stepped over aggressively and asked, "Why are you here?" It was hard to tell from her short communication bursts but her royal Draccario accent was very thick. D'erik also had a royal accent but it wasn't as pronounced as hers.

"Exactly my point, Gen," D'erik conceded graciously. "Why *are* you here?"

"Beats the hell outta me," Bastille answered quite honestly. "Ooof," he groaned as he rolled up to a seated position. "You two talk funny. What accent is that exactly?"

D'erik moved a more cautious distance away. "Sky Security is literally three minutes out. Suppose we did untie you, my scruffy friend. Would you be able to talk more freely?" D'erik offered.

"Yes, untie me, Draccario, and give my gun back, and maybe I won't kill you both where you stand. Final offer."

"Oh," D'erik was clearly flustered. "Gen, what do you—"

In a flash, Gen produced a knife and tossed the seven-inch blade squarely between Bastille's crossed legs. It lodged into the oak floor, pinning just a bit of his pants leg into place. Bastille didn't even flinch. He stared the girl down and sensed just a hint of amusement in the corner of her eyes.

"Join us when you're ready," she said, and then turned and walked out.

D'erik gestured around the corner, indicating where they might be waiting, and then exited quickly.

Bastille rolled onto his knees, pulled the knife from the floor, and cut away the fabric binding his hands. Rubbing his wrists, he looked once more around the little storage area. All kinds of foodstuffs were packed away on the shelves and sorted. Canned vegetables and fruit lined this whole pantry. Bastille dusted what he assumed was flour off his pants. He inspected some of it more closely on his fingertips, curiously, before blowing it off. Then he followed through the door, flipping the knife around casually.

Much more daylight filtered into the living room through the huge floor-to-ceiling windows. It was a seamless blending of architecture and natural surroundings. There was a hint of modernity and technology, but it was masked by a more rustic veneer.

Through the window, Bastille could see his banged up Mustang. Not pretty. It stood out in that garden like a baby with a face tattoo. Completely out of place in its pristine, natural surroundings. He winced, seeing the landing struts buried deep into an otherwise beautiful garden.

"Hm. Sorry about the flowers," he conceded.

D'erik sat at the table, sipping tea from a dainty porcelain cup. He motioned to another steaming teacup across from him. Gen stood with her back to them at the window. Bastille figured she probably didn't realize that the sunlight through that dress fabric left little to the imagination. Yet for some reason, it all struck him as being… overly produced. Whatever that meant.

He spun the knife in his fingers and thought: What the hell? He sighed, set the knife down on the counter. That was the right play. He could see Gen's shoulders relax a little. He knew she was tracking his every move in the window reflection. He then slid into a chair across from D'erik. Lifting the flowery cup to his lips, he breathed in the fragrance. "Chamomile?"

D'erik looked pleasantly surprised. "Very good, Captain. You are a discerning polymath."

"Nah, I don't do arithmetic," he confessed.

"A regular Renaissance man, if you will," D'erik clarified.

"Ha, yeah, you got me," Bastille said, rolling his eyes. Who were these weirdos? He watched them sip their tea for a moment. So many stories he'd heard about this extremist group. So many myths and cautionary tales. All from the KACorps intel, though. "Everyone thought you all got, uh, sucked up to heaven. Or blasted into a black hole somewhere."

"Oh, goodness, no," D'erik chuckled to himself. "No, far from it. Historically, we separatists really just wanted our religious freedom."

"To do your weird sh*t out where nobody could stop you?" Bastille said dryly.

"Our freedom to not be hunted down and exterminated like vermin by Colonel Wexell," D'erik answered rather pointedly. "So, yes, we headed off into the great unknown to start over. Pilgrims, if you will."

"Hm. *General* Wexell now, I hear," Bastille said. D'erik glowered at the name. Bastille looked back toward the windows and changed the subject. "You build this Shadow Moon yourself, Pilgrim?"

D'erik studied him for a moment. "Yes, in a manner of speaking. Not from scratch, but yes. The water canopy, the cloaking device, oh, hmmm—"

He cut himself off, but not before Bastille noticed the warning look that Gen gave him.

"So, like a fancy bio-dome," Bastille shrugged.

"Oh, ho ho, but so much more. So much more," D'erik caught another look from Gen and trailed off.

"It's incredible," Bastille said.

D'erik smiled and accepted the compliment with a nod. "Care for some more tea, Captain…?"

"Bastille. Jacques," he said finally.

"A pleasure, Captain Bastille," D'erik replied. "My name is D'erik, and this feisty little one is Gen-wa'ar. She goes by Gen."

"Yeah, little dip," Bastille said sarcastically. "She your daughter or what?"

"Haha, no, no, my friend, daughter indeed." D'erik was very amused by the idea. "No, she is my mother."

Bastille almost choked on his chamomile.

"I know why you're here, Captain," Gen said, turning fully from the window. "I know who sent you."

Bastille leaned back, hanging an arm over the chair back. "Enlighten me, lady," he answered coolly.

"Dash Strouthers," she said with her quiet confidence.

Bastille tensed up and pushed the empty teacup and saucer to the center of the table and stood. "Okay, enough. Suppose you ask your friends to come out of hiding," he growled with a wave to the room.

Gen studied him for a moment and then nodded. A half dozen Draccario guards de-cloaked from their vantage points around the living room, weapons at their ready. A few more stepped into view on the porch; more were down by the Mustang.

"Very good, Captain," Gen all but clapped.

"Why stop there?" Bastille challenged, circling a finger in the air, "Are any of these theatrics really necessary, little dip?"

"It's Genwa'ar, you—" she checked herself. Taking a breath to recenter, she barked out a command in the Croix mother tongue, "*Klaaven-daœ eraaliyum, ka.*"

Instantly, the walls and furniture dissolved from their holo-construct states. The scenery and the Mustang outside shimmered and ghosted away into a million tiny cube patterns, leaving nothing but a large, secure white room with Gen, D'erik, Bastille, and a half-dozen guards at the ready.

Gen lifted an eyebrow, and her hand flew to her hip, annoyed.

"What?" Bastille shrugged. "It was a thousand little clues. I'm sorry. The wood grain on the floor had a slight digital residue to it; the Mustang was missing a few modifications; the chamomile tea—"

"The chamomile was perfect," Gen interrupted. "I personally coded that one."

"The chamomile *was* perfect," Bastille admitted, "but it reflected weirdly when I stirred it with the spoon. I'm sorry, some of the physics are off in your… game engine, or VR booth, or whatever."

"Is that it?" Gen was tapping her foot now.

"Well," he scrunched up his face almost apologetically. "D'erik seems a wee bit…" he trailed off.

In a huff, Gen pointed a remote at D'erik, and when she clicked it, he dissolved into nothingness with a lingering, "Oh dear."

After that, the Draccario guards also blinked out of sight.

"Okay," Bastille approached her more seriously, "the only true thing you've said so far is the part about Dash Strouthers."

"Ugh." Gen waved a hand in the air dismissively. "You were mumbling the name while we held you unconscious. I was just playing a hunch."

Taking out the Mauzer in one smooth motion, she pointed it right at his chest. "There's a *huge* bounty on your head, Jacques Bastille. Every data stream across the StarNET. Dead or alive." She took two steps toward him. "Tell me why I shouldn't blast you now and collect what could be a very handsome reward."

"Because," Bastille also took a deliberate step forward so the barrel was firmly nestled into his sternum. "Your people have kept this Shadow Moon a secret for a hundred years or more; you wouldn't risk coming out of hiding now. Over me. And you've already got unlimited resources, and life as you know it is five by five. Why wreck all of that? Besides, you don't have what it takes to pull that trigger. I don't care how old you really are inside that lolita skinbag. You're no killer."

She shrugged and leaned in conspiratorially. "Maybe I'll just kill you out of boredom." Bastille waited for her to make up her mind one way or another. She stood there, biting a fingernail, deep in thought, before snapping out of it. She holstered the Mauzer and commanded, "*Tchlaak.*"

A digital doorway materialized behind her, and she walked out. After a moment, she poked her head back in and said, "Well? Are you coming or not?"

"Unbelievable!" Gen exited in a huff.

"Where are we going?" Bastille called after her.

"The Bath House, Captain. You stink."

Bastille stopped short. A Draccario Bath House? That couldn't possibly mean what it did back on Earth. Or things were about to get weird.

- 6 -

DRACCARIO BATH HOUSE

Phaedra the Shadow Moon

Bastille followed Genwa'ar closely down an endless maze of corridors. Most of them had expansive see-through walls, so you could look out over the city. It reminded Bastille of one of those tube farms a gerbil might live in. Gen did not speak to him along the way, but she nodded and said, *"Shin'sey,"* to everyone in passing. She appeared to be some sort of royalty around here. They repeated it back, always with a slight bow. It either meant "good day" or "have no fear of the orang-utan behind me, he's a harmless simp." Judging by the lack of eye contact the Draccario snobs gave him, it was probably the second one.

Gen walked past one door and then stopped to reconsider. "Actually," she said, turning them both back to the entrance. "I think you'll find this quite interesting."

She unlocked the door with an amulet on her ring finger, held to the keypad. It slid open, and they stepped through. Bastille halted just inside the door.

"What the hell?" He looked at row upon row of Cryo-tubes with a variety of naked teenage bodies inside. There were way more varieties than just the Mizuke units he'd seen at Bender's place. In fact, this tech made Bender's lab look like a barnyard shed. "What's this? Some sorta pervy playground?"

"Good heaven's, no." Gen looked at him, her lips curled into a contemptuous sneer. "I'd almost forgotten the gutter minds we had to put up with all those years ago. You might need a leash."

Bastille rolled his eyes. "Spare me the sanctimony, your majesty."

Gen took a cleansing breath and continued, "These are brand new Byno-Cores for our advanced citizens. Grown to the age of perfection. Ready to be Recycled."

She walked over to inspect the side chambers. Small rooms off the main lab. One of them was occupied. "Come," she waved him over.

Bastille joined her, and they peered through the portal together. There was a young Draccario guardian in uniform; there was a scientist or engineer-type; and then there was a naked older lady. Over a hundred years old. They all stood in front of one of those young Byno-Cores—also female—strapped to a vertical slab. She did not look conscious.

"Um," Bastille shifted uncomfortably, "maybe they'd like some privacy for their weird sh*t."

"Hush. Privacy is forbidden," Gen explained with another warning look. "Now I'm sure you are used to some crude, backwater Re-cycle methods to obtain your new," she looked him up and down, "first-class meat-suit—"

"It gets the job done, sweetheart," he said, scowling back. "Trust me."

"Hmph," she objected. "And that flea-ridden skinbag is the result of how many surgeries and curative maintenances?"

Bastille sighed. "Uhhh, I lost count after eight," he admitted.

She stifled a condescending laugh. "How your kind ever made it off-planet, we will never know."

Bastille ignored the jab. The scene inside that chamber was too wild. The old woman stepped over to the teen girl and placed a hand behind her neck—possibly over her Relay box—and the other hand she placed over her own Relay. Then a blue electric energy field emanated from the foxy granny and quickly blossomed from little sparks into a whole charged frenzy. Lightning shot from the old lady's eyes and mouth into the teenager's face and chest. Both bodies rocked and shook. And then it was over, and the old body slumped to the floor. The teen Byno-Core inhaled deeply and came alive.

"Holy sh*t," Bastille whispered. "Did she just—"

"Re-cycle? Without any technological assistance? Yes, she did. That's not even that remarkable to *us*. We perform twelve or more of these Re-cycles a week," she searched his stunned face.

"I mean, but how?" was all Bastille could muster. He watched the engineer and soldier pick up the old shell and toss it into a spare parts bin. Then they ran some tests on the young girl, who looked exhausted and disheveled but was otherwise… okay.

"You know…" Gen inhaled deeply, lifting her chin. "Since we're here, we could get you a Relay booster."

Bastille turned to her, his eyes narrowing.

"No," she held up a hand as she explained, "it's basically a long overdue upgrade to all of—"

She waved her hand over his face and abdomen.

"—this."

"And what's the catch?" Bastille studied her. "I wake up one day and suddenly discover I'm a toaster oven or a royal foot stool?"

Gen looked very annoyed at the question. She knocked on the door, and the engineer came over. "*Shin'sey*, have you got an extra thirium Relay booster?"

His eyes jerked to Bastille and then back to Gen. "But I would need council approval for—"

"I *am* the council," Gen reminded the underling. She locked him in a steely, unblinking gaze. The same one she'd used on Bastille when he was tied up. Only this time, it actually worked.

"Of course." The engineer bowed apologetically, then skittered off around a corner for all of two seconds, and then returned with a small container. He handed it to Gen and then excused himself back to the Re-cycle room.

"Better, faster, stronger, smarter, and, of course," she leaned in with a smile, "younger."

"That's not gonna make me younger," he argued.

"It'll roll back the years," she promised and popped the latch to open the kit. Bastille looked closer at the small rectangle cartridge and then stepped back warily.

Gen sighed, turned around, and pulled her collar down. "Oh, for heaven's sake, it's the same as mine, you big baby."

Bastille leaned in to double-check. It did look exactly like the one in her hand. He exhaled deeply and shrugged. "What the hell? Why not?"

Gen turned back around. She removed the cartridge from the box, and when Bastille hesitated, she grabbed his shirt and pulled him down closer to her level.

"This better not hurt," he warned her as he submitted the back of his neck toward her.

She snapped it into place over top of his Relay box. "It is a maintenance upgrade. You won't feel a—"

And that was the last thing Bastille heard before his Relay overloaded; his system went into shock, and he dropped to the floor.

Fzzzzzzzht.

* * *

NeoTokyo, Eno District

Eno's Ghost was the most popular cabaret for academy hangouts, and tonight the club was packed; pockets of fighter jocks and wannabes crowded the tiny space. This was where those who had earned their wings came to regale the rest of the flight virgins with seaside tales worthy of generations of Salty Dawgs.

Lieutenants Dash and Step raised shot glasses full of XXX Ghorkin Ale with newly pinned Captain Johnny "Walker" Sato.

"To Walker!" Step held a freshly charged tumbler full of neon green liquid aloft. "Braved the dark waters, faced down Leviathan and the Kraken, and not only lived to tell the tale but soiled his knickers in the process."

"Here, here!" A small circle of friends echoed, and everyone laughed and downed a shot.

These celebrations also brought in what the Naval cadets referred to as the Señora Remora—named after the little fishies that swam in the shark's shadow, feeding on its glory and conquests. One particular starry-eyed guppy approached Walker and tugged his sleeve to get his attention. "Excuse me, Captain. Did you get any Viddix footage of the Kraken?"

"Viddix footage?" Walker paused for effect as he had when he rehearsed this over and over in his bunker the night before, "Sweetheart, I was so close I chopped off a piece of the mighty beast's tentacle to carry home as a trophy."

Step and Dash exchanged a knowing look. They knew where this was headed. "Be right back." Dash gestured toward the restrooms on the other side of the crowded bar.

"Take your time," Step said, shaking her head. "Walker's just getting revved up."

Dash threw her a thumbs up and pushed out of earshot as Walker was explaining how he just so happened to have the squid tentacle with him in his front pocket, and did she want to touch it?

Halfway across the room, the bar's techno beat became drowned out by an alternate atmospheric groove pulsating from the pit—a circular space with stadium seats, descending in concentric stair steps down to a low-level stage. Everything from karaoke to unsanctioned MMA fights to alligator wrestling took place in the pit. Now there were dozens of cadets all crowded around, blocking the view.

Probably some stripper, Dash thought to himself. *Must be a good one, the way everybody is mesmerized, even the ladies. Oh, what the hell since I'm already here...*

He diverted toward the pit and pushed through the back wall of cadets because curiosity got the better of him. It wasn't a stripper. A young Japanese woman with electric blue hair danced to the pulsing, organic beat. And not "danced" in some base, lewd fashion, but almost a balletic movement mixed with traditional Nihon Buyo arts forms.

Transcendant.

She had some props, like her ornate paper fans that snapped open and closed and umbrellas she spun high into the air and drifted back into her hand; even the length of fabric coiled around her arms would unfurl, floating upon the air and waving around in trailing patterns as she lithely moved across the stage. She wore the white garments of the Mighty Draccarios, but Dash had never seen anything like this before, religious or not. It was simultaneously the most erotic yet non-sexual thing he had ever seen.

And every now and then, she would look up at him at the apex of one of her stretches, and their eyes would meet. Hers were electric blue. They glowed from within. It was beautiful. *She* was beautiful. And mesmerizing.

Dash watched until he thought his bladder would burst and then pushed quickly away to the bathrooms. Rushing to the urinal, he cursed the six beers he'd downed, which recycled through him now. Had he known they would interrupt the magic of that moment, he would have sworn them off early in the evening. Hell, early in the year.

Through the bathroom door, he could hear applause and cat calls. Quickly finishing up, he flushed and ran out the door, back to the pit, but she was gone and the satisfied spectators were dispersing. A couple of cadets in the show center were stripping down to their skivvies. By the size of these two gorillas, it looked like a round of bare-knuckle fights was the next order of business.

Dash looked around, but the girl wasn't anywhere to be seen. He swore under his breath and made his way back over to his rowdy group of aviators. As he approached, they parted to let him rejoin the group. Several were smirking at him. And then suddenly, he saw her. Right there in the middle of his friends.

"Dash, this is Mizuke Blue. Mizuke, this is Lieutenant Dash Strouthers, the one you were asking about." Step smiled, pulling Dash closer into the action.

"Nice to meet you, Lieutenant," Mizuke curtsied gracefully.

"Y-yeah, same," Dash returned the courtesy bow, although he felt like he'd butchered it. He lifted a thumb over his shoulder toward the stage. "Hey that… that was…"

"So *hot!*" Walker chimed in. Drunk as balls.

"*Inspired*," Dash corrected him as he shouldered him back out again.

"Thank you, that's exactly what I was going for. Hot and inspired," she smiled, holding out her hand. Dash reached for it, and the smallest electric shock jumped from her fingers to his.

Fzzzzzzzht.

* * *

Draccario Bath House

Bastille jerked forward as a blue-haired attendant connected a coupling to the Relay at the back of his neck.

"Whoa, whoa, easy captain," Gen said, pushing against his chest to settle him.

Bastille looked around, and he was standing waist deep in a salted, milk bath. His sudden moves had disturbed the half-dozen other bathers sharing this particular spacious tub. More like a pool by the size of it. As his senses returned, so did his awareness that Gen was completely naked. They all were.

He withdrew quickly from her small hand on his bare chest, scrambling back toward the pool's edge. He went a little lower in the water to reduce his exposure.

And then he saw the woman who had just plugged in his Relay.

"I'm so sorry," she apologized. "It must have been a bad connection."

She was also completely naked. But unlike everyone else reclining in the hot medicinal waters, she was completely out in the open, flapping in the breeze. And damn gorgeous. All of these people walking around were completely… perfect. It was like being surrounded by Greek gods and goddesses. They were young and old, every color and ethnicity, but all of them were lean and chiseled and perfectly coifed and manicured, and—Bastille realized he was staring at her chest.

"What? I'm sorry. No, it's a bad coupling, uh, Relay, not your fault. I'm okay, I'm—gonna sit," he said, getting a little flushed around the gills.

Gen also sat down again beside him. Bastille felt her eyes penetrating into his core. "I'm sorry," she observed, "you're ashamed to be naked."

"No, what? No, I'm not—I've…" He stopped there and looked at the back of his hand where a cut used to be. "What is in this water? My cut is gone."

"A blend of minerals, mostly," Gen smiled. "Some repair NITs. We have radically boosted your immune system through light receptors on your skin and the air we are breathing, thanks to the thirium upgrade on your Relay box. Increased oxygen and atmospheric pressure. A whole regiment. You'll feel better than new. Anyway, you must be hungry. *K'heel oein va'an tuhr*," she said softly to the attendant, who rose nimbly to fetch the first course.

Bastille stared at his hand. As he flexed his fingers, small sparks arced between them. "Um," he showed it to Gen.

Gen nodded back, visibly amused at his discomfort. "Yes," she said, holding up her own palm, conjuring a small, electric fireball, and then snuffling it out just as quickly. "You'll learn all sorts of new tricks."

"Sorry, little dip. This—I'm not used to this… and I can't even remember the last time I was naked with this many people. It wasn't bath time, though. Actually, it's a funny story if—"

"No, thank you, Captain. That vulgar tale you may hold in your own private confidence," she admonished.

"Your loss, kid," he shrugged.

"I am not a kid," she bristled again. "I helped lead these people here 150 years ago. We are not perfect people, as much as we discipline and engineer our society to be. This planet does not have unlimited resources, as you incorrectly asserted. We have kept ourselves separate for a season to heal, to grow in knowledge, and to innovate. But we cannot live outside of the universal life circle forever. Society at large needs us. Mother Earth needs us. And," she added sadly, "we need them."

"Hm, that is an incredibly naive way to get everyone killed," Bastille said.

"It's just the truth," she replied, sipping a red drink from a chalice. She handed it to him.

He took a sip. If it was a wine, it was the best one he'd ever tasted. It hit the tip of his tongue like a tangy plum and as it rolled back it blossomed into its full oakiness. "Mmm," Bastille nodded, handing the cup back to Gen.

"Yeah," she said.

It was a lot to take in. The people, the technology, even the architecture. The wall structures blended seamlessly into the large ceiling bubble. Oblong window portals let artificial sunlight pass through and reflect off the dozens of eternity pools. Nudes entered and exited the long hall at the other end. Among them were probably a dozen blue-hairs, clearly some sort of lower-ranking or subservient class. But everyone was smiling and friendly, as though they were out on holiday.

There was a sense of civility and ease among everyone there. Gen had been correct; these were highly disciplined people, and their self-control and physiological enlightenment allowed new heights of community, openness, and discovery. Anywhere else, Bastille imagined, this would quickly devolve into some sort of sexual frenzy or competition. What was it that kept their baser selves at bay?

Whatever it was, Bastille was not there yet. Not quite able to emotionally rise above. All of this was a huge turn-on. These milky mineral waters were barely able to conceal that fact. Anyway, the best he could afford them, he supposed, was the courtesy of not drooling while he stared. That's as evolved as he could manage.

Bastille leaned back into the waters and let the healing vitration do its job. His whole body tingled. A couple of attendants returned carrying large trays of food and drinks. They stepped carefully down the stairs into the water. The male attendant closest to Bastille busily prepared the tray arrangement.

Bastille couldn't help but notice the guy's manhood dangling there a couple of feet from his face. "Really? You wanna put that thing away before you poke an eye out?" He shielded his eyes with his hand.

Gen nodded to the attendant, who bowed quickly and then removed himself from the water. The other attendant moved the tray into position in front of them and then took her leave as well.

"I mean, I don't wanna sound vulgar, but please congratulate your engineers on the most perfect breasts and penises and bodies I've ever seen. That man's junk should be in a museum."

"There is so much more to beauty than these simple, clumsy meat-suits we wear on the outside, Captain," Gen said, adding some fruit to a small plate along with a scoop of red sauce that she dipped a piece of bread into and offered it to Bastille. "*Sha'afule?*"

He took it and bit into it cautiously. Then, pleasantly surprised, he dug in greedily. He didn't realize how famished he was. The flavors popped in his mouth and fizzled as he swallowed them down. There was a strawberry essence to the dip, and the bread was a pure, fluffy slice of heaven. But somehow meatier.

Gen smiled to see him enjoying it so much.

"You're not gonna eat? This stuff is incredible," he said, stuffing his face.

"Today is my fasting day," she replied, leaning back again. "You know what they say: 'Abstinence makes the heart grow fonder.'"

"Very clever, little dip." Bastille stuffed another meaty morsel into his mouth. It had a decidedly familiar flavor to it. "Is that lobster?"

"Mm, more or less," was all she'd concede.

Bastille was watching her face when she became suddenly serious, distracted by something back over his shoulder. He spun around to discover one of the Draccario guardsmen from before had de-cloaked, activated his weapon, and leveled it at him.

Bastille surmised the beam was not electrical in nature; otherwise, everyone in the pool would have been fried with him. None-the-less, a not-electric beam shot from the tip of the guardian's staff and blasted his chest. It didn't have quite the pain of the Mauzer shot, but it was instantly effective as the captain was blasted from consciousness with little to no warning.

Fzzzzzzzht.

* * *

NeoTokyo, Eno District

Dash Strouthers woke up in a sweat. The city lights beyond the window shades leaked an amber glow into the room. Next to him on the bed, he discovered Mizuke's naked form nestled back under the covers he had displaced. He sighed. Helluva night. He climbed gently from the bed and rubbed his eyes with the heel of his hand.

Dash checked over his shoulder again to make sure he hadn't dreamt it, but the goddess was still there, fast asleep. He slid the Vancinex injector from its case atop his dresser, stepped quietly to the bathroom, and closed the door. This triggered a soft light that pulsed off and on a few times before settling on with a high-pitched, fluorescent hum. A cadet's quarters were not the highest-class spaces. He was lucky to have his own room. Once he made Captain, he looked forward to an upgrade. Of course that was dependent upon him getting KACorp's neural implant to communicate to the ships. He didn't love the idea of them poking around his melon like that and dropping in a computer.

Dash sat on the edge of the tub and pressed the silver tip of the gun against his forearm.

This is for medicinal purposes. Calm my mind. It's fine, he assured himself. He hesitated. Slowly pulled the tip away, reconsidering. Wrestling. *It's fine!*

He pressed the gun into the base of his neck and fired off a full dose. A smoky cloud residue shot from the tip. For whatever reason, users had different olfactory triggers from the injection. For Dash, it was always pine trees. Just a sharp, woodsy aroma that lingered for a split second and then vanished. He exhaled a blue plume of smoke.

He set down the gun as he moved to the sink. Splashing some water into his face, he looked up into the mirror. Much to his surprise, Jacques Bastille stared back at him from the other side of the mirror plane.

Fzzzzzzzht.

* * *

Phaedra the Shadow Moon

Bastille awoke. His arms were held in place by a couple of round metal hand bracers out to the side. His ankles were also secured. He was floating in the middle of the room like a giant "X." He could feel wires down the back of his bare back and knew that his Relay box had been tapped into again.

The small, circular room around him had a wide, mirrored band along the wall. Probably an observation space on the other side. There was not much else in the room. He wondered how long he had been out.

'*Thirty-two minutes and forty seconds,*' a creepy electronic voice said from no particular direction.

Bastille looked around. He saw no one. Did he perceive that audibly? Or was that just in his head?

'*We have a direct uplink to your mind,*' the man answered.

"What's going on?" Bastille asked his captor aloud. "Where is Genwa'ar?"

'*She is of no concern to you. You are being held on account of a security breach.*'

"Security breach?" Bastille's mouth twisted into a half-smile, "Is this because I peed in the pool?"

A mild electric shock jolted his system and sent goosebumps up his spine and almost wiped the smirk off his face. Almost.

'*At 014.132 you released a virus into our system that penetrated our security firewalls. Do you deny this?*'

Bastille had no clue what he was talking about.

'*When you were plugged into the uplink, you faked a cerebral short-circuit which masked the virus—*'

"I didn't *fake* anything," Bastille interrupted. He continued audibly to drown out the intruder's voice in his head. "I was unconscious, when I snapped awake, everyone was naked. I ate some strawberry lobster goo and tried not to think about making babies with the hot waitress with the blue hair and the big—"

The next electric shock made the back of his eyeballs feel like they were under siege by a thousand shards of glass.

"—eyes."

Fzzzzzzzht.

* * *

NeoTokyo

In the bathroom, Dash watched in the mirror as Bastille finished screaming.

"What the hell is going on?" Dash whispered, not wanting to wake Mizuke in the other room. She obviously wasn't hearing the strange man screaming inside the mirror. "Why are you… in there?"

Bastille didn't look so good, but there was nothing Dash could do. The mirror separated their two worlds. But then Dash noticed something out of the corner of his eye and spun to see a young girl sitting on the edge of his tub.

"I'm not going to hurt you," she said, rising quickly. "I'm Gen."

Dash pressed back against the wall, rubbing his eyes. "Oh my God, I'm trippin' balls. How did you get in my bathroom? Why is there a sh*ttier old version of me stuck in my mirror? Is this an intervention?"

"Shut up and listen. We haven't got a lot of time," Gen moved forward and talked through the mirror to Bastille who had a trickle of blood from his nose. "Bastille, this is the only way I could talk to you here in the subspace of your unconscious mind. Otherwise they could have tracked me. They think you're attacking them. They think you're a threat. They're going to drain you of any intel of value and then Re-cycle you."

"I didn't do anything," Bastille objected, but then reconsidered. "Okay, I may have entertained a few… hundred impure thoughts—"

"What are you two going on about?" Dash interrupted, blinking hard at them both. "Subspace of the what now?"

He reached out a finger and touched the arm of the one called Gen. She was real. He jerked back. Gen cocked her head to one side quizzically and then understood, "This is Dash Strouthers, isn't it?"

Bastille nodded, "More or less. Lieutenant Dash Strouthers meet Gen. Goes by little dipper."

"Not little dipper," she corrected. "So, he's been ghost-lining inside of you and now, what, turned loose into our system?"

"So it would appear." Bastille wiped some blood from his brow with his forearm.

"So *what* would appear? You two don't even make sense." Dash was close to hyperventilating. He put his hands on his knees to keep from falling over. "I think I'm stroking out. Does anyone smell syrup?"

"He kinda does whatever the hell he wants," Bastille added, holding himself up with the wall and the sink, but barely.

Dash opened his mouth to speak but no words were forming.

"This is impossible," Gen said, "we should not be here."

"Thank you," Dash conceded, gesturing at her with both hands.

"Best I can tell, they're like memories," Bastille explained. "But like lucid, interactive memories? All I know is that every time I plug into a new network, he gets stronger. More sentient."

A tremor rocked the small room, flickering the lights, and Gen looked behind her and said, "Uh-oh! They're getting closer."

She glitched out of sight just before—

Fzzzzzzzht.

* * *

Phaedra

Bastille was revived once more. Only now, the security chief stood in front of him, face-to-face. Well, face to helmet anyway. The chief was completely covered in light tactical armor. His voice was calm and filtered. "Your virus has proven to be very tricky and skillfully programmed, but in a short matter of time we will isolate it, and when we do, we will destroy it. And then we will destroy you for bringing it into our safe haven."

"W-where?" Bastille was still trying to figure this thing out, too. "Where have you tracked it?"

"Excuse me?" the chief replied.

Bastille explained irritably, "I need to know where the virus is headed. Security? Weapons? Climate Control? Communications?"

The guard studied him for a moment. "It's going exactly where you sent it. Science Lab Archives."

"What?" Bastille's eyes darted around as he searched for answers. "That doesn't even make sense. Why would he head to archives?"

"You have one chance to help us put a stop to this thing," the chief warned, clapping the shock stick against his free hand.

"Couldn't if I tried," Bastille shrugged awkwardly. "Hit me, boss."

"Fine," the guard took a step backwards, raising the sparking baton. "Let's do it the hard way."

Bastille braced himself for what he knew was coming. Didn't help, though.

Fzzzzzzzht.

* * *

NeoTokyo

Dash checked the corner of his bathroom mirror frame when Bastille suddenly returned. Followed quickly by the woman calling herself Gen. She flickered in and out; her imaging was less stable than Bastille this time.

"Dash is headed to the Science Lab Archives," Bastille announced, not wasting any time now.

"No. I'm what?" Dash was entirely confused.

Gen considered the new info. "DNA coding, Genealogy, Experimental Sciences, History of Our People, what is he after? What are you after?" She poked a finger into Dash, which was all too real and made him even more uncomfortable.

Tap, tap, tap.

A knock on the bathroom door. They all froze. "Dash?" Asked the soft, sweet voice of Mizuke, "everything okay in there?"

Dash clamped a hand over Gen's mouth. "Yes, Mizuke, sorry, I'll be out in a second. Just finishing up in here."

"Please come back to bed, honey," she pleaded.

"I will be there in two seconds," he said, and they all listened to the sound of her retreating footsteps. He spun back to Gen, saying, "And you have one second to, to, to beam yourselves outta here."

"Mizuke?" Bastille clarified.

"Yes, Mizuke—wait," Dash pointed an accusatory finger, "how do you know Mizuke?"

Bastille looked to Gen and explained, "His wife. Mizuke."

"Well, whoa, first off, not my wife," Dash clarified, and then smiled sheepishly at the thought, "but I dunno, gosh, maybe one day—"

"We've gotta get you off of Phaedra," Gen interrupted, back at Bastille.

"What about this guy?" Bastille aimed a shaky finger at Dash.

Sometimes Gen was on the side of the mirror with Dash, sometimes she was on the side with Bastille.

The walls around them were all slowly turning black and flaking off. It was really freaking Dash out.

"From what you've told me," Gen continued, now on Bastille's side of the wall, "whatever he is becoming, he is quite versatile. And he's latched on to you. So, I suspect if we can get you back to your ship, he will follow."

"Well, that's gonna be easier said than done, little dip," Bastille replied.

"I'll help you," she said, leaning in closer. "On one condition."

"And that is?" Bastille pressed.

And then she was gone. He looked through the mirror and she was there, elbowing Dash out of the way. "You take me with you," Gen answered.

"Out of the question," Bastille said. "Are you out of your *functured* mind?"

"I am," Dash said matter-of-factly. "I'm completely outta *my* functured mind."

"No discussion," Gen snapped and patted Dash's chest. "And you? Live your life. With any luck, you'll never see either one of us again."

Another tremble and light flash, and Bastille and Gen were gone from his tiny little space. Dash checked the shower, but no one was there. He checked the mirror, and this time it was his own timid reflection staring back at himself.

"Oh, thank God," he let out a huge sigh of relief. "I'm young and handsome again. And not at all crazy."

He picked up the Vancinex gun and studied it carefully. Unscrewing the base of the handle, he popped out a cartridge and drained a neon blue liquid into the sink. He flicked on the faucet. Some of the serum vaporized as it mixed with the running water.

Pine Trees.

Dash took a deep breath, savoring the smell and then killed the lights.

Fzzzzzzzht.

\- 7 -

BATTLE DRAGON

Phaedra the Shadow Moon

Pitch black. Bastille's guard activated a wrist-comm, which cast a small glow onto his helmet, "Delta5, do you copy? Brek, status report."

Brek responded breathlessly over comms, "Sir, some sort of an EMP blast knocked out power and electronics throughout the whole wing. Stand by."

The emergency lights blinked on inside the little interrogation space. The captain of the guardians faced the observation glass. His mask's hyper-vision (HPV) allowed him to peer through the wall with a thermal scan as Brek and the team on the other side frantically attempted to restore power. They'd be flying blind in there with no power. And worse, there was no protocol on the books for such an event. It was mild chaos, which had the captain's full attention. Otherwise, he would have noticed what was going on behind him.

Now released from his electromagnetic restraint, Bastille slowly stood up and jerked the intrusive wires from his Relay box, still a little dazed. Flexing his achy muscles, he re-seated one hand-shackle around his fist.

The guardian spun around. "Stop right there. On your knees *now*, Captain Bastille."

"Not on the first date, sweetheart."

The guardian reacted in an instant, closing the space between them with a sideways flip. Bastille saw the boot coming at his face an instant too late. It connected, followed quickly by a barrage of punches.

Bastille rolled out to diminish the force of an armored knee connecting with his bare chest. Then he blocked three of the next five combo punches before landing a well-timed haymaker across the guard's helmet. The guard went sprawling.

As the enemy sprang a little wobbly back to his feet, Bastille circled more cautiously this time. The new crack along the helmet's visor made Bastille smile. He traced a line down his own cheek with a finger and chided the guard, "You've got a little something on your face, here."

Bastille knew that he would have been no match for this guy had it not been for the Draccario Bath House and the thirium vitration his body had been infused with in the short time he had been on Phaedra. Gen was right. The air contained purer oxygen levels at a higher atmospheric compression level. Bastille had never felt stronger, even in the midst of this hailstorm attack from his relentless captor. He was almost certain now that Gen had been restoring him for an escape she had orchestrated. She was significantly craftier than he had given her credit for. Just as dangerous as he'd first suspected, though.

Over the next few moments, both combatants would spend time on the floor as they traded blows and attempted to outmaneuver each other. Bastille knew if he could grab the guardian, he could most certainly out-wrestle him into submission, but the guy was flipping and jump-kicking off the walls and table, impossible to pin down. Like trying to grab a cricket.

Bastille finally landed another blow to the helmet, splintering the visor and sending the guardian careening into the closest wall. But even then, the warrior recovered quickly, ripped off the damaged helmet, and quickly tossed it off to the side. He was a silver-haired guy with sharp-looking, chiseled features, as they had all been bio-engineered for. But there was a drop of blood coming out of the corner of those perfectly formed lips.

Bastille moved in to finish, but the guardian held a hand open, conjuring one of Gen's blue fireballs. Apparently, he hadn't really felt endangered until right at this moment. The guardian climbed slowly back to his feet. He'd lost a lot of steam, as had Bastille. In matches this close, Bastille found, it usually came down to sheer willpower, which one of them was too stubborn to stay down. Bastille could tell the guardian was trying to buy some time.

"You will not be getting off this planet alive, Bastille. Genwa'ar had no business allowing safe harbor to Ma'kobi skinbags like you. This ends now."

"Ma'kobi—?"

The security door beside them snapped unlocked. The guard threw the glowing orb, and Bastille intercepted it with the shackle, which exploded into tiny shards all over the room. Bastille ignored the tiny spurs hitting his skin and lunged forward to punch the guard's gut. Only, once his fist connected, a concealed ten-inch blade from beneath the skin on his cybernetic arm shot forward. It pierced the slats of the body armor into the guardian's torso, retracting again in the same instant.

The guardian was stunned. So was Bastille.

"Easy there, old timer. Nice and easy," Bastille said as he helped lower the elite warrior to the ground. Drops of blood began to splash the white tile on the floor.

"Stop! What are you doing?" Gen ran in, tossing some clothes to Bastille. She was no longer wearing those formal flowing robes of a royal Draccario councilor. She had donned a brown and tan layered travel ensemble with olive pants that tucked into her tactical boots. She shoved Bastille aside. "Marcus."

"Gen," Guardian Marcus winced, "Bastille cannot be allowed to live. Do not be blinded by the Qu'-Nadi scrolls. He will be the death of the separatists."

"Shh, Marcus. *Kleev'an da'ar shuk thaalta.*"

"...*shuk thaalta*?" Marcus managed, but he had lost too much blood and couldn't continue. Gen brought up a communicator and looked at Bastille with that fierce gaze that melted lesser mortals.

"This is Genwa'ar. We need a medic in Interview Lab 3. Marcus is down, and the prisoner has escaped.

He is headed for the flight deck. I repeat, he is headed for the flight deck."

Gen motioned to his clothes. "We are leaving, Bastille. Get dressed."

Bastille wasted no time and pulled them on quickly. Gen grabbed a pen stick from Marcus's belt, ripped the cap off with her teeth, and injected it into his neck. The impact was immediate, and Marcus was revived.

"Don't move, Marcus. Help is on the way. Just lay there and keep pressure on the wound. It has missed your vitals, but you've lost a lot of blood."

"And the prisoner?" Marcus croaked weakly.

Gen motioned—behind her back—to Bastille, who grabbed his boots and stepped out into the hall.

"I'll find him. But Marcus, he's not the monster we thought. You're still alive. If he had wanted you dead, you'd be dead. We'd all be dead. Now stay here 'til the Med-unit arrives. They're three minutes out."

Marcus nodded and breathed as evenly as he could.

"I love you, Marcus," Gen said and kissed him on the forehead. She then stood and darted out the door behind Bastille.

"Gen—" Marcus attempted to sit up but couldn't. He could only whisper, "Be careful."

Out in the hall, Bastille monitored the main access door, which was sealed shut. On the other side, a team attempted to cut through as sparks flew everywhere. Gen pulled on a backpack and headed in the opposite direction.

"Are you coming?" she asked, very annoyed.

Bastille stayed put, gesturing at the interrogation room. "Who was that in there? Boyfriend? Husband?"

"I guess you would call him a concubine," Gen conceded, and then motioned up the hallway. "Can we…?"

"Wait, what is that?" Bastille needled her. "A *love* slave?"

"We don't have time for this," she said, rolling her eyes and turning away.

He fell in behind her. "Is he like a fancy hooker? Good for you, little dipper."

"That is *not* how it works here."

"Hold on," Bastille said, grabbing her arm. "You just told them I was headed to the flight deck."

"Yes, *flight deck.*" She moved so close that he thought she was about to slug him. "Because I moved your ship two weeks ago to the falls at the edge of the settlement."

"Two weeks?" Bastille straightened up, his brow furrowed. "How long have I—"

She spun on her boot heel and walked away. Bastille chewed his lip a moment, then gave in and lumbered after her. He followed down the corridor and around a corner as the main doors blasted apart behind them. Four guardians entered first in delta formation, scanning everywhere for threats. Once they yelled "Clear!" they were followed quickly by the Med-unit who made a bee line for Interview Lab 3.

* * *

Clang. A rounded exit portal irised open at the edge of the settlement. The high city wall blended in seamlessly with its jungle environs, hidden beneath vines and ivy. Hard to believe that this lush greenery, the colony, and everything had at one time been a desolate space rock, possibly a gigantic meteor, orbiting lifelessly through the galaxy. It was some next-level terraforming. Bastille was impressed the more he saw of this miniature Eden.

Bastille stepped through the portal beside Gen, and she sealed it behind them. Gen marked the time on her WristCom. Bastille wondered why there'd be a security wall on a planet that was completely off-grid. Unless this was less of a city wall and more of a holding pen for—

"We've got to be quick now," Gen warned. "There is a trigger alert on all access points. We don't want to be here when the scouts arrive to investigate."

Gen cinched up her backpack and jogged off along a minimal trail through the underbrush. Bastille followed closely. It'd be really easy to get lost without her. Checking over his shoulder, he already couldn't identify where the portal had been if his life depended on it. They settled into a good clip, and Bastille breathed in all of the exotic scents. And then sneezed it back out again. It'd been a long time since he'd smelled fresh vegetation like this. An explosion of perfumed flowers, trees, and other forestation; it was amazing. But it was killing his sinuses.

He was so caught up in his own nasal drama that he almost tripped over Gen when she stopped short. He opened his mouth to give her a piece of his mind, but she clamped a hand over it and pulled him to the ground. Her attention was focused on the canopy above them.

A large, ominous shadow passed overhead, and Bastille heard the swish-swooshing of gigantic, leathery wings. He climbed back further into the underbrush to conceal himself more, crouching right next to a huge aromatic bud. The orchid was a little overwhelming and drove his nose crazy. In the shafts of sunlight, he could see all the dust and pollen dancing around, taunting him.

He watched Gen peek around the nearest tree. Her eyes bulged, and he followed her gaze just in time to see a huge beast land in the clearing beside them. Bastille could not believe his itchy, watery eyes. It was a real, live-flying megasaur. Its scaly body was huge and muscular, maybe the size of a full-grown whale, stem to stern. It had a long, thick neck and a tusked, metal mask over its face. A nose ring that could cradle a full-grown gorilla hung in its nostrils, which flared open and shut.

"A Battle Dragon," Bastille whispered, his mouth hanging open.

"Shhh," Gen swatted at him and then added softly, "Are you crying?"

He jerked a thumb toward the offending flower beside him. Gen just shook her head at him.

Another low growl brought their full attention back to the huge problem ahead of them. Indeed, it was a Battle Dragon. There was a saddle on its back and riding atop it was a single dragonrider. He, himself, was ornately armored and held the reigns in one hand and a long rifle bowcaster in the other. The two of them surveyed the forest for any movement. There was an eerie calm. The only noise was the dragon as it adjusted its stance, dug its huge claws into a wide swath of underbrush, and harrumphed from time to time. It snorted once and rippled its mighty muscles. The damn thing could sense them close.

Bastille stifled a sneeze, and Gen whipped around, glaring at him. His eyes were red and puffy, and once again he jammed an angry finger at the massive flowery culprit by his head. He wouldn't be able to hunker down there any longer. They were going to have to blow their cover and run for it. She shook her head and mouthed to him, "It's like trying to escape with a toddler."

He was about to respond when she clapped a hand over his mouth again. The dragon had begun a low, bellowing noise.

"The dragon knows we're close," she whispered next to his ear. "I guess the Council approved deadly force. This is about to get really tricky."

"You think?"

Another loud roar echoed through the forest, and Gen shouted "Move!" and broke into a run.

Bastille jumped up with another sneeze and followed along behind her like his life depended on it. Because it did. Gen moved elegantly through the underbrush and somehow dodged every branch and vine that grabbed at her. Bastille was slapped left and right as he tripped and crashed along awkwardly in her wake.

He chanced a look to his left, and the Battle Dragon's golden eyes were locked onto him. The beast chewed ferociously on a metal bit the size of an oak trunk in its teeth, but held steady. The dragonrider leveled his rifle weapon in their direction.

Bastille jumped forward and dragged Gen to the ground a split second before the huge concussion blast exploded plants, leaves, and dirt everywhere to their right. Barely had the blast subsided, then the two of them scrambled forward through the dust cloud on their hands and knees. They jumped to their feet again and continued on in a full sprint.

Gen dropped a canister behind them, which instantly spewed smoke, filling the whole area. It provided visual cover but would also throw off their scents. One whiff of those fumes would effectively scramble the dragon's acute sense of smell, hopefully long enough for them to get airborne.

Bastille could see a break in the tree line in front of them. He braced for another bowcaster blast from behind, but there wasn't one. Instead, the ground below them began to shake with the weight of the galloping monster clambering after them.

Gen called back over her shoulder, "You should be in range. Start the ship. *Start the ship*."

"Where? I don't see—"

"Start the ship, Captain!"

Bastille pulsed out a search string from his HUD and sure enough connected with the ship's mainframe. He began preflight, shorting several steps in the process. Popping the canopy.

Another laser bolt from the dragonrider flew past Bastille, and it all happened so fast he didn't quite understand it all at the time, but it looked like Gen turned and deflected the blast with a lightning ball from her own hand. It exploded into a tree close by, splintering the base into a thousand shards, which Bastille took down his right side. The blast sent the huge, Redwood-sized trunk slowly toppling across their path. Gen and Bastille barely escaped the branches and foliage that ripped at them as it crashed to the ground.

Bastille momentarily slowed to check on their pursuers. The Battle Dragon was scrambling to climb over the tree, but it clearly wasn't built for this kind of terrain. There were too many trees for it to spread its wings and vault the obstacle, but the fallen tree was too bushy at that point to just push through without getting entangled, so it poised there with its claws atop the redwood and reared back its head.

Bastille connected the dots just in the nick of time. He turned and broke out of the tree line into the clearing, only it wasn't a clearing so much as a gigantic ravine. Off to the left, he could hear the roar of a huge waterfall. Again, something he hadn't seen in years and would have loved to stop and have a picnic, maybe with that pool waitress from before.

Gen was ahead at the ravine's edge, gathering a rope coil that had been concealed there. Bastille timed himself and dropped into a power slide the last few feet of the way.

Gen yelped as he grabbed her and the rope in passing, and their momentum slid them right over the cliff. As they cleared the lip, a huge blast of fiery napalm raked across the top of the ravine. The heat alone was enough to singe the exposed skin of Bastille's shoulder. The top of the rope burst into flames.

"Ungh!" Bastille held on firmly as they were jerked to a halt at the apex of their jump and then swung back toward the Mustang. Ah, his beloved ship, clinging there to the side of that mountain, camouflaged in ivy and vines.

There wasn't any good way to slow their collective momentum, so Bastille cradled Gen close, and they smashed ungracefully into the ship's hull. *Gong.* Birds scattered everywhere. Some sort of squirrel lizard jumped into the ravine and spread its arms. The extra skin stretched taut, and it glided off to safety, chittering angrily as it went.

The burning rope was severed at the top, but Bastille managed to grab a fistful of vines before they both fell to their deaths. Breathing heavily, he lowered Gen into the open cockpit just below them and then shimmied down himself. It was a rather awkward angle to enter. Gen took the RIO seat behind him and strapped in. Bastille triggered the cockpit to close while firing up all the engines. Gen jacked the control cables into her Relay box as Bastille grabbed the throttle.

Thankfully, Bastille's sinuses began to clear the instant the cockpit was sealed and the filtered air blew across his face, instantly clearing his head. Even the abrasions on his neck and hands began to clear up. This new thirium upgrade was awesome.

"Bastille!" Gen smacked his sore shoulder, pointing straight up above them.

"Ow, I see it. I see it," Bastille said with a growing sense of dread.

The Battle Dragon's mighty head snaked over the edge of the cliff. It was even more terrifying and huge, this close-up and personal.

"Oh, hey, Sizzlepants…" was all Bastille could manage to quip out. The initial awe of the dragon's existence was long past. It had been replaced by a complete adrenaline panic. The dragon reared its head again. Bastille had never done battle with a dragon. No one had. He didn't know if his ship could withstand a direct hit from a blast of napalm, but he wasn't going to stick around and find out.

"Releasing land lock," he shouted, punching the controls.

The clasps at the end of the landing struts popped free, and the Mustang ripped clear of the vines and roots and fell back toward the bottom of the canyon.

"Engaging cloak!" Gen yelled back.

"What cloak? This ship doesn't—" Bastille was shocked to look out the window and see his ship ghosting away into thin air. "What the hell did you do to my ship?"

"Upgrades, Captain. Now get us away," Gen said, watching the ground rush toward them.

"Have I really been here two weeks?"

"Nineteen Days. Now, would you—" she gestured frantically toward the sky.

Bastille goosed the throttle and pulled back on the stick as a wall of fire sprayed down from the heavens. They dodged most of it. Bastille watched the flames impact a boulder outcropping and shear it in half like a guillotine. Being so close to the blast radius, the ivy on their fuselage erupted in flames. Even inside the armored Mustang, they could feel the heat. Flames stuck to their wings, and the ship soared like a phoenix rising from the smokey canyon.

Bastille was all too happy to watch the horrifying Battle Dragon diminish into a speck on the horizon. He knew there wouldn't be any pursuit. At least from the dragonrider.

"Ready water canopy in thirty seconds," Gen warned.

"Roger that," Bastille said, pulling the Hydros online.

They made short work of the water barrier before they exited the other side and the Ion drives kicked in.

"Plugging in coordinates," Gen announced.

"Whoa, wait a minute, little dip, what do you mean? Where do you think you're taking us?"

"The AlphaN1 wormhole," she said casually. "Earth."

There was a long pause.

"No dice. I told you that's the worst idea ever. Look, you've been living on your little bubble planet for way too long. Why would we go back to that hell hole?"

Bastille watched Gen on his monitor. She closed her eyes for a long moment. Once she made up her mind about whatever she was wrestling with, she answered, "To overthrow General Wexell; destroy the Fort Royale slave market; and raise the *Bellevue*."

Gen input the flight information into the NAV computer and punched "Engage." The sub-light drive began to spin up for action.

Bastille punched "Disengage," and the drives whined back down. He then keyed another sequence, locking Gen out of the control panel. "Bullsh*t," he growled. "None of that has anything to do with me. In case you hadn't noticed, I've got a few problems of my own I need to take care of first."

Gen tried to re-engage the sub-lights to no avail. Finally, she gave up with a frustrated sigh, and un-strapped her restraints.

"As the *former* Ma'kobi King, with a contract out on his life from the *current* Ma'kobi Usurper," she paused to let that much sink in. "All of this has *everything* to do with you, Captain Bastille."

She flicked a switch near her headrest, and her seat mechanically lowered, giving her access to the living chambers below deck. She jumped down, and her boots clanged all the way down the gangway.

"Hey, wait, what?" Bastille checked the scanners again. He had to raise his voice to be heard down below. "Uh, don't you find it strange that your Draccario brethren haven't sent out fighters in pursuit?"

"Stop using that foul word," she yelled back.

"Brethren?"

"No, you imbecile," her insult floated back up from below decks. "The D-word! Look, right now the Council of St. Croix will be meeting in an emergency committee to vote. The vote will pass unanimously, with the exception of Bly'nette Olferr'n, who will counter-vote just to be contrary, and *then* they will begin pursuit."

"Well?" Bastille pressed. "How many?"

"How many what?" Gen shouted back.

"How many ships will they send after us?" He asked, getting annoyed. He could hear her clanging back up the short corridor until she was standing beneath his seat. He could just see her angry face through the foot controls.

"Ships, Captain? No, I'm afraid you don't understand. They won't send a few ships. They'll send *everyone*. The entire planet will break orbit and begin pursuit." She let that sink in and then turned and disappeared back up the bulkhead towards the captain's quarters.

"That—the whole *Shadow Moon* is—" Bastille sputtered.

"Now who's the naive one?" Her taunt echoed up from below.

Bastille shook his head. It was all too much to take in. But first things first, he flipped through the angles and flight charts. What was clear was that Gen was right. For now, there were no pursuers on the scopes. He punched another button, switched over to autoNAV, and lowered his own seat. "Coming down," he warned. Before it even finished moving, he slid out, bypassed the small ladder, and landed with a thud. Then he proceeded down the short passageway to the cramped living quarters.

He rounded the corner angrily, but stopped short as Gen stripped off her shirt. He turned back around immediately and talked over his shoulder at her. "Okay, first thing? This is my ship. Not a bath house. No more getting naked whenever you feel like it. It just ain't natural," he bristled.

"On the contrary, Captain, it is the most natural." Her tone was very frosty.

"My ship, my rules," he said firmly. "Take it or leave it."

She ignored him, climbing into the bed naked. She slid beneath the covers. Bastille heard the rustling sounds and chanced a look back.

"What the—" he stopped, watching her fluff the pillow. *His* pillow. And lay her head down. In *his* bed.

"I assume we will be sleeping in shifts to maximize our limited space?" she asked snidely with a cocked eyebrow.

"I, I, uh—" was all he could manage.

"Very good. Then I volunteer for first shift," she said, rolling onto her side, her back to him. "I haven't slept in a week."

"Now just wait a minute, little dip. We've got a *lot* to talk about. Battle Dragons. Shadow Moons. Cloaking devices. And you don't just dump that Ma'kobi King bullsh*t on someone and then roll over and go to sleep."

"It's a long journey, Captain. We'll have plenty of time to fight, I assure you," she replied curtly. "Oh, and one more thing?" She propped up on an elbow and looked back at him.

"What now?" he growled, clenching his jaw.

"The part about this being your ship may be true. But I've discussed our route with Dash Strouthers, and he agrees with me that the best thing to avoid trouble is to head to the G9-Gate on the other side of Tamora." She laid back down with a very self-satisfied smile on her face.

"Talking with—" Bastille looked around, confused. "The other side of Tamora? There is a huge asteroid belt between us and Tamora," he added incredulously.

"Be that as it may. Dash, you may continue," she said into the air, leaving it at that.

There were some clicking and popping sounds as the ship came off autoNAV and adjusted trajectory, and another bump as the Ion drives spun up to speed. Bastille braced himself as the initial pulse kicked the ship forward, and the Mustang bolted lithely across the starry galaxy.

Bastille punched the wall, denting the thick metallic bulkhead, and then headed back towards the cockpit.

"I'd conserve that energy, Captain," Gen admonished playfully after him. "Now that we're away from the super-optimized Phaedra environs, we'll need to mind our—"

Bastille triggered the cabin door and it slammed closed with an obnoxious *clang*.

Outlands
System
Qu'Nadi

- 8 -

THE SS DAYSTAR

Planet Earth, Somewhere over the Pacific Basin

The *SCV Bellevue* galleon was the belle of the St. Croix fleet. It powered across the Pacific, 500 klicks south and east of NeoTokyo. The massive hospital warship was the most technologically advanced vessel on planet Earth, currently on its maiden voyage. Thirty feet off the ocean surface it floated along the ground-effect cushion created by its massive turbines and wings. For the past three weeks, it had harbored in NeoTokyo, treating patients, onboarding supplies and personnel, and fueling. Now, it was on its way back out on a two-year tour of duty that would take it into all the war-torn areas around the globe that needed it most.

As with any military hospital, this one never slept, but occasionally there was a downtick or slow cycle in the action during the pre-dawn hours. This particular morning, a woman's scream from below deck echoed through the Maternity Ward, on Level 66.

Room 6610 buzzed with activity.

Mizuke laid on the hospital bed with her knees pulled tightly to her chest. A doctor sat between the stirrups, focused on the bald little head crowning down below. Nurses—both human and Byno—busied themselves here and there, suctioning up blood and bathing the area with specialty oils and decontaminants. Monitors constantly beeped and reported her vitals.

Dr. Vance could easily have been 150 years old. His scraggly features would be better associated with a hobo than a world-renowned surgeon. Whereas most St. Croix elders would go through and Re-cycle themselves in order to be young again, Vance had avoided that. In fact, he was suspicious—paranoid is probably the better word—of that whole industry, probably because he had helped launch it.

He wore his gray hair like a badge of honor. A long, French-braided hippy badge of honor. He was casual, easygoing and supremely confident—a type of confidence one generally forgives in the rare case of the truly super-genius. A lesser doctor could imagine they knew everything and were God's gift to medicine. This was due to a critical failure to realize that learning things and knowing things were two entirely different skills. And it tended to be a Darwinian fatal flaw that worked itself out sooner rather than later. Yet there were others whose casual bedside ease was the direct result of successfully negotiating trauma after trauma— saving life after life. It was a point of pride for Dr. Vance that, in a matter of nano-seconds, after having only just met, he could know your body better than you. Of course this was from years of study, but it didn't hurt that he was also an enhanced empath.

He monitored the baby's heartbeat without even requiring a computer. He knew the baby was strong and well. Every few seconds, he pushed two fingers around the baby's head as it breached, coaxing the skin around to stretch open further.

"I hope you like mucous-colored hair," he joked with a crooked smile, "because that's what this baby's got."

Dash snorted, grateful for a moment of levity—anything to distract from the whole grisly ordeal. He stood by Mizuke's head, gripping her white-knuckled hand and propping up her head at the same time. He would have fainted a few times himself had it not been for Dr. Vance's keen eye. All of that KACorps survival training did not prepare Dash for the gruesomeness of this bloody ordeal giving birth.

Mizuke did not laugh, however. She was breathing quick, shallow breaths, and Dash could see she was concentrating with all her might to overcome her constant and severe pain. And unlike their gym workouts, they couldn't just stop and catch their breaths with a baby poking out. They had been at this for five hours and made great progress. But the toll on Mizuke was obviously tremendous. Some nurses massaged her legs to keep them from spasming. Dash wondered if the blood vessel on her forehead would burst open like a horror film alien.

Dash knew that Mizuke was reconsidering the St. Croix "natural" birther process. But it was too late for an epidural. They'd been told in the beginning that they could have done a Caesarian extraction completely drugged up and finished hours ago, had her stomach mended with their advanced healing nano-tech, and been laying there enjoying the new baby in her arms. But, no, she had to do things the hard way, which seemed to be the St. Croix motto, Dash discovered. Funny how your mind picked times like these to attack you about things outside your control.

"Okay, ready for another push, Mizuke? This one is gonna be the one. Time to kick baby girl out of the house," Doctor Vance instructed.

Dash kissed the knuckle of her hand, and Mizuke nodded, bravely. They were a good team. Time for the big push. Dash knew she didn't really have a choice. The baby was in a precarious spot. He liked to think he was sharing in the pain. Mostly as Mizuke squeezed the blood from his hand with each push.

Suddenly, a loud *kaboom* was heard that shook the whole ship and rattled things about the room. Everyone stopped and looked around, concerned. Another explosion was even bigger and closer. The lights flickered. The ship's alert siren began to blast through the halls.

"Nurse, go see what the hell they're doing out there!" Doctor Vance yelled, never taking his eyes off the baby.

Dash looked back toward the door, watching the Byno-Nurse roll away. His instinct was to follow her into the action. Action he felt he could understand and would be comfortable with. Explosions. Danger. *That* he was more than prepared to cope with. Watching a human come out of his wife's most intimate places was overwhelming. And in the middle of it all, he had the most absurd stray thought that this kid wasn't even born yet, and she was wrecking his favorite playground.

Another explosion. Mizuke shook Dash's hand and he spun his attention back to her. "Let's do this, Doctor," she cried.

"Okay, Mizuke, take a deep breath and push." The doctor pressed a hand against her abdomen.

Mizuke bore down into this contraction. Dash and the nurse on the other side helped pull her upper body forward to help put the squeeze on the baby.

"Looking good, Mizuke. Here we go. Great progress. Here comes the head." Doctor Vance smiled.

The small head pushed out of her body, and Dash caught the first look at his brand-new daughter's face. It was nasty. It was covered in goop and slime and blood. And it was probably the most beautiful thing he had ever seen.

The Byno-Nurse rolled by the door, pausing in the entrance long enough to announce, "We're under attack, Doctor. Allied vessels." Then she was off again.

"Dammit." It was the first time the doctor had lost his cool.

"They're gonna blow a hospital ship out of the sky?" Dash asked. "Are the KACorps trying to start a war with the Croix?"

"No, those shots are warning shots," the doctor dragged an arm across the sweat of his brow. "They mean to board us. Take whatever they want, and then cower behind the legal system and claim some sort of technological imminent domain."

Dash stood. "I can help if I can get to my fighter."

"No, Dash." One look from Doctor Vance settled him firmly back into place. "What do you think they're gonna do to you if they find a KACorps Test Pilot on board a St. Croix vessel? And if they find out your wife is a St. Croix Advance-Tech Engineer?"

Dash shifted nervously and replied, "They wouldn't dare."

"This isn't NeoTokyo, Dash. These are international waters."

Sadly, the doctor was right, and Dash knew it. Since the rise of Colonel Wexell to power, the Kytos Alliance had splintered into a half-dozen factions, all grabbing for resources and fealty. But one thing they all had in common was that they hated the Croix. "Draccarios" was the slur they used. Only the small test corps at Bravo Bay remained neutral. As long as they remained off-radar, they could help the Croix, NeoTokyo, and any others trying to fend off the evil regime's growing control.

"W-what do we do, then, Doc?"

"Well, *we* are gonna finish having a baby," he said plainly. "Then *we* are gonna patch up Mizuke, get you both back on your ship, and get you on your way."

"Aaaaaaaahhhhhh," Mizuke cried out. "Can we get on with this?"

"Yes, Mizuke," the doctor soothed as he supported the baby's head. "Everything's fine. The first hurdle was the head. We're past that now. The next step is the shoulders. One more big push will do it. Ready?"

Mizuke spat out a string of expletives in Japanese, totally uncharacteristic of her, but they were drowned out by another string of explosions outside, which rocked the whole boat and flung Dash to the floor.

Fzzzzzzzht.

* * *

Deep Space

Captain Bastille's eyes flashed open, like waking from a dream where you're falling and about to hit the ground. Only he knew all of that had been no dream. It took a moment before the world rushed back around him into focus. He heard Gen nearby before he saw her.

"Captain, wake up. We've got a problem," she said with a frantic edge to her voice.

Bastille went from drowsy stupor to fully alert in a couple of heartbeats, as any good soldier is trained to do from bootcamp. He sat up in the bed and threw the covers off. At some point, he and Gen had traded sleep shifts. He recognized that the ship's proximity alert was sounding off.

"Asteroid belt?" he wondered aloud, pulling on some socks.

She shook her head. "There's another ship out there." She fidgeted with the belt of her own light-grey tactical jumpsuit. Nervous energy, Bastille noted.

"I thought you said they wouldn't pursue," he said grouchily as he wiggled his toes into his boots. He stomped the heels on the floor to seat them firmly in place.

"It's," there was no easy way for her to say this, "it's not one of ours."

Bastille jumped up, pulled a shirt on, and ran down the passageway. *Clank clank clank clank.* His boots hit the metal floor in rapid-fire succession. Gen padded lithely after him. The pant legs of this new outfit were wrapped around each of her calves down into a foot wrap that doubled as a shoe of sorts. It rendered her as silent as a house cat.

Bastille pulled himself up into his jumpseat and punched the elevator. "Going up," he said as he rose into the canopy. A thousand possibilities raced through his mind, some worse than others. When the ship came into view, he was relieved to see that it wasn't another bounty skiff. But, as Gen had surmised, it wasn't a Draccario vessel either.

"See," Gen pointed to the hull as her RIO seat rose and locked into position behind him, "*SS Daystar.*"

SS. Scout Ship—or at least that was the original foundation of this vessel. A long, sizable spacecraft built for speed and stealth. This one had been completely modded up into a gunship, though, so his relief was short-lived. Yet, curiously enough, there were no other markings on it anywhere.

Odder still, it was just floating there. Anchored in place. Right here at the edge of the asteroid field. No lights. No motion, no activity.

"What do you think, Captain?" Gen asked, perched forward on her knees, so she was right behind his ear.

"I don't know whether to blast it out of the sky or go up and knock on the front door," he said, honestly perplexed. He rubbed some sleep boogers out of his eyes.

"Are they sleeping?" Gen wondered aloud. "Or dead?"

"There's no external damage to the ship," Bastille pointed out as he punched the controls over to manual and edged closer. "Nothing recent, any—"

"What are you doing?" Gen interrupted, gripping his headrest nervously.

"Easy, little dipper," he said, looking back at her worried face and smiling. "We're just going in for a little looky-loo."

"Yes," she said sarcastically as the mystery ship loomed closer, "most of my people's cautionary tales ended with this proverbial 'looky-loo'."

"Funny," he replied, eyes darting over the ship surface, "that's how most of our best stories began."

He pushed forward on the throttle and closed the gap between them. He gently circled the ship, paying close attention to the mounted turrets. Most of them were forward-facing. It was obviously an attack vehicle. Designed to punch a hole and keep on truckin'. Bastille pushed into what he felt was their blind spot—7 o'clock low—to complete the walk-around.

"Seen enough, Captain? Can we get on with it? Imminent death awaits us inside the asteroid belt," Gen whispered, as if she didn't want her voice to carry across the negative space and awaken anyone.

Bastille noted that the more nervous she got, the thicker her royal accent became. "You're a scientist, for

God's sake. Show some professional curiosity at least," he chided.

"As a scientist, I know that curiosity and mortality rates have a rather high correlation, especially when stupid levels of testosterone are involved," she bit back, still a whisper.

"Oh, really?" Bastille chuckled.

"That's just science." She shrugged.

"We can take you back to your beloved bubble planet any time you want," he replied, not taking the bait.

She punched his headrest. Bastille slowed the ship as they approached the rear.

"I'm gonna do a low-level scan for any life signs," he said, flicking a sequence into the computer.

"Captain, I do *not* approve. The odds of us randomly running into another ship in this part of the galaxy are infinitesimally small. Impossible, actually. So either we just won the interstellar lottery, or—"

Bastille picked up where she left off. "—or they were waiting here just for us? No way."

"These are strange days, Captain," she warned. "It merits an abundance of caution. It's no time to play fast and loose. You're not listening to me, are you?"

His finger hovered over the engage button for a moment as he second-guessed himself, but then he exhaled a long, slow breath and punched it.

Immediately, the *Daystar's* lights flicked on, and the docking hatch at the back opened. The vessel sprang to life. More importantly, Bastille noted, none of their weapons engaged. He drifted their own ship higher just to be safe and flicked off the weapon's safety, and one finger hovered over the trigger with his other hand easing the throttle, ready for action. But after the bay doors opened, there was no other movement from the ship.

"Feeling lucky?" Bastille whispered.

"No, I've just had a hundred heart attacks. I'm not feeling 'lucky,' I'm feeling sick to my stomach. Can we go now?"

Bastille laughed. His own heart was beating loudly in his chest, but he wouldn't give Genwa'ar the satisfaction of knowing that. He swallowed hard and scanned the readings.

"Life scan says there are about four or five life forms aboard that ship," Bastille said as he looked into the docking bay. There was a large insignia on the floor. An insignia that matched the three markings tattooed on the dead blue-haired goddess in the captain's quarters of his burned up ship on Da'karh. The same one he saw on all the Mizuke BLU units in Bender's lab. He exhaled slowly.

Yeah, this was no random lottery.

"Looks like they're inviting us in," he said, finally. Not at all what Gen wanted to hear.

"Captain, you're not thinking we are—" her question trailed off as she felt their ship pulse forward.

"Relax," he said casually, "when it's your time, it's your time. What's the worst that could happen?"

"Death, dismemberment, torture—" Gen sputtered. She was livid.

"Stick with me, little dip." Bastille kept a keen eye on the *Daystar* as it grew in proximity.

"And those are best-case scenarios," she continued.

"Nah, this'll be a hoot," he said.

"A *hoot*?" Gen over-annunciated the unfamiliar word.

"Yeah, you know, fun, like a party," Bastille explained.

Gen snorted derisively. She was not having fun. She was mad. Or scared. Or both. "You're gonna be the death of me yet, Bastille." She slumped back in her seat and chewed her pinky nail in deep thought.

* * *

The Mustang touched down inside the docking bay, right atop the mystery insignia—the tri-mark. It was spacious in here. There was easily room for ten more Mustangs, and this wouldn't even be the main storage hangar, most likely. Although these blockade-runners were not the largest ships in the fleet, they were still impressively sized. Also noteworthy was the fact that a ship this big could be manned by a skeleton crew of 3-6 people, depending on their skill levels. Therefore a favorite of marauders and brigands. Bastille, did not mention this last part to Gen. Her imagination was already working overtime.

As the H2 powered down, Bastille kept an eye on the monitors. One of them showed the bay doors closing ominously behind them. He glanced up periodically at the entryway at the other end. No movement there. He double-checked his Mauzer and shoved it back into its holster. He waited for the ship to signal that the hangar bay was pressurized once again before he opened the hatch that hissed loudly.

As soon as all was clear, he climbed out of the cockpit, slid down onto the wing, and then jumped down to the ground with a metallic thud. He turned to help Gen after him, but she ignored the hand and flipped down, steady and nimble, landing in a squat. Rising slowly, she scanned the surroundings.

Ka-clang!

The sound of a chamber unlatched at the far end of the hangar snapped their attention aft. They both straightened as four human forms walked through the portal and spread out in a line. With barely a pause, the group made their way toward Bastille and Genwa'ar.

"Uh-oh," Bastille spoke to Gen over his shoulder. "These look like the Assassin Quartet from Gannon."

"The w-what?" Gen stepped closer behind him.

Bastille flashed another smile. "I'm kidding, I have no memory. These could be my parents, for all I know. Come on."

"Idiot," Gen seethed.

He began walking forward to meet their hosts. Everyone stopped about 20 feet away from each other. Bastille looked the group over, not missing any detail. Halfway through the process, he realized what he was doing. He was deciding in which order he would kill them. It was a professional practice. Second-nature. Just one more puzzle piece in the mystery that was his own sordid past.

The two men on the ends looked ragged enough. They had the lanky cut of engineers or lab techs. Not as slick as the KACorps low-level grunts. These were probably your garden-variety underworld thugs. Those two would be the ones keeping this ship afloat. Safe enough to let them live the longest. No one looked over thirty years old, which didn't mean anything either. They could have been as old as Gen. He noticed they all carried weapons at their ready. Holstered, but not belted down.

There was one gigantic mountain of a man in the middle, heads taller than the others, with a scar that went from the top of his tattooed head down the side of his face and neck and disappeared under his body armor vest. The tattoos told an intricate and bloody tale of his time at Tomar's Ranch, a penal colony on the Rangoor Nebula. But mostly, Bastille noted his itchy trigger finger. He was a wild card and would have to die first. He had some sort of shoulder harness on. Backpack maybe? Anyway, not the leader.

The leader was the blue-haired Asian woman second to the right. The bottom half of her face was covered by a tactical balaclava, a black material pulled up over her nose and mouth. Her short, spiked hair reminded him of a pufferfish. She, too, had a long scar on the side of her face that narrowly missed those piercing blue eyes. Everyone clearly deferred to her. It was slight but they were all a tiny step behind her. That meant she was not only the leader, she also had guts. Moxy. Bastille would take that into consideration. If she had been the leader standing *behind* everyone, that would have showed some sign of weakness. But, no, this one was unafraid. He respected that.

Wait, was she… *crying*? Was that a tear rolling down her cheek? She reached up and pulled the coverlet down, and Bastille gasped.

"Mizuke," he said, his mind reeling.

"Dash?" She stepped toward him. "He said you would be here," she said and ran to him, throwing her arms around his neck and planting a huge kiss right on his lips. Bastille's memory was fuzzy, mind you, but even so, he knew that this ranked as one of the top kisses he'd ever laid into. Electric. It caught him off guard, and he even found himself kissing back. The others shuffled nervously.

It was as if a lost soul mate had been restored to him, and he had to remind himself that this woman belonged to a part of him that was not, well, technically him. Bender definitely had not wiped everything clean. This body clearly remembered her body. His emotions were going haywire. He pulled away reluctantly, but the instant yearning was palpable within him.

"Mizuke, I—I am Captain Jacques Bastille," he said softly. She cocked her head to one side and then pressed his own Mauzer against his chin. He hadn't even noticed it had been lifted out. Oh, she was good. He raised his hands slowly.

"I know who you are, Captain Bastille," the waterworks were over and now she was all business. "Ah, ah, I wouldn't, if I were you, Genwa'ar," she warned, pressing the gun tip further into Bastille's neck.

Gen had pulled a small caliber weapon of her own and aimed it squarely at the woman. She didn't blink. Didn't move.

"Mizuke, what happened to you?" Bastille asked, more intrigued than mad.

"I don't think you're in any position to ask questions, skinbag," she replied with a leer.

"Actually—" Bastille held up a finger and signaled the ship with his Relay. Weapons spun up, guns swung around facing them all, and a single red targeting dot showed up on Gigantor's chest. The big guy grunted his disapproval, trying to wipe off the dot to no avail. "See? I've got you right where you want me." He grimaced awkwardly at his own lame wordplay.

Mizuke leaned back, confused. "What?"

"I mean, what are you doing here?" Bastille asked.

She studied his face for a moment, a look of hurt; then slapped him hard. "You skin snatching sonofabitch," she spat. "I am Captain Mizuke Strouthers of the *SS DayStar* is all you need know. Sent here to stop a traitor to the Kytos Alliance."

"But Mizuke, you are St. Croix. Isn't that right, Captain?" Gen stepped forward, lowering her weapon. She explained more excitedly, "This is great news. Dash has returned, and we are on our way to earth to stop General Wexell."

"Well—" Bastille was about to deny it, but held back when Mizuke powered the Mauzer down, spun it back around, and handed it to him, butt first.

"This quarrel does not involve you directly, Captain," then looked past him and pointed an accusatory finger at Gen. "She's the traitor we're after."

"Me?" Gen looked confused by this. She raised her gun again. Mizuke stepped around Bastille and walked right up until her chest touched the tip of Gen's gun. Gen steadied the gun with another hand.

"She's using you, Captain Bastille," Mizuke sneered.

"To get back to Earth, I know. Little Dipper is a little bossy," Bastille replied, his brow furrowed. "And delusional."

"No," Mizuke explained, "she's *tricked* you into taking her back to Earth. To turn you over to General Wexell. Collect the bounty. Maybe those Dominion Fugs strengthen themselves against KACorps with their own alliance with the Draccario separatists."

Genwa'ar cringed at the slur.

Mizuke continued, "Feel free to interrupt anytime, Genwa'ar."

"S-she's lying," Gen said off of Bastille's confused look. "She's lying," she repeated, but more pleading with him the second time.

"Really?" Mizuke stepped aside. Lifting a small analyzer from her belt, she powered it on as she walked toward the Mustang. Guided by a cadence of shrill beeps, she moved to the wingtip and stopped. Gen slowly lowered her gun. Mizuke found what she was looking for and triggered her hand device. A Draccario tracking device de-cloaked. "Right where they said it would be," Mizuke looked back at Gen.

Gen squeaked to protest, but no words came out.

"Genwa'ar, you're under arrest," Mizuke said with a snap of her finger. "Moose. Peanut."

Out of the corner of his eye, Bastille saw the big guy turn away. What he carried on his back was a large, armored backpack. Only it was less of a backpack and more like a saddle of sorts. Suddenly the top flap opened, and a dwarf popped up with a stunner and fired it once at Gen whose body instantly seized with an electric blue energy field. She dropped her gun and fell to the ground, twitching.

"Hey!" Bastille shouted, yanking out his Mauzer and leveling the gun at the little man, but as quickly as he'd emerged, he disappeared back into the pack. The big guy turned back around again. Bastille ran at Moose, holstering the Mauzer as he closed the space between.

"Captain, wait—" Mizuke tried to stop him, but he was on a rampage.

Moose reached down to his belt and lifted off the thin baton dangling from it. He snapped the trigger, extending it to its full length, and swung the club at Bastille's fast-approaching head. Bastille ducked it, rolling low. When he came back around, the hidden sword blade emerged from his wrist. With one stroke, he sliced cleanly through the big man's weapon, severing it in half, and glanced his cheek.

Bastille punched into Moose's chest and sent the blade up under his breastplate, not aiming for vitals but not really caring what he hit. Before the big man could even recover, Bastille sliced once more across his thigh. As Moose was forced to kneel, Bastille retracted his blade, stepped up onto that knee, and swung his own leg across Moose's broad shoulders. He reached into the pack, grabbed the little guy, and threw him to one side.

As he completed the complicated head-scissor takedown maneuver, Moose went flying, bleeding out of at least three places. Bastille ended up with the backpack sniper pinned to the floor, gasping for air, a blade through his shoulder as well.

"Don't kill Peanut," Mizuke pleaded.

"Touch her again, Peanut, and I'll bleed you out," he seethed, inches from the little man's face. "Got it?"

The pain from Peanut's shoulder was a loud roar in his ears, but the sniper nodded his head and said, "Yesssss."

Bastille retracted the blade, stood, blood dripping from his forearm, and walked coolly past Mizuke.

"Tend to your wounded," he said in passing. Then he bent down, scooped Gen up in his arms, gingerly, and started back toward his ship.

"She will be the death of you—of us all—if she's not stopped," Mizuke warned him.

Bastille turned and moved toward her. She stood unflinching. "And I will be the slow and painful death of each one of you if you hurt her again. That is a binding Ma'kobi blood oath." His breath was heavy. It blew wisps of Mizuke's spiked bangs from her face.

Mizuke was unyielding. "She is unconscious but unharmed, Captain. Bring her to our Med-unit and our flight surgeon will tend to her," she said earnestly.

"How can I begin to trust you or your crew after this?" Bastille spat.

"Because two weeks ago, Dash Strouthers contacted me. A man that's been dead and gone for more than a century. He sent us here to intercept you. To help," she replied calmly, letting the info sink in. "Do you think a Croix guardian such as her would go into custody willingly? And your reputation, well—it speaks for itself. This was the only way. Let my medic take a look at her."

Bastille studied Mizuke's face and then softened. Looking back down at Gen, he knew Mizuke was right. "Okay, where is this Med-unit?"

"Zimmer." Mizuke snapped her fingers and one of the rugged, mechanic guys at the end stepped forward.

"Hai."

"Show our guests to the infirmary. Take good care of our two guests, and then look after Moose and Peanut," she said, indicating the other two who were still writhing on the floor in pain.

"Yes, Cap'n. Follow me, *Shu'uma*." He gestured toward the exit.

Bastille followed behind, triggering the Mustang from his Relay. The guns locked down tight, the canopy slid closed, and it switched into sentry mode. He stopped at the flight deck entrance, checked back over his shoulder, and saw Moose had risen to his feet, picked up Peanut carefully like a baby, and was limping along behind them.

"Sssssss," Peanut hissed, trying to mask the pain. "I'm okay, buddy. You did good." He patted his large friend on the shoulder. "You did good."

Zimmer watched it all and leaned in with a thick Islander brogue to Bastille and confided, "Tha' big dude be a giant fluffy teddeh bear. Oughtn'ta cut him up like 'at."

"I s'pose we'll all know what's what next time around, won't we?" Bastille replied gruffly.

Zimmer caught his steely gaze, swallowed hard, then turned and lead through the doorway.

- 9 -

ZIMMER'S MISTAKE

Deep Space

"What do you mean you've done all you can do?" Bastille asked. His tone was even, but the way he leaned in towards Zimmer lent it more menace.

Zimmer hunched over Gen's body in the infirmary. She was hooked up to all sorts of monitoring apparatuses, beeping, humming, and analyzing. He confirmed one more mobile scan and then threw his hands up desperately.

"She ain't like us, man. She's gentetically altercated. Total bonzai! She *is* stable. But inna computer terms, it's more'n like, I dunno, sleep mode than a coma. Her skinbag is fixin' 'erself right up at a super high cycle, but her mind shows zippo activity."

"So, the pocket monkey fried her brains with his stunner?" Bastille rose to his feet.

"Th-that's one theory, but I don' tink so. It's more'n like… like… it's more'n like she left, Cap'n."

Bastille pulled the Mauzer from its sheath and laid it on the table by Gen's inert form. "Dead, you mean. You mean you've killed her."

Zimmer got even more frazzled. "No, no, no! Absotively not," he grabbed a stylus and drew on the brain monitor screen, "see in ta case of brain dead, you get a flat line. Like so. No residual hubbub and noises. But hers," he scribbled back and forth along the line. "Hers is completely wonky like this," he drew accordingly, "again, as if she left home. But check this—" he pulled up an alternate monitor for Bastille with lines and lines of code scrolling out in real time.

"What am I looking at?" Bastille checked over the computer language that was vastly unfamiliar.

"That was the last transmission from her Relay. Two seconds before Peanut's stunner even fired. And this piece?" He circled that last piece of code. "This piece is a, uh, complexicated search blonk. A back-door lock, if you will, that is running an infinite lorp."

"A lorp?" Bastille asked.

"A lorp," Zim said making a round, loop motion with his hand.

"A loop. For what?"

"For when she comes a'traipsin' back," Zimmer smiled, hoping this good news would stem his own death sentence. Sweat beaded up on his forehead.

"So your theory is that she ejected away to safety but left herself a breadcrumb trail to find her way back?" Bastille clarified.

Zimmer thought about it a second and then snapped his fingers. "Exactamundo! Whew. He gets it." His shoulders slouched as he finally relaxed a little bit.

"Fine. Where'd she go?" Bastille squinted at the frazzled tech.

"That I canna know. We can run a systemical scan, a little program I've got, but I don't tink she here. On board. I tink she go back home."

"Home? That's a long way away," Bastille said incredulously, "she couldn't transmit that much data that far that fast."

"Maybe using the ship's Relay or tapped into your Mustang, but I dunna tink it's as far as you tink," Zimmer suggested, lifting an eyebrow.

"That means the Draccario—uh, the St. Croix Shadow Moon is closing in fast," Bastille holstered his Mauzer studying Gen's face carefully. He relaxed his furrowed brow a bit.

Zimmer exhaled slowly, relief softening his face. Until Gen's body began to seize violently.

Bastille and Zimmer both took a step back as the aggressive tremors increased. "What's happening, Zimmer?"

"I dunno! Just... dunna touch anyt'ing."

After a full minute, the body went inert again as quickly as it started. Zimmer stepped forward again and double-checked her vitals. The monitors all read the same.

"Is she back?" Bastille put his hand on her forehead.

"No," Zimmer punched some code into the computer, "all systems are same as before. Lorp is lorping. Zippo bonkers."

"Fantastic. Now we've got two ghosts on the loose," Bastille mumbled, slumping back into the chair beside Gen.

"What's 'at again?" Zimmer peered back over his shoulder.

"Nothing," Bastille replied, dodging the question. "Anyway, from a tactical standpoint, we'd be better off on the far side of the asteroid field. I should go inform Mizuke."

Zimmer indicated a round, mirrored bubble on the ceiling in the corner. "I'm sure I's Captain watches everyt'ing with keen interest, *Shu'uma*."

The infirmary door slid open, and Mizuke strode in snapping her portable monitor closed. "Yes, good work, Zim. Double-check Moose and Peanut. The nanoids should be almost done stitching them back together. Then ready my Mech suit."

"Hai!" Zimmer bowed sloppily and scurried away.

"Captain?" She motioned to Bastille. "This way."

Bastille rose to follow.

"You're right," she said two steps ahead of him, "we need to punch through this asteroid belt and get to the other side. Trouble is, we're down a few crew members if you hadn't noticed." She threw him a perturbed look. He responded only with a non-committal, "Hm," and she continued, "So, I'm gonna need your help driving."

"Any sign of the Shadow Moon?" Bastille asked, ducking a low portal as their boots clang clang clanged down the tight corridor.

"Not a single blip on the radar," she replied. "We've scavenged an old D/U/G unit loaded with a swarm of SAT-drones. We'll scatter them in our wake. If our pursuers bump into anything, DUG will shoot us a warning."

They stepped into an elevator, and Mizuke punched up the bridge. Bastille stood behind her, taking in her blue-cropped, messy pixie cut. Very different from the traditional shoulder-length bob of the Mizuke from the flashbacks. Her black uniform was a turtleneck tank with detached sleeves that ran all the way from her fingers to her sinewy biceps. Her bare shoulder was inches from his face. And being so close, he could breathe in that jasmine scent she wore.

"Pardon?" She said, tucking some hair behind her ear and turning towards him with those big, electric blue eyes.

"I didn't, uh, that is—what's this word Zimmer keeps using? Shoomah?" Bastille stammered.

"*Shu'uma*," Mizuke corrected, studying him curiously. "It's an old Ma'kobi bounty phrase. *Shuliah* meaning something like Phoenix. *Umannta* literally translates as Deathmark."

"Phoenix Deathmark," Bastille rolled the words around, confused.

"When a dead man rises from the grave and becomes the hunter. He is the *Shu'uma*."

"Hm."

"Or," she pursed her lips thoughtfully, "he could be saying *Shyoomah,* which is 'street mongrel who licks himself.'"

"Of course it does." Bastille cracked a smile. The doors whisked opened and Mizuke walked over to the helm, where Tanner Crest busily tended to his task of keeping them all afloat.

Bastille followed closely.

"You remember Tanner from our welcoming party," Mizuke said, more of a statement than a question. "He is our flight engineer. Plotting us the least suicidal route through the asteroid belt."

"It's all jazz." Tanner threw a little salute, but didn't break from his computer work in front of him.

"You'll be here beside him," she indicated the pilot's seat.

Bastille sat down, and it automatically slid forward into position. Mizuke leaned in over his shoulder. Bastille could smell that perfume again, which had not only imprinted on his mind but would forever trigger that memory of their first passionate embrace as well as the yearning of a thousand others before.

He knew Mizuke could feel it, too. That tug of familiarity. She would know every inch of his scruffy face down to his moody eyes that changed color with how he was feeling on a given day—green and blue and grey and brown. He could feel her eyes on him. He turned to her expectantly. She cleared her throat and continued.

"It's standard fly-by-wire," Mizuke began, then added, "just take it easy on the corners. Give her some breathing room to ease in and out of the flight vectors.

This ain't no Mustang. But it's no box turtle either. She's pretty yar. She'll surprise you."

"I bet she will," Bastille agreed, looking back at her.

"Hm," she said, her hand on her hip. A single eyebrow lifted.

"Yeah, yeah, I got it, Professor, I got it," Bastille laughed. He actually didn't know if he had it or not, but because of the relaxed comfort he felt in this seat, he knew deep down that this wasn't his first time helming a Sea Scout. He trusted that muscle memory would kick in and guide them through the rocky mine field. Or they'd all quickly become floating space garbage. Either way, no sense in getting all worked up over it.

"And where will you " Bastille shouted into her face. He thought she'd headed for the door already, but she was still right by his side, studying his hands on the controls. He continued a little softer, "Ahem, and where will you be?"

"I'll be in the MechRoom, keeping giant space balls at a comfortable distance, pew pew pew." She fired some imaginary guns with her fingers and then blew the resulting smoke from her fingertip barrels.

She handed the end of the Relay cable to Bastille. "We'll be one and one after you dock to the Neuralnet." She patted his shoulder as she leaned toward his ear. "So be careful what you think."

"See you on the other side, Captain," Bastille said casually.

"See *you* on the other side, Captain," she echoed over her shoulder as she walked out.

Bastille snapped the Relay into place at the back of his neck, and his eyes glowed white.

Fzzzzzzzht.

* * *

Planet Earth, Miramar Settlement

Captain Michael "Dash" Strouthers had only just plugged the umbilical cord into the life support Relay at the base of his neck and cinched his restrainers into place. Something wasn't right. Maybe. Sitting there in the cockpit of the H2X-Ø Mustang, prepping for pre-flight, there was a strong sense of déjà vu.

As the canopy halves slid forward and back into place, the ComLink in Dash's HUD crackled to life with a friendly female voice, *'Captain Strouthers, radio check. Radio check one, check one,'* relayed Major Stephanie "Step" Phillips from her position up in Flight Control.

Dash paused, trying to blink away the fog and confusion. He hadn't had one of those Jacques Bastille memory interruptions in years and now of all times the neural glitch was impeding his flow state. Dash noted with dismay that his responses to other stimuli around him were mechanical. Rote. As if he knew what to say like this were a scene in a play.

"R-radio check: Affirmative, Step. Read you, uh, loud and clear?" Dash stammered a bit.

"You sure, Dash?" asked Step and then continued over their private HUD link, *'Cause you don't sound like you're ready to make history.'*

"Step—" Dash began but couldn't form words to the uneasiness about him. Especially on the eve of such a huge undertaking. If he told anyone about the aberration they'd ground him indefinitely and someone else would break the water-launch to space record. Bump that. The monitor in front of him showed the cockpit seal as solid. Everything looked 5x5. He ignored his apprehension and trusted the monitors. "Step, I'm, uh, snug as a bug."

"That's the spirit, then. What say we light this tuna?"

"Yep," Dash said, hitting a button labeled スタート. The whole cockpit sprung to life with readouts, monitors and heads-up displays. They all began cycling through their startup sequencing and settled one by one into ready status. 3.4 seconds from cold boot to all systems go.

Dash began going over another checklist in his head. Everyone else's lines, which he shouldn't know unless this were all some sort of a dream.

"Flooding the tubes," he said to himself and then looked over to where the nervous looking Seabee punched a huge red button.

"Flooding the tubes," echoed the Seabee into the comm, watching the water levels rise around the mid-sized fighter.

Dash leaned his head into the headrest and took some deep breaths.

"Bird's sexy," he mumbled to himself.

"Damn that bird's sexy, Dash. Bring her home in one piece, yeah?" The Seabee smiled through the portal at Dash, adding the hang-loose, all-ready signal.

Dash signaled back, adding, "Uh, right, you ain't seen nothing yet."

The Seabee threw him an odd look. Dash knew he wasn't pulling off this charade convincingly, but somehow he had a self-awareness that he should not have had. Somehow in this déjà vu moment he knew had enacted this scene before. And this self-awareness wasn't nearly as troubling as the scene's impending climax which barreled toward him quickly. Hadn't he done all of this before? Hadn't the ship… *exploded*?

He heard himself answer another exchange with Step who cleared their moon dance with SkySAT. Saw the photo of Mizuke. He blinked and it shifted into a picture of the dead, blue-haired woman from Jacques Bastille's crash-landed freighter. Wait, was that part of a different dream? He blinked again and it reverted back. Something was off, but he didn't have the bandwidth to consider it as he raced down the tube and broke free into open water.

"Welcome to the party," he mumbled to himself.

"Visual confirmed, welcome to the party," crackled the voice of his friend, Lt. Colonel Vincent "Gator" Gordon, who slid his ship into position off his wing.

It felt like time was compressing. Whole scenes were not being played out chronologically. They were clipping forward several minutes at a time. One minute he exited the launch tubes and the next he whispered: "Let's get vertical."

Step echoed, "You are clear to begin Level Two maneuvers. Let's get vertical."

Dash engaged the atmospheric drive. He shot out of the water leaving Gator behind and heard the first celebration from Step and her crew on comms. The Mustang climbed into the sky with the Ranger squadron alongside.

"Ranger Force in position," Dash said along with Gigsby's gruff female voice on the other side.

"I'm uh, I'm increasing the power to 45%," Dash said.

"Roger that, Dash. Shoot the stars!" Step replied.

The Mustang increased its speed and the Rangers began to struggle to keep up. As the distance between them increased, Dash knew he should be calling out the speeds, but he stopped after "Mach 15… um, Mach 18…"

Dash reached down and engaged engine number three. "Ions coming online."

"Ions coming online," Stephanie echoed to Base. "10 seconds to Sub-Space."

"To the moon, Alice," Dash said to himself as his finger hovered over the Ion drives. A very shaky finger. His whole hand was shaking. He was sweating profusely inside the gloves, and in that moment, he made a decision. "Abort! Abort moon dance, repeat abort!" Dash yelled.

"Dash, what's wrong, all systems are clear," Step answered back.

"No go, no go!" Dash confirmed as he pulled back on the yoke and began to arc the Mustang back and away from the space canopy. That's when another less familiar face popped up on the screen.

"Captain, what are you doing?" asked Colonel Wexell very calmly. Very sternly puffing away on a cigar.

"Colonel Wexell…?" A quizzical expression twisted his face. What was this?

Wexell leaned into the monitor. "Sorry to interrupt your moment of glory, son," she glowered at him, "but our program will receive so much more funding if this test flight is unsuccessful, so, ciao."

Dash was now thoroughly confused. He watched as the Atmos drives were switched remotely over to the Ion drives. He tried to undo it, but it wouldn't respond. Something else had taken over his ship. And in that instant, he saw Wexell smiling up at him from the screen before the entire ship erupted in a ball of fire.

Fzzzzzzzht.

* * *

Deep Space

Bastille's eyes snapped open. Alert. His breathing heavy. He looked around to gather his bearings. Dash was right. These neural glitches were incredibly disorienting. And they'd somehow gotten worse since Phaedra. His eyes began to adjust to the bright ceiling lights. It appeared he was laying down in the infirmary of the *Daystar*.

How did I get here?

He looked around but he was alone. Connected to a bunch of monitors which beeped and processed his every move. One of them sounded some sort of alarm.

But something didn't feel right. He could hardly move. He was strapped down by safety restraints. He raised his head as much as he could to look down and saw that he had rebooted somehow into Genwa'ar. He was Genwa'ar! He lifted a hand and wiggled the fingers. Her fingers. He took shallow, gasping breaths as her breasts rose and fell.

He yelled and a girl-scream pierced through the room. He strained with all his might against the harnesses but they were secure. He heard movement to his left and saw Zimmer running back into the room.

Zimmer's look of surprise melted into pure disdain as he took in the scene before him, flipping off the alarm. He looked down at Gen.

"Well, well, it look'n like the Draccario skinbag is back," Zimmer said with a sneer.

Bastille tried to talk but his mouth was so dry. He couldn't quite get any words out. Zimmer smiled and back-handed her.

"Shhh, sh shhhh," Zimmer said a-fixing a mouth restraint into place which muffled her protests even more. "We don't want to alert the others." He pressed a tranq device into the base of her neck, squeezing out a sedative.

"Nah, we's gotta some special tests to run on ye backstabbin' princess. D'ya like games?" Zimmer said tugging down the zipper on Gen's jumpsuit.

Bastille could feel the drug's effects instantly. Zimmer's face elongated and mixed into the ceiling lights, which began swirling around as the room spun and the darkness slowly took over.

Fzzzzzzzht.

* * *

Bastille awakened. He took a second to let his senses come fully alert. It was relatively dark except for some ambient light from a window or another room behind him. His head lay on a soft pillow. He brought his hand up to touch. It *was* a pillow. He rubbed his large manly hands together. Checked the scar on his shoulder before he sighed in relief.

It was good to be back in his own skin. He heard a flush from the adjoining room, a door opened, and light flooded the area briefly before it was pitched back into darkness. He was in bed. He was under soft covers that smelled of a jasmine flower. He didn't recognize anything else. Especially not the warm female form that slipped back into bed behind him. He could feel her warm breasts press into his back as she threw a gentle arm around him and kissed his shoulder.

Bastille waited. Perfectly still. The woman's breathing became steady, and within minutes she had fallen back asleep. Bastille carefully slid out from under her arm, peeling back the covers.

He sat up on the edge of the bed. Behind him, a large window portal showed a million stars twinkling against the black expanse. He looked back at his bed-mate and pulled down the corner of the blanket, which had obscured her beautiful face.

Mizuke.

She sighed in her sleep and turned in the other direction. Bastille rubbed his face. It didn't take a rocket scientist to put this one together. What was Dash going to do? Their thing was a hundred years ago. Did he even care? He didn't even have a body now. Plus, he was more computer than man. Bastille was chewing on the Dash problem when he remembered Zimmer.

He felt around on the floor and found his shorts. Pulling them on, he then slid his hand up under the mattress and removed the Mauzer he knew would be there.

Checking out the window, Bastille could just barely make out the asteroid belt behind them, receding in the distance.

"Everything okay?" Mizuke asked sleepily, through a yawn.

"Yes, of course," Bastille said, walking over to the bed. "I'll just be a minute, okay?"

Bastille moved some of the hair from her eyes, pushing it back behind her ear.

"Mm-hmm," she said, burrowing deeper into the covers.

Bastille watched her fall back asleep. Shaking his head clear again, he stood and walked from the room. He was now on a mission. It was a little chilly out in the hallway since he just had on his skivvies, but his bare feet padded soundlessly along the corridor.

He took the lift back down to the infirmary. When the elevator doors opened, Moose was standing there beside the lab entrance, rifle in hand. On guard. He straightened when he saw Bastille approaching. His large frame blocked the entire doorway. After his own time in the infirmary, Moose looked to be completely patched up. This could have been another epic battle if he was back at 100 percent because this time he knew Bastille's tricks.

Bastille walked right up to the towering menace, looking him directly in the eye, even though he only measured up to the big man's chest. Bastille had no interest in Moose. Not now. Not even before; he was merely an obstacle preventing him from reaching Peanut. Now he was an obstacle again. Peanut was apparently Moose's best friend. So, of course, he'd fight to the death before he let anyone hurt his small companion. Which is why Bastille had jumped to brutalize him so quickly. Take him out of the equation. Now, Bastille just hoped Moose didn't hold the same affection for Zimmer. They stood there, staring each other down.

Moose sized him up and then, very intelligently, he stepped aside.

Bastille nodded and triggered the door. It slid open smoothly and noiselessly. He could hear Zim cursing at Gen in the adjoining room.

"C'mon! I know'n you're in t'ar. I's a-seen ya! Ya canna hide f'rever." Zim was almost naked, threatening her, occasionally jolting her body with a low-level shock he administered to her exposed abdomen.

"Stop," was all Bastille said as he strode forcefully into the room, gun cocked and locked onto Zim's back.

Zim spun around, surprised. Clearly, he was not understanding why a man in his underwear was pointing a dangerous-looking gun at him. Before he could wonder where his guard was, Moose ducked through the door and stood just inside.

Bastille motioned with the gun for Zim to step aside. Zim complied, talking nervously as he moved.

"*Shu'uma,* you'n be hap t'hear she back. A brief bounce but I did it—"

He never finished his thoughts. Bastille pulled the trigger on the Mauzer. A blast that had barely moved Bender's large frame catapulted Zim back against the wall. He didn't even have time to scream. And that was just the stun setting. Bastille walked up to Gen and zipped back up her uniform, noting every bruise and red mark on her skin. Then he removed the gag from her mouth and the other restraints from her body. He was seething.

With little warning, he fired the Mauzer up to full power, turned on Zim, and blasted his unconscious form into a million dust particles. It took a full minute for the blind rage to clear, and his breathing returned to normal.

He pulled some pillows up under Gen's head. He could see the nanotech repairing the gash on her cheek at a remarkable rate. He spread a blanket over top of her and then raised the side rail back up to prevent her from rolling off. On the wall, he slid the room lights to about fifty percent.

Bastille walked up to Moose. "No one comes in here and nobody leaves without my orders, got it?"

Moose stiffened and grunted out an affirmation.

Bastille walked past him and out the same way he came in. The entire ship was at rest now. Bastille went back to Mizuke's chambers and slid the gun back under the mattress. It sizzled as the hot barrel singed it a bit. He climbed under the covers and wrapped his arms around Mizuke, who made some mewling sounds and pressed her naked body back against him. He may not know who he was. He may not know where he was going or how he was going to keep himself alive to do whatever he needed to do. But what he did know was that this felt right, here and now. This was home. Mizuke was home. His eyes fluttered closed.

They were both back asleep, breathing heavily, within minutes.

\- 10 -

RE-ANIMATION

Deep Space

Captain Jacques Bastille stood beneath the shower head as a dozen tiny salt water jets rained down upon his scalp; the steaming brine cascaded down his body and pooled at his feet. He hadn't moved for a while. He stood there, leaning his forehead against the cool stainless steel surface, soaking. When he darted his tongue across his lips, he could taste that familiar, tinny flavor in the water that every starship eventually acquired, no matter how first-rate their water conditioning system.

It was frustrating to know that fact, yet to not know *why* he knew it. To be cut off from your own past was to handicap your very future. A shallow history provided a limited basis for predicting things to come. So much of every waking decision was anchored upon data points of desire and truth. Pleasure and pain. People who have loved you. People who have hurt you. How you might react and who you might react to depended on a systematic self-discovery process that took a lifetime to calibrate.

Bastille couldn't foresee five minutes into the future because he could barely glimpse a few weeks into his own past. Pieces of the puzzle were slowly coming together, but there was so much that was still shrouded in darkness. He could meet someone and instantly know that he recognized them, not knowing why. He could taste a piece of food and remember that it was his favorite flavor. Yet at other times, there was food he knew he was supposed to hate, but now he didn't mind it. His tastes were evolving. Everything was changing. Unhinged. Constantly shifting like lightning sand because there was no past to anchor it.

Somehow, though, it all proceeded toward an endgame, which he half expected not to survive. He was rebuilding every relationship from scratch and this left him extremely vulnerable, and Bastille found that to be the most exhausting part of all.

Mizuke's voice crackled through the comm system, interrupting his reverie. "Captain, we're ready for you on the bridge. Bring the duffel."

Bastille stirred for the first time, snaking his hand out of the shower to the return button beside it. He mashed it, and after the chime, he answered, "Be right up."

Bastille had no idea how long he'd been standing there, but the prune pattern on his fingertips suggested a twenty-minute set at least. A random thought occurred to him that once upon a time he would have yard-whipped any crew who showered longer than two minutes on board an active-duty ship. Such extravagance had not been tolerated with limited resources. What an odd detail to manifest.

He absent-mindedly played with a piece of blue hair clinging to the silvery shower stall. Touching the center of the strand, he swirled it around in a circle, gathering it expertly into a little ball, which he collected and flicked down the drain. He spun the lever to fresh water and rinsed off all the healing salty residue, then shut the water off and stepped out of the shower. Steam tornadoes rose up off his broad shoulders, dissipating into the coolness around him.

Bastille was confounded by the fact that he could explain the engineering behind a drop of water leaving his skin and falling into the drain system. How it moved into the ship's recycling flow through the water main and purifiers and back out to the shower or lavatory systems. But he couldn't remember where he'd gotten the bullet dimples in his abdomen or the scar tissue on his shoulder and back that resembled a seaweed attack. He could dismantle, clean, and reassemble his Mauzer in under three minutes, but he couldn't recall where he'd acquired it and could not explain the dent or the small fissure at the base of the handle. All these observations were loose threads that should have been attached to stories. Instead, there was a wall of darkness. More like an impenetrable fog where he could see movement and shadowy glimpses, but only vague shapes beyond. Nothing ever coalesced.

He held his arms out to the side and closed his eyes as he stood before the dry rack, which blasted him with a cyclonic heat wave. At the same time, the exhaust system sucked most of the moisture ions from the air and returned them to the water mains.

* * *

Fifteen minutes later, Bastille stepped onto the bridge, where everyone was crowded around a map table cluttered with digital star charts, documentation, and flight paths projected all over it. They looked up when he entered and tossed down the duffel he'd retrieved from the Mustang.

Mizuke pointed to a patch of red dots on the other side of the asteroid belt. "DUG has picked up a signal from the shadow planet that passed through his drone swarm about 45 minutes back. We have no idea how long it will take them to work through the asteroid belt, but once they're past the radiation interference on this side, they'll presumably be in range to send Genwa'ar back aboard. Which we must be prepared for."

That explained Moose's presence up here on the bridge. No sense in guarding a comatose Byno-Core if they were out of tactical range and if the ship's one deviant existed only from the knees down. Peanut was parked in the saddle-platform on Moose's back, leaning over his shoulder with a pained look on his face as if he were trying to work out an extremely advanced calculus problem. Or maybe the wound Bastille had inflicted had nicked his lungs, and now, even though he was ninety-seven percent healed, it still hurt to breathe.

Peanut raised a MediPen to his mouth and drew a breath. When he let out a puff of smoke, the painful expression dissolved into a deep, calm satisfaction. Eyelids at half mast. Yeah, he was feeling no pain. Unfortunately, this was a process he'd have to repeat every hour or so now for the next five days, until he had healed completely.

Bastille couldn't help but notice Tanner glaring at him across the war table. "Who piddled in your porridge?"

Tanner bristled even more at this. Mizuke held up a hand to stop Tanner from overreacting. He nodded at her submissively.

"Zimmer," she explained, "was his brother."

Bastille straightened up and gestured toward the door. "Zimmer was a psychopathic sex-deviant who was running some kind of S&M experiment on my friend. Isn't that right, Moose?"

Moose grunted. That was Moose for "yes."

This caught Tan off guard a bit. Bastille continued, "Check the ship log. He was abusing Genwa'ar while we slept." He clapped Moose on the shoulder. "So, we stopped it. From ever happening again."

Peanut gave Moose a little bump on the shoulder. Tanner struggled with the accusation about Zimmer, but everyone present knew it rang true nonetheless.

"Ain't right, though," Tanner said. His Islander brogue wasn't nearly as strong as his brothers but still noticeable. "Yeah, he was a perv. And a monster on the sonic wafers. Devil's candy. One of the reasons we had to accept these deep-space missions. Get him away from people."

"And the law," Peanut added.

"Well, that too," Tanner conceded. He shifted back and forth uncomfortably. "Don't make it right, though."

"Technically it was strike three. Anyway, it's done. Runway behind us," Mizuke added, looking each crew member in the eye. "Nonetheless, he *was* our chief engineer, and now we're shorthanded. Out-gunned. And time is of the essence." She walked over to the duffel bag and bent down to inspect it. "According to Dash, your bag contains six *seklas*."

This caused a generally impressed murmur from the crew. Mizuke pulled out six bricks, wrapped neatly and safely. She stacked them on the table's edge.

"*Seklas*?" Bastille asked, since everyone else seemed to be in the know.

The question disturbed Mizuke. In part because everyone in the entire universe knew what a *seklas* was as well as its extraordinary value. But more disturbing than that, there would be far more vital information she needed him to recall for the mission at hand, to which he may not have access.

"Seed bricks," she replied casually, handing one off to him. "The most valuable commodity on the black market. Draccario invention. Each brick contains the raw seed DNA needed to jumpstart a colony's worth of food growth, vegetation and basic animal life. In short, gentlemen, this is how we're funding our mission."

"And what mission is that?" Bastille pressed.

The answer came behind them from the doorway.

"To crush General Wexell at Fort Royale. End the slavers. Raise the *Bellevue*. Restore the Alliance of Kytos," Genwa'ar said, stepping onto the bridge.

Bastille's Mauzer cleared leather a split second too late. Gen aimed a stunner at him, and he took the full force of the blue electric bolt into his chest. It spread to his limbs and snapped his mind off instantly, like a light switch. Around him, alarmed voices echoed away into the fog.

Fzzzzzzzht.

* * *

SCV Bellevue

Dash Strouthers sat in Dr. Vance's office, hugging Mizuke in his arms. Tears streamed down her cheeks. The doctor moved around the desk and perched closer to them both.

"I'm sorry, but the fertility tests have resulted in some potentially sensitive findings. Mizuke, you are unable to have children," he said gravely. "Because it's illegal for your kind."

"I don't understand," she sobbed. "My *kind*?"

Dash looked up to say something when the whole scene he was in jumped back five seconds earlier, as if he were rewinding a Viddix playback. The doctor re-appeared on the other side of the desk, moving around closer to them both. "Unable to have children," he repeated. "Because it is illegal for your kind."

Dash squeezed his eyes shut. His mind was playing tricks again. Had to be those KACorps neural implants. Either that or residual Vancinex hallucinations. Even though he'd kicked the habit, he'd read that the side effects could linger for years. When he opened his eyes again, he flashed to a hospital bedside, holding Mizuke's hand in the delivery room. She wailed loudly. Her feet up in the stirrups, and Dr. Vance between her legs delivering their baby. The infant's head had just crowned.

"I hope you like mucous-colored hair, because that's what she's got," the doctor quipped.

Mizuke's wailing dissolved into a piercing ring tone, and the scene fluttered backward and then proceeded again as the head crowned again. Dash looked closer to the wall beside him, and it was artifacting and pixellating, as if data were in the process of corrupting. The lamp also glitched and settled again. Mizuke screamed in pain, but the sound dropped in and out into a static white noise.

Dash shook his head to clear it, but the scene around him slowly began to disintegrate. How was this even possible? He reached out to touch the computer monitor, and it jiggled like a mirrored gelatinous blob. Dash tried to speak, but an electronic discord of notes screeched out. Then suddenly, the whole scene flashed away.

Now, Dash was standing inside a large laboratory with Dr. Vance. The artifacting had gone away, and the room was crystal clear. Beside them was a long row of Cryo-tanks emitting a blueish glow.

Dash stepped closer to one of them. Identical nudes in every tank. Where had he seen these containers before? In a dream? It was. Bender's laboratory in

Jacques Bastille's world. Dash looked closer at a sign on the glass which identified it as a "Mizuke, BLU." It was a Biosynthetic Lifeform Unit.

"Now understand, Dash, they are biosynths. As such, they are not equipped to bear children," the doctor explained. "But they can serve in any other capacity. Everything else is fully functional."

"That's great, Doc. I want one. She's perfect," Dash said, but then winced painfully.

The doctor watched him closely. "Dash, your nose is bleeding."

Dash drew a finger across it, and sure enough, there was blood. "Doc?"

The doctor pulled out a penlight and shone it in his eyes. "How are you feeling Dash? Have you been having any trouble with the—"

The doctor continued talking, but disharmonic tones came out of his mouth instead of words. Dash couldn't understand the digital gibberish.

"Fshhhhh fshh," the doctor said, making no sense. Pulling a specialty device from the cart beside him, he motioned for Dash to turn around. "Fshhh fshhh. Fshh fshhh fshhh fshhhhhh fshhhhh!"

Dash turned around as the doctor pulled out some cords and jacked one into the back of his neck.

Then, in another bright flash, he was back in the delivery room on the 7th floor of the *SCV Bellevue*. Room 38. He stood beside Mizuke while Dr. Vance worked down by her feet.

"Aaaaaaaaahhhhhhh," Mizuke cried. "Can we get on with this?!"

"Yes, Mizuke. Everything's fine," the doctor reassured her. "The first hurdle was the head. We're past that now. The next step is the shoulders. One more big push will do it. Ready?"

Mizuke spat out a string of expletives in Japanese, totally uncharacteristic of her, but they were drowned out by another string of explosions outside, which rocked the whole boat and flung Dash to the floor.

Fzzzzzzzht.

* * *

SS Daystar

Captain Mizuke knelt close by Bastille, finishing a threat to the crew: "—next person to open fire on my ship will be airlocked."

Bastille awoke with a sputter. Mizuke cradled his head and he rolled off to the side coughing and hacking until his breathing returned to normal, "These memory flashes are brutal." He wiped a trickle of blood from his nostril.

"Compromised memory nodes. The past is unraveling, Bastille," Gen said, standing off to the side, strategically out of reach.

Bastille slowly climbed to his knees and then stood with an assist from Mizuke. He braced himself against the ship's bulkhead. Reaching out two fingers on his non-mech arm, he tapped the wall a couple of times just to feel the cold steel on his knuckles. It was getting harder and harder to tell the memory spikes from reality. "Gen's back," he said, spitting some blood from his mouth. "Everyone's cool with this?"

"Not Gen." Mizuke stepped in and laid a steadying hand on his arm. "Well, not inside, anyway. This is Dash. Or some backup amalgam version of Dash."

"What?" Bastille was confused by this latest wrinkle.

"Dash 2.0," Dash saluted.

"You're the ronin? Messing with my head?" Bastille looked him over suspiciously.

"Yeah, it was gettin' a little crowded in there, mate," Dash said with no trace of the royal accent. "So when I found this tiny meat-suit that Gen left just a-layin' around…"

Dash shrugged at the inevitable result.

Bastille shared a look with Mizuke. "You buying this?"

She chewed on the question for a moment before answering with her own, "Do we have a choice?"

Bastille groaned. Before Phaedra, he wouldn't have thought any of it feasible. Not without a roomful of specialized Re-cycle gear. But after what he saw there—and experienced at Bender's horrific laboratory—he'd have to entertain some strange new possibilities.

\- 11 -

PEANUT'S SUICIDAL PLAN

The *DayStar* crew had settled around the bridge, scoping out the newcomer. Genwa'ar carried herself differently as Dash. Less poised and regal. More slouch and swagger. Whereas before she walked as gracefully as a panther, now she moved stiffly like her own legs were unfamiliar. Or rather, his legs. Man, this was going to get confusing.

Dash wore a black cap with his long hair tucked up under. Black tactical pants and flight jacket on instead of the usual flowy St. Croix eco-threads or matching jumpsuit. He also chewed on a black perkweed cigar. He finally sauntered over to Bastille, blowing smoke up toward the vents. The white cloud smelled like a pleasant blend of molasses and sandalwood.

"Dash Strouthers of the Kytos Alliance Test Corps," said the 170-year-old test pilot now inhabiting the 16-year-old's Byno-Core. He no longer had Gen's strong Draccario accent anymore, either. That was one of the give-aways.

"Got it." Bastille eyed the stranger cautiously. "Shouldn't you be dead?"

"Shouldn't you?" Dash replied, flicking some ash from the cigar tip. "Look, I figured you'd be gunnin' for Genwa'ar and I couldn't risk being expulsed from this meat-suit by that bloody Mauzer." Dash indicated the weapon on Bastille's hip.

"I'd have done the same," Bastille said as he coolly tapped the pistol butt. "Might still."

Peanut and Moose observed everything silently as they nursed their steaming cups of kuraac in the corner. It was a potent home brew that former prisoner's made that would jolt an elephant. Peanut also kept one hand on a small pistol just inside his vest.

"A shame to be limited by skin and bones again," Dash said with the slightest scowl. He pinched at his toned little-girl's arms. "Helluva thing to get used to. Imagine the freedom to course through an entire computer network in the blink of an eye, yeah? You think the Mustang is fast?" He elbowed Bastille playfully in the ribs.

Bastille moved a step away from him, toward the pile of star charts on display. "Well, I'd say you definitely gave the Draccario—the Croix—a run for their money. Speaking of which, what happens if Gen comes back and you're still, uh, occupado?"

"Unclear. I could be ejected. Or maybe I have squatter's rights and she gets stuck in some sorta holding pattern. Or we may form some sort of hybrid system merger like you and I had going on. Dang, I can't get used to these wibbly-wobblies," Dash scratched at his left breast. Then wiggled it a little. "I mean, how are you supposed to get any work done with these things bouncing around?"

Peanut almost spit out his drink.

"Oh, for the love of…" Mizuke smacked his hand away. "Cut it out!"

Dash turned his attention to her. "And you are Mizuke Blue. We had a thing going once, didn't we?"

"Once," was all she'd concede. "You don't remember?"

"There's a lot of holes," he said, tapping a finger to his temple. "Memory gaps. And the ones I do have… well, there's no emotion attached to them anymore. No feeling. It's like reading a history book about someone else's life. I don't know how else to explain it." Dash looked her over, focusing on the scar on her face. He reached up to touch it but she grabbed his hand.

Peanut leaned forward just a bit, but Bastille held up a subtle hand to wave him off of whatever action he'd been about to take.

"We're not doing that now," Mizuke said firmly. "We've got a Shadow Moon that could de-cloak any minute now, and we've got a boatload of prep work to do."

Dash turned his attention to Bastille. "And you look like shyte. You really let ourself go, yeah?"

"Hmm," Bastille grunted back at him.

"And yet, you've still got some of my old emotions bouncing around in there. Which is why the two you—" Dash pointed at Bastille and Mizuke.

"Okay, we are definitely not doing *this* right now, boys," Mizuke pulled away from them both with raised arms and headed over to Bastille's bug-out bag on the floor. "Seed bricks. That's what we're doing. We've gotta get these *seklas* to the black market. Bastille?" She tossed a brick to him which he caught. "You've got the most experience there. Need you to find us a buyer. Whatever memories you've got, Captain. We're open to suggestions. Dash, you need to brief us on that Shadow Moon."

"Aye a crazy piece o' work that place," he said.

"Yeah, well, you were on the inside. What did you find out while you were poking around in their mainframe? Moose? Peanut? Ready the ship to break anchor. If we're not mobile in twenty minutes, I'm sending someone out the airlock. Understood?"

Everyone grumbled various "ayes" and snapped to work. Bastille turned aside to Mizuke, privately, "Listen, now that your soul mate's home, so to speak, I'll understand if you—"

"Stop. That is not my Dash," Mizuke cocked an eyebrow as they both watched Dash settle into the pilot's chair. "And I sure as hell am not the same girl he abandoned all those years—"

She cut herself off.

"Hm," Bastille grunted. He considered the conflict in her eyes before dropping it. Then, he announced to no one in particular, "I'll be out in the Mustang."

"*My* mustang," Dash corrected, through teeth clamped onto the cigar butt.

Bastille paused at the door and turned back. "You are a spectral ronin. A rudderless soul. A temporal anomaly in *our* reality. A blip. Just, try not to screw anything up while you're here."

He exited. Dash flicked the smokey butt of the perkweed at the empty doorframe. It splintered into dozens of glowing embers when it ricocheted off the wall.

* * *

Bastille sat in the cockpit of the Mustang, jacked into the NavCOMM. He scrolled through files that flashed across his HUD. Names, faces, flight logs, and star-chart locators flickered past at an incomprehensible rate. What used to be a clunky process requiring hand motions and eye signals to perceive and negotiate data was now sped up a hundredfold—the speed of thought. Bastille wasn't even sure who or what it was he was looking for, but cross-referencing old communiqués and decrypting flight records and shipping invoices, he kept landing on the Vega System. Specifically the Mandreen Settlement part of the Vega System.

He looked up from the cockpit, and Moose and Peanut were headed his way, dragging binders behind them to lock the Mustang down for their hyper-dive. Peanut fit easily under the belly of the ship to secure the mag-chocks around the landing struts. He took a second pair around to the nose strut and locked it down tight when he engaged the magnetic harness.

Moose lifted him up onto the Mustang's wing, and he walked along the surface up to the cockpit next to Bastille to check it out. "All good, boss?"

"You boys ever been out to the Mandreen Settlements?" Bastille threw it out casually.

"In the Vega System?" Peanut clarified, nervously scratching at his beard stubble.

"Is there any other?" Bastille watched the color visibly draining from the dwarf's face. Moose didn't look so good either.

"I'm hoping there is," Peanut answered. "Otherwise, this will be a one-way trip to hell."

"So you've been before?"

"Yeah, we've been." Peanut aimed a thumb over his shoulder at his partner. "And I reckon Moose would rather be back in the torture dungeons of Tomar's Ranch."

Moose shrugged and added a rudimentary hand sign.

"Exactly what he said," Peanut grumbled. "It's a run-down, garbage port that makes the Thegas red zone look like a damn seminary."

"Don't stop there." Bastille gestured for him to continue. "Lay it all out for me."

"I mean, okay, so the black market is a shadowy, highly decentralized—"

"Sh*thole," Bastille cut in.

"—more like a living, breathing organism. A parasite. But if the beast had a head, it would be found at Mandreen. That's the rumor. Only the real problem is that it's heavily under Ma'kobi control. And not just any Ma'kobi, either. Tavi6. The Savvy Tavi. Take all your worse nightmares and double it. That lot would just as soon gut you and jack your ride," he patted the Mustang's side, "than waste time brokering a deal."

"Well, it doesn't look like we've got a choice." Bastille mulled over his next words before he continued, "Listen, I need to know that you boys are up for a fight."

"It's a seven-day trip," Peanut said, jutting his chin up. "And I swear by the forty jugs of Artemis, we'll be ready, sir."

"Good. Cause if there's dying to be done," Bastille assured him, "it ain't gonna be us."

Peanut looked relieved at this news. Bastille noted their unspoken concern. Whatever had happened to him over the past month, it had softened him in their eyes. He was not the bloodthirsty Ma'kobi legend of old. Bastille could tell there was still a lingering question on Peanut's mind.

"Out with it, Peanut."

"Well, sir, it's just that…" he looked to Moose who nodded him forward. Peanut swallowed hard and continued, "The real Captain Jacques Bastille assembled the Ma'kobi clans, ran off those KACorps pigsacks, and established the brotherhood. Why would someone like that retire from the Ma'kobi life at the top of his game? We even heard he became some sorta… *farmer*?"

A fair question. There was probably a fair answer, too. Only Bastille had no clue what it was. "I dunno," he sighed, tapping his forehead, "it's still a mystery up here. A lot of blank space. But when I find out the answer, I'll let you know. Deal?"

Peanut rolled this around a bit and then accepted it. "Deal," he said, smiling for the first time.

"Good," Bastille said, climbing out of the cockpit. "Then let's go tell Captain Mizuke about your fantastic suicide plan."

Peanut stopped. "My—" his smile dropped, and he shook his head at Moose.

Moose snorted back at him, amused.

"All right, not you, too," he said, twirling a finger at Moose.

Moose complied by turning around and presenting the perch on his back to Peanut.

Peanut jumped into the saddle and tapped twice on his shoulder. Up there, he looked like a child riding piggyback. That is, a highly acrobatic little child who was also an efficient killing machine, to be exact.

Peanut whispered to Moose, "Maybe *you* should retire and take up farming."

Moose grunted and then lumbered forward to follow after Bastille.

"You could always kill me and collect the bounty," Bastille yelled back at them. "Save everyone a lot of bullsnipe."

"The thought has definitely crossed our minds, boss. Only Moose figured out if we just hang around long enough you'll get yourself killed. Then, *viola*."

Moose lifted his fist with the brass knuckles on the forefingers. Peanut knocked his own wrist gauntlet against it with a *clang*.

"You mean voilà?" Bastille suggested.

"Tomato, potato," Peanut shrugged.

"Well, good luck with that plan, pocket monkey," Bastille called back to them.

"Tick-tock, skinbag!" Peanut shot back.

Bastille smiled to himself. They might all live through this after all.

* * *

Bastille, Moose, and Peanut stepped onto the bridge. The monitors were fed data and Viddix streams from Dash's Relay box. He was seated in the pilot chair, poring through a digital mound of footage. He paused only briefly at pertinent data points.

"Oh good, I wanted you all to see this," Mizuke said, turning over her shoulder to Dash. "Can you bring up Project Libellule again?"

On-screen Viddix flashed to some star charts. Wreckage reports filled the space, and then some blue prints popped up.

"Dash found this information going through the St. Croix files on Phaedra. An experimental stealth barge, far as we can tell. Abandoned by them almost fifty years ago. They were planning a large-scale assault mission, it looks like, to recover it before you showed up and threw off their plans. There's something inside it they want badly."

"Something they referred to as the *Fists of Ma'kobi*," Dash added. "So, yeah, you showing up on their doorstep the week after this discovery had their council pissing themselves."

"I don't suppose we know what the Fists of Ma'kobi are?" Bastille scanned the blueprints closely.

"No," Mizuke said. "But after we trade the *seklas* on the black market, we should head over to the wreckage site and take a look. It's in the Qu'Nadi system."

"Anything the Croix are fixated on should definitely be on our radar as well," Bastille agreed.

"You get any leads on the black market?"

"He sure did," Peanut was happy to chime in, "so get out your suntan oils and beachies cause we're headed to the tropics of the Vega System."

His announcement had the desired effect on the entire crew.

"As in, M-mandreen?" Tanner stammered. "The garbage planet?"

"You got a problem with that?" Peanut asked aggressively.

"I think anyone with a pulse has a problem with that," Mizuke answered. She walked to the huge portal window and looked out across deep space with her back to them all. The G9 Stargate loomed before them. She turned back around, resigned. "Welp, set coordinates for the Vega System, Dash. I'll breathe easier once we've unloaded our hot cargo. Bastille?"

Bastille simply nodded. That settled, the room broke into activity as everyone took places for the hyper-dive.

"Have we battened down the hatches?" Mizuke boomed.

"Aye, Captain," Peanut affirmed heartily.

"Hoist the anchors, Moose. Let's get underway," she said.

"Aye, Captain," Peanut replied for Moose, who jerked a huge lever.

Outside the Sea Scout, four stationary probes were retracted into the ship. They rotated and slid into place along the ship's surface, like missing puzzle pieces in their storage slots. The iridium core began to spin up, and Dash dropped the ship down onto the G9 jump gate surface, which glowed and sparkled as they submerged beneath it. A few seconds later, they were completely engulfed in hyperspace.

* * *

Bastille stripped down to his shorts, peeled off his shirt and dropped it beside the bed. "What else did you find out from Dash?"

Mizuke was already lying naked in the bed. She stared up at the ceiling as he climbed beneath the covers. "I can't really explain it," she began. "He's in there and sounds like himself from time to time, but it's not him. It's like a machine-hybrid version. A construct. I'd swear he doesn't have a heartbeat, but I know that can't be possible."

"Well, Bender and the Outlanders had access to some pretty dark and muddy tech. A lot of banned stuff from KACorps. From what I saw, anything's possible." He rolled up on an elbow to watch her. He wanted to broach this next topic very carefully. "You know, in one of the memory splices that I had since the accident, you and Dash were having a baby—"

Mizuke's eyes grew cold, and she snapped, "That's... not possible." She sat up, looking at him as though he'd stabbed her. "Why would you say that?"

"I'm sorry, Mizuke. I didn't realize—" he paused to reword his thoughts. "I'm trying to unravel all of these flashbacks or whatever they are and that one didn't make any sense."

Mizuke climbed out of bed and went over to the window portal. Bastille just gave her space. Didn't say a word. She scratched at the back of her head and then exhaled loudly. That had always been her way of doing an internal reset. She turned back around and looked him over with tears in her eyes. "The day I found out I was nothing more than a Biosynthetic Lifeform Unit was the worst day of my life." She clutched her arms around herself, rubbing her tattooed shoulder absently, and continued, "Worse than all my time with the… with the slavers. Me. A lab rat. I couldn't believe it. Wouldn't."

She moved back over toward the bed and sat on the edge. Bastille laid a hand on the covers, close to her knee. She placed her hand on his and said softly, "It doesn't matter. Everyone here's got baggage. Scars. Hell, we've all made tough choices. Some of us are forced to live with those memories every day. And now we've got Dash 2.0 up there, and I couldn't care less because I'm on Mizuke 3.0, and I'm never, ever going back." She looked straight at Bastille now. He studied her eyes. They were normally a dark brown, but when she got super-excited or angry they turned black as midnight. Like now. "You have a gift, Bastille. A clean slate. No memory. No dead weight. No baggage."

"We've all got baggage, Mizuke. You just know where your baggage is and what trips the detonator. My baggage is a bunch of hidden landmines," Bastille explained. "But I know I had a fresh start when I retired as Ma'kobi king. Not that it mattered in the long run. And I had another fresh start after the accident. A fresh start with you. The *real*… you. Mizuke 3.0, the badass renegade captain, with her badass crew and her badass ship."

She smiled and intertwined her fingers with his.

"And with her badass tits," Mizuke said, blushing a little at the word.

Bastille laughed, and pulled her down on top of him. "God, yes, I would wrestle a sea condor to get just five minutes with those things."

Looking deep into his eyes, she shook her head and sighed. "How is it that a practical stranger in my bed feels like—"

She paused, searching for the right words.

"—home?" Bastille finished the thought.

She nodded and ran her fingers through his hair. There was no denying it. He felt it, too. The heat was palpable.

Mizuke grabbed a fistful of his hair and pulled him close. Their lips mashed together in a rough kiss, tongues darting out in search of each other. He rolled on top of her. She wrapped him in her arms and legs, and her hot breath panted in his ear as they moved together as one, deep into the night.

- 12 -

THE STONE SCORPION

Long ago, the Vega System became the designated spot outside of the Kuiper Belt to dump trash, refuse, and convicts. What had begun on the Mandreen surface became so unmanageable that garbage transports had begun dumping contents into orbit. Then, as that cluttered up, they continued to move further and further out. Gigantic SuperStructures flew in, dropped off thousands of containers of trash, and then flew off. Because of the location of the four planets in this system, it created a nice little gravitational array, keeping all the refuse floating in protective orbit around Mandreen.

Since the Ma'kobi had moved in, that airspace was now also littered with the shells of burnt-out ships of all shapes and sizes. A graveyard scattered across the galactic space around the Mandreen Settlement. These random obstacles bumping and crashing through the area made the approach to Mandreen treacherous. In fact, anything more than a low ion thrust was ill-advised.

However, Captain Mizuke Strouthers and her crew piloted the *DayStar* in and out of the largest debris, several notches above the recommended velocity. They blasted some of the mid-sized space trash into dust. Occasionally, small satellites would bounce against the hull, but the shields would scatter them back into space. It was a painstaking, dirty job, which they'd been at for the better part of an hour.

On the bridge, Tanner was running eyes—pinpointing on the giant HUD various targets as they became problems. Objects were highlighted on-screen as they entered the flight path for the helm to figure into his trajectory. Dash Strouthers, still inhabiting the Byno-Core of Genwa'ar, was flying. Sweat beaded up on his brow. Of course, he was the most capable to fly this route because of his machine-like speed and reflexes. Anyone else would have killed them all hours ago. Dash, eyes glowing white from the HUD sync, was at one with the *DayStar* as it danced lithely through the cosmic wasteland.

Down in the Mech room, Mizuke was suited up. Her Relay umbilical was jacked into place. Equally focused. Her arms and legs were encased in a power suit that held her twenty feet off the ground. She, too, had a gigantic HUD with a three hundred and sixty-degree view all around her. She spun her hips, and the suit swiveled left. She locked onto a mid-sized projectile that was headed their way. Just before it hit, the ship banked left, avoiding it all together.

"Dammit, Dash," she complained into her head-set. "Gotta leave me something." The lights of her helmet cast a red glow across her eyes and face.

"Fine," Dash called back. "High right, b12. It's all yours."

Mizuke swiveled right and back, extending her right arm. Outside the ship, a bank of ferocious cannons came about to bear. She locked onto the object and pulled a trigger—a very controlled, very professional short burst.

The left side of the satellite exploded, forcing the entire piece of space junk to redirect off and to the right. The point wasn't so much to destroy the larger debris as it was to interrupt its course away from their flight path.

"Good scat, good scat!" Mizuke repeated, her eyes flashing. She lived for this stuff. Sometimes, in the monotony of the space routine, you could go for months without ever climbing back into the Mech room. Especially on long deep-space missions like this one, where you had to conserve ammo for any unforeseen incidents ahead. But Mizuke had now suited up twice within two weeks.

"Good scatter, confirmed," Dash agreed. "Nice shooting, Captain."

* * *

The entire *Daystar* crew was so preoccupied with their forward targeting that no one noticed when one of the burnt-out looking vessels snapped to life as they passed by. It didn't even register on the scopes as it tracked along in their wake, taking advantage of the clutter-free flight channel they created. If they had noticed, they might have been impressed by the ship's colorful paint job. From that distance, they might have even misread the odd pattern all over the hull as a wild, orange and red speckled design. But that would have been false. There were over three hundred individual flames, signifying a host of victory marks. Trophies. Kills.

Had they added up those tallies and known anything about the Vega System, they might have deduced correctly that this was the notorious *Stone Scorpion*, one of the deadliest ships responsible for twenty percent of the rubble around Mandreen. The *Scorpion* crew usually shot first and asked questions later, but their interest piqued at this rogue, singular vessel gliding purposefully through the graveyard at breakneck speeds. A ship like that deserved the honor of being boarded and pillaged alive. Might even get some new conscripts out of it. Not to mention, there had been many rumors recently that *the* Jacques Bastille might be alive and headed their way.

The bay doors at the belly of the *Scorpion* opened and a deadly array of Sig cannons pushed forward into place. They dared not lock on weapons radar too soon, or that would alert the unsuspecting *DayStar* crew before they could cripple it. And that would take the sport right out of it. And so the cat-and-mouse game continued.

* * *

Ironically, the *Scorpion* crew was so preoccupied with *their* forward activity that they missed an H2 Mustang decloaking behind them. At that moment, they may have had a small chance at evasive maneuvers. As it was, their first alert was when Bastille's missile barrage was almost upon them. As calculated, the trajectiles closed half the distance and *then* locked onto their targets.

Bastille imagined the ship's helm staring blankly at a half-dozen radar blips suddenly materializing out of nowhere. He imagined the captain being alerted at the last minute as the ship began to pull up sharply to avoid impact. Lastly, he imagined their second surprise when the missiles didn't strike them underneath. Those were just ghost-signals. The real missiles high above would all race to a less fortified part of the ship connecting the bridge to the main body, and their final realization would be that by pulling up, they had exposed themselves to a cunning strategist and played right into his hands. And then, the impact.

The explosion was precise. The *Stone Scorpion* lurched, bleeding metal and Enginion fluid down the left side. Three of the four stabilizers flamed out, but they miraculously stayed afloat and mobile. They pulled up and retreated into the heart of a nearby debris field. Bastille followed. They countered with a battery of munitions, launching everything they had at the Mustang. Bastille's HUD lit up like a firefly convention, and he skimmed his ship as close as he dared into the space junk careening around him.

Dozens of smaller explosions blasted the satellite junk all around him, but the Mustang shot through it all unscathed. The cyrenium shell did a great job of deflecting that blanket of particulate matter that ricocheted in every direction. Bastille arced high above the *Stone Scorpion,* vectoring over to its dead side. As he figured, the marauders rolled their ship so their guns would be facing him once more. They locked onto him, and once again, his HUD danced with a dozen separate warnings.

"Any time, *DayStar,*" Bastille calmly advised over comms.

"Get clear, Mustang," Mizuke ordered.

Bastille pulled out and away as Mizuke fired from the *DayStar.* It was a great shot. A direct hit on the *Stone Scorpion.* The conning tower was blown clear, and the entire bridge went spiraling off into space. It impacted what was left of an old asteroid mining rig with a flash of color and a huge ring of fire.

The *DayStar* opened up on the rest of the ship, a chain of explosions destroying the right side faster than any internal safety measures would be able to seal off below decks from damage. The *Stone Scorpion* rammed headlong into a flotilla, and the resulting fireball forever merged the two structures into a new large, metal tombstone, which would float here around Mandreen as a testament to 78 Ma'kobi cutthroats who had been outwitted by the cutthroatiest Ma'kobi of them all.

"Good scat, Mustang," Mizuke said into comm.

"Good scat, *DayStar,*" Bastille replied. "Peanut's survival instinct just saved all of our lives."

"Yeah, he's pretty proud of himself over here," Tanner piped up. "You think they'll send any more interceptors?"

"No," Bastille said, powering down his weapons. "No, we just took out their number one gravedigger. We've got their full attention. And fury."

"Copy that," Tanner said.

"Expect them to hail as soon as we clear the rubble." Bastille flipped his missile safety back on.

"Roger that. Great shooting, Jacques." She flicked her finger across the comm trigger to close her mic.

"You, too. This might have kept us alive for another few hours, but I wouldn't break out the bubbly just yet," he cautioned. "Looks like we'll be clear of this in another twenty minutes. Then it's all jazz."

"All jazz," Tanner echoed, and then punched Dash in the arm. "I taught him that one. 'It's all jazz.'"

Dash glanced askew at Tanner, annoyed. "Do you mind? I'm trying to keep us alive here," and then back to the monstrous task at hand of avoiding a thousand and one collisions.

Tanner raised both hands and said, "Sor-REE!" under his breath.

Back on their six, Bastille triggered the cloaking device again as he pulled up and out of the *DayStar's* wake. He rolled through a gigantic hole in a tattered supercarrier and disappeared out the other side, back into his protective escort mode. He knew nobody else would be sent out. They had just won an audience with the Magistrate of Mandreen, Savvy Tavi.

In fact, the entire Mandreen Settlement would be abuzz with activity. All they knew was that something special was headed their way. Bastille intended to push the Psy-Ops to their limit.

It was said that once upon a time, the ships were made of wood and the *men* were made of steel. Back then, a vessel's flag was its signature marquee. Out in open water, it quickly defined friend or foe. Bastille and the other Ma'kobi crews had less of a need for physical flags. But every modern ship had a signature broadcast signal that other vessels could identify once they opened communications. Every frigate, schooner, and fighter was issued a single set of codes. The Mustang, as with most smugglers, had three or four of these—three innocuous diversions and the real ID.

Bastille took his comm offline and switched it back over to its original broadcast signature. There would only be one unique ID like this in all the space lanes. They may not see his ship on their radars yet, but as they opened up hailing frequencies to the *DayStar*, they would know beyond the shadow of a doubt that the ghost of Jacques Bastille, the former Ma'kobi King was upon them. And all hell would break loose.

- 13 -

THE MANDREEN ORDEAL

Mandreen Colony in the Vega System

Flying low over the Mandreen surface, it was easy to feel overwhelmed by the sight of an endless supply of refuse that stretched out from horizon to horizon. There were dozens of individual ground fires down below, indicating subterranean factories. The thousands of little caterpillar-like objects moving about from this distance were actually Rovers, colonists trekking across the dump on their gigantic, Enginion-powered forty-eight-wheeled vehicular systems.

The Rovers were covered head to toe in gear so as not to expose skin and lungs to the dangerous chemical cocktail that hung over the planet's surface like a suffocating, noxious blanket. On other, more affluent planets, bots would have taken over this dirty work long ago. But not here. Here, human life had no choice but to subsist amid the rubble and swamp gas.

Bastille's Mustang took point, leading the *Day-Star* to the Mandreen Colony proper. He had decloaked once they burned into the atmosphere; there was nothing further to gain from stealth and obscurity. In this world, reputations were hard won, and Bastille would need to flaunt the family name lavishly, even if he himself had no clue about the breadth of the shadow he cast.

A veritable who's-who of scoundrels and their vessels slid into tight escort formation around the Mustang and the *Daystar:* the mining juggernaut *Corleonis,* the cunning fast-boat *Steadfast,* the deadly *Terp* galleon, and the falsely decrepit-looking warship, *Vicar's Delight.* They all slowed to navigate over the high city air gates and received clearance to land in the Northern Tower.

Bastille circled the tower once and then aimed into the mouth of the massive structure. The city itself had some fortifications, but clearly their largest defense lay in the garbage belt around the Vega System and a hundred other unscrupulous crews like those aboard the *Stone Scorpion.* May she burn in hell.

The landing struts touched down, and Bastille powered everything into standby. Behind him, the *Day-Star* dwarfed his tiny craft as it settled onto the black granite flooring, beside a large fissure. This tower had been built strategically around that seemingly bottomless expanse. Giant doors squealed shut as the tower entrance was secured. Steam or gas of some sort shot up around both spacecraft, purging them of atmospheric chum.

"Okay, oxygen levels are all jazz," Tanner read from his display, confirming Bastille's own readings. "We won't be needin' masks. Though you might wanna breathe through your mouth hole if you're sensitive to vomitous smells."

Everyone turned to look at Peanut. Moose patted his back sympathetically, but Peanut ducked away from it. "What? I'm not gonna puke on anyone." Peanut objected with a scowl and then added quickly, "Again. Probably."

A delegation of bodies had begun swarming out of the doors at the opposite end of the hangar. They were double-timing it in the direction of the ships.

"Steady," Bastille said, scanning the intimidating squad. "Let them come to us."

The soldiers, armed and masked, formed ranks upon ranks, line upon line, filling the hangar with a massive army. Bastille double-checked his Mauzer, but knew it wouldn't be much good to them. As the last of the soldiers double-timed it into formation, the entire division snapped into place. This was a lot of decorum for an off-world garbage colony like Mandreen. You wouldn't expect that level of pageantry out here on a former penal colony.

Bastille noticed a regally dressed figure in colorful robes moving through the ranks toward them. Flanked on either side by a couple of guards, it made Moose seem like a small puppy.

"That important-looking rooster is Savvy Tavi," Peanut relayed to Bastille. "We maybe shouldn't keep him waiting. And, by the goddess, do *not* mention his legs."

"His legs," replied Bastille, clearly confused.

"Just… don't," Peanut pleaded.

Moose grunted to second the motion.

"Any last thoughts?" Mizuke chimed in.

"Nope," Bastille said. "Stay calm and stick to the plan. Just a nice friendly, 'Howdy-do'. Let's do our business and get the hell outta here."

A deep breath from the other end: "Okay, let's take a walk," Mizuke said, pulling the balaclava up to cover her nose and mouth.

Bastille saw the yellow warning light on the *DayStar's* underbelly rotate as the service platform de-elevated. He could see all eight boots as the lift moved, slowly revealing shins, then knees, then thighs, and then belts. Peanut would be tucked in protective custody on Moose's back.

Bastille triggered his own cockpit, which hissed as the seal broke in half and slid open from front to back. He wrinkled his nose. Whew. The stench was palpable, but not nearly as bad as he'd expected. He grabbed the duffel from the back seat and stepped off the wing, letting gravity drag him down to the hard deck. His boots clanged loudly on the surface. Then the service elevator bottomed out with a resounding thud, and the crew of the *DayStar* walked forward to join him.

As briefed, they all fanned out as they moved toward Tavi6, but kept a step behind Bastille. Back on board the Mustang, his targeting computer busily ran an algorithm calculating targets and impact zones. If there *was* a double-cross, blood would be spilled.

Bastille stopped. Squared up to Tavi6. Dropped the duffel between them. Tavi6 moved his hand up to his black ornate mask with golden inlaid designs. He unlatched the bottom of the shroud, and escaping air decompressed forth. Tavi6 bent forward slightly and pulled off the entire headdress in one motion.

A 72-year-old Haitian with long white dreadlocks stared menacingly back at Bastille. He looked as regal as a lion. And indeed, he was King of this Jungle. He stepped closer, and beneath his fancy robe, where feet should be, Bastille caught sight of a hoof. And then another. They clomped across the floor until the two men were a meter apart. Tavi6 cocked his head to one side as he examined Bastille.

"You look ridiculous in this albino skinsuit, brother." He broke into a huge smile. Bastille exhaled slowly and forced a smile as well, bowing ever so slightly but never breaking eye contact. They clasped each other in a warrior's forearm handshake and then Tavi6 turned to Moose and laughed.

"The Mighty Moosimus Rex! Where's that little parasite of yours?"

There was a brief pause, and then the top flap of Moose's pack lifted up. Peanut stood and turned around over his shoulder, looking as grumpy as ever. "Savvy Tavi. This better be important, I was in the middle of a wank!"

Moose grunted.

Tavi6 laughed a big-bellied laugh.

"Moose, I warned you to pop that zit on your ass before you came back here," Tavi6 said, walking over and smacking him on the shoulder. "Good to see you boys again. And what have we here?"

"Tanner Crest," Tanner said, extending his hand. Tavi6 walked right past him and over to Mizuke. She did well. Didn't blink and held his gaze. Just as instructed. Tavi6 reached out and slid her facecover down.

"Hm," he said, sizing her up and looking back at Bastille. "I imagine you belong to this one, now, am I right, Bastille?"

"I am Captain Mizuke Strouthers," she seethed at him. "I *belong* to no one."

Not as instructed.

Tavi6 leaned in closer to her. "You might want to change your mind on that before we get too far, little one. See, on this planet, things that belong to no man? Well, that's called garbage."

He held her gaze. He had one blue eye and one brown eye. Both were cold as steel. He then looked past her to Genwa'ar's petite Byno-core. "And how about you, sweet pea? To whom do you—"

Dash pointed at Bastille before Tavi6 even finished the question.

The Haitian smiled at this. His humor returned. His demeanor softened again. He turned back face-to-face with Bastille, looking him up and down. Toe to hoof. He spoke in little more than a whisper now: "I wouldn't have believed you were still alive." He poked a finger at his face and said, "Hiding in a dead man's skin. And a pale, chewed-up skinbag at that. Tsk Tsk."

"At least," Bastille answered in a most measured tone, "it's all human."

Behind Moose, Peanut groaned out a "holy sh*t" that only Moose could hear. "Was I not clear about the leg thing?"

Tavi6 straightened to his full height to look down his nose at Bastille. Then he reached down and held his robe open. It was just a peek at his hairy bull haunches, which indeed ended up in a wide hoof the size of a dinner plate. "Ain't science grand," his eyes flashed with pride.

"Huh," was all Bastille could muster, staring down at the animal legs before him.

Tavi6 let the robe fall back into place and then paced in front of Bastille. *Clomp, clomp, clomp.* "I wasn't sure that was you out there at first. But there's no other ruthless, cold-hearted bastard that could have breezed in here, dancing out among the rubble. Who else could have taken out the entire *Stone Scorpion* stem to stern as brilliantly as Jacques Bastille: Ma'kobi King? My hat is off to you, brother. Now, tell me why I do not kill you where you stand."

Bastille calmly held his gaze. "If you think you've got what it takes, then roll the dice. *Brother*," Bastille overemphasized the last word; the corner of his mouth turned up in a half-smile.

Peanut nervously drummed a finger on Moose's shoulder. Mizuke fidgeted with the butt of the gun in her horizontal holster at the small of her back. Dash reached over and put a hand in Mizuke's hand. She appeared to any onlooker like a little sister would take her big sister's hand when she was scared. It took Mizuke a little by surprise, but it had the desired effect of calming her down and taking the edge off. Mizuke gave Dash's hand a little squeeze and then worked a little harder to settle her thoughts and her breathing. As instructed.

"No more blood will be spilled this day," Tavi6 announced. "Because today is the day Jacques Bastille returned from the grave!"

The Mandreen army pumped a fist in the air, and as one voice said, "A'uuh! Shu'mah!" three times.

This pleased Tavi6 greatly. He turned back around, beaming charismatically at Bastille. "Come. I have prepared a feast in your honor." Tavi6 put an arm around him and led him forward. "Come!" He turned around to snap his fingers at Mizuke and point to the duffel. The message was clear.

Mizuke shot another pissed look at Dash, who pleaded with his eyes. Mizuke dropped down and scooped up the duffel. Moose held out a hand for the assist, but she ignored it and brushed past. "Tanner, stay with the ship. Get the Mustang aboard. Keep her warmed up," she said, throwing the strap over her shoulder.

Tanner looked all too happy to oblige. The rest of the *DayStar* crew fell in behind Bastille and Tavi6. The two giant guardians brought up the rear. Peanut was at eye level with the bigger one.

"What's your name, handsome?" Peanut teased him, crossing his legs comfortably, like he was chilling on a couch in his living room. The beast ignored him. "I bet it's Cletus, isn't it? You look like a Cletus." Cletus didn't answer. Didn't even give any recognition to Peanut. "So, Cletus, are you from around here in garbage city?"

"Peanut!" Dash hissed up at him. "Stop taunting the Murder Mountain."

"What? Just making friends," Peanut leaned over the side to stick his tongue out at Dash.

Dash sped up to catch Mizuke again. The whole entourage marched on silently, except for the rhythmic shuffling of leather, buckles and hooves.

* * *

At the edge of the Vega System, all was silent. All was still. And then a large, shimmering apparition passed in front of the stars, subtly warping their light in a spherical fashion. As if a specter were passing through. Trash and debris were pushed aside, cutting a large, invisible swath for what could only be Phaedra, the Shadow Moon. The graveyard magically parted for this unseen force.

One of the dead satellites was brushed aside with the other refuse. The movement triggered a small beacon aboard, which began transmitting immediately.

* * *

Under the Mandreen Colony, a pair of boots thundered down the helter-skelter maze of hallways, turning this way and that. The corridors were a patchwork quilt of metal and wood and a thousand different objects that were anything but hallways in another life. The boots belonged to a Mandreen Rover named Kamo, who had just received the faint warning transmission from an outermost satellite along his safety net.

Kamo burst into the Great Hall, where Tavi6 hosted a giant feast for at least fifty of his top officers. The whole room buzzed with the air of a Viking victory celebration. There was music and laughter, large cuts of meat, and very few utensils or table manners. At the head table, elevated from the rest on a platform, sat Tavi6 and the *DayStar* crew. Most of the *DayStar* crew, that is. Mizuke and Dash sat at a small, improvised table at the base of the stairs. Mizuke was livid, but had been told that protocol would not allow women onto the royal platform and that they should be honored just to be eating in the main hall with the rest of the warriors. All men.

"You can sit down here at the kid's table or you can make a scene and get us all killed," Bastille had told her privately. "It's your decision, Captain. And to be clear, I stand with you either way, but I'm recommending that we not go to war here and now with 1000 years of bone-head tradition."

"Affirmative," Dash said, already gnawing on a drumstick twice as big as his arm.

"Let's just get it over with and be on our way," Mizuke conceded. "This whole place gives me the creeps." She tore off a piece of bread and angrily chewed on it.

It had taken Bastille's firm assurance to calm her enough to stay on mission and take her seat. But she wasn't happy about it. The day she had escaped from KACorps captivity—disabling her slave collar and bashing her owners' heads in with it—she had been reborn. A whole new life. A whole new Mizuke BLU. From there, she had fought long and hard to gain her independence and become the respected and feared starship captain she was today, and she had every one of the scars to prove it. She hated Tavi6 for the emotional collar he was attempting to hang around her neck. And for making her remember what it was like to feel less than. But simple minds would not be changed by temper tantrums. Only strength spoke to strength. And that time was not just yet.

Dash, on the other hand, preferred to be separated out along the edge of the room where he could keep an eye on the whole lot of them at once. This being a former Penal Colony, he didn't trust anyone in this entire Vega System. Especially as a young, genetically enhanced 16-year-old girl. There were looks on these monsters' faces that hinted at some deeply unpleasant ideas churning in their little garbage planet minds. And even though he was just borrowing Gen's meat-suit, he would protect it with his life.

It was a humbling position to be in. Days ago, he had been nearly invincible, cruising within the *DayStar* and Phaedra's mainframes beyond limitations. Growing and evolving in power, purpose and self-awareness. But none of their crew was safe here. The sooner they all got what they needed and put some hyperspace between them and Mandreen, the better.

Bastille sat on the stage to the right of Tavi6. They were chowing down on a main course that could only be described as giant bugs, almost like roaches. They were two or three feet long and roasted right in their shells. Some sort of Mandreen delicacy, no doubt. Like the natives in more cultured areas of NeoTokyo, who might serve up a turtle in a half shell or an entire seabass. But that was so long ago and now so far away. And probably destroyed when Wexell and her own Dominion death squad took over the Earth.

Dash watched with interest as Kamo ran in and hurried right up to the Murder Mountain guards. They blocked him with their spears at the base of the stairs. Kamo showed them a black tablet and said something Dash couldn't overhear. The head guard looked up to Tavi6, who gestured Kamo forward. The Rover ran up the stairs and around behind Tavi6, thrusting the tablet in front of him and whispering in his ear.

Tavi6 directed whatever was on the screen, through a couple of hand motions, onto a giant Viddix array in front of them. The bedlam through the entire hall grew quieter as they all watched the screen. There was some footage from various outposts. It showed satellites and junk pushed to the sides. Creating a path for some invisible force.

Tavi6 spit out his mouthful of food onto the floor. "What the hell is this?"

Bastille simply said, "Shadow Moon."

Tavi6 looked at him and understood immediately. "Show me infrared," he commanded.

Kamo had already uplinked with the war room. Tavi's command was loud and clear. Kamo responded without delay, and the view switched on-screen to infrared. Lights turned to blacks. Positives to negatives. But nothing showed up.

"Heat signature," Tavi said, drumming an annoyed finger on the table.

Again, the screen changed, and heat patterns showed up all over, but the source of the motion remained invisible. Kamo was visibly shaking, though, because generally, 'Kill the Messenger' was one of the early stress relievers his master favored.

Tavi6 stood, getting revved up. "Fire up all the beacons. Broadcast simultaneously. Spray that damned garbage with every channel we've got," he growled. "Map it in 3D."

Somebody in the war room deserved a medal. These requests took time and specialized coding to accommodate, but the 3D map was drawn up in less than a minute and began refreshing. As more and more beacons came online, more and more space was filled with digital signals. As that space filled, a clear picture began to form of a massive moon pushing through the debris.

"Yup," Bastille confirmed, using a sharp bone to pick some gristle from his teeth, "here come the Draccarios."

"Target that moon. Light 'em up!" Tavi6 bellowed with a withering look to his head Lieutenant. "Recall our entire fleet. Notify the Rovers to push underground."

"You don't seem too worried," Bastille observed of Tavi6 who shrugged it off.

"Worried? Hell no! *Excited.* Been years since we've seen a battle worthy of our Ma'kobi forces. Long overdue. You'll see." Tavi6 slurped a wiggling tentacle into his mouth.

Hidden ships fired up throughout the garbage belt and began navigating home as quickly as each captain dared. Missiles and weaponry were launched against the Shadow Moon, but were repelled left and right by the same mysterious force field as the trash.

The space all around exploded as ordinance struck the burnt-out ships and other debris. Phaedra pushed steadily forward.

Mizuke had moved to the edge of the stairs, blocked out by the huge guardians. She wanted to be part of the strategizing upstairs but could not proceed, unbidden. Bastille threw her a warning look to stay put. Other officers began to crowd forward, too, to await direction.

Dash, however, remained seated. His stomach didn't feel quite right. He cursed inside. What were these horrid cramps? He knew he shouldn't have eaten the giant cockroach. He leaned forward on the table; nobody around paid any attention.

"You won't be able to fight them off, brother," Bastille counseled Tavi6. "They will tear this planet apart. You should evacuate while you can."

"Ha!" Tavi6 snarled back at him. "This planet has many, many surprises, my friend. There are so many levels of garbage on the surface that we can safely remain in our bunkers for 200 years and never come up for air. Let them bomb away." He flung his arms out wide. His foot soldiers banged their spears on the ground in a show of solidarity.

"They're not here for you. They're here for me," Bastille warned. "They're here for Genwa'ar."

"Who?" Tavi6 asked, spitting out a bone and sucking some more meat from a shell.

Bastille gestured down to the table at the edge of the stairs. Dash's head was slumped forward, not moving.

"Check on Dash," Bastille called out to Mizuke.

Mizuke turned and began pushing through the warriors toward Dash. When she pulled him up, he immediately began convulsing. Shaking hard.

"What are your women doing?" Tavi6 asked with a furrowed brow, more annoyed than anything.

"I don't know, but I've got a hunch we're not gonna like—" Bastille stood.

Suddenly, Dash was still again. Or was it even Dash? The Genwa'ar Byno-Core took in a large breath, then raised her head up and slowly stood, climbing onto the chair, then onto the table. She looked around and finally found Bastille—glowing, white eyes narrowed.

Bastille swore and then turned to the crew around him and announced, "Gen's back."

"That's okay, boss. You two are best friends, right?" Peanut searched for a bright side. "Besides, she doesn't have a weapon."

"You don't understand." Bastille shook his head. "She *is* the weapon."

Tavi6 looked confused but heeded the warning quickly. "Guards, kill the bitches!"

"Just Gen, not Mizuke," Bastille corrected, but he saw Tavi6 was not understanding. "Not the blue hair."

"Just the little one," Tavi6 added, slightly annoyed. "Bring me the BLU."

Gen flexed her head left and then right, cracking her neck. Loosening for battle. Her hands began to glow a blueish color. The officers in the front, who were so eager to lay hands on her, took a step back. One of the guards threw a spear at her. She stretched a hand out and snatched it from the air. The whole staff began to glow as she spun it around and infused it with some sort of kinetic energy. She launched it mightily towards the head table.

Bastille just barely got Tavi6 down in time, rolling under the stone surface before the projectile hit the wall behind them. The explosion drilled a large hole through it. As the dust settled, Bastille looked up, his ears ringing. He coughed and sputtered.

"What the hell was that?" Tavi6 screamed, shaking some rubble from his long white dreads. One cheek was bloodied from the explosion. "Some sorta voodoo magic?"

Bastille was equally shocked by the blast. "Oh yeah, the Draccario scientists developed some fancy energy powers. Watch out."

"Now you tell me," Tavi6 said.

They looked over the top of the table just as Gen leapt right into the middle of the first enemy rush. She kicked and flipped and punched with those glowing, blue fists. Men around her screamed and exploded and died. About the time they began piling on her, she would jump up and over into another unsuspecting group. At one point, she literally ran across the shoulders and helmets of six guys before dropping back down to the floor to kill another five.

The guards moved forward, and Mizuke finally saw her chance to break protocol and race up to the head table, where everyone was up and accounted for except for poor Kamo. He lay facedown on the dinner table with most of his back splayed open, a piece of the spear handle sticking out of him.

"We've gotta get you back to your ship," Tavi6 said. "You are no longer welcome here, Jacques Bastille."

They all jumped through the hole in the wall and down into the next room. It was part of the kitchen where workers were also trying to recover from the concussive blast. Bastille counted about four dead in the immediate vicinity. One of the ovens had flames shooting out of it, too, as loose, angry roach-creatures scampered to safety.

The *DayStar* crew moved quickly through the room as Tavi6 led them. Moose took up the rear, and Peanut whipped out a snub-nosed scatter blaster and mounted it aft. He latched himself into his tiny chair and watched the doors.

"All clear, Moose! All clear. Go, go, go!" Peanut yelled, slapping the sides of the chair loudly, like he was heeling a horse. Moose double-timed it, rejoining their company.

As they ran out of the kitchen, another explosion rocked the hallway, and one of the Murder Mountains was thrown bodily through the breach, slumping dead to the floor, bleeding from a massive head wound. Warriors began to pile out after him as the fight moved to the small, confined hallway space. Bastille knew that would work even better in Gen's favor. Fish in a barrel.

Damn, he had underestimated that little dipper.

"War room says the Shadow Moon has settled into a low orbit," Tavi6 yelled at Bastille, who was neck and neck with him as they turned this way and that down the patchwork corridors. "You won't be able to leave the same way you came in."

"I'm open to suggestions," Bastille called out, checking behind them again to make sure Moose and Mizuke were close by. They were two steps behind.

"My men have loaded your ship with gold for the seedbricks, fuel, and supplies and are currently uploading a map of our central planetary mining shaft."

"Mining shaft?" Bastille asked dubiously.

Tavi6 pulled up at a large security door and began keying the code. "Mining shaft. Through the planet's core. Totally safe. Our Rovers go back and forth weekly. Most of them even live to tell about it."

"We've got company," Peanut screamed.

Gen had run past their corrider and then backed up when she caught sight of them. Her chin was tucked, and her fists balled as she marched toward them. Her fiery gaze was fixed on them, unblinking.

"Hold still, ya damn grasshopper," Peanut took aim and started blasting. Gen twisted this way and that and finally tucked into a side alcove as the hallway exploded again with his suppressive fire.

Tavi6 got the hangar door opened and waved everyone through. Peanut laid down a couple more rounds, jacked a grenade in the lower chamber, and sent that down the hall for a visit. The security door closed just as the grenade exploded, sending dust and debris shooting beneath it before it clanged shut.

They all ran across the giant hangar space toward the *DayStar*.

"Fire it up, Tanner!" Mizuke shouted into the comms.

"Aye, Captain," Tanner replied.

They had to cross the huge chasm on a utility bridge. Each one of them gulped as they looked down into the dead space below them. An explosion behind them jerked the security doors open. Not all the way. Just enough. Gen slid under the door and flipped back up to her feet. That motivated everyone to cross the bridge faster.

Tavi6 swore again, "That little girl is really starting to get on my last nerve."

"Just think," Bastille added with a wry laugh, "they've got a whole planet of them right up there."

They all cleared to the far side; Bastille indicated the bridge. "Peanut, take care of this!"

Peanut laid down some fire, and the bridge exploded into bits, starting with the middle and dissolving a good 50-foot section that dropped down into the abyss.

"Now get to the ship and lock everything down," Bastille barked as he slowed to assess Gen's next move.

"Aye," Peanut answered as Moose took off after the others.

"Is the Mustang—"

"Already aboard," Tanner chimed in over comms, before Bastille could even get the whole question out.

"The mine shaft starts about a half mile below, inside this crevasse," Tavi6 said, gesturing as he explained. "Stick to the gold line. It'll take you right to the core. Right into the back gate."

Bastille had been watching Gen approach from the other side. He wasn't convinced she couldn't jump it. But she stood on the other side, glaring at them. Her hands weren't glowy and blue anymore. Maybe she'd drained her battery. Or whatever she had going on inside. But she stared at him hard.

Bastille suddenly registered Tavi's words. "Wait, when you say back gate—"

"Hyper-gate." Tavi6 smiled back at him. "Surprise," he said, holding both hands out.

"You idiot, you opened a wormhole in the middle of the planet?" Bastille cocked his head to one side, incredulous.

"Hey," Tavi6 shrugged toward Gen. "They aren't the only ones who can build cool sh*t."

"Not bad for the King of Garbage Mountain," Bastille said, patting the man on his armored shoulder pad.

"One man's trash," Tavi6 winked and then turned back around, frowning. "What's she up to now?"

Gen sat calmly on the floor, cross-legged. She put her hands on her knees in some sort of lotus position, closing the tips of her fingers together. And as if that weren't creepy enough, she smiled at Bastille.

"I don't like this," Tavi6 said, truly spooked. "The hair on my neck is standing up." He brushed it down with his large, calloused hand.

"I don't like it either," Bastille said. "Ahhhhhh!" Suddenly, Bastille dropped to a knee, holding his Relay box.

Fzzzzzzzht.

Fzzzzzzzht.

Bastille blinked hard. "Aaaarghh! She's trying to force her way aboard."

"What?" Tavi6 stepped back, leveling a weapon at Bastille.

"She's trying to, I dunno, broadcast herself inside of me. Take over."

"How is that even—well, fight it, dammit!" Tavi6 said, wide-eyed. He wiped some sweat from his brow with the back of his hand.

"I'm…trying—" Bastille said, and then slugged Tavi6 across the face so hard it spun him around.

"What the hell—" Tavi6 growled, touching his lip and seeing blood on his fingers.

"She's…she's—" Bastille was losing the battle.

"Fight it!" Tavi6 flipped his gun in his hand so the butt was aimed forward. "What if I knock your ass out!?"

"No, then she'll grab complete control," Bastille said, kicking Tavi6 with a front kick that slid him back across the floor. Bastille's hand shook hard as it slowly bent down to his own Mauzer. He fought it with his other hand as it cleared leather in slow motion. She was too strong. Tavi6 was up again and grabbed the gun, too. Helping Bastille out. Between the two of them, they struggled to keep the nose clear.

Behind them, the *DayStar's* engines roared to life.

"Bastille, what's going on out there!?" Mizuke called out over the comm link.

"Unnnnnngh" was all Bastille could reply. The nose of the gun came up slowly and began to point at Bastille's leg. Together, they wrestled it away, and it began moving toward Tavi6's body, inching closer to point blank range with his head.

"Shhhhhhhhit," Tavi6 said through gritted teeth. "Shoot the bitch. Mizuke BLU. Shoot. That. Bitch."

A missile launched from the *DayStar* and impacted the far edge of the ravine, rocking Gen's body high into the air and backward. It slid motionless, about thirty feet and lay crumpled on the floor.

At the same time, the Mauzer blasted a shot, barely clearing Tavi6 and Bastille, who both flopped to the ground with the recoil. They lay there, panting hard.

"I'm cool, Tavi. I'm cool." Bastille still gripped the gun.

"She gone?" Tavi6 yelled frantically. Not convinced.

"She's gone." Bastille slowly pried his own fingers off the butt of the gun and held up both hands.

Tavi6 finally exhaled. Relieved. "Now," he said, gulping for air, "get your glitching ass off my planet."

"Roger that," Bastille said, rolling to the side. He put a hand out and helped Tavi6 back to his feet.

Tavi6 handed the Mauzer back and squeezed Bastille's forearm tightly.

Bastille returned the weapon to the holster, snapping it back into place. Then he turned back toward the ship.

"Bastille," Tavi6 yelled after him.

"What?" Bastille said, annoyed.

"Good to see you, brother." Tavi6 grinned.

Bastille saluted and hobbled toward the ship.

Climbing aboard the lift under the ship's belly, Bastille called into his comm, "I'm coming aboard. Let's fly."

The elevator rose. Tavi6 watched him disappear slowly into the belly of the *DayStar*. "Jacques Bastille," he said, shaking his head to himself. "Holy sh*t."

He turned again toward Gen's lifeless body and raised a comm to his mouth.

"Status Report," he growled out, back fully in charge.

Behind him, the *DayStar* lifted up off the ground and swung gently overhead. Tavi6 could see through the front windows to the bridge. Bastille, now at the helm, threw him a salute. Tavi6 nodded back. Then Bastille nosed down and dove straight into the abyss. The rumble of the engines echoed loudly, and Tavi6 turned and walked away as the sound grew more and more distant.

- 14 -
EXIT STRATEGY

Mining Shafts under Mandreen

"We don't need the suit," Bastille repeated into the comm, straining to hold the ship steady.

"We need the suit," Mizuke argued back, powering up her Mech-World office. The view outside the *DayStar* came to life around her in full 360-degree panorama as she stretched and flexed her limbs and digits, ready for action.

Bastille didn't have time to fight. He was too busy navigating the ship deeper into the Mandreen tunnel system. Following that gold line on-screen that Tavi6's people had uploaded into their NAV system was proving quite tricky. He wasn't sure how the Rover transports had managed, but the *DayStar* was having trouble squeezing through some of these edifices and around some of the corners at such a high rate of speed.

He flipped the ship around another corner and grazed another wall.

"You're scratching my ship!" Mizuke chided him.

"I'm not scratching your ship," he yelled back, fully focused on the rapidly shifting obstacle course unfolding before him. "How much longer, Tanner?"

"Two minutes at this rate," Tanner replied, clinging to his own arm rests for dear life. "Are you sure Savvy Tavi didn't send us down here to die?"

"Not gonna die," Bastille muttered under his breath, clipping another stalagmite.

"Are you trying to kill us?!" Mizuke shouted through the headset.

"Not gonna die," Bastille repeated louder as he threw the ship left and right to keep from splattering against the underground caverns.

It would have taken a long time to build out this mine shaft. And it was as rickety as any mine shaft Bastille had ever seen during his old asteroid mining days. Definitely not up to code. He half expected to barrel around a corner into a collapsed wall of rubble. He lost any sense of direction or which way was up. The digital gyro-compass to his right was spinning like a top. Some moments they were horizontal, and others they were headed straight down into the planet core.

"We sure could use Dash right now," Mizuke said. "Do you think he made it aboard?"

"He's a big boy," Bastille answered brusquely through intense and violent vibrations. "He'll be fine."

"Will we?" Mizuke countered.

"Mm," Bastille grunted back.

Moose sat to the rear of the bridge, strapped into the jump seat. Peanut sat beside him with his eyes closed as his body jerked left and then right, like he was on a roller coaster. He peeked through his fingers briefly, hoping maybe they would tell him a different story than the painful one his aching body kept relaying, but it was just in time for the *DayStar* to whip around a corner straight into the smallest gap they'd encountered. He hoped it was an optical illusion—that it was actually a giant hole farther down the pipeline. It was not. He squeezed his eyes shut again. "Oh, sweet goddess," he squeaked.

"Clear us some room, Captain," Bastille shouted. He grabbed the throttle and gave it a small boost.

"Slow down, give me some space to—" she started twisting around to bring one of the weapons forward to bear. She barely had time to line up the shot, when Bastille was in her ear again, like a drill sergeant. "Now, Captain, take out the top left bank now!"

"Why are you accelerating?" she asked incredulously. She pulled a trigger to launch a barrage of ordinance into the wall.

The ridge exploded into a thousand tiny chunks and opened it up just barely enough. The *DayStar* blasted through the debris while pebbles rained down all over the ship.

"Because the last thing we want is to get wedged down here 12 miles below the planet surface," Bastille explained, jerking left down a side tunnel to stick to the gold line on-screen. "Now keep it hot."

Finally, the space opened up, and there was the Mandreen gateway before them, illuminating this whole massive chamber in a golden glow. Bastille breathed a sigh of relief. There were stalagmites and stalactites as big as skyscrapers that he deftly threaded the *DayStar* around.

"Baby, are we glad to see you," he said, aiming right toward the center. He slowed the ship down as the tunnel surface began to ripple. Seconds later, the *Corinna's Night*, a Mandreen warship, materialized before them in the middle of it. He banked high left just in time to avoid a head-on collision.

The attack frigate had heeded Tavi6's orders to return to base when the planet came under attack. Now a foreign ship was bearing down on them. So they opened fire, cannons blazing.

Bastille swore as he maneuvered in the cramped space to avoid a direct hit. "Return fire."

"Way ahead of you," Mizuke said. Squeezing the dual triggers, she unleashed a barrage. Not as easy as it sounded because of the evasive, rolling motion of the *DayStar* as they ducked for cover back down between the stalagmites grown up from the floor.

"Not the gate," Bastille scolded her, watching some of the loose shots hit the edge of the wormhole.

"You just keep us off the walls, Captain." She managed to strafe the entire left side of the enemy's sloop.

"They've got a weapons lock," Tanner confirmed from a red-flashing HUD.

"Are they insane? They're going to wipe out both ships at once," Mizuke said.

"It's your job not to let that happen," Bastille answered.

"Incoming!" Tanner screamed.

The screen lit up with target indicators.

"I'm on it! I'm on it! Break right, Captain, let me —" As the ship rolled, the two missiles came into Mizuke's sites, and she blasted them to smithereens with a short burst. The explosion caused the warship to lurch left and opened a lane of portal access.

"That's us," was all the warning that Bastille gave his crew.

"You just gonna ram them?" Tanner's voice got really high-pitched.

"Light em up," Bastille ordered.

Mizuke did so. She threw a low-caliber weapon burst in their direction. Again, they weren't trying to nuke the whole grotto. *Corinna's* crew must have figured out what they were after. They turned their own weapons on the hyper-gate. The right side of the portal began to spark, meaning the wormhole could destabilize any second. Bastille had to close a lot of distance really fast.

"Hold on," he said as he punched the Ion drives without even spinning them up to one hundred percent. The *DayStar* skipped across the cave straight into the mouth of the wormhole. The spinning walls collapsed behind them, only they didn't completely fold up on themselves. Instead, it began to destabilize and invert. The entire area was slowly sucked into the ruptured portal piece-by-piece.

Corinna's Night tried to thrust away, but the negative gravitational pull was already too strong. The whole warship was drawn backwards into the small, unstable fissure. It was a process much like threading a warehouse through a coffee mug. Somewhere on the other side of hyperspace, the entire ship was reduced to particulate matter along with the entire core of the Mandreen planet as the wormhole crumbled in upon itself.

Bastille imagined that Tavi6 would not be too happy about having his whole planet destroyed by the rogue wormhole, even if his citizens made it out alive. So much for barricading themselves underground for the next 200 years. Bastille didn't have long to think about it, as the metaphysics of the hyper-dive overtook them at such a rate that it rendered the *Daystar* crew immediately unconscious.

Fzzzzzzzht.

* * *

SCV Bellevue

Dash Strouthers looked around the large laboratory space. He recognized the vats as the same ones in his Jacques Bastille visions that held the Mizuke biosynths. Only now they were all empty. Drained. When he looked down into his own hand, he saw it held a blaster. And then he heard a painful yelp and discovered Dr. Vance down on the floor, clawing his way forward.

"Dr. Vance," Dash holstered the weapon and sprang to his side, "what's going on?" He knelt beside him as the doctor sputtered and coughed.

"Wexell attack." He coughed some more. "Th-they're gonna make it look like the Ma'kobi or KA-

Corps, but it's the Dominion death squad," he practically spat this last part, such was his hatred for them.

"What did those Fugs do to the Cryo-tanks?" Dash surveyed the area, looking for any sign of the biosynths.

"They took them. They took them all," the doctor said, weaker with every word.

"Who, Doc? Who did they take?" Dash was frantic for answers. None of this made sense.

"T-took them all," the doctor repeated. He heaved a gurgling sigh and went limp.

Dash laid the dead man's head gently on the floor. He went over to the Cryo-tanks and almost slipped in the clear, gooey liquid all over the floor. The drainage from the vats had spilled everywhere and collected in puddles. Everything was still fresh, Very recent. But where were the BLU units?

If those Dominion Fugs found a St. Croix engineer on board, there was no telling what they would do to elicit all of her tech secrets. Emboldened by Colonel Wexell, they had attacked a hospital frigate in broad daylight. They were capable of anything. If they were no longer deterred by the threat of a fourth World War, that is exactly what would happen next.

Dash saw a bunch of boot prints and drag marks all headed through the same access way. He followed them through that door and paused as he heard explosions from different decks of the ship. A woman screamed behind him, and he turned to see a Dominion thug dragging a woman along by her blue hair. Mizuke!

He ran toward the officer. The man took one look at Dash's uniform and shouted orders at him, "What are you waiting for, Captain? Clear this whole area and bring all the BLU units to the holding area. I found this one trying to escape, and I just passed three more barricading themselves in two doors down—"

He didn't finish. Dash shot him neatly through the forehead, and the man collapsed to the ground. The woman cowered in fear.

"Mizuke," Dash grabbed her arm. She looked up at him, and although she looked identical to Mizuke, it was not her. It caught Dash off guard, and he pulled away.

"I-I-I am 132," the woman said, her teeth chattering. "I am BLU-132." She looked confused and very frightened.

"Hey, hey, you're okay. What's going on here?" He held out a calming hand to her this time as he approached.

She scampered back from his touch, but the wall prevented her from going any further.

"Shh, I'm here to help," he said gently. "Please tell me."

"Dominion s-slavers," she whispered hoarsely, pointing up the hall.

Dash heard some more boots running in their direction. He helped the biosynthetic woman up, triggering the door beside them and pushing her inside.

"Wait until it's clear. Ten minutes, if you have to. Lock the door. Then make your way to the lifeboats, two hallways over. Do you understand?"

She was crying but nodded. "Th-thank you," she whispered. "I am BLU-132."

"Okay," he smiled sadly and closed the door just as two more grunts ran around the corner.

"What happened here?" The taller lieutenant barked at him. His nameplate read, "Charles."

"I dunno, sir," Dash lied. "Looks pretty fresh if you ask me."

"What's your name, soldier?" He wasn't even looking at Dash; he was bent over, checking the corpse.

"Captain Strouthers, sir," Dash answered.

"Well, come on. Colonel Guissman needs some backup with the other BLU units," Lt. Charles ordered.

Dash followed mechanically behind them. They entered a holding area. Actually, it was a rec room that had been converted into a holding area. There were two Fugs and a Reek—Re-cycle Geek—all together grouped in the doorway.

On the other side of the room, a huddle of identical, naked, blue-haired Mizuke biosynths cowered together. These would be the full-grown servants freshly released from the Cryo-vats back in the lab.

"Holy sh*t, Colonel," said Lt. Charles. "I *told you* the Draccario scumbags kept all the hottest BLUs for themselves."

"Hah," Colonel Guissman scoffed. Dash could see by Guissman's uniform insignia that he held the highest rank in this small squad. Guissman shaved the head of one of the Mizukes for transport. The Reek outfitted her with a Bio-Ring. That was the official name. But it was a slave collar. Mizuke was on her knees, shivering, even though she had more clothes on than the others. Her face was bleeding from a gash around the eye. Her shirt sleeve had been ripped off her shoulder, and Dash could see she had a fresh tri-mark branded onto her shoulder.

The Reek said, "Can you believe this squiffer has been running around unmarked for years? Poor poppet, I bet she thought she was a human."

"Shut it, Bender," Guissman snapped.

"Aye, yessir, your eminence, sir!" Bender snapped a sloppy salute.

Mizuke looked up at Dash with tears in her eyes.

"Mizuke," he said quietly.

She shook her head with a cautionary "no" as a huge lock of blue hair was shaved off and dropped to the ground. She was almost completely shorn; she looked mangy like a wild dog.

Dash didn't even realize he'd pulled his gun until he shoved it into the leering mouth of Lt. Charles next to him and decorated the wall with his brains. He dropped three more before the Colonel had even unholstered his own weapon.

Guissman yelled something into his comms as he drew his gun. Dash sent a single shot through his comm, hand, and neck simultaneously. Blood splattered the wall and dotted Mizuke's face.

The Reek they'd called Bender clambered away into the hall, man-handling another Dominion Fug as his human shield. Dash nicked the guard's shoulder with another shot and dropped him, but the chubby one called Bender escaped.

Dash slid to a knee beside Mizuke.

"We have to get out of here. Mizuke, are you okay to walk?" He wiped some blood from her face with his sleeve. She was still shaking, too stunned to stand.

"Wh-what am I, Dash? Am I a poppet? One of them?" She turned back to the Mizuke BLUs still huddled in the back like scared little children. "Am I one of those sex dolls?"

"No, Mizuke," Dash said, cupping her face to look her in the eyes. "Not exactly. You are my wife, and I'm getting you out of here." He helped her struggle to a knee, but she yanked him closer, angrier now.

"Did we or did we not meet at the sailor bar on NeoTokyo… Eno's Ghost?" Her eyes searched for the truth.

"Yes, we did. That's all real, Mizu, please. We *have* to go now."

She refused to budge. Her electric blue eyes were unblinking.

"Okay," Dash admitted. "You… began as a biosynth but you're not—"

"Aughhh!" She shoved him away and slumped back to the floor. Eyes filling with tears. Betrayal.

He approached her again, more gently. "Mizuke, I promise to explain everything. But we have to go now." He tried to coax her toward the door. "Please?"

"Go?" She shook her head, snapping out of the daze. "We're not going anywhere with this thing," she indicated the slave collar that all the biosynths wore. "You go to your ship, Dash. Signal the Croix. Bring back some help."

Dash was dumbstruck at the thought. "I'm not… I can't leave you here," he protested.

Just then, every screen lining the room and hallway fuzzed out, and the emergency messaging was replaced by a single smug face—an older, stocky woman with a calm, military demeanor. She was speaking but muted at first. Finally, the audio patched through and synched up with the signal.

"I repeat, attention, insurgents. I am Colonel Wexell. And this Draccario super vessel, the *SCV Bellevue*? It's mine. Unless there's any objection, Commander?" She waved to someone off-screen, and *Bellevue's* commander was pushed forward onto his knees.

The banged-up officer angrily ranted, "You will not get away with—"

Blam! Wexell shot him in the face. "No speeches," she said and set the smoking blaster aside. She took a moment to pour herself some of the commander's scotch.

"Those of you who know my name know that you have no choice but to surrender. A new day is upon us, ladies and gentlemen. In the next sixty seconds, my men will sweep the whole ship. If you resist, for every one of my people that you kill, I will kill thirty of yours."

Dash looked around the room at the six dead soldiers and then at the cowering women in the corner. A couple had picked up weapons from the dead Fugs and raised them shakily, aiming at Dash.

"Stop. What are you doing? We'll go. Okay, we're going," he said, grabbing a better hold of Mizuke, who had lost too much blood to fight him. He thought the others might shoot him in the back, but they held their fire. So he advised them, "You all should get to the lifeboats. Now." He opened the door and peeked into the hallway, which was clear for the moment. Cradling Mizuke close, they moved out slowly.

"Listen," on the hallway monitors, Wexell continued her appeal to the passengers' sensibilities. "To be honest, I'm *exhausted*. The last ship had a young captain, head full of the most scandalous anti-Dominion bigotry. They hurt my crew. They hurt my *feelings*. So we cut out those men's tongues and fed it to their women." She might as well have been reading a weather report for all the lack of emotion she portrayed. She calmly sipped what looked like a tumbler of Scotch as she morbidly continued. "Next we skinned them all alive and fed them to the sea birds. Some real circle of life, cradle to grave stuff at work. The point is this: if you want to negotiate with a lady, I am honored to be that lady. But if you force me to be the darkness… I swear to you and your bratty little children that the horror stories they tell of this place will make our last war party seem like a spa day. I implore you… to choose wisely."

Wexell stood and opened a semi-opaque lid beside her. It was an old-time record player from way before the Colonial Uprising. She dropped the needle onto the spinning record, and a 1930s jazz riff began to play. Then she smiled at the camera, raised a glass, and walked out of frame, leaving that music playing over a horrifying shot of the dead captain bleeding out. The music echoed eerily through the ship's halls.

And then the explosions commenced.

Dash hurried Mizuke along as fast as she could manage. He knew what was next. He'd studied these kind of piracy tactics at the academy. These marauders would surround the outside of the *Bellevue*. Interlinked cables would connect each of their perimeter ships. When a signal was given, all the shipmates would throw a switch together. A blue light would shoot from one ship to the next, repeatedly, until an electric grid had been cast over the entire vessel.

It went exactly as Dash had learned. Like clockwork. Suddenly, within the *Bellevue*, gravity ceased to exist. One moment they were dusting themselves off from the fallout and debris, and the next everyone was kicking and floating in zero gravity.

The weightlessness actually benefited Dash and Mizuke, as they could now move more freely. Mizuke held tightly around Dash's waist as he maneuvered them forward, skimming the walls expeditiously. They took a lift down to the hangar deck and exited. As their momentum floated them past, he grabbed hold of the bay doors, and they both jerked to an abrupt halt.

Dash triggered the door. When he reached for Mizuke, her slave collar suddenly activated, and her whole body stiffened. An electric haze surrounded her as she flew off down the hallway, held fast by an invisible lasso. She disappeared into the smoke and fog.

"Noooooooooo!" he yelled.

Dash was about to pursue when he heard Mech-forms clang forward through the clouded haze. Headlamps swept this way and that, along with the laser guides on their rifle scopes. Within the ZeroG environ, they walked on the walls and ceiling spread out in a delta formation. These were no minute-men, day players you picked up from the docks; these were Special Ops in stolen KACorps gear. They were Dominator warriors with augmented chromium exosuits. A death squad otherwise known as Manglers.

Dash retreated through the hangar door and shut it behind him. To deter his pursuers, he blasted the controls with his sidearm. When he spun around, everything that hadn't been bolted down floated freely inside this spacious garage. Ships and materials alike. He spotted his HX-45 Marauder and pushed off the wall in its direction. He hurried inside the open cockpit of the ship, which hung weirdly upside down as it drifted. He powered up the ship as the bay doors were blown open behind him.

A Mangler wrenched the burning doors aside and stepped through, cautiously scanning for targets. He saw Dash in his cockpit, and his eyes widened. Before he could respond, Dash pulled the trigger, and a missile from the HX-45 cut the Fug in half as blood and hydraulics spewed from within.

Dash oriented his ship toward the mouth of the hangar and throttled forward, blasting through some ship debris and dodging payloads floating freely. Even before he exited into the full sunlight, his HUD had locked onto the closest enemy ships.

Four advanced drone missiles preceded him out into the open air. The AI warheads he launched immediately found purchase in three of the sloops around the *Bellevue* perimeter. This collapsed the anti-gravity field, and every person in the ship crashed to the floor. The Dominion Manglers hung awkwardly from their magnetized boots until they released the power locks and dropped to the floor.

Outside the *Bellevue*, the HX-45 burst out of the hangar into the sun. "Mayday, Mayday, *SCV Bellevue* is under attack from Dominion assault teams," Dash repeated a couple of times into his headset.

He'd gotten the enemy fleet's full attention now. He pulled back and circled around under the belly of the hospital ship and flew to the other side of the bow, where Wexell's flagship sat high and clear from the battle.

Dash launched a full array of drone missiles at the ship. The enemy immediately fired back at him. He flicked the joystick right and slid back under the cover of the *Bellevue*, but suddenly his whole system jammed and he had zero control of the HX-45. With ordinance closing in all around and no computer response, he flipped the eject button, and as he cleared the cockpit, the neural link to the Marauder was severed.

Fzzzzzzzht.

- 15 -

NO SKINBAG LEFT BEHIND

Mandreen Colony

Bastille opened his eyes. His first feeling was relief that the hyper-dive hadn't left him puking up his toenails like the last time. But something wasn't right. He blinked as the confusion dissipated and his eyes focused. It was a dimly lit room he found himself in, but something hung in his face. He moved his head slightly. It was hair. Long blonde hair.

Now looking down, he saw the curves of a 16-year-old body and a flight jacket that was all too familiar. Genwa'ar. Somehow, during the hyper-dive from Mandreen, he had been dislodged from the Dash Byno-Core on the *Daystar* and re-seated into Gen's vacant meat-suit here. In hell.

*Sh*t.*

These things needed to come with owner's manuals. Or at least seatbelts. He quickly became alert to a shuffle of feet by the large door. He peered through a couple strands of hair to see a massive guard near the entrance to the room, which had stone walls and appeared to be a cave. It was one of Tavi's royal guards. A very Spartan appearance. Short-cropped beard. Engraved helmet with the nose guard that came down for protection. Strategic armor plating that covered sinewy muscle. Some of his battle tattoos could be seen through the breaks in the armor. On the neck. The abdomen. The thighs. Or were they bull haunches? Hard to tell in the shadows.

Bastille noted the Relay box on the centurion's neck. Whoever was driving this Byno-Core had lived more than one life. There was no telling how old he was. Prime skinbags like this one cost a fortune on the black market. The fact that Tavi6 had never Re-cycled into another body had not escaped Bastille's notice. The Magistrate of Mandreen was obviously opposed to it for himself, but not for some of those closest to him. He had always been a little superstitious about the process, equating it to ancient demon possession tales from their upbringing. But he was also a calculating and wealthy man, so building up an elite force around himself of the best-trained men in first-class meat-suits made tactical sense. Bastille knew this because he was the one who'd taught him that over fifty years ago. How a person could look down his nose at human Re-cycling, but butcher himself through animal augments was a mystery to him.

Bastille scanned the rest of Gen's body, which he currently inhabited. He was upright, chained to a rock wall. So this was not just a cave, but a dungeon. He was definitely on Mandreen. He was clothed but still disheveled from that blast she took back on the flight deck.

Bastille moved his hand slightly, and an iron manacle chaining him to the wall clanked softly. The noise brought the guard to full attention—his long-rifle and bayonet leveled directly at Bastille. No more sense in playing dead. He put some weight on his legs and slowly stood. He pulled his head upright and shook the hair from his eyes. Tilting his head left and right, he cracked some kinks out.

The guard glared at him, then raised his fist and hammered on the door twice, *bang bang*, growling in a deep baritone, "She wakes."

The door lock snapped and creaked open, and the guard backed out of the room. Bastille held his gaze the whole time, smiled crookedly, and even winked just to further mess with his head. After the guard exited, Bastille frowned and licked his lip. That dumb smile of his had split his parched lip, and now there was the taste of blood on the inside of his mouth.

Bastille moved quickly. Testing the chains, he gave them some hard tugs and realized there was no give in them. Scanning the rock where they were connected to the wall, there was no weakness there either. But this was no ordinary body. This was Genwa'ar. She had lived for decades on the Shadow Moon. A lifetime of stored-up strength and power. Powers, which Gen had unleashed on Tavi6 and his Royal Guard no less than an hour ago.

Those goons would be back soon enough. Bastille's imagination went wild with scenarios of how they'd want to repay Gen for their dead comrades and take the penance out on her flesh. Which, for the time being, was Bastille's flesh. They would probably stop short of killing him because this body could still be used as a pawn against the Shadow Moon invasion. Bastille cleared his mind.

Looking to narrow his focus, he concentrated on his right wrist constraint. He balled his fist and breathed out slowly. He didn't even know which muscle to flex to trigger any sort of super-witchy power. At first, he strained his arm and wrist, but that only gouged the metal further into his forearm.

No, this power had to have a deeper, internal trigger. He visualized his arm moving forward and breaking free from the manacles. He even closed his eyes because, of course, they saw zero progress, which made his mind laugh at the absurdity of this task. But Bastille still focused. He silenced the unbelief. He strained forward. He willed his hand to break free.

Had his eyes been open this time, he would have seen a blue glow forming, ever so faintly, inside his fist. He could feel it beginning to work. The heat. Slowly, the iron cuff began stretching, and the bolt into the wall slipped out a few inches.

Bastille opened his eyes. Ecstatic. He couldn't believe the progress. It actually worked. He watched the blue-ish glow diminish and the power surge wane.

But still, he could wiggle the chain around. It was definitely loose. He closed his eyes to focus his mind again.

He was in the middle of his second attempt when the door clanged loudly and the original guard re-entered, holding his long-rifle. The bayonet was aimed at Bastille's head. This guy was taking no chances. He was followed in by one of the Royal Guard Murder Mountains—who had to duck to enter the room—and finally by Tavi6 who was absolutely livid.

"Tavi," Bastille said warily, "wait, before you—"

Wham. Too late. Tavi6 punched Bastille in the stomach, and he sucked air, alternating between coughs and gasps. Unable to breathe for a few seconds until the sharp pain abated. Tavi6 grabbed Bastille's tiny throat and slammed his head back against the blackstone wall. Their faces were now inches apart.

"You don't speak. You don't utter a word unless I command it. Do I make myself clear?" Tavi6 increased his grip, and Bastille could do nothing but hang there, feet dangling off the floor, and choke. Face turning red. Eyes beginning to roll back into his head.

"General—" one of the guards prompted softly from behind, snapping Tavi6 back into the present. He released Bastille, who collapsed back against the wall, knees buckling as his feet touched the floor.

Bastille gulped air down as the blood rush subsided, and he edged away from the black void of death. He had no idea what would happen to him if this Genwa'ar host body were to die, but he didn't care to find out. His mind raced, but he discarded every option as quickly as it surfaced, lest he trigger Tavi6 too far beyond the man's limited self-restraint.

Tavi6 rubbed some sweat from his forehead as he collected himself. He threw a warning look at the guard who'd spoken up. The guard straightened, eyes forward.

Tavi6 continued to his prisoner, "You will call off your people's attack on our planet. The man they are looking for—Jacques Bastille—is no longer here. Escaped." Tavi6 leaned in closer and added, "You will call off the Shadow Moon or suffer unspeakable things."

Bastille unsteadily climbed to his feet again. He looked Tavi6 in the eye and then went for it: "I *am* Jaques Bastille."

Tavi6 crossed the space between them in an instant, brandishing a blade he yanked from an ornamental neck pendant. He held it to Bastille's throat. "What… did you say? And choose your words smartly, as they could precipitate your end."

Bastille repeated slowly, cautiously, "I am Jacques Bastille, King of the Ma'kobi."

Tavi6 regarded him for what felt like a full minute. Bastille waited for that one smooth stroke of a blade that would spill the lifeblood from his throat. But Tavi6 stayed his hand. Instead, he pushed backwards and away, eyeing the little girl's Byno-Core very skeptically. Then he smiled warmly.

"Interesting play." Tavi6 picked absently at the tip of the knife, then pointed it at Bastille. "Two hours ago, I would have slit your throat. But I've seen things since then. The universe—don't know why I'm surprised—is a fun, exciting new space." Tavi6 tapped the flat side of the blade against Bastille's forehead and then holstered it smoothly.

"What an easy problem to solve, *Brother*," Tavi6 smiled. He pulled his shirt open to the collarbone, exposing a wicked scar pattern that spiderwebbed across his chest and shoulder. "If you are indeed my brother, tell me a little story. Two people in the entire universe know how I received these markings. If you are Jacques Bastille, tell me. How did it happen? *Brother*."

Bastille deflated a bit. He had such little knowledge of anything before three weeks ago, much less something that happened fifty years into the past.

Tavi6 moved forward a little. "I'll even give you a hint: Caverns of Lycendale."

Bastille peered deeply into the fog of his own mind. Straining. But it was still just a hodgepodge of swirling gray shapes. Hard to discern. The name held no purchase in his memory. He took a flying leap and said, "You… were surprised… by a bull lizard. And, uh, and it impaled you on its electric tail-spike and bucked you into the riverbed."

Tavi6 looked surprised. He looked over to his men and then back to Bastille. Walking over, he held out both hands to receive his brother back, and at the last second, he slapped him so hard across the face that blood shot from his nose.

Tavi6 grabbed a fistful of Bastille's long hair to make sure he looked him in the eye. "Not. Even. Close." And then he slugged him again in the belly, doubling him over. He was winding up for another hit when the whole room rumbled and shook, and the two lights flickered. Like a mini-earthquake.

Tavi6 let go of Bastille and triggered his wrist-comm. "Status report."

"Wormhole—collapsing—" Bastille spat out a mouthful of blood between gasps.

Over the radio, a harried man explained, "Sir, there was a skirmish at the planet core with the *Corinna*. The wormhole has destabilized. We are reading high levels of Hawking radiation."

Tavi6 regarded Bastille for a moment, then spoke back into the comm device, "Evacuate everything we've got. But quietly, Captain. If we can get outta here without alerting the Shadow Moon, perhaps the temporal rift will suck them into oblivion."

"Roger that, sir," the captain cleared the comm.

Tavi6 turned to the original guard, gesturing back to Bastille, "End this. Painfully. And then join us at the fleet rendezvous."

The guard nodded his compliance.

"You! On me," Tavi6 barked at the murder mountain who lumbered after him. The door clanged ominously closed behind them.

Another tremor shook the room. Rubble was shaken loose from the walls, and sandy grit trickled down from the ceiling. The remaining guard set his long-rifle down and then snapped off his breastplate, removing the whole upper piece in one smooth motion.

"You are gonna be late for takeoff, my friend," Bastille warned him, working at the manacles. "I'd keep that armor on."

The guard turned around and snapped off his belt, and the plates across his thighs came off, too. Hairy thighs. Beastly thighs and hooves.

"I'm serious. I have been with all manner of skanks and scalawags. Probably got Chlamydia, Herpes, Clav9… it'll melt that donkey dick right off. I'd reconsider."

The guard bent down and pulled the knife from his long-rifle. He approached Bastille as the room began to rumble some more and fall apart at the seams. Bastille closed his eyes. He concentrated everything he had on that Relay box. He did as he saw the old lady on Phaedra do during her Re-cycle. He slowly moved one hand behind his head to cover his Relay. He focused every thought on one single task. The guard held the knife to Bastille's throat as his other hand began to yank at his belt.

Bastille focused more and finally began to sense it—to see it in his mind's eye. A tunnel formed ahead of him. A light. A path.

The guard leaned in for a kiss, and Bastille wrapped his loosely chained hand around the man's Relay box. Then he gathered all his energy and focus.

"Ahhhhhhhhhh," Bastille screamed and suddenly, blue light shot from his glowing eyes and mouth straight into the guard's face as his life force transferred over into the new meat-suit. Gen's body went limp in the chains as the guard stumbled backward and steadied himself.

Bastille was now inside the guard's Byno-Core. He held a hand up to his face and waved it around. "Ha! Haha! I did it! Suck it, Bender! I Re-cycled myself!" He kicked with his new bull haunches and his hooves clomped the ground. He studied them closely. "I… just don't get it."

The room exploded with rock and debris as a section of the flooring fell into a dark abyss. Bastille rummaged for the guard's keys and quickly unlatched Gen's body from the wall. He caught her before she hit the ground. Lifting her up, he threw her over his shoulder, grabbed the long-rifle and ran to the door. He briefly considered his pile of clothes and armor on the ground and decided there wasn't enough time. Pulling the door open, he raced out into the corridor, mostly naked, with Gen's limp body bouncing helplessly on his broad shoulder.

The halls were completely deserted. Bastille ran past a section of wall that had collapsed. On the other side, he could hear engines firing up. He climbed through the gap in the wall and then shouldered his way through another weakened inner door. Through the broken ceiling, he could see the flight deck above them.

"Here goes," he said, crouching low. With a grunt, he sprang up through the crumbling floor, landing solidly as his hooves slid across the blackened tiles. "Hell yeah, now I get it."

Fires had broken out around him as the last of the fleet pushed out of the crumbling confines of this shuttle bay. Bastille saw a couple of ships running last-minute pre-flight checks and ran toward one of them. The pilot perked up at the sight of a naked guard running toward him with a petite offworlder slung over his shoulder. He popped his top hatch open. "Sanji, what are you doing?"

"Brought you a present," Bastille said, laying Genwa'ar's Byno-Core gently atop the lower wing of this catamaran. The ship was chewed up, but Bastille liked that it had a large outrigger folded up on the left side. Once deployed, that large engine would take this ship interstellar. He climbed onto the wing beside Gen. The pilot stepped out of the cockpit to get a closer look. "No time to explain," Bastille said, and stabbed the pilot's exposed neck with the bayonet. When he yanked it free, the pilot dropped to his knees, clutching at the blood spilling down his chest and onto the wing beneath him.

Bastille attempted to climb into the fighter with his current half-breed body, but it was just too big for the small ship. He wouldn't be able to maneuver at all with him and Gen both inside the confined cockpit. And he wasn't about to leave Gen's advanced Byno-Core behind. He crouched back down above Gen on the wing. The pilot lay right next to them, watching helplessly as life drained from his body. Bastille slid a hand behind Gen's neck and cupped the Relay box. Then he leaned his forehead against hers, closed his eyes, and concentrated. It wasn't working.

With his free hand, he reached behind his own neck to cover his own Relay box. He didn't even know if he had the Re-cycle energy to perform this again. But he had to force it one more time, or he was a dead man. As the world exploded around him, he strained harder until he began to see that small point of light. The gateway. Then he kissed Gen on the mouth as a blue light flashed and his life energy was channeled from the guard back into Gen's body.

The guard's meat-suit flopped down as Gen-wa'ar's frame revived with a huge intake of breath, coughing, and sputtering. Bastille had successfully Re-cycled again. He would like to have been at home in the

Dash Byno-Core—wherever that was—but being back in Gen's meat-suit would have to do for now. It was like upgrading from a clunky freighter to a nimble starfighter.

Bastille rolled the guard and he slid off the wing to the ground below with a grunt. The half-breed, now back in control of his own body, began to revive. But it would be too late. Bastille saw the pilot was in his final death throes and he shoved him off the skiff as well.

Climbing quickly into the cockpit, Bastille closed the canopy and fired up the engines. The last of three fighters took off up the ramp, and Bastille nosed forward to follow. A huge ceiling girder dislodged and crushed the lead fighter, batting it to the floor. The remaining two fighters and Bastille's catamaran powered safely over and through, just barely escaping the crumbling fortress.

* * *

Bastille trailed the fighters as they raced down toward the planet's core to shelter themselves among the surface canyons from the Shadow Moon above. The Croix pounded the colony relentlessly with a barrage of advanced weaponry, unaware of the unstable wormhole expanding beneath the surface. Bastille followed a ravine as more ships gathered with them along the escape vector, mostly top-dwellers who'd been slow to get the news of the attack and subsequent tactical retreat.

The small, disheveled convoy pulled up from the ravine, kicked in the ion drives, and jettisoned into space as the Mandreen Colony continued to dissolve around them. Already on the west side of the planet, the event horizon sucked space junk down from orbit into its gaping maw. The Shadow Moon council must have realized what was happening because they finally ceased the bombardment and began evacuation maneuvers.

Once Bastille and the others reached the debris field, the convoy slowed down to cautiously pick its way through to the rendezvous point. Bastille climbed to a safe distance from Mandreen and then turned to watch the Shadow Moon's final struggle. It had ceased any forward momentum. It no longer gained any distance, but it was not losing any ground for the moment.

Bastille was proud of Tavi6's plan and that it worked as well as it did. He vowed to congratulate him next time he saw him, right before he killed him. Bastille slipped his own skiff left to avoid some space junk hurtling past.

Suddenly, the Shadow Moon's surface began to crack and split open.

"Hell yeah!" Bastille pumped his fist.

His celebration was short-lived, though, as a gigantic starship tore through the front side of the moon like a hatchling from an egg. It was a silvery, bulbous superstructure that Bastille would have loved to document longer, but the Shadow Moon's surface began to crumble back toward what was left of the Mandreen planet. And Bastille wasn't exactly sure what would happen when Phaedra's surface impacted the Mandreen surface, and he wasn't about to stick around to find out.

He fired his thrusters, spun his ship around, and dove headlong into the thousands of tumbling objects between himself and deep-space. Weaving in and out, rolling, and dodging, he pushed faster and faster through the minefield. Minor debris pelted the exterior, but the shielding held.

Behind him the planet's surface exploded and a massive shockwave pulsed forward consuming everything in its path.

Bastille really wished that he had his Mustang right about now. He powered up the catamaran's outrigger, which he lowered until it locked into place. All the while, he searched the garbage horizon for a clear shot through the debris. Finally, and for an instant, there was a small tunnel of opportunity. The Nav-COMM beeped a path confirmation, and that's all he needed. He punched the sublights and launched forward through the last of the debris and out into deep space.

- 16 -
UNDER COVER

Deep Space

The *DayStar* floated in a gentle tumble, its shell pinged from time to time with particulate matter emanating from the newly exploded jump gate in their wake. Genwa'ar was the first one on the bridge to regain consciousness. Her wicked, fuzzy-headed migraines dissipated, and the world around her snapped into focus. She leaned forward and vomited all over the floor. Felt better for it, but not one hundred percent herself. Looking at her manly hands, she knew in an instant that she had mistakenly landed in Bastille's Byno-Core.

Even after all these years, the one-on-one Re-cycle process they'd perfected on Phaedra was considered experimental. This latest Croix technology for long-distance Relay-casting was even murkier. Only used as a last resort. She wasn't sure what had transpired, but she felt lucky she hadn't ended up inside a satellite. Or a hair dryer. As she considered the whole thing, she couldn't help but laugh. After all this time, all the fighting, and conniving, *she* was now the infamous Ma'kobi King. On the outside, at least.

"What's so funny?" Peanut asked just before wretching up his own royal dinner.

Gen spun her head and got her first clear look around the room. Peanut unbuckled himself from his chair and dropped to the floor, where Moose was stirring, too. Gen checked her holster and felt better that Bastille's Mauzer sat securely in place. She quietly snapped off the safety strap, calculating the time and distance to her closest kill. Of the two of them, she'd target the hulking silent one first. Next, she would really enjoy frying the small man who had attacked her when she and Bastille had first come aboard.

It was possible that this small band of misfits could be helpful on her journey, but the risk of sabotage was too high. As much as she hated to purge them all, Bastille was really the only one she needed to accomplish her mission. And now, for all intents and purposes, she *was* Jacques Bastille.

From the helm, Tanner triggered the comms, "Captain, you better get up to the bridge."

Radio silence.

"Captain?"

"I—I'm here," Mizuke said, entering the room behind them. She braced herself against the door. "Give me a sec, dammit. Stomach is in knots."

Peanut assisted Moose to his feet, and they moved forward to the star-chart table, adding, "Where the hell are we?"

Gen slowly shuffled back from the rest of the group for a cleaner shot. She felt conspicuous but reminded herself that nobody could possibly know that this Bastille meat-suit contained their mortal enemy. Mizuke moved along, still a little groggy. She steadied herself against any firmament along the way toward the helm, including what she would assume was Bastille's massive barrel chest.

"All good, love?" She said, patting Gen.

Gen was taken aback at the "love" bit but forced another smile and gave an unconvincing "Mm-hmm" as Mizuke passed by to join the others.

"Liar," Mizuke said with a chuckle. "Tanner, where in God's green universe are we?"

Gen slowly reached down for the Mauzer and began to slip it from its holster, but she was deeply conflicted. A lingering scent of jasmine in the air had her heart pounding faster. Something about this Mizuke woman was stirring her. Not her, but this body. Responding on its own. Confusing her. She shakily raised the Mauzer to their turned backs, her pulse quickening.

"I guess we're wherever Dash surfaced us," Tanner answered.

Gen looked around suddenly at the mention of Dash's name. That would complicate things if he were somehow aboard. He could jigger everything up. Shut down engines and cut the air supply. And she wasn't powerful enough, especially not in Bastille's body, to fight a ghost-line, even with the mods she'd installed after Bastille arrived on Phaedra. No, it wasn't safe to reveal her hand just yet. She slid the Mauzer back into the holster.

"I'm gonna need to reboot, uh, well… everything," Tanner said, and heaved a frustrated sigh at the star charts that refused to stabilize or lock on to their current position. "Our systems are scrambled from that hyper-dive."

"Saved our lives," Peanut said with a thumbs-up to Gen.

Gen couldn't answer because she didn't know what Bastille had done in those final moments. Instead, she just shrugged it off like it was all in a day's work. Moose also gave her a congratulatory chip on the shoulder, which almost dislocated her arm. This was not going to be easy, pretending to be Bastille. He was obviously friends now with these delinquents.

"Alright, well, that's gonna give us all time to get cleaned up," Mizuke observed. "I want this puke deck swabbed and the systems back online within the hour."

"Roger that, Cap'n," Peanut said, still massaging his stomach. "I'm kinda hungry again."

Mizuke walked past Gen and pulled her along by the scruff of her lapel, "You're with me."

As they exited, Peanut gave a knowing smile to Moose. "Ow, owwwwwww," he howled after them.

* * *

In the captain's quarters, Mizuke lithely shed the last of her clothes and stepped into the bathroom headed for the shower. Gen stood in the bedroom, fumbling with some of the unfamiliar buttons and clasps of her own ensemble. She opted instead to just pull the coat and shirt off over her head. Looking into the mirror before her, Gen saw Bastille's spiderwebbed scar, touching it absent-mindedly.

"Your brother's an arrogant asshole," Mizuke called out from the shower. "Did being around his high holiness again trigger any new memories?"

"What? No," Gen responded, covering her royal accent to sound more like Bastille. She stepped into the bathroom. Mizuke was just a silhouette on the shower door.

Mizuke poked her head out and said, "I can't hear you out there, you're gonna have to come closer." And then smiled wryly and disappeared back into the steam.

Gen swallowed and removed the last of her clothes. She considered the Mauzer one more time and then set it aside. She had seen Bastille naked in the bath house back on Phaedra, but that was just briefly amidst the commotion of his arrest. She hadn't seen him in as much detail as she could now. She ran her hands down over his front, checking the mirror again, very impressed. "Down boy," she said to herself. Finally, she took a deep breath and entered the shower.

Mizuke stood under the hot spray, water cascading down her beautiful body. Gen took in every curve. Her brow furrowed when she noticed the troubling scars all over this poor woman's back and the mysterious tattoo on her shoulder blade. Gen reached out to touch it. Mizuke looked back at the fingers trailing across her skin.

"I had a chance to have that erased," Mizuke continued thoughtfully, "but some things you never wanna forget."

She moved to the side and pulled Gen under the spray, drawing up close. Gen let the water drench her short hair and run down her face and beard. When she reopened her eyes, Mizuke was right there, looking deep into her soul with those startling blue eyes. Her scent and the soothing spray massaging her back—it was all quite titillating. And then Mizuke leaned forward and kissed her—a warm, passionate kiss.

Gen's eyes were wide open. None of her training had prepared her for this moment, here with a rogue Mizuki BLU unit. This one was unlike any others she had known. Yes, it was common on the Shadow Moon of Phaedra for love, companionship, and sex. Yes, their citizens took autonomous lovers. Gen had definitely had her share through the years, as any 220-year-old would, just never from this side. The man's side. It was primal and powerful and intoxicating. She couldn't concentrate on anything else, and so finally she surrendered to it and grabbed Mizuke's head in her hands and kissed back hard, prompting a surprised but accepting little moan from Mizuke.

* * *

Gen lay in bed, spent. She rested gently with Mizuke draped across her chest, snuggled close. Mizuke's steady breath indicated she was almost asleep. Gen reached her hand up and ran her fingers over her own lips and through the scraggly beard on her face. One strange sensation after the next.

She really wanted to lay there and relive that last half-hour in every torrid detail—all the things Mizuke had done to make her feel incredible. She wanted to wake her up and take her again and again. But she knew the more they interacted, the longer she stayed, the greater the risk of exposure. So far, Mizuke had fallen for her in the most intimate way. No, she couldn't stay any longer. Gen pulled away, and Mizuke groaned disapprovingly.

"Where are you going?" Mizuke smacked at Gen's butt.

"Uh, check the Mustang." Gen paused to see if that would sell.

It did. Mizuke pushed her away and snuggled back into her own pillow, "You're such a man."

Gen looked back at Mizuke which was another mistake. She was getting stirred up all over again down there. Sigh. The male body was a real nuisance.

"Go," Mizuke said, turning her back on Gen. "Go check your beloved ship."

The spell was broken. Gen peeled herself from the bed, getting dressed as quickly as possible.

* * *

Peanut walked into the infirmary to see what he would falsely assume to be Jacques Bastille. Gen, still driving the Bastille skinbag, was seated on the floor, surrounded by cables and jury-rigged electronics hardwired into monitors. There was even a patch panel from the wall that had been removed, and this rig was somehow tied in to the ship's core processors. "You wanted to see me, boss?"

Gen peeked over the top of a circuit board she was fusing together and waved him over. Peanut could not make heads nor tails of the mess in front of him, so he just stood there waiting for Gen to complete whatever it was she was doing. She seemed very intent and focused. At length, she finally spoke up.

"I've got a little theory about this memory loss," Gen tapped a screwdriver to her head. "I'm not one hundred percent sure that there's any actual data *missing*, so much as *unreadable*. So, I've got two choices: one, I cut through my own skull and have you manually remove the faulty neuron chips from my brain—"

"Ewww, hard pass." Peanut paled at the thought.

"As I figured, so, two, I've created an array to copy and transcode all the data from the neuron chips into this spare Relay box, using my own Relay as a base station and processor."

"Oh s-sure, of course. What's the catch?" Peanut asked.

"For one, the process cannot be interrupted," Gen warned. "Once it begins, it is crucial that every last nanobyte is downloaded. Until then, I am completely frozen in time and space. Until you reboot my system and re-upload all the data."

"Wait, um, what?" Peanut shifted uneasily.

Gen held up a finger for each part of the three-step process she outlined, starting with the thumb: "Download. Reboot. Upload."

"Okay, now I'm no bio-engineer or even much of a mechanic." Peanut rubbed his troubled forehead.

"Sigh. It's not about engineering," Gen explained. "I've done the engineering. It's about having someone you, uh, trust to flip this switch when the process is finished. Just turn the lights back on." Gen pointed at the remote.

"Where did you learn how to do all of this? This is some high-level quantum mechanical crap, boss."

"Oh, you pick things up here and there," Gen dodged, hoping that would satisfy the little man.

"Uh-huh," Peanut answered, unconvinced. "So, how long does this process take?"

"That part is unclear. Depends on how much is in there to decode. Could take an hour, could take a week," Gen shrugged.

"A week—" Peanut said, eyes darting back and forth, "—a lot can happen in a week."

Gen silently agreed.

"But it's the only way," she said, tapping her head, "to get all the important stuff back."

There was no arguing against that. Peanut paced the floor deep in thought. He didn't look completely convinced. He scratched his armpit absently and then mused aloud, "I mean, if we're really taking on General Wexell we could use all the advantages we can muster. In that sense a week isn't so—" Peanut broke his reverie when Gen's Relay snapped into place. She was now seated on the MedBed and keying a sequence into the system interface.

"Wait—" Peanut said, tapping out a nervous little drumbeat on the shelf, "—when do we start?"

"I just did," Gen said as the computers began to click and flash a jumble of light-speed-coded images across the screen. She handed Peanut a remote and pointed out the two highlighted buttons. Basically, idiot-proof. "Reboot. Re-re-reload."

"But how will I know when it's done?" Peanut furrowed his brow.

"You'll kn-kn-kn-know," Gen winced against the electronic invasion and sat back. Inside, she was quite pleased with herself. Yes, there was a high risk this procedure could fail, but at least this way, she would be incapacitated while the download took place, with less chance of giving herself away. Especially given that palpable magnetism between Bastille and Mizuke that was throwing her meat-suit's hormone levels way out of whack. Anyway, once the process was over, she would know everything Bastille knew. More in fact, because currently, Bastille knew nothing. Wherever he was, he was still just a blank slate.

"So, why are you hard-wired into the ship?" Peanut finally asked.

"The d-d-d-data flow of the neur-neur-neural ch-chips is a fr-fre-fre-frequency that can't b-b-be–"

"You know what, forget I asked," he said and slid up into a chair opposite of Gen to begin the wait.

Just then, a massive explosion rocked the ship. All the lights blinked off and on. Peanut looked at Gen. Her eyes glowed white and her face was void of expression. He jumped down and checked the monitors, but it appeared that everything continued to transfer uninterrupted.

Over the comms, Captain Mizuke called "Status Report" to the bridge, and Tanner answered, "Two Bounty Skiffs are flying patterns around us. Outworlders, Captain."

"I'm headed to the Mech Room. Fire up the suit and put some distance between us if you can," Mizuke ordered. "Bastille, what's your position?"

Peanut swore as he moved to comms. "Sorry Captain, Bastille is, uh, in the infirmary until further notice. Um, downloading his brain or something into a Relay box or—? Said we prolly shouldn't shake up the ship too much for the next few hours or, you know… a week."

Static silence on the comms. Peanut cringed.

"All available hands to the bridge," Mizuke growled. "That's an order."

"Aye, Captain," Peanut said and bolted for the door.

* * *

"Damn Snakes," Captain Mizuke swore from the Mech Room, as she finished climbing into her suit. She was lifted high into the air, and the room around her came alive with an ocean of stars. "Where are they, Tanner? I've got nothing on visuals."

On the bridge, Tanner had the helm. He frantically searched the monitors for the slightest registration, but all was still. He shook his head in frustration. "Neither do I, ma'am. They appeared out of nowhere, laid down a few blasts and disappeared again."

"Two ships?" Mizuke clarified.

"Two ships," Tanner said.

"Since when do Outworlders work in pairs?" Mizuke wondered.

"It's a whole new world out there, I guess," Tanner replied.

Just then, a blip registered on the radar, followed by two more blasts, and then it disappeared. From another quadrant, the same thing. So far, shields were deflecting.

"Captain, they must be completely powering down their ships after each bombardment. And then powering up again on a new course."

"You can't power a ship up and down that quickly. That thing was on the scope for all of four seconds."

"Yes, ma'am, they must have figured something out."

"Well, they shouldn't be able to thrust or change vectors if they're powered down, correct?"

Tanner thought that through. "Theoretically, that is correct."

"So the next time they appear, I want distance, speed, and location and after they disappear, I want a list of possible trajectories. I'm gonna light up the sky until we punch metal."

"Can't we just outrun 'em?" Peanut joined Tanner on the bridge, and Moose lumbered in after him.

"They'd just report our location, and suddenly every bounty-hound in the system would drop down on top of us," Mizuke said.

"Here they come," Tanner warned.

Boom, boom, boom.

The *DayStar* shook some more before the enemy specks dropped off the radar.

"I'm gettin' real tired of this, Tee," Mizuke snarled.

"Alright, sending you coordinates… *now*, Captain," Tanner responded. "Possible trajectories on our bogies. Light 'em up."

The captain swung the cannons around and lined up her sites along the computer's trajectory, and fired a rather large spray of ordinance into the black night.

First round, nothing.

Second round, still nothing.

Third round, a small explosion. She targeted that explosion and launched a couple torpedoes in their direction. Suddenly, the ship popped back on radar as the Outworlder powered up to escape. But it was too late. They were blown into stardust.

The second ship also fired up and took off across the sky.

"Shall I pursue them, ma'am?" Tanner asked.

"No, I got this," Mizuke said.

"Are you sure at that range—"

"I said—" she squeezed off a round, leading the target by a respectful distance and holding her breath until the two shapes vectored together in a giant explosion, "—I got this."

"One in a million shot, Cap," Peanut whooped.

"Tanner, get us outta here. I want as much distance between us and that jump gate as possible," Mizuke ordered.

"Aye, Cap'n," he responded.

"Peanut, I need to see you in the infirmary," the Captain added.

"Roger that, on my way." He looked up at Moose who appeared slightly apprehensive. "What are you worried about, you big baby?"

* * *

Peanut walked into the infirmary. The captain sat close to a monitor, trying to decipher the lines of code streaming by.

"What the hell, Peanut?"

"I know, it's a huge mess. Routed through the mainframe, blah blah blah, into the black box, and then when it's done, I hit this button here, reboot the skinbag, then reload all the data."

"Peanut," Mizuke said with a look of concern. "There are maybe three top-level engineers in the universe who know how to do something like this."

Peanut snapped his fingers and pointed at her. "That's what I thought too, but Bastille was all—" Peanut lowered his voice to mimic him, "—'You just pick some things up here and there.'"

Mizuke checked the system pad. "What time was that?"

"I dunno, he called me at 1745, I reckon." Peanut shrugged.

"Well, he left our, uh, *meeting* about 1630. That means in an hour and fifteen minutes, he created a cluster array, hardwired into the ship's mainframe, bypassing our security measures, retro-fitted not one but two

Relay boxes and inserted a make-shift hack straight into his own brainstem."

Peanut kicked at the floor absently, "Sounds hard."

"No, Peanut, it's impossible," Mizuke said, followed by an exasperated sigh. She did not like the conclusions her mind was presenting to her. "Okay, I want Moose down here around the clock. I want binders on this meat-suit and those binders do not come off until we have a full understanding of who it is we're dealing with."

"Jacques Bastille, ma'am," Peanut added as tactfully as he could. "Right? I mean, up in your, uh, *meeting* did you… notice anything, I dunno, different?"

Mizuke crossed her arms defensively. Come to think of it, three orgasms were *not* normal. She suddenly felt a little gross. She ignored Peanut, turned on a boot heel, and walked out.

Peanut turned back around to regard the body. The eyelids danced around as if Bastille were in deep REM sleep. His finger tips also tapped, and occasionally his leg spasmed, too. Peanut hit the comms.

"Moose to infirmary," he said. "Stat."

He then moved over to the shelves, opened a bottom drawer and pulled out the security binders. "I swear, Bastille, we're gonna have to put a bell around your neck or something," he huffed, annoyed at the skinbag.

- 17 -
THE RUINS OF OTHELLO

Qu'Nadi System

The NavCOMM in the small Mandreen catamaran chimed out an incessant warning when the Qu'Nadi system finally appeared on the scopes. Jacques Bastille uncurled his small body from his uncomfortable sleeping position in the upright seat. He tapped the screen, and the alarm was silenced. He yawned and stretched out his arms and legs as far as they could go. One advantage to still being in Gen's small body was the extra space. His feet barely touched the floor.

Catamarans like this were not ideal for long, interstellar trips. Do-able, but barely. For one, unlike his Mustang, they had no sleeping quarters. He'd been stuck for days in this same cramped cockpit. He could not wait to get back on land and, even more so, back into his own skin. Sure, the eyesight and reflexes of a

16-year-old superhuman were pretty fantastic, but there was a strong difference between male and female biology. Or maybe it was chemistry. Anyway, right now, the raging hormones of a teenage girl were undeniably loud and distracting.

He thought of it like flying an unfamiliar ship where the controls were much more sensitive. And some were opposite of what he was trained for and sent him messages that were gibberish to decode. Much like the bounty ship he'd commandeered on Da'karh. Only with this body, he couldn't just reboot it back into EarthPrime. In fact, it had taken him three days to figure out that he wasn't angry or depressed about his whole situation; he was just ovulating. Not to mention, his blood sugars were low and he needed to eat something. He had felt like the world was collapsing cruelly around him, but after some food and a nap, the emotional surge dialed back to a dull roar.

He really didn't know how Genwa'ar could stand it—because she handled this same body with such grace and poise. Meanwhile, he had raged against the sub-console when his deep-space communications went down one morning. That's where the dent in the panel came from as did the dried blood on the knuckle of his right hand. He needed to get back into his own body as soon as possible, but he didn't know where it or the *DayStar* were located right now. He knew where they were last headed, though.

Planet Othello in the Qu'Nadi System.

Wasn't much of a lead, but it was the last known whereabouts of the so-called Fists of Ma'Kobi. Hell, Tavi6 and his entire force could end up here, too, for that matter, since they had been, shall we say, liberated from their permanent living situation on Mandreen. He wasn't sure what his brother's next play would be. He would be rallying to go to war against the Draccarios, that much was for sure. Although Bastille figured that a thousand Ma'kobi warships still wouldn't be enough to battle that juggernaut, *Phaedra's Deliverance*, which he'd seen hatch from the collapsing Shadow Moon.

Actually, there was one ship that could give it a run for its money—the *SCV Bellevue*. Bastille smiled. Even though he could not remember a single battle he'd ever fought on that converted hospital frigate, he knew that under his command, with the right crew, they could take on any force in the universe. The entire idea of it intrigued him because he had no empirical evidence to back that up. But in his heart, he knew it was truth.

Right now, he had no memory of what had become of the ship. Surely it must be in that bastard General Wexell's clutches. A ship that size wouldn't just disappear. And it would explain the recent Dominion show of force. Command the *Bellevue*, control the Milky Way.

Bastille reached up and brushed tears from the corners of his eye.

Dammit!

He couldn't wait to get out of this body.

* * *

As it neared Othello, the Mandreen catamaran raised its outrigger back into storage and fired a couple of retros to slow its approach. It was a beautiful planet, as lush as the Earth had been before the surface wars. Othello was much larger, though, which meant that gravity would not be comparable. It was reading about 2.7g. This was closer to Jupiter's gravity, which was three times what you might experience on Earth. So mark up another bonus for being in a small, nimble superhuman meat-suit.

Bastille had crawled into the lockbox behind his cockpit seat and pulled out the armored flight suit and helmet. That and the squawkbox rifle were standard fare for every long-range Ma'kobi fighter. He knew it would be large for him, but he wanted an extra layer between himself and whatever this planet had to offer.

Settled back into the cockpit, he banked left to circle against the planet's rotation and scout more ground. His NavCOMM searched for readings of any sort, particularly signs of civilization. Plenty of life readings in general. The planet was teeming with animals and vegetation. This could have possibly originated from all the DNA packed into the *seklas* or seed bricks the Croix settlers would have terraformed here to jump-start their Edenic infrastructure. Or it could be that this utopian paradise had already evolved to that point on its own. Hard to say with that crazy group.

The computer alerted Bastille to some energy readings it found around the equatorial line. There was a larger continent to the west, which was separated by an island chain, and then a smaller land mass where the energy spike was geotagged. Double-checking the results, he noticed a landing beacon he could lock onto.

Just on instinct, though, he decided to run a HALO drop. That stood for high altitude, low open. It was meant for paratroopers but he'd used it from time to time with spacecraft. Upon burning into the atmosphere, he killed all power and instruments. Then he let the catamaran simply plummet like a meteor for miles and miles until the ocean began to rush up at him. Muscling the controls manually, he glided into a ground-effect position two meters off the water and fired everything back up. He was 2000 km off-shore, so if he had done his job correctly, he would be close to invisible on radar, right up until the moment where he made landfall. As the engines kicked on, the water behind him plumed up into dual rooster tails, and he zipped forward to the smaller mainland.

It was early evening, yet with the twin suns in the sky, he could imagine it would never be completely dark here, except in some rare eclipse moments. Hence the lush vegetation and climate. Finally, he made landfall over top of a beautiful coastline. Breakwaters burst over the protective reefs. He could almost smell the stale, sulfur smell of the sea water and hear the bird calls echoing across the sky. He pulled gently back on the yoke, and the aircraft climbed to the top of the cliffs. As he cleared them, he picked up another, more familiar signal.

The *DayStar*.

Seeing that signature actually gave him goosebumps, and he started crying again. Happy tears. His only friends in the universe were here waiting for him. Hopefully, Dash was with them. Bastille had not seen nor heard from him since Tavi6's warrior feast. For all he knew, Dash could be back on the Draccario warship.

Bastille figured he'd have to be extra cautious when approaching his team. After the dust-up on Mandreen, they'd just as soon blast Genwa'ar into a thousand particles as risk having to fight her head on. Not to mention this unfamiliar catamaran junker begging to be shot out of the sky.

He throttled back a bit as he came into view of the buildings and homes on the outer edges. They were all overgrown with plant life, which he expected, but they had also sustained structural damage as if they had been bombed out. As he passed over the first colonial residences, he got a better look. The roofs were gone, but the walls were intact although burnt out. The insides had been gouged as if some construction-sized earthmovers had been rooting through the rubble.

The closer he got to the city, the more damage he saw. No dwelling was unscathed. Whatever force had driven them from their homes and off-planet had been very thorough. Home-to-home, actually. Not some large-scale plague or atomic attack, but a meticulous ravaging. He slowed down even more and readied his weapons, even though there were still no life forms reading on the scopes.

Despite their torn-up condition, Bastille could fully appreciate the artistry of St. Croix architecture. If it was possible to describe a building as being fluidly dynamic and seamless, this was it. Grass became hills became trusses became archways became walls became windows became roofs became walls again became rocks became hillsides. Their air travel and skywalks would have negated the need for many roads.

Bastille finally spotted the *DayStar* gleaming in the sunset between a couple of taller buildings. He breathed a sigh of relief to see they hadn't crash-landed. That ugly thought had crossed his mind, along with a dozen others. He circumnavigated a skyscraper for a better view and froze as he cleared the other side.

The entire back half of the *DayStar* had been ripped off. It was completely gone. Not in pieces laying around the area, just… gone. The exposed interior and ground around it were charred, but the front half of the ship sat there unscathed, creating an absurd optical illusion from the front.

One thing was for sure: Whatever had gone from home to home, destroying in its path, was still out there. Bastille immediately dipped the nose of the catamaran into the closest rooftop—or what was left of it—and nestled his landing struts into the rubble. He cut the engines as soon as possible.

Wasting no time, he popped the canopy, which hissed loudly when the seal broke. He grabbed a small supply pack and a Standard Issue Squawk Box Rifle Cannon (SIS-BRC). He hopped down from the lower wing into what used to be a living room and stumbled to a knee in the process.

"Sh*t!" he said, catching himself. This extra gravity would take some getting used to. He clambered up a half-crumbled flight of stairs and squatted down by a shattered open window. He positioned the long gun so he could survey the area with the advanced rifle scope.

As he scanned the area in the vicinity of the *Day-Star*, he saw no signs of movement, human remains, or anything sentient. The crew definitely wasn't on board, or his ship-to-ship scan would have registered something. There were a bunch of taller buildings around, but if they had escaped the ship, Mizuke would know better than to take them up there. She would have taken them…

…there. Into that underground entrance, fifty meters off the *DayStar's* gangplank. Bastille was still checking the area when the gunsight glitched for a second. It was very quick. Almost like a shimmer or a signal hit. Could his eyes be playing tricks? His ill-fitting power suit was already augmenting his muscles to counter the increased gravity, but even the short jaunt up the stairs had winded him. Not to the point he should be hallucinating, though.

He heard a whisper of air movement behind him and then a loud screeching of metal. He whipped around to watch in horror as his ship was lifted straight up and out of the building by a gigantic dragon. The dragon ripped the skiff in half like it was a loaf of bread and inspected the innards as oils and fuel spewed out.

Bastille quickly triggered a sequence into his wrist-comm. He knew he had one shot at using the remaining ordinance on the ship as well as the leakage that was spewing on the undercarriage of the mighty beast. The dragon was about to lose interest in the wreckage, when the ship began to beep and whir and come alive.

What seemed like an eternity later, but was possibly only seven seconds, the catamaran exploded into a thousand fiery shards. The dragon reeled back as it caught fire and plowed through a building structure below, furious.

Bastille didn't need an invitation to move. He jumped right out of the window, sliding down the building's angled front face for about five stories, and then jumping to his feet near the bottom, where the engineered wall fiber merged seamlessly into an unkempt grassy terrace. Pieces of his destroyed ship ricocheted off the building behind him, littering the area with burning flotsam. The fuselage crashed through one of the archways right after Bastille scrambled past, exploding behind him.

He rounded the building and stopped there to catch his breath. Peeking back around the corner, he checked the dragon's progress. It had finally righted itself and was clawing up to the sky in a cloud of black smoke. One wing definitely seemed a little gimpy after that. Another explosion went off, and the dragon roared back at it defiantly.

Bastille ran safely into an alleyway of buildings at his top speed, such that it was. His plan had a couple of bugs in it, which he allowed. One of them was whether or not the door he was aiming for was even unlocked. Worst case scenario, the squawk box would handle that, though. Secondly, the dragon was punishing the wreckage of his catamaran, but it would begin hunting again. These things were savagely smart. And unlike the "domesticated" version back on the Shadow Moon, this feral Battle Dragon had no rider to reign it in. It was living, breathing carnage. And it was pissed as hell.

Bastille stopped inside another alcove, worried his poor little heart might burst. In most other Byno-Cores, it may have by now. Very evenly, he sucked air in through his nose out through his mouth. He heard the enemy dragon screech. It was way off in the distance, and that gave him hope. But, then he heard an echo—high to his right. No, not an echo. Another shadow passed over the buildings as a second airborne beast entered the kill zone. Bastille pressed himself deeper into the corner and let it pass. He was about to step forward when a third screech reverberated from another part of the city. Bastille swore. Three of these things? This was getting ridiculous.

One of the dragons took off into the sky. Bastille made a run for safety and made it beneath the *DayStar*. He tucked himself behind the front landing strut, gulping for air. Now the top dragon was circling above from a keen vantage point from which it could watch the entire city for movement.

The first dragon, the wounded and angry one, was now tracking the alien scent along the ground. Bastille looked back where he had run from and could hear the thing rooting through the same alleyway he had passed through just a few minutes before. But those two didn't worry him as much as the third one, that he couldn't see or hear.

He looked back toward his destination. The miracle door. Fifty meters back on Earth on a good day was a solid six- to eight-second sprint. This body with Othello's gravity and this flight suit, backpack, and cannon? He'd be pounced before he got ten steps out into the open. He was losing time. Those things were closing in.

The earlier explosions messed with his ears a little. Some lingering tinnitus, maybe. There was a faint ringing, almost a buzz, that began to get louder and louder. Bastille almost couldn't concentrate.

Suddenly, the *DayStar* dipped on top of him. Exactly as if a gigantic weight had settled upon it. There was a deep, guttural wretching sound, and then some sewage splashed down in front of Bastille. And in the middle of the sewage was half of a man who bore a resemblance to poor Tanner, the *DayStar's* engineer. Albeit, a very digested Tanner.

This could have been a primal thing the dragon was doing. You don't fight on a full stomach, so it may have just been prepping for battle. But at the same time, knowing the intelligence of these creatures, Bastille took it as a personal display of force. Sort of a dragon-y, "Look here at your future, mortal."

Bastille turned again to the door. Was his mind playing tricks again? No, it had been closed up until this point, and now it was clearly propped open by about six inches. Bastille quietly pulled the cannon over his back and cinched it tight around his shoulder. It would be of no help here. He was just going to have to kamikaze run for it.

Three things happened next, almost simultaneously. The first dragon, the wounded one, broke into the town square and saw Bastille. Unmistakably clear. Then, gunfire from a nearby rooftop erupted, which drew the attention of the Alpha perched atop the *DayStar*. And lastly? Bastille ran. He ran as fast as that 16-

year-old superbody could run, and then he pushed it one step beyond. As he cleared the ship's shadow, he could see two human forms jumping from the rooftop, firing as they fell toward a second-story balcony. One was a hulking mass doing the daring parkour. The other was a tiny man on his back spraying down suppressive fire.

Moose and Peanut!

Bastille would have been dead if not for their intervention because the distance to their sniper's nest was four times as great as his own to the safety door, and the Alpha Dragon covered that in three seconds. Bastille could hear the other two dragons echoing a warning cry. The door kicked open all the way, and Bastille dove headlong inside as it slammed shut behind him.

Hands grabbed at him in the dark and pulled him back further into the cavernous hallway and around a corner, which was a good thing because the fire-spray that erupted at the front entrance would have cooked them instantly. Liquid flames entered every crevasse around the iron door, and the hallway lit up brightly. Bastille scrambled to his feet to follow along behind his rescuer, who he could see now was Mizuke Strouthers.

He followed her through another hallway and down a stairwell into a basement. They navigated a whole network of doors and shafts until they finally got to a larger holding area. That's when Mizuke spun around with a Mauzer in her hand. His Mauzer.

"That's far enough, Miss," she said, panting. They were both out of breath. "Now, we just saved your bacon, and we'll be needing to know who owes us that life debt," she fired it up, and it hummed readily.

Bastille held both hands in the air. He reached for his helmet and pulled it off slowly. His blonde hair cascaded down his shoulders. "That's twice you've pulled my own gun on me, Love."

"Nooooo way," she said incredulously.

Just then, Moose and Peanut ran in from another entrance, huffing and puffing. Well, Peanut was huffing and puffing, but Moose was Moose.

"Who we got?" Peanut said, dismounting.

"Says she's Jacques Bastille," Mizuke answered with a smirk.

"Funny. We already got ourselves a Jacques Bastille," Peanut said, throwing a thumb towards a back room.

Bastille smiled evenly. "I doubt it, pocket monkey. But this, I guarantee, you put me in a room with *that* Jacques Bastille, and only one true Ma'kobi King emerges."

Mizuke and Peanut looked at each other and shrugged.

"Sure," Peanut answered while Moose stepped behind Bastille to relieve him from his Squawk Box and pack.

Peanut then led the way as Mizuke and Moose fell in behind. Mizuke kept the Mauzer trained on him the whole time. They walked through another door, and the area suddenly looked a lot less bomb shelter-ish and revealed some advanced research and development laboratories. It even had electricity. Those Draccario engineers sure thought of everything. Well, not *everything,* or else they wouldn't have been eaten alive and run off by their own house pets. But they had certainly thought of a lot.

At the main lab, they walked in, and Peanut stepped to the side. Bastille froze in the doorway until Mizuke nudged him forward with the nose of the Mauzer.

"What the hell did you do?" Bastille said. He went over to a large tank in the middle of the room. It looked like all the Cryo-tanks he had seen before, only this one had his old body floating in the middle. That was the good news. The bad news was that it was cut into two distinct pieces: an upper half and a lower half.

"It took the three of us a few days just to figure this much out. But the body and tissue are being pre-served now," Mizuke explained. "There may be a way to repair it somehow, but it's not like the Draccario techs left any instruction manuals laying around."

"Wh-what happened?" Bastille said, leaning his forehead against the glass. He was starting to hyperven-tilate.

"You're not gonna faint are you, little girl?" Peanut broke into a wide, toothy grin.

With the strenuous activity of the last 10 minutes and the planet's extreme gravity and thinner at-mosphere, Bastille's body was shaking. He realized he hadn't eaten since he hit the Qu'Nadi System, and he suddenly regretted all of it. As the world around him slowly blacked out, he fell to the ground like a rag doll.

Fzzzzzzzht.

- 18 -

THE KYTOS ALLIANCE

Neo Tokyo

Dash Strouthers slowly became aware of his surroundings. The last thing he remembered was getting blasted from the sky in his HX-45 Marauder somewhere over the Pacific. It was during an attack lead by Colonel Wexell's Dominators and those damned Manglers. Or, wait, maybe he had been eating a giant roasted bug on Mandreen with Savvy Tavi and his Ma'Kobi warriors. Both felt like real memories, and neither felt like a dream. But it didn't make sense. Shouldn't he be dead right now? Wexell's slavers were never too keen on leaving witnesses alive.

Dash was hooked up to a mobile medical box, monitoring his vitals. An IV ran fluids into the crook of his arm. This wasn't the *Bellevue*, though. It couldn't be because there was no motion in the room. He decided he was land-based. Besides, this wasn't a full-fledged Med-unit like they had on the hospital transport, rather some sort of makeshift field hospital.

Nobody was in the small room with him. He wasn't restrained in any way, but that didn't mean much. The door looked solid, and the room was sparse enough to be a holding cell. Dash systematically tested his muscles to make sure everything was operational.

Feeling pretty good, he went to roll onto his side and yelped as a sharp pain bit into his abdomen. Tears streamed down his face as he sat up, sucking shallow breaths to keep from passing out. Ignoring the searing pain, he carefully peeled up his shirt to reveal a bandage. Something had gotten him bad. And while he couldn't be certain without an x-ray, it also felt like the time he'd busted a rib in boot camp.

Suddenly, the door swooshed open, and shadowy figures rushed in. Dash surged to his feet—

"You wanna fight auuggghh—"

—and then crumpled to the floor.

"Dash, you idiot, what are you doing? Lay down," Major Step Phillips said, rushing to help him back up to the bed.

Gator was at his other arm, scooping him up off the floor. "He's for sure ruptured his seams again, Major," Gator said, none too happy about it. "Can't believe you tried to take on an entire Mangler squad by yourself, what were you thinking?"

"Th-they, aughhh, they got Mizuke. That was real, right?" Dash winced as they laid him back down.

"Yes, I know." Step situated Dash's head down on the pillow. She swung his legs atop the bed. "A whole sh*t ton o' sunshine has gone down while you were out. NeoTokyo is under curfew. Draccario citizens are being rounded up and hauled off God knows where by Wexell's Fugs. The whole planet's on the brink. The *Bellevue* attack was an act of war. News outlets already have a name for it. They're calling it the Surface Wars."

Dash settled a little easier. The pain began to disappear all at once. He opened his eyes and saw Gator withdrawing a Vancinex shot from his stomach.

"Dash," Gator said, "I hate to do this, bud, but we are on a super tight schedule. We've got to get to the sub tonight or we won't make it back to Bravo Bay. And Dash," he leaned in closer in an excited whisper, "word is KACorps just delivered the H2 prototype."

"The wh-what?" Dash fell into a bit of a fog as the drug dulled the pain receptors in his brain.

Step chimed in, "It's called the Mustang. Top Secret joint project between the Draccario and KACorps Black Ops. Supposed to even the odds against the New Dominion faction. But we gotta get back there tonight before the lockdown."

"With or without you." Gator shrugged.

"Eat a dick, Gator," Dash struggled to say. "I'm not going anywhere."

Gator smiled. "Not quite, partner," he said, holding up one more Med-gun and wiggling it around.

Dash eyed it warily. "What's that one gonna do?"

"This one opens a beautiful can of whoop-ass. You're gonna feel like you can out-wrestle a sea condor in heat, but it wears off quickly, so pace yourself."

"And mind your squiffing bandages," Step implored him.

"Yeah, try not to bleed out all over the place," Gator added with a wink.

"Hit me, asshole," Dash said.

Gator did. The mist from the metal tip had barely evaporated when Dash sat bolt upright in the bed. He looked like he was screaming, but no sound came out. Gator and Step looked at each other .

"Breeeeeeeathe," she said, placing her hand on his chest.

Dash took in a long gush of air. When he exhaled, his breath was frosty. He took another deep breath. And then another. And then his face returned to normal.

"Fun," Gator said, and stood up.

Step rose as well, and Dash leapt to his feet, shaking his arms and legs like a track runner prepping for their heat. They steered him toward his clothes and helped him pull some things on.

Gator took Dash's gun and stuffed it into the back of his pants; then after a nod, they exited.

* * *

NeoTokyo was one of the first underwater cities they had built before the Third World War. It was finished around the time of what had come to be known as the Earth Singularity, an explosion that vaporized 1/8 of the Earth. The planet hemorrhaged and wreaked havoc around the globe for decades until the environs finally stabilized into a proliferation stage.

Meanwhile, the air became toxic. The ground shifted, and temperatures rose, as did the waterline. Continents were unrecognizable. If it hadn't been for NeoTokyo and the Space Colonies, mankind could have been completely wiped out.

That was almost 200 years ago. NeoTokyo was the center of life and commerce on the planet. Other pockets and underwater cities had sprung up around the world, such as Miramar, but politically speaking, NeoTokyo was KACorps territory. Wexell's New Dominion campaign threatened to upheave all of it.

Dash, Step, and Gator took the Redline tube down to the Dockside District. An elderly subway guard worked his way down the crowded car, visually scanning each face with his advanced helmet tech and cataloging them. Just routine. He was on complete autopilot. At this hour, everyone was headed home from work and attempting to get a jump on the curfew.

The guard perked up when an overhead chime noted the Dockside stop approaching. Three unblinking LED blue lights on his visor swept the car from head to tail. But nobody moved. No one would be foolish enough to head to the docks this time of night. He scanned the crowd as the trains slowed to a stop. The doors opened. The guard looked around, but everyone remained in place. The doors closed, and the train started back in motion again.

The guard shrugged and continued scanning the crowds. He came to Dash, Step, and Gator, and the facial recognition posted an error in his HUD. He scanned the three again. Nothing. He lifted his visor and saw an augmented reality puck on the empty seat before him.

Suddenly, he was barking commands into his comm and running for the front of the train.

* * *

As the train pulled away, a hologram shimmered and disintegrated, revealing Dash, Step, and Gator in special holo-gear. Those sucked up a lot of power, and the batteries were drained, so the oversized coveralls were useless now. They all unzipped and stepped out of them. Gator rolled them up and stuffed them back into the duffel, then slung it over his shoulder again. Signaling with a hand motion, they all moved quietly between the vacant buildings toward the Seagate.

Huge portals all around them showcased the vast oceans just outside. This see-through titanium window technology was newer. The ocean would have crushed the early iterations of this dwelling space if it hadn't been shrewdly constructed within the rocks and reefs of the ocean floor. But those were windowless, reinforced capsules. Now, you could watch a pod of whales drift by, peeking curiously in, as they did now, on three humans running quickly along the hallways.

Gator rang for the lift, and they took it down to the lowest level where they spotted the HX-45 tethered in a tank, suspended just over the waterline. Gator triggered the sub with his Relay, and the top hatch opened. All three of them climbed down the ladder. Dash followed the other two and missed the last couple of rungs, crashing to the floor.

"Dash!" Step rushed to his side.

Dash didn't even attempt to get back up. The meds had worn off. "I'm, I'm just gonna take a little nap right here if you don't mind," he smiled weakly.

"I'll grab a blanket," Step said, patting his shoulder sympathetically. "With any luck, when you wake up, we'll be back in sunshine-y Bravo Bay."

Dash gave a thumbs up and winced as the Marauder shuddered to life. "Ow," he said loudly enough for Gator's benefit.

"Sorry," Gator said back over his shoulder from the elevated cockpit. "But if that hurt, then this next part is not gonna feel very—"

He mashed a button, and the HX-45 unclamped from its dry dock battens and dropped to the waterline with a splash.

"—pleasant," Gator finished.

"OWWWW!" Dash groaned.

"Tickles, don't it?" Gator said, goosing the throttle, which immediately pulled them below the surface. He guided them out of the back gates and away from NeoTokyo as quickly as possible.

Had they been civilians, they would have had to out-process and have their digital visas stamped, and never would have made it into open water. But being part of the KACorps Black Ops gave them certain privileges. The D/U/G guarding the exit let them pass without delay. For now, anyway. Who knew what the future would bring as the Surface Wars spread.

Step returned with a blanket, pillow, and another Med-gun. "Looky what I found. A night cap."

Dash ignored her, staring past her into the distance. "Step, they marked Mizuke for the slaver's ring. We've gotta find her."

"We've got our whole network on high alert," Step assured him, sliding her hand into his. "We'll find her, Dash. And we'll bring her home. We just—it's just hard to know who to even trust right now. Those Dominion spies run deep."

"The whole world's gone mad." Dash winced as she adjusted the pillow under his neck.

"Well, you still have us," she squeezed his hand.

"Hey," Gator interrupted. "Speak for yourself, lady. I voted to leave him for fish food. A lot of trouble for one lousy pilot."

Step leaned in close to Dash, whispering, "He didn't sleep for four days since you went off-grid."

Dash smiled back. Step held up the Med-gun and he nodded. "Hit me."

"Sweet dreams," Step pressed the metal tip to his neck and pulled the trigger.

Fzzzzzzzht.

* * *

Othello's Ruins

Jacques opened his eyes and lifted a hand to push back the long blonde hair tangled everywhere. Fantastic. He was still in the Genwa'ar host body. It occurred to him that this was the first time in the past week that he'd triggered a Dash memory. Ever since he'd landed in Gen's Byno-Core he hadn't had even the whisper of a flashback. Until now. Maybe it was Dash's way of revealing that he was still around. Somewhere.

A hand moved under his pillow, and it was not his own. His two tiny mitts were accounted for. He looked over, and Mizuke lay there, nestled close, watching him slowly come back to life.

"What?" He stretched out with a yawn.

"You're adorable," she said, playing with a strand of his hair.

"Hey, my eyes are up here, lady," he smirked back at her.

"This is weird, Jacques Bastille," Mizuke admitted.

"No kidding," he agreed as he propped up onto an elbow. "The sooner I get back to my own skinbag, the better."

"Yeah, but your other body is a little—" she made a chop-chop hand motion.

"I know," he answered, shaking his head sadly. "I know. It's not ideal. We'll figure it out. Somehow. I cannot stay like this much longer." He held up one of his own hands, checking the details on the front and back of it. Mizuke took it in her own hand, intertwining their fingers.

"I was worried about you," Mizuke confided, wiggling a little closer to him.

"Well, we're hardly out of—"

"No, shut up and listen. I've been on my own for years now. Me, my ship, and my crew. My job keeping everyone alive. I didn't think I could ever…" She paused and searched for the right words. "I didn't think I could ever do… this… kind of thing again. And then, there you were. And I knew you instantly as if I'd known you forever, and yet I don't really know you at all. You're a complete stranger. And I hate the fact that part of me missed part of you when you were back on Mandreen."

"Mizuke—"

She put her finger against his lips, cutting him off. "Shhhh. I'm not—I mean I don't want… anything. I just need you to know that once upon a time, I was dead inside. Completely dead. And now, I'm beginning to feel things again. Even just… a glimmer of hope. And I *hate* you for that. I *despise* you for that, Jacques Bastille."

She grabbed a handful of his hair, as if to emphasize her words, and then she leaned in and kissed his lips. And he kissed back. A kiss that ended as abruptly as it began.

"What's wrong?" Mizuke said as he climbed quickly from the bed.

"Yeah, this body feels *very* strange right now," he said, straightening his tank top. "I like all the things you just said. For the record, I totally agree with all of it. I just—this," he indicated his chest, "and this," he indicated lower, "not me. I need me. I need my mind, my body, my memories—I need me. Before I go crazy."

"Of course," she said, climbing from the bed to dress alongside him. "I get it," she assured him. Mizuke watched him over her shoulder. He seemed to be deep in thought.

"By the way," he said. "What actually happened to the other body, old half and half?"

"It was insane, actually." Mizuke scrunched her brow, recalling the scene. "First we figured out it wasn't you. It was Gen. That was a whole thing. And then, Gen had this idea that she could somehow mind-control the dragon. The big dragon. It's hard to explain. I think she was delusional, myself, but after we landed, they attacked the ship, and we're all running for our lives. They grab Tanner—he's screaming—and we turn around, and Genwa'ar is face-to-face with the Alpha."

"What do you mean face-to-face?" Bastille pulled his head through a turtleneck and looked back at Mizuke.

"They were both standing there, like eight feet from each other, staring at each other. Like—I dunno."

"Like what?"

"Like—this sounds dumb—like they knew each other? And then the next minute, this thing claws her in half, and she's lying there bleeding out. And it just… flies off."

"Huh," Bastille said as he pulled his boots on and then stood. "Seen any signs of Dash?"

"I, honestly—I thought he was with you." Mizuke stood and took her pistol from under her side of the mattress and holstered it across the small of her back.

"Maybe. I don't know where the hell he went," Bastille said, waving at the air. "And Gen is floating around somewhere, too, now?"

"I don't know. I really don't know how this works anymore. It's not like anyone else is skin-surfing right? Just you three, apparently. If it's a superpower or a genetic leap in evolution or a Draccario magic trick, then it's a very small, exclusive club."

"On Phaedra, all of them could do it." Bastille said, trying unsuccessfully to do something with his long hair. "They've always been light years ahead of the rest of us. Dammit, this hair is a rat's nest. I should just chop it like yours and be done."

"It's fine." Mizuke stifled a laugh and walked over. "Let me," she said, pulling his hair back. Breaking it down into three strands, she very quickly fashioned a nice, loose braid.

"I get that the mind and body are just organic computers," Bastille mused, still on the superpower comment. "If anything, Gen and the Croix have found a genetic loophole that they're exploiting. Ow."

"Hold still," Mizuke said, grabbing his shoulders to steady him. She then finished the top-half braid and then held up two hair scrunchies. "Pink or black?"

Bastille snorted and folded his arms across his chest. "Could we not?"

Mizuke chuckled at his discomfort and then slipped the black scrunchy into place, leaving the rest of the hair to dangle in a pony. She gave an approving nod. "One thing you should know, Jacques, when Gen was on the ship, as you, she tied into the mainframe, hardwired her cerebral cortex through her Relay box, and downloaded all the damaged memory out to storage and back."

"What?" He turned back from the mirror and faced Mizuke.

She nodded. "She rebooted your system. The Dash 2.0 was wiped and reloaded. Everything back in place."

"How is that—nevermind." Bastille rubbed his forehead, trying to comprehend the whole scenario. "So you're saying I might have all my memory back?"

"Yes. If you get back into your own body, you may have full, one hundred percent access to everything again." Mizuke smiled. It really was the first great news they'd all had in a long time.

Bastille's face lit up. He was so excited he threw his arms around Mizuke and kissed her full on the lips. A knock on the door caused them to take a step back. Peanut stood there sheepishly.

"Uuuhhhh, I don't mean to interrupt, ladies. I reeeeeally don't, trust me," he shifted back and forth awkwardly. "But Captain, you're gonna want to see this. Captains. Plural. You two."

"We got it," Mizuke scowled at him and headed out the door, pulling on a jacket. Peanut stood there, staring back at Bastille who stopped right in front of him.

"What?" Bastille said, trying to read his friend.

"Just trying to wrap my head around the two of you—"

"Don't," Bastille interrupted, annoyed. "I meant, what's going on up there?"

"I think Dash is back?" Peanut replied, scrunching his mouth into a frown. It was more of a question than a statement.

They both exited quickly and caught up with Mizuke at the lift.

* * *

In the medical vat, something had been activated. The whole area glowed blue. Inside, a tiny NIT swarm encircled the Byno-Core's midsection, ever so slowly stitching both halves back together. From the inside out. The nanoids were about six percent done with the repair procedure, the monitors showed.

"How long?" Mizuke asked, checking the vitals.

"About 45 minutes ago, we came in because we heard strange noises and thought maybe those dragons had, I dunno, snuck up on us. Or Tanner was back from the dead. It's been a long week, okay? Scared the crap outta us. But when we finally busted in, this thing was goin' apesh*t. Stitching away just like—" Peanut gestured both hands at the machine.

Bastille took a step closer and turned aside to Mizuke. "Dash or Gen would both have the knowledge to do this. It could be either one of them."

Mizuke nodded. "The question is, when they're through with repairs, are they going to take back control of that body? If so, we're gonna have problems."

She was right. The team didn't need an internal battle to fight as well as the three fire-breathing monsters to deal with on the outside. Not to mention the small matter of not having a functional ship to get them off-planet.

"I calculate about 12.5 hours at this speed before this skinbag is done," Peanut said, pointing to one of the computer readouts.

Bastille became aware again of that ringing in his ears. It was faint, but still there. Hopefully, he didn't have the onset of tinnitus. But it was very persistent, whatever it was.

Moose came into the room a few seconds later and gestured to Peanut.

"The SkyLizards are back." Peanut translated for them.

"What could they want?" Mizuke wondered. "They've never hung around here before."

"Breakfast?" Peanut shrugged.

"Do you think the dragons are making that ringing sound?" Bastille asked, jiggling a finger in his ear.

Everyone in the room looked at each other and then back at him. "What ringing sound?" Mizuke asked.

"The—" Bastille looked around at their clueless faces and then pulled his finger from his ear. "Nothing. It's gone now."

It wasn't. It was getting louder.

"You okay, boss?" Peanut squinted at him.

"Yeah, so have you got a good vantage spot to see these dragons?" Bastille asked.

"Thought you'd never ask," Peanut said proudly. "Come on. Front row seats."

They started out the door, and Bastille took one more look back at the MedVAT. Seven percent.

* * *

After a few minutes of climbing stairwells and jumping small crevasses between buildings, they arrived at the watch tower. Peanut carefully led the way, pointing out obstacles or loose rocks along the trail. Moose pulled up the rear. He had to duck through most of the low-hanging portals.

As they emerged onto the enclosed observatory deck, Bastille looked around. This was like an above-ground bunker. It reminded him of the control towers at the old airbases. Obviously, this one was fortified with something more than the rest of the city, making it impervious to attack. It had to be, since this area and the laboratory deep below the earth were the only intact areas left in the whole city. They moved quickly through a connecting breezeway between the two, keeping a close watch on the open sky through the exposed ceilings.

They climbed one last flight of spiral stairs before finding themselves inside the overwatch tower. It was a breathtaking spectacle. An unimpeded 360-degree view of the entire city.

"There's a hatch at the top of this ladder, here, but we're not dumb enough to open it. This room completely shields us from the dragons. They can't see us, or smell us, or hear us," Peanut bragged. "We can watch the bastards completely unnoticed."

He looked to Moose for backup, but Moose lifted a finger to point out the window. Mizuke saw it, too.

"Then why is the Alpha looking this way?" Mizuke said quietly.

"Bugger me," Peanut said, backing away a little bit, startled.

The largest of the dragons sprang into the air and casually flapped toward the tower. As it did so, the ringing in Bastille's ears grew louder and louder. He began to wince, but nobody else seemed to be affected. Bastille couldn't explain how, but he knew that the Alpha was responsible for the noise.

Peanut whispered, "We better get back down. Big Fella knows we're in here." His foot was already at the top of the stairs. The others nodded in silent consensus, and Peanut led the way back downstairs.

The dragon landed just outside the tower terrace and stood there, his eyes piercing through the smokey glass windows. Peering right into Bastille's soul. The others had gone, but he hadn't been able to move.

Mizuke was halfway down the spiral when she heard a door latch and realized Bastille wasn't with them. "Jacques!" She yelled and they all turned and quickly ran back upstairs. As they re-entered the tower, they just caught Bastille exiting the top hatch. He stepped out on top of the tower. And the dragon, whose tail wrapped halfway around the building, stood right there, waiting to strike.

Bastille closed the hatch behind himself. This was a one-way trip. The ringing was excruciating. The dragon flared its nostrils and moved closer. Its hind feet were on the terrace below, but its front feet gripped the tower top. The Alpha raised up to his full height, staring at the unfamiliar human female in front of him.

Bastille also rose to his full height, such as it was, and walked forward. He looked the dragon right in the eye. The dragon blinked. He snorted once, and steam shot from his nostrils and singed the hair off Bastille's arms, but he showed no fear. Didn't even flinch. The dragon blinked again, and a second inner eyelid, like the membrane of a cat's eye, pulled open. The minute that his naked eye was exposed, the ringing stopped. More accurately, the buzzing became understandable, as if an ancient uplink had occurred.

Fzzzzzzzht.

* * *

NeoTokyo

Dash watched the little Draccario pug as its breathing returned to normal, as it calmed and settled into this little staring contest, as his own breathing calmed. He looked into those steely gray eyes. A creature so ugly, it was beautiful. And then the uplink clicked.

'*R'zar,*' the tiny creature said.

Fzzzzzzzht.

* * *

Othello's Ruins

Bastille heard the dragon's thoughts and blurted out, "R'zar!"

'*Who are you?*' The beast snorted menacingly. '*Why do you possess the Dragon-eye?*'

"I am Jacques Bastille," he said, hoping that was enough. Truth be told, he was just happy to not be dead yet. Or swiped in two.

'*This name is unfamiliar. Your form is unfamiliar. But your essence is… true,*' the dragon said as he studied him closely. '*I accept your claim to an alliance with the—*'

A loud screech to their right announced that the other dragon was bearing down fast. The one Bastille had wounded by self-destructing the catamaran. The angry lizard dove to snatch Bastille, but the Alpha batted it away with his tail, growling back. The dragon retreated. The third circled high in the sky. Watching. Waiting.

'He said I should rip you in two and dine on your flesh.'

Bastille waited, not knowing how to answer that. Was this some sort of dragon humor? He held out his arms to the side as if to say, 'Here I am; come and get me.'

'We have much to discuss. Come, Dragon-eye.' R'zar craned his neck forward, as close to the roof ledge as possible.

For the first time, Bastille noticed the scales beneath its ear canal jutted out to form little prehistoric stairs. Something you would never notice unless a dragon submitted itself to you.

Bastille carefully climbed up until he was on the back of the mighty beast. He turned to the roof, and the hatch was open. Moose was standing there with the Squawk box leveled at them. The others stood in his protective shadow, wonder and confusion on their faces.

"It's okay," Bastille yelled. They were not buying that. He smiled and tried not to seem nervous. "Wait for me below. I'll be back," he assured them. "I think."

Moose lowered the gun. Peanut watched the other dragon circling high overhead. Mizuke pulled them all back below, into the tower's safety.

'*Hold on,*' the dragon commanded.

Bastille found that he could wedge his legs up under the scales, where they overlapped. The scales were as hard as granite, but there was a protective skin layer overtop that made the dragon hide feel like so much a leather saddle. Kind of like the Cyrenium shell on the Mustang. But that's where the comparisons ended. There were eight or nine foot-long, coarse hairs. Bastille wrapped one around each hand like the reins of a horse. It was the perfect grip. Satisfied, the dragon leapt into the air, its powerful wings sweeping them higher and higher into the thermals above the city, where they could relax and soar.

It was truly a sight to behold. And for a pilot, this was the closest thing Bastille would ever have to free-flying on his own. No cockpit in the universe would match this feeling. The wind whipping at his face, the huge creature moving beneath him so smoothly as they glided aloft.

'*I am R'zar,*' said the animal, bellowing proudly.

The name carried a weight to it. The word resonated within Bastille, and he knew immediately that there was an ancestry and a nobleness and power with that name. Perhaps one day he would fully understand in his own language the fullness of the name, but for now, just the name itself when it was spoken aloud gave him goosebumps.

- 19 -

AIRBORN

R'zar, Ga'al, and Tr'm—those were the three dragons that ruled over the Ruins of Othello. R'zar led the pack high into the air and bore Bastille up and over a particular mountain ridge, where an ocean of clouds cascaded down the leeward side in slow motion. In the valley below, there appeared to be a large, abandoned Draccario space port.

Draccario. That name would have a completely different implication throughout the galaxy once word of these Battle Dragons got out. No longer those laughable little test tube lizards. They were now a force to be reckoned with. They could be communicated with, harnessed—not 'tamed', not 'domesticated' because those words required mastery and servanthood. This would be a partnership of the deepest levels, a covenant of man and beast. They could conceivably provide the tipping point in a land war or aerial battle. He doubted they'd be much help in space, but Bastille knew that an alliance with the Battle Dragons would bring their suicidal mission against General Wexell further into the realm of survivability.

Nobody knew the full capabilities of these magnificent beasts. There was no military course devised—outside of fiction—that factored in a dragon battalion.

'We shall be your fists,' R'zar said, clearly overhearing Bastille's every thought. There would be no secrets here.

They glided down in large, winged circles, landing gently at the mouth of a gigantic, fortified hangar. R'zar hunched his right shoulder down, and Bastille slid down to the ground. The dragon approached the doors, and Bastille watched, intrigued, as a scan flashed over the dragon's face and the huge metallic doors began to groan and creak and slowly ease apart.

Bastille followed R'zar inside. The dragons must have nested here for 20 years or more. Rooftops and bones littered the entrance. The skeleton of some massive sea creature that would have made one helluva feast. Broken walls, mounds of junk. Wending through it all, Bastille struggled to keep up. He still had not fully acclimated to this planet's gravity or Gen's Byno-Core.

As the main hangar doors closed, the dragon fired up its chest cavity that contained a molten core—not agitated enough to spew forth, just stirred up enough to cause his chest to glow a deep orange, which cast a strange soft light about the room.

Bastille struggled on through the boneyard. Finally, the path cleared up, and he reached the edge of the tide of garbage, where his foot came down on a metallic ramp leading upwards. The dragon plodded forward and mentally triggered a switch at the top.

Lights began to *clack, clack, clack* all the way up the cavernous interior. Bastille knew immediately what this was. It was an A-Class freighter. No, it had to be bigger than that if this was just the cargo hold. Double-A Class, perhaps. Whatever the Draccario engineers had built with all their technology, this was the pinnacle. The pinnacle 20 or 30 years ago, that is. And they had knowingly designed it with the Battle Dragons in mind. Hence the cyber-link capabilities.

Inside the cargo space, there were holding areas for six mighty beasts. Beds, if the analogy didn't seem so base for these majestic warlords. Thrones, more like. R'zar had chewed down the barrier between two of the spaces to create one large enough to accommodate himself. Someone had underestimated his size and growth. For all Bastille knew, the dragon could still be growing through his "teen" years.

As R'zar passed a huge stack of trees—roots and all—he pulled one into his space and plopped down, taking a huge bite out of a prickly green section. Bastille knew that smell. Pine. That supported his initial speculation that all of this area's vegetation derived from seed bricks. No wonder it all seemed familiar.

He sat down on a nearby block and watched the dragon's sharp teeth grind away at this snack. He waited patiently because he knew the beast would talk in its own time. They were off to a tenuous treaty of sorts, and he didn't want to upset or dishonor it and risk a vital alliance—or worse—a ride back to the city. Anyway, he was grateful to not have been sliced in half like Gen or chewed up like Tanner.

* * *

Bastille had moved to the floor. Scraping together some loose pine needles, he had fashioned a small pile into a pillow. Any chance to rest in these extreme gravity conditions, the better. A half-hour must have passed when R'zar swallowed the last big mouthful and then emitted a huge noise that reverberated through the hall and could have been a dragon sigh or a belch. Bastille was unsure. The dragon closed his eyes.

'*Our alliance with the Croix has ended,*' the large one finally spoke.

Bastille rolled over to his side and propped up on an elbow to observe the dragon more carefully.

'*They became blinded by petty ambitions. Fractured at the top. They no longer wish to know the ways or the truth the universe holds, much less to serve it. They wish to rule it all. Such ambition is not the dragon way,*' R'zar explained.

"But there is one Battle Dragon who rides with the Croix," Bastille recalled.

'*T'mor. The traitor. The runt will be ended when next we encounter,*' the beast promised. And a dragon promise—interwoven with a keen intuition bordering on prescience—is the highest promise of all. Once spoken, it cannot be broken.

Bastille worded his next question very carefully. "What—happened here?"

'*A prophecy arose of an epic armageddon. And one who would lead us into battle. Back to Mother Earth. Fight-*

ing broke out as to who that leader would be. Factions formed. A peaceful society was splintered. At that time, the dragons had selected no riders, and so ill, unsuitable choices were foisted upon us. Weak ones. Weak of heart. Weak of spirit. We rejected them and were forced into battle for our own freedom. We lost two great ones, but the dragons prevailed and drove them back into the heavens. For years, we awaited the one,' he said. After that, the dragon remained silent for some time. Bastille thought maybe he'd gone to sleep.

"And now—?" Bastille pressed.

'And now, you take your place atop the Scarlet Libellule, *and we ride out,'* the dragon explained.

"The *Scarlet Libellule*?" Bastille asked. He recalled the name from Dash's briefing aboard the *DayStar*.

The dragon raised its head and opened its eyes, and a low rumble began. Bastille thought it was the dragon himself, but the vibration grew until the whole cargo bay shook with energy. Bastille jumped to his feet. This ship was not wreckage, as had been reported to them. This ship was alive. The *Libellule* was operational. He looked back to the dragon, who flashed inside his mind the image of the bridge. That was a neat trick. Like downloading a file from the StarNET. One minute the ship was a complete mystery, the next minute he knew the entire layout. Just by hanging out with R'zar, he was beginning to know things he'd never learned.

Bastille nodded and took off running. It took three minutes just to clear the steerage hold. By the time he made it to the conning tower, the ship's engines had been preheating for a good fifteen minutes. Bastille got his bearings and slid into the captain's chair. He felt like a child in the large throne-like space. Once again, his short legs barely reached the floor.

He triggered some monitors that surrounded him with readouts and ship stats. He didn't even need wiring to clip into the ship through his Relay box. He could connect instantly. Once he did, several more monitors powered up, and systems were cycled into place. It's like the ship was launching itself.

Or wait, someone else was obviously at work here. And it wasn't R'zar.

"Dash," Bastille said and smiled to himself. Dash was back.

The ship quivered as the hover-thrusts came online. The *Libellule* eased off the ground. Outside, years of garbage and built-up vegetation rattled off the areas where they had accumulated. The landing struts shook free of their holds. At the same time, Dash triggered the doors of the outer hangar. Not just the front lock they had come in through. The full topside hangar portal.

The ceiling and the sides all began to crack open and peel away in another amazing feat of engineering. Dash triggered another button, and the very walls and floors of the bridge became a monitor surface. It was as if Bastille's chair was floating in thin air with a 360-degree view of his entire surroundings. Light began to pour into the hangar space, and from his vantage point, Bastille could watch the whole majestic process unfold before him.

His pupils dilated as the fullness of both suns filtered through. Below, the cargo doors of the ship remained open. Bastille assumed that was so R'zar could enjoy his view and the other two could come and go as they pleased.

The ship inched forward as the hangar widened enough to let it pass. With precision, Dash threaded the needle in a graceful maneuver; Bastille was convinced he was just showing off now. He looked back over the ship. No wonder they had to keep it separate from the city. It was half the size of the entire city.

As they passed over the ridge line, the shadow of the ship swept down over the city and over the courtyard, where half the *DayStar* still stood. Ga'al and Tr'm flipped excitedly through the air. Some sort of dragon happy dance, Bastille supposed, as he watched them in wonder. They were so lithe and nimble for such large creatures. It was uncanny.

The *Libellule* settled into a station above the city and then hovered there. Again, Bastille was unsure what technology was at work because the extra mass of the planet would have made this huge ship impossible to keep aloft for long with any engine tech he was familiar with. This actually felt more like they were floating.

Bastille kept forgetting about the mental link with the dragon, so he called out into the air, "What about the others? My team?"

'We have prepared for them as well,' the dragon assured him.

Bastille saw an indicator for another, smaller cargo hold. He pressed it, and a monitor brought it to full screen. *Damn! It's the back half of the* DayStar. That would have all of their weapons and supplies, and more importantly…

"The Mustang," Bastille said as his ship auto-piloted out of the cargo hold and down to the planet's surface, settling beside the *DayStar* wreckage. After a minute, the melted lab entrance opened, and Moose and Peanut peeked out cautiously, armed and ready.

Bastille triggered the ComLink and his voice echoed outside the ship. "Hey, pocket monkey, what are you waiting for, engraved invitations? Saddle up. Let's go."

Peanut broke into a smile and waved with both arms. Mizuke stepped outside beside Moose and Peanut.

"Ahoy there, sexy pants! You're also invited aboard." Bastille chuckled to himself and then continued, "And the lady with the blue hair can come along too if she wants."

On the monitor, Mizuke smiled back, held up a hand, and flipped him the bird. Then all three disappeared back inside to grab pertinent gear. Bastille unbuckled from the seat and made his way down to the ship's main hold.

Ga'al and Tr'm busily hauled in a half-dozen more gigantic trees and dropped them, crashing onto the already huge pile. Ga'al roared a warning bellow at Bastille but kept his distance. Seems he still held a grudge from his charbroiled wing. But cranky as he was, he would give them no further trouble.

Unless R'zar was dead.

R'zar heard the thought and harrumphed. A puff of smoke from his nostrils hung in the air. Bastille got the point. R'zar wasn't going anywhere anytime soon. He shook out his mighty wings for emphasis, dusting

Bastille with leafy residue from his earlier snack, and then he, too, took off to forage.

* * *

A couple of hours later, the Mustang climbed its way up to the *Libellule*.

"Permission to come aboard," Mizuke's voice crackled over the radio.

"Permission granted," Bastille said, watching their progress from the helm.

The Mustang spun around in a tight little arc and expertly maneuvered into the lower hangar. Bastille sealed the doors behind them. He turned his attention to the main cargo hold where two of the dragons were settling in. R'zar had returned with another one of those sea creatures impaled in his talons, still squirming. It most resembled an armor-plated squid, and one of its tentacles wrapped fiercely around the dragon's leg. It would not last much longer out of the water.

Tr'm was the last one aboard. He was always on high security alert. He had been circling way overhead the whole time. Bastille wasn't sure what the diligent lizard was expecting, but he was glad for its vigilance.

After the Mustang was on board, Tr'm flipped acrobatically and dove toward the hangar. At the last second, he nimbly unfolded his wings and landed on deck without so much as a scratch from his huge talons.

Bastille triggered the comm, ship-wide. "Welcome aboard the *Scarlet Libellule*. Humans and mighty dragons alike. We will be pushing for the stars in twenty minutes, so batten down the hatches and ready for deep space. Over."

Bastille jumped down from the captain's chair. "You've got the bridge, Dash. Give us twenty, and then take us out."

Bastille exited. He was most curious to see the condition of his old body from the MedVat. If it was one hundred percent repaired, then he wanted it back as soon as possible. It should hopefully be the same Re-cycle process he'd performed on Mandreen.

The other big question was: where had Genwa'ar gone? There was a small possibility that the dragon killed her, and she was lost and gone forever. But he doubted that. Doubted that she could be taken out so easily.

Even though the Battle Dragons were on their team, R'zar forbade anyone but Bastille to enter their lair for the duration of the interstellar trip. It was for their own safety. As their travel extended to weeks, when the dragons' food supply was sure to run low, they'd accumulate a certain bloodlust that even their code of honor would not be easy to temper. They would arrive on Earth cranky, hungry, and twitching for battle. And at that moment, Bastille would unleash hell into the very heart of Fort Royale. General Wexell would not know what hit her.

Through the intercoms, he heard Peanut say, "Sir, we are a go for launch."

"Roger that, we are go for launch," Bastille echoed through his Relay box.

That was Dash's cue. The engines revved up, the ship banked, and the city slowly became smaller and smaller in the rearview monitors. They slipped from the atmosphere and arced away from Othello on their way out of the Qu'Nadi system.

Bastille entered the Captain's Quarters, where Moose and Peanut had brought his body. It was secured to a hover pad floating there in the foyer.

Mizuke spun around as he stepped closer. "Wow, quite a day," she said. "I wasn't sure we would see you again." She hugged him close, adding in his ear, "Idiot."

"Yeah, you lost me twenty thousand qubits," Peanut grumbled. Moose grunted happily. Peanut snapped back at him, "I said I'm good for it."

"Tsk. Lucky, I guess," Bastille said, nicking her chin playfully with his knuckles.

"Mm," she said, smoldering back at him.

Peanut tapped the hover bed. "Well, shall we leave you three alone, orrrr—"

"No, we've gotta try something first." Bastille pulled away from Mizuke and motioned with his hand. "Spin the body upright."

Moose and Peanut guided the bed so it was standing vertically.

"Moose, hold on to me," Bastille said, indicating his own shirt.

Moose looked at Peanut, who just shrugged. Moose grabbed a handful of Bastille's shirt between the shoulder blades.

"Don't we need to hook up the Re-cycle units—" Mizuke started to ask.

"Hm, watch…" Bastille reached out his hand, concentrating all of his will, his essence, and then he touched his hand to his old bod's Relay. A blue spark popped between them. Bastille placed his other hand over his own Relay and then kissed the other Byno-Core. Suddenly, in an electric blue tornado flash, the male skinbag inhaled deeply, eyes slammed open, gasping for air as his heart began to tick again for the first time in days.

The 16-year-old girl body slumped to the floor. Moose caught it, held her up like a rag doll, and then casually tossed the meat-suit onto his shoulder.

"Holy sh*t," Peanut said. "You gotta teach me how to do that."

Bastille calmed his breathing and heart rate down as much as he could. He was much more disoriented on this Re-cycle than any of the times before. He had been in Gen's meat-suit for so long, he had acclimated. It was great to be back in a familiar space. He blinked rapidly, worked a few muscles, and finally decided all was well.

"Okay, cut me loose," he said confidently.

Mizuke triggered the hover bed restraints, and Bastille stepped tenderly forward. And then collapsed to the ground.

Moose set down Genwa'ar and helped Mizuke and Peanut lift him back to his feet unsteadily.

"Easy, boss," Peanut cautioned. "It's gonna take a sec to get your, uh, boy legs back. I dunno how this works," Peanut confided to Moose.

"I got it," Bastille said. "I'm good."

They reluctantly let him go, and he stood there on his own, flexing his hands, turning his head, and tapping his feet. Generally, getting the feeling back throughout his body. Recalibrating his mind and body.

"Well?" Mizuke prodded him.

"Time will tell," he said, running a finger along the tiny scar that encircled his abdomen.

"No, I mean, is it all there?" She asked excitedly, "Your memory?"

Bastille searched inside and then frowned. "Nothing. Nothing except what I carried with me," he clarified. "Nothing from before."

"I can't allow that," Genwa'ar said.

They all spun around, and Gen was sitting up groggily on the floor.

Bastille reached for a weapon at his side that wasn't there. Peanut took a step behind Moose, who situated his large frame between Mizuke and Gen.

"Identify yourself," Bastille commanded.

"Relax, mate, it's Cap'n Dash Strouthers at y' service," he said, holding his hands up peaceably. There was no hint of the royal accent, either.

They all breathed a sigh of relief.

"Explain yourself," Bastille said, pulling on a shirt.

"Those memories, all the data that Gen recovered, were from a very different Jacques Bastille. A murderous brigand. The day you get those memories back, you risk becoming the darkness again. In some cosmic way, I think that's why I'm here. To prevent that from happening," Dash explained. It was more of a warning than anything.

"That 'data'—those memories are me!" Bastille growled, thumping his fist to his chest. "It's who I am, and I have a choice—we all have a choice—to be driven by our past—no matter how blisteringly sh*t-riddled it is—" this last part was to Mizuke, "—or we can choose to move forward."

Dash stood to his feet, not backing down. "Bastille, you wanted this clean slate. You wanted to leave the Ma'Kobi life behind, remember? Re-cycle into someone new and start over from scratch? A complete reset. That's why you went to Bender in the first place. That's why you stole the seed bricks to secure your retirement. Your freedom. But then General Wexell sent out those bounty hunters to Da'Karh, and well, here we are. Back in the fight."

Bastille shifted uneasily. That *had to have* been the original plan. He could see the truth of Dash's logic. Everything lined up.

"Well," Dash continued, "you have the fresh start you've always wanted, Jacques Bastille. Colonial Farmer? Space Trucker? Exotic dancer? Whatever you want to become."

"What is she… I mean he… I mean, what's going on, boss?" Peanut said, stepping to the front.

Bastille waved him off and kept on Dash. "We've got a cargo hold full of Battle Dragons, one of the most advanced warships in the universe, a super-powered meat-suit—we are *not* going farming," Bastille said, squaring up to Dash.

"Agreed." Dash did not back down. "General Wexell wants you dead. We've got an intergalactic war brewing between the Croix, the New Dominion, and the Kytos Alliance, and you are the best hope for peace and freedom. Yes, we *are going to battle*," Dash emphasized the last part. "After that, if you're still alive, we can discuss who it is you want to be next. Until then, captains, I'll be on the bridge, checking supply levels."

Dash stepped back, turned on a heel, and walked out the door, veering sharply left towards the bridge.

Mizuke waited for a response from Bastille, but he stepped toward the door without so much as a word. "Wait," she said, grabbing at his arm, "where are you going?"

"Dragon conference. If I'm not back in 15 minutes, dunk me in the Cryo-tank. Sew my ass back together." He walked out the door, taking a sharp right toward the cargo bay.

Moose and Peanut scratched their heads.

"Are the dragons gonna recognize him in that body?" Peanut asked with genuine concern.

"Go check into your quarters," Mizuke ordered softly. "Get some food. Rest. Something tells me we're gonna need it." She gestured at the hover bed. "Take this with you."

"Aye, Cap'n," Peanut said as he and Moose backed the hover bed out of the room.

\- 20 -

DRAGON RULES

Ka-clang. The door to the dragon's lair opened loudly. R'zar, Ga'al, and Tr'm were alerted to a new scent. A new presence. R'zar, curled up and resting, barely even moved. Ga'al dined on a pine core, but the head of Tr'm was high and alert, golden eyes watching Bastille's every move.

"R'zar!" Bastille bellowed.

'I said no visitors,' R'zar roared back.

Bastille took giant steps into the cargo hold, and the door clanged shut behind him. And latched. Ga'al and Tr'm were instantly to their feet, fully attentive. R'zar opened one eye, curiously. He was not going to stop the other two this time. If a man could not mind his boundaries, he would pay the price. Especially a stupid man he'd already dealt with once before.

Bastille continued forward, his heavy boots echoing across the vast chamber.

Clang, clang, clang.

R'zar opened his other eye.

Ga'al was the first to pounce. And he was fast, too. He was halfway across the distance when Bastille shut off the deck's gravitron via his Relay box. Ga'al struggled to adjust his flight to no avail and flew past Bastille, whose magneto-boots held him firmly to the floor. Bastille continued towards R'zar, who was now beginning to float off the floor, as was Tr'm. Ga'al slammed into the wall behind him, disoriented, flopping around, and getting very angry.

Just as Bastille figured. Worthless in space.

But Tr'm was smarter. And even faster. He had a talon hooked into the floor. Pushing slightly backward into a wall, he launched forward, flying directly at Bastille.

Bastille smiled and cranked the gravitron up to three hundred percent, and Tr'm slammed to the ground with the other two. The force was so strong, even Bastille had to take a knee. The dragons were pinned flat by the artificial gravity well. Bastille triggered it off again, and the dragons floated freely in the air, able to breathe again but squirming and clawing at anything they could. Bastille walked on, closing the space between himself and R'zar, who firmly gripped the floor with his own talons buried deep in the skin of the vessel.

Ga'al howled in frustration as he continued banging around in the corner like a drunk pterodactyl. Tr'm hit the ceiling and launched again at Bastille, who again dialed up the gravitron. This time, Tr'm spun like a cat, landed on his feet, and sprang forward to close the gap. With a single talon, he raised his front paw and swiped across at his prey. A death strike.

At the last second, Bastille extended the blade from his right forearm. He brought it low across his left side, a glowing blue deflector that received the dragon's talon, sharply interrupting its deadly path. He saw a look of surprise in the dragon's eye as the super-strength manifested, and as he batted the talon away, sparks flew.

The force of the creature's momentum moved it right into the position Bastille had anticipated. Extending the blade again, he caught the soft spot of its shoulder that was now in range, stuck his blade between the scales, and at the same time, flipped off the gravitron. He flung the massive beast over his shoulder and sent it screeching headlong into Ga'al.

It was not a mortal wound—a pin prick, really—but one Tr'm would not soon forget. Or forgive. As Ga'al and Tr'm crashed together, Bastille turned the gravity up one more time, and they spilled to the floor in a tangled, growling heap.

Bastille turned back around, panting heavily from the exertion. R'zar was right there in front of him, eye to eye. He hadn't seen him move, much less heard him approach, but there he was. His chest glowed vividly. A single claw extended slowly from the scaly fist and tapped ominously on the metal floor. He could have ended Bastille right there, but he stayed his hand.

'*You have my attention, boy,*' he growled.

Bastille retracted his own blade into his forearm. "Mighty R'zar, I am Jacques Bastille. Your Dragon-eye. I ask one final time: Would you yield to our alliance, my friend?" he shouted, then braced himself for what he figured would be his own fiery end.

If a dragon could smile, R'zar would have smiled. The very idea of yielding to a tiny human was laughable. But, then again, this was no ordinary human. Instead, R'zar moved his face even closer. He blinked twice, then his inner eyelid slid back, and he peered right into Bastille's soul.

Fzzzzzzzht.

* * *

The tiny dragon peered up off that table into Dash's eyes and forever imprinted on him.

Fzzzzzzzht.

* * *

R'zar recoiled.

'Shapeshifter! What trickery is this? Do you realize you almost died?' R'zar scolded him.

Bastille let out a breath he didn't even realize he'd been holding. "It was a risk I had to take, R'zar. This is my true form. Know this," Bastille explained, beating his chest with a fist.

R'zar studied him.

Bastille felt a bump against his shoulder.

'Leave him,' R'zar warned Ga'al.

Bastille turned, and Ga'al was right there. Tr'm too. Crowding into him. Bastille stood his ground. They snorted hot fumes, which singed some of his body hairs. Then they parted to his right and left and circled around behind R'zar.

'*You should be honored,*' R'zar said.

"Honored?" Bastille asked, eyebrows raised at the absurd thought.

'*Yes, honored. That is as close to a dragon apology as it comes,*' R'zar turned and headed back to his own space. '*No one else enters that door,*' R'zar bellowed.

"No one else," Bastille promised, with a slight bow. "If they do, they are dragon food." This last piece was thrown out to Tr'm, who nodded, yanked off a large tentacle from the sea squid, and dragged it into his area for a little post-battle snack.

On his ComLink, Mizuke piped up: "Captain, you better get up to the bridge. We've got company."

"On my way," Bastille said, heading toward the door.

* * *

As Bastille strode onto the bridge, Peanut and Moose took a respectful step back.

Mizuke threw him a dirty look. "What the hell was that?"

"We cannot win without the dragons. And they will not fight for us without the Dragon-eye. What did you want me to do?"

"I dunno." She shrugged and cocked her head to one side. "How about a little heads up? 'Hey, I'm off to become dragon lunch, so—'"

"Mizuke," Bastille put a calm hand on each of her shoulders and looked her right in the eye, "they just needed a stern talking to."

"Uh-huh." She gave him a half-smile and then pointed to the main screen behind him. "Well, they're not the only ones."

Outside, the bedraggled army of the Mandreen Forces—or what was left of them—was gathered. At the head of the contingent was one hell of a flagship. It had bits and pieces of a dozen recognizable space vessels—old and new—cobbled together. The entire command deck was a heavily modded-up Space Shuttle. On the side panels and down the payload bay, it had almost as many victory marks as the *Stone Scorpion*. The name of this legendary ship was *Challenger IV*.

"Your brother would like a word," Mizuke said ominously.

"Interesting," Bastille said, squaring up to the screen and standing a bit taller. "Okay, put him through."

Tavi6 appeared on-screen before them. The monitor showed a facsimile of their bridge, too, from floor to ceiling, so as Tavi6 stepped forward, it was almost as if they were inhabiting the same space. Bastille walked forward to meet him.

"Jacques Bastille. I'm of the mind to crush you into stardust and salt our supper with your remains."

"Funny," Bastille said, unflinching, "I was thinking the same thing."

Tavi6 jabbed an angry finger at Bastille and said, "You destroyed our whole planet."

"You left me there to die. Only I was in this body," he stepped aside to show Genwa'ar, waving "Hi" from the helm. "But you did leave me some company. Sanji, I believe, was his name, and some bullsh*t story about a childhood scar."

Tavi6 was taken aback. "Bastille, look—"

"Enough!" Bastille held up a hand and cut him off. "We don't have time. How many of your ships are in fighting shape?" He pressed in closer.

Tavi6 had to stop and think about this. He looked off screen, probably to his Ops Officer before answering. "Thirty-two war vessels and skiffs."

"Well, we're taking them with us," Bastille informed him.

"Wait just a damn second—" Tavi6 began.

Bastille ignored him. "How many civilians?"

"Seventeen," Tavi6 said, more than a little confused.

"Alright, the civilians and two warship escorts will head to the Qu'nadi system. The Planet Othello is an abandoned colony left over by the Croix," Bastille ordered.

"The Draccarios," Tavi6 spat.

"The Croix," Bastille corrected. "There is a home base there for an entirely new community. Top-notch dwelling and tech. *And first-class garbage.* Yours for the taking."

"Uh-huh." Tavi6 considered it and then leaned in closer. "And in return?"

"You and the other fighters will join me in my attack against Fort Royale. Any survivors can stay on

Earth or return to Othello," Bastille stated the terms simply.

"You are going up against the New Dominion Army of General Wexell, headquartered at the virtually impenetrable Fort Royale, and you want us to join you?" Tavi6 studied him closely. "Are you mad?"

Peanut and Mizuke exchanged a look and nodded a matter-of-fact "Yes" off to the side.

"This is not a request," Bastille growled. "Release your civilians, assemble your command staff, and have them here within 30 minutes. The Ma'kobi King has spoken."

The gigantic screen returned to a view of deep space, showing the massive army of ships spanning out before them.

Peanut exhaled loudly, breaking the room's awkward silence. "Think they're gonna do it?"

"Well," Bastille asked over his shoulder to Dash, "have any of their weapons come online?"

"Negative," Dash answered, eyeing the scopes in front of him. "All systems… normal."

"I give it 50-50." Bastille nodded and then looked over at Mizuke. She gave him a skeptical "We'll see" type of shrug.

Dash flipped open a weapon safety latch and hovered his hand over the trigger.

They all turned again to watch the screen. Waiting. Waiting. Waiting.

"Bastille," Mizuke pointed lower on the screen.

"I see them." Bastille grinned from ear to ear.

Civilian ships began peeling off from the larger group. They raced past the *Libellule* and onward to Othello. Dash secured the weapons safety, and everyone breathed a sigh of relief.

"Okay," Bastille clapped his hands together and rubbed them gleefully.

"M'kay," Mizuke echoed. "Helluva gamble, Captain." She patted his shoulder in passing.

Peanut collapsed dramatically back into his seat. "I need a drink."

* * *

Minutes later, a dozen smaller shuttles approached their ship and were directed to the lower hangar. Moose and Peanut were sent down to greet the emissaries.

"Captain Mizuke, why don't you join them, too. Welcome everyone to *your* ship," Bastille said, with a twinkle in his eye. "Make sure they know they're not on Mandreen anymore. They'll be taking their orders from a woman. And anyone who has a problem with that can take it up with our Dragon Council."

"Mmm, with pleasure, Captain," she beamed and strode purposefully from the room. She was going to enjoy this.

Dash threw a look back at Bastille.

"What?" Bastille asked, bemused.

"Nothing, Captain. Not a damn thing." Dash shook his head and resumed monitoring the scaled-down fleet before them.

"Very good. I'm going to get cleaned up. We'll meet in the CIC in half an hour."

"It'll only take them fifteen to get everyone there," Dash advised.

"You are correct. That'll give them a good time-out to sit and stew," Bastille said, heading out the door. "You've got the bridge, Dash."

"Aye!" Dash saluted back at him.

- 21 -

MA'KOBI CONSCRIPTION

Bastille marched into the Command Intelligence Center (CIC) of the *Scarlet Libellule,* and immediately the unrest across the room was quelled. He half-smiled at Mizuke because this crowd was much more demure than the last time they'd all tangled on Mandreen. Apparently, she had laid down the law. They all snapped to attention when he stepped into the room. "Shu'ma! U'aah!"

Jacques Bastille. Enemy of the New Dominion Fugs. Escape artist from the belly of the Croix. Destroyer of the planet Mandreen. Conjuror of AA-Class warships from thin air. Benevolent donor of high-class, abandoned cities to Tavi6 and his refugees. The man who would not, could not be killed in battle, by man or beast. He held the respect of everyone in that room. Even Tavi6.

"Admiral Bastille," Tavi6 began as he bowed slightly.

"*Captain* Bastille," he corrected him. Then Bastille turned to address the room. "This is not the KACorp's Navy. We do not use the Kytos Alliance's playbook. We are a brotherhood of independent ship captains. We have joined forces temporarily against a common enemy. There are 32 warship captains. There will be 32 equal shares from the spoils of this battle."

There were some hearty "Ayes!" around the room at that unexpected news.

"Brother, that is extremely generous," Tavi6 said, watching him closely. "But what is *your* stake in all of this?" His eyes flicked from Bastille to Mizuke and back.

"Same as anyone. Freedom. Revenge. Take your pick." Bastille climbed the stairs to the upper deck and stood beside Mizuke. "Now," he continued, "have we determined the status of the Croix vessel?"

Everyone shifted awkwardly. They avoided eye contact. Scratched at their scraggly beards.

"C'mon," Bastille was a little agitated, "they're damned slippery, but they're not impossible to track. I know *one* of you has a position lock on them."

Liz T'arn was a haggard old skipper. She stepped forward at Tavi6's reluctant nod. "Sir, our scouts lost them at the edge of the Scorpio Nebulae. Vanished into thin air."

That was surprising news for Bastille. He turned aside to Mizuke and thought aloud, "There's no hypergate there. No wormhole."

Mizuke shook her head and confirmed, "None."

"No, sir," Liz continued, gathering steam as she waved a perkweed cigar around. "If anything, they were headed away from the closest jump gate." This received nods and "ayes" from a couple of other captains in the know.

Bastille considered that for a moment and then had an outrageous idea. "Could they have developed some sort of jump technology?"

A murmur went around the room.

"Aye," Liz said, jamming a thumb toward Tavi6. "That was our thinking, too, Cap'n. Only thing'a make sense less'n they're a'ghosts."

Bastille looked over at Mizuke. He could tell by her knowing look that they were on the same page. He put a hand against the ship walls beside him, looking the room up and down with fresh eyes. "What are the chances—" Bastille started to ask her, but Mizuke had reached the same conclusion.

"I'm on it," she said, and rushed off toward the bridge.

Tavi6 stepped cautiously up the stairs until his hooves were one step lower than Bastille. It was his people's protocol. A sign of respect. He dared not go higher without an invitation. Those were the Mandreen ways. "What are you thinking, brother?"

Bastille turned but addressed everyone, careful to include the whole group in the decision-making process. "Wexell, no doubt, has gotten word that we're headed that way. Earth at top speed through the closest hyper-gates, we're talking, what—?"

"Two weeks of travel time," Tavi6 said, confirming the math quickly in his head. "Yeah, give or take."

"Two weeks. So in two weeks, she's expecting a battle. In two weeks, they'll be completely dug in, and we will have the fight of a lifetime. But if we've got a jump drive on this ship—a working hyperdrive—we could be there in under three days, ladies and gentlemen."

Another strong murmur from the crowd, and Tavi6 held up a hand to quiet the motley horde. "Even with the element of surprise," he shook his head dismally. "I'm sorry, but this is still just a suicide run."

Bastille put a reassuring hand on his shoulder. "Ah, but our goal is not to defeat their entire navy, brother. Which, by the way, is all spread out, is it not? Patrolling against the KACorps resistance, guarding the jump gates? We have the ability to jump behind their main lines and straight into Earth's atmosphere. We can hit their Fort Royale headquarters hard and fast before they even know what's upon them."

There was a buzz of excitement in the room. More and more of the ship's captains could see the plan unfolding to their advantage. There were still a lot of details to work out, but it was sounding crazy enough to be feasible.

"If you cut off the head of the beast," Bastille said, pounding a fist against the wall beside him. "The Dominators will collapse and scatter."

Someone whispered in Tavi6's ear, and he relayed it to the others. "Yes, exactly, but what of the Draccario forces?"

"The *Croix*," he paused to let the name-correction sink in, "have a different end game, don't they? They don't want to take over the whole planet. They just want to return the Earth to its so-called former glory. To do that, they're the ones that are gonna have to completely subdue General Wexell, the New Dominion forces *and* the KACorps resistance. And, by the way, the Kytos Alliance will most likely stage from their outposts on Europa and Saturn and Mars. Wexell may know that we are headed her way, but she has no clue about the most advanced Croix warship bearing down upon them."

"You don't know the forces that Wexell has amassed since you left," Tavi6 said, rubbing his forehead, still unconvinced. "We're gonna need a miracle."

As if on cue, a deafening roar echoed throughout the halls of the entire ship, and immediately silenced everyone in the room. Long after the vibrations died down, everyone held their breath, fearing for their lives. Everyone except for Bastille, who crossed his arms and tried to keep from laughing.

Finally, Tavi6 spoke up, whispering, "What the hell was that?"

"That," Bastille said with a wink, "is our miracle."

* * *

They had their work cut out for them. Over the next seventy-two hours, nobody slept. Everyone worked to prepare the fleet. The best part about joining forces with the Ma'kobi of Mandreen was their superior scavenger and engineering prowess. More than anyone across the known universe, they knew how to build, shape, and improvise with limited resources. They were able to bring twelve of their ships into the cargo holds. Another seven ships docked externally to the *Scarlet Libellule*, reinforcing the connections into an extension of the hull itself. Thirteen of the ships would have to be left behind. There was some debate about sending them through the hyper-gates, but that would be of little use. By the time they arrived, the battle would have been over for a week.

Those captains and crews and their weapons were also divided up and applied to the active duty crews and ships, but most were assigned within the spacious *Libellule* itself. They would fight under the command of Captain Mizuke Strouthers.

There was a singularity of purpose. Quarrels, if any broke out, were quickly resolved. You could say they had a sense of destiny within them. Or perhaps they were energized for the epic battle ahead. Mostly, it was because nobody wanted to be sent to those bloody cargo bays like that idiot Captain Arkin.

Arkin wasn't one hundred percent on board with leaving his ship behind and voiced vehement concern about being assigned to Captain Mizuke. He even went so far as to draw down on her during one especially heated moment. That was the last straw.

Mizuke knocked him unconscious with the butt of his own gun, and he was dragged below to the Dragon Council. He never returned. Word spread quickly, and any other strong opinions were kept in check. His second, Quartermaster Jeffries, was promoted to Captain, and the rest of his crew seemed almost relieved to have the obnoxious tyrant gone. But up to this point, nobody had seen what was behind those bay doors and lived—except Bastille, who moved freely in and out to strategize with R'zar.

Everyone had a guess as to what was in there—everything from some sort of Space Chupacabra to the Devil himself. And no one was convinced the mysterious beasts could be contained by the steel-hybrid walls. Some even assigned them mystic powers and swore they moved throughout the fleet at night.

Dash enjoyed fueling that rumor. He had grown very adept at jumping into the ship's network and back into Gen's body when it suited him. More than anyone, he knew every capability of every ship in the fleet. Moose and Peanut enjoyed watching him move things around in strange ways and freak out the superstitious Seabees.

The *DayStar* crew knew that was how legends were created. And the leadership status of Jacques Bastille, Ma'kobi King, would not be so easily challenged by this rag-tag group any time soon. It was hard to tell where the stories of the "Ma'kobi Shu'ma" left off and the truth began. They made sure that rumors also leaked back to General Wexell that Bastille and his superhuman armada were headed to Earth.

"We need to talk, Captain." Dash pulled Bastille aside during a lull in the final preparations.

"Speak your mind, Dash," Bastille said, handing off a small tablet to an ensign.

Dash indicated the others in the room and Bastille nodded and cleared the CIC to give the two of them some space.

Dash struggled with how to express his next thought. "I need to give you something vital to the success of this mission," Dash said cryptically.

"Great. Let's have it," Bastille said with a nonchalant shrug. He wasn't sure what it could be, but he had grown to trust Dash.

"Well, it's not that easy," Dash admitted, drawing closer to Bastille. "I have sorted back through so many of your memories, trying to extract a single important bit of information. But I can't disentangle it from… another memory."

"Why don't you just tell me the info?" Bastille suggested. "If you've seen the memory, can't you just describe it?"

"Won't work." Dash shook his head. "I need to install the complete memory bit, which will give you muscle memory and certain other data points you're gonna need next week when we get to Bravo Bay."

"I see." Bastille furrowed his brow in thought. "But they're connected with some bad… stuff?"

"Yes, and there's no good time to do this install on you," Dash continued, "plus we have no idea how it's gonna fully affect you."

"We?" Bastille cocked an eyebrow at him.

"Yes, I ran this by Captain Mizuke first. She doesn't see any way around it either," Dash said, scrunching up his face as he braced for Bastille's response.

Bastille looked at the ground, thinking through it all. He kicked absently at a scuff mark until it was erased. Then he turned back to Dash with a renewed sense of resolve and said, "The good with the bad."

"The good with the bad," Dash nodded and began rolling up his sleeves.

Bastille watched him prep, pulling open a toolkit beside them. "Have I objected with every fiber of my being against you being the sole gatekeeper of my former thoughts and memories?" Bastille asked.

"You have," Dash nodded with a wry smile. "Hourly."

"Okay, then where do we go? Do I lay down here or—"

Dash looked around the room and shrugged.

"Right here it is, then," Bastille conceded, taking a seat.

Dash held up his right hand, and a blue glow was already forming around his fingertips. Bastille threw him a hang-loose and turned around, adding, "To the moon, Alice."

Dash slowly reached out and cupped his blue hand around the Relay box on the back of Bastille's neck. Their eyes immediately glowed white hot.

Fzzzzzzzht.

* * *

Beneath the Miramar Settlement

A younger Jacques Bastille and a band of Ma'kobi defectors emerged from the rocky tunnels beneath Bravo Bay, their weapons drawn and ready. On a hand signal from Bastille, the group dropped quickly into a crouch to conceal themselves where the tunnel opened into this private grotto. Two of General Wexell's scout hover cycles sat empty on the small flight deck. The enemy's position blocked the ramp to the H2X-1 Mustang, which was their ride out of here.

Bastille scanned the area through his long-rifle scope for any signs of movement. "Dominion Fugs," Bastille whispered. "Two, maybe more."

"Always something," Reid scowled back at him.

"Could be anywhere," Bastille said.

For years, Bastille had heard rumors of this mysterious access portal, which led right into the back door of their Ma'kobi headquarters. These emergency tunnels had been dug long ago during the cove's former life as Miramar. What had once been a top secret military base of operations had grown into an extended flotilla city for the Ma'kobi brotherhood and their families. Now these neglected caverns would provide Bastille and a handful of loyalists with a perfect escape as General Wexell and her forces stormed the Ma'kobi water town above.

"This is gonna slow things down," Reid said. "But if I can sneak aboard the Mustang, I can fire it up and draw them out while you bring the others around."

"Okay," Bastille agreed. "But take Augie with you for backup. I'll find our long-lost defense drone."

Reid nodded, pointed at Augie, and motioned him into formation with a silent hand signal. They both moved out together, using the large rocks as cover.

Bastille intended to smuggle this small squad with him into retirement. A fresh start. Freedom for one and all. And he'd hoped to do so undetected, but an entire Dominion brigade arrived just as they were executing their escape. Occasionally, a top-side explosion shook the walls, and small pebbles dropped into the water. But for the most part, this area was too far removed from the battle action to be in any immediate danger, the two scouts notwithstanding.

Bastille moved over to the water's edge and knelt down. Then he triggered the display on his wrist-comm and punched in a directive. The water began to bubble and stir, and then a silvery dome breached before them. It was D/U/G.

"Hello, I am Defensive Underwater Guardian, or DUG," D/U/G said loudly.

"Shhhh, not so loud, idiot," Bastille reprimanded the old machine. He plugged an ancient memory stick into the activation panel on the D/U/G. It whirred and hummed, and the lights shifted from red to blue positive.

"Maintenance mode granted," D/U/G said a lot softer. "Voice print to confirm."

"You know who I am, you little sh*t," Bastille replied.

"Voice print approved, Dash Strouthers. Now upgrading records and doing much needed system maintenance for the first time in… thirty-six thousand, one hundred and twenty-seven days. Stand by."

"Fine, but call me Captain Bastille now," he instructed.

"Heard. And you can still call me… DUG," the bot said.

Bastille thought it was quite handy that this old skinbag of his still had access to an old defense-bot after all these years. He turned around to the remaining two guys guarding his back. "Okay, I don't know how long this will actually take, but once it's fully back online, we'll have a permanent ally guarding this entrance." Bastille removed the stick and closed the access portal, and the newly reactivated D/U/G sank beneath the waters to finish 98 years' worth of system maintenance and upgrades.

Bastille tapped his men on the shoulder, and they followed him back into the labyrinth of tunnels. After a few turns, their eyes adjusted to the iridescent blue glow of the wall lights that had been placed here a hundred years ago. When he'd first seen them, he assumed they were electronic, but they weren't. They functioned a lot like deck prisms on the old ships and were fitted into the cave walls, channeling light from the bay down into the caves. He appreciated the lights, but did not love the fact that some of them leaked. A thin creek of runoff water swirled at their feet.

Bastille rounded the last switchback to the straight-way. There was his first mate, Finn, standing watch. His loyalty was undisputed, but he was always restless due to a recurring wafer habit that constantly pushed him to the edge.

"Well?" Finn stepped off the wall, eager for news.

"Looks like Bender's information paid off. The Mustang is up there getting prepped as we speak. DUG is coming back online, so those codes worked as well. Should prevent anyone from following us out. This plan might just—"

"Stop," Finn reprimanded him. "Don't jinx it, Cap'n."

"Might just work," Bastille finished with a smile for his jumpy friend. "Where are the others?"

Finn pointed his rifle barrel back up the tunnel, "Anxious as hell to get moving."

Bastille could barely see the small group of refugees fifty meters ahead. Six in all were seated on the rocks, catching their breath. The youngest of the group was Kyra. Normally, she was a precocious and high-energy 10-year-old. But the stress and physicality of the half-day tunnel journey had worn her and her mother out. The whole team, actually. Bastille looked forward to giving them some good news for once.

"Almost there, Finn," he clapped his buddy on the back. "Take two guys with you and check on Reid and Augie. See if they need help rounding up those two Fug scouts. The rest of you come with me to grab gear and rally the troops. The sooner we make orbit, the better."

With a nod, they were all off. Bastille pulled the straps of the duffel on his back to cinch them a little tighter and then headed off toward the stragglers. He ignored the rumbling explosions and fighting far, far away. Wexell's forces would be so consumed with Ma'kobi Bay that no one would notice an old KACorps Mustang slipping off to some hidden corner of the galaxy along with this tough little group and eight seed bricks to start all over again.

They had closed half the distance to the families when a metallic scraping sound began echoing through the enclosed chamber. Bastille thought it might be a cave-in, but then he saw the cause. Between him and the civilians, a set of bars was dropping from the ceiling, cutting them off.

"Kyra! Everyone! Run! Run to me now!" Bastille shouted at them, "Leave the stuff and run!"

Some ran, others ignored him and began gathering packs and gear. Kyra was in the lead, but it was too late. The bars latched into the cave floor before Bastille and his advance team could get to them. He stood on one side and Kyra on the other, both out of breath.

"What happened?" Kyra asked wide-eyed. "Are we trapped?"

Bastille reached through the bars and lifted her chin up. "Hey, I'm gonna fix this." He smiled at her.

The rest of the group arrived, inspecting the bars with growing panic. Kyra's mother pulled her daughter back from the bars as Bastille tried to muscle them up, but they were stuck.

"Stand back," he said, firing a round from his Mauzer, but it had no effect on the titanium hybrid bars or the surrounding rock.

He grabbed a loose rock and began banging at the bars with mighty blows. Sparks flew, but after a minute, the rock crumbled into worthless pieces.

"Bastille!" Finn yelled. "It's no use. We need heavy explosives."

Bastille spun around to his men behind him. "There is probably a standard issue squawk box on either one of those scout ships." That's all he needed to say, and the two Seabees took off running in that direction. He turned back around to Kyra and her mother. "That's the only thing that's gonna move these bars."

"And cave in the whole tunnel in the process?" Finn whispered.

"No, not if I—"

A booming, electronically modded laughter echoed from way back in the cavern, where they had all come from. That menacing cackle was unmistakable. General Wexell.

"Little cave rats," the general began, "the battle is over, the Ma'kobi council is dead, and I have decided *unanimously* to rid my new outpost of all the vermin and filth that has weakened our New Dominion to its knees."

"Bastille," Finn pointed at the ground.

Bastille followed his gaze and saw a trickle of water snaking its way along the cave's bottom. The trickle became a stream, and the entire group began to panic further, throwing themselves against the bars, trying to move them or bend them. Anything.

The taunting continued. "Jacques Bastille, you have been found guilty of Re-Cycling your Byno-Core as well as high treason against the New Dominion Army."

"No!" Bastille yelled angrily.

The water began to flow more freely and very quickly rose up to their knees. Bastille had a difficult time even staying at the bars because the fast-flowing current kept pushing him back. Some of his men had already been swept away. On the other side of the bars, the stragglers were being pushed against the large grate. Kyra was reaching through, crying.

Bastille could hear a giant rumble behind them as the water level rose. He fiercely began attacking the wall, but his feet were slipping, and he had to use one hand just to hold onto the bars and keep himself from being washed downstream.

"I knew this was a trap. You just lead us down here to die, you traitor," one desperate man was screaming, his face pressed into the bars.

Kyra's mother was the only one *not* in a panic. "Bastille, you must go. You *must* go now!"

"I'm not going anywhere," Bastille yelled, tears stinging his eyes. "Not without you two."

She lifted Kyra up in her arms to hold her higher above the rising waterline. "Kyra, say goodbye now."

"Nooooo," Kyra cried. "He has to fix this. He promised."

"Kyra," her mother kissed her neck choking back her own emotions.

Kyra sniffed and resigned herself to it. "Goodbye, Father."

Kyra's mother hugged her close and then lifted her eyes once again, "Goodbye, Bastille. Go!"

Bastille saw the wall of water behind them an instant before it pounded them, submerging the whole area. "Noooooooooo—" he screamed as the water slammed them all backwards, ripping him from his family. The last thing Bastille saw at the moment of impact was that Kyra's skin fragmented and glitched, and then he was smothered in a bubbled torrent of ocean water.

The duffel on his back protected Bastille well as he bounced along the cave walls at the front edge of the wave. Sometimes he surfaced for air; other times he was twisting and didn't know which way was up. He didn't fight it. He could barely form a cohesive thought. He had just lost his entire family, which, apart from his own freedom from the Ma'kobi life, was the one thing he had actually cared about.

Bastille continued to slam from surface to surface. The darkness was closing fast, but he could barely make out a light toward the end of the tunnel. And hands. Bastille didn't care. He wanted to meet his maker. He wanted to hold him accountable for what had gone down here today.

His lungs burned for air. The light approached swiftly. The faster everything went, the more time slowed down. Stretched out. Until he could almost live an entire lifetime in a single heartbeat.

Suddenly, hands grabbed at him as he rushed past, lifting him from the water. Voices were yelling something at him and then he passed out.

Fzzzzzzzht.

* * *

Scarlet Libellule

Bastille lay in a fetal position on the floor of the CIC aboard the *Scarlet Libellule,* shaking violently. He rolled onto his knees and pounded the floor angrily. There was a reason that life brings us every moment, especially the traumatic ones, spread out across a continuum of space-time; it allows the human body and the fabric of the psyche time to absorb. To react. To bend and to cope. Even to forget. Bastille had no such luxury. In a single instant, Dash had uploaded an entire cargo ship full of feelings and emotions upon him, and his body and mind were in complete shock.

Dash could only kneel there beside him and hope Bastille had the strength to fight through. There was a defibrillator close by for the worst-case scenario. It didn't look like he would need it, though.

Bastille's breathing normalized as the emotional numbness and shock began to blanket the pain; his mind was healing at an incredibly fast rate. Dash realized that the roar in his own ears was not adrenaline or Bastille's screams, but R'zar—linked to Bastille's mind—who was himself absorbing a tremendous and sudden overload. The link was probably, in fact, the only way Bastille had survived—by apportioning out some of the pain between two incredibly resilient minds.

Bastille slowly returned to his senses. He was gulping down air. He rolled onto his back. He was a mess. A trickle of blood ran out of his nose. Dash let him just lay there for a good ten minutes, staring at the ceiling. Deep pain in his eyes.

"Why—?" was all Bastille could finally muster.

Dash offered a hand and pulled him into a seated position.

"While the Croix attack from the stars and Mizuke, Tavi6 and the Battle Dragons attack the surface, that is our back door way in."

"You're a bastard," Bastille said.

"No, no, you're welcome," Dash said as he stood to his feet. "Now we're ready to make the jump home."

He reached down, but Bastille slapped his hand away. "Speak for yourself," Bastille growled. "I can't feel my legs."

"Take your time, Captain. I'll go ready the crew," Dash said and left the CIC.

Bastille held his hand up in front of his face. It was still shaking violently. He grabbed it with his other hand and massaged the palm. For the first time he questioned whether or not he really wanted the rest of an entire lifetime of painful memories back. He was fairly certain that, after spending the last fifteen minutes recovering from one memory, all of them at once might indeed kill him. And his dragon.

- 22 -

RETURN TO BRAVO BAY

Fort Royale, Formerly Miramar Settlement

Conditions were *not* perfect.

The Earth was still in as rough a shape as ever. The sky was so clouded with dust and ash that, from the surface, you could rarely see the moon up in the sky. Or what was left of it. Back during the Surface Wars 150 years ago, eighty percent of the moon's mass was blown away. It would forever be a hanging crescent, slowly eroding into the night sky. This wreaked havoc on Earth's tidal and weather systems, making the sea a churning, angry mass.

The new hub of General Wexell's very powerful dynasty was located here atop the ruins of the Miramar Settlement. This was her glorious Fort Royale. She'd stolen it from the Ma'kobi brotherhood and driven them into the stars. Because here in the Caribbean, the surface was more livable than any of the metropolitan areas from civilizations past. Everywhere else on the planet, humanity was forced underwater to survive. Here you could be outside for three hours and not contract radiation sickness. It was rather idyllic.

The island was twenty times larger than it had ever been in the past. Its footprint had multiplied as ships fused together into a large patchwork of buildings. It now resembled the bastard love-child between Venice and Shanghai. This was an engineering brainstorm began by Bastille. And even though NeoTokyo was the largest underwater city on the planet, Miramar had the most people topside. Over ten million.

And today, every one of them was on edge. Old and young alike. Their factories had been pushed into high gear one week ago at some intel that General Wexell had received about forces amassing for battle from the planet Mandreen of all places. More Ma'kobi sewer rats to deal with. But that, in and of itself, was not the most worrisome news. No, the more alarming part was that Jacques Bastille had returned from the grave and was leading this new revolt.

So it had been a week of very little sleep and horrid rumors and misinformation stirring the whole flotilla city into a panic. Everyone was nervous and jumpy. So when the surface dwellers heard the giant *KABOOM* in the sky and spotted a massive UFO flying straight for them—broadcasting the Ma'kobi King's signal—it caused instant, widespread pandemonium.

Armageddon had begun.

* * *

The *Scarlet Libellule* survived the hyper-dive. Barely. Even now, upon their re-entry just topside of Earth's atmosphere, half of their internal systems were down. Rebooting. Communications, down. Weapons, down. Flight controls: sixty percent. Shields were up, fortunately. But so was the enemy's Ion canopy below them.

The ship instantly began to draw fire from Wexell's air defense drones. Tavi6's *Challenger IV* and the Mandreen forces began to blow the couplers holding their ships to the *Libellule*. Each one fired up and peeled away from the main ship to engage the enemy that had swarmed up from the surface of the planet like a hornet's nest.

From the cargo bays, ships also launched out into the sky in every direction, often engaging an enemy before they had even cleared the ship.

As the *Libellule* continued its rapid descent, it appeared to be free-falling alongside hundreds of parts, equipment, and debris of all shapes and sizes. Finally, the ship regained full responsiveness and corrected its path, slowing its descent and separating away from the debris cloud.

Ground weapons from Fort Royale were engaged at this point, and the *Libellule* rocked with explosions and flak. It maneuvered to a more satisfactory position and then launched a full broadside attack back toward the ground turrets.

Meanwhile, the rain of debris was largely unheralded by both sides, except for those who maneuvered out of its path as it plummeted towards the ocean. As the junk rained down into the water, the debris disintegrated into much smaller pieces. This agitated the sea condors who had just swooped in for their morning feast.

One piece of space junk slowed down significantly before it hit the water. Almost like it was being careful to mind its precious cargo. As it hit the water, its exterior exploded into smaller pieces, and the Mustang emerged from its cocoon, engaged its Hydros, and rolled out into the open water, unnoticed by anyone on the scopes.

With the Ion shield over the city still in place, the *Libellule* had to perform evasive maneuvers to avoid a collision. But it couldn't simply hover over the city like a fat bulls-eye, so they had to fly defensively, taking massive hits along the way.

Somewhere in her own Command Center, General Wexell had gotten over her momentary shock and was now smiling to herself at the short-lived offensive.

"Send in the carrier groups," she bellowed. She held a hand up and balled her craggily fingers into a fist. "We will squeeze them 'til they bleed."

The carrier groups were already inbound from the blockade they had formed around the planet, beyond the moon. They were long-range vessels, so they could sit miles away in space and bombard the ships below. The first barrage of firepower sent two of Tavi6's ships down in flames. And the *Libellule* took a direct hit as well and was now listing to the port side.

Aboard *Challenger IV*, Tavi6 screamed at the monitors, "Is that all ya got!? Ya cowards," he punched a button on the console before him, and the payload bay doors opened. Inside the cargo space, a large Apolloclass rocket rose into firing position. "Houston! We've got a solution," he proclaimed, and launched the giant rocket toward the carriers. The whole ship vibrated as the old-school technology blasted out and away. The missile wormed its way up toward the carrier group. When the lead carrier locked onto it and was about to fire, it self-destructed, dispersing a dozen smaller satellites. Small, but effective.

As Tavi6 punched in another sequence, the satellites began jamming the frequencies of the entire Dominion flotilla, replacing it instead with his favorite playlist: the Mandreen Symphony recreating the "Carmen" opera. Tavi6 waved his arms majestically in time with the music as he directed his battle skiff to peel away and head straightaway against the entire carrier group. A few other ships turned to follow his suicidal ascent.

The carrier group launched another barrage of firepower, but the satellites were doing their job and the weapons were not tracking well in the second round.

"Status report?" Tavi6 asked of his helm.

"We've got ten inbound carrier class. Beyond that, we've got another thirty battleships turning around to join the fight."

"You got that, Bastille? It's about to get real toasty up here," Tavi6 said into the comm.

"Hold the line, no matter what," Bastille commanded. "We're about to go radio silent."

"Roger that. We'll toe the line til we're out of toes," Tavi6 replied. He leaned back in his seat, and rested his hooves on the console, and said flatly, "Well, sh*t." And then to his crew, he added, "I give us 30 more seconds til we're toast."

"Fifteen," the worried helmsman said, indicating a super-carrier locking on small range weapons.

"Nobody said anything about a Leviathon-Class Supercarrier! That's cheating. Our scramblers are not gonna work against that asshole," Tavi6 said, cranking up the music even louder. "Launch everything we got!"

"Aye, Captain," the helmsman replied.

* * *

Inside the large cavernous grotto beneath Fort Royale, the Mustang had settled onto the old, abandoned landing pad. Two burnt-out hover cycles were scrapheaps on either side. Bastille stepped down, all armored up. Dash followed, still in Gen's bio-form, followed by the hulking mass of Moose, carrying Peanut in the hunting blind upon his back.

Part of their regimen on the journey had been to keep the gravitron aboard the *Libellule* dialed up similar to the gravity on Othello. This meant that stepping out onto Earth's reduced gravity suddenly made every one of them feel like a super-soldier.

'*Welcome back, Captain Bastille. It's a great day to knock on death's door,*' D/U/G relayed as it bubbled up to the surface. It was covered in barnacles and showing signs of wear from the salt water after all these years, yet fully functional.

"DUG, secure this quadrant. Nobody enters the bay," Bastille ordered.

'*Aye, Captain,*' it said as it armed itself and sank back below the water line.

Bastille led them quickly to the heart of the tunnel system. He stopped at the entrance, watching the slow trickling water at his feet that had eroded a small crevasse into the bedrock after all these years.

"Captain?" Dash pressed.

"Let's move out," Bastille said, breaking from his reverie.

They triggered the visors in their suits, and the darkened tunnel suddenly burst into light with the enhanced vision. Bastille moved around all the rocks very deftly, made the turn around the switchback, and then slowed to a trot as he hit a straightaway. They all knew what was ahead, but still, none of them was fully prepared.

"*We* got this, Captain," Peanut said as Moose shouldered the Squawk Box.

"Wait, Moose," Bastille said. He walked up to the rusted grate. Bones and skulls lay piled against the floor. One small, boney arm stretched through the grate and lay on the ground. Bastille squatted and picked the small hand up gently, rubbing it tenderly.

Time was precious, but nobody dared speak a word. When Bastille stood back up, there was a fire in his soul. "Cut it down," he ordered, walking back a few steps.

Moose took a deep breath, then leveled the Squawk Box cannon and fired a single shot. The grate, the pile of bones, and the debris disintegrated before them in a fiery explosion that echoed down the tunnel.

"Well," Peanut said, "that's gonna wake somebody up."

"Good," Bastille said, moving forward through the mangled, steaming grate. "Let 'em come."

Moose and Peanut looked back at Dash who gave them a nod. Then, they all hurried to catch up to him as he swiftly ran up the tunnel.

* * *

A young lieutenant ran frantically into the Fort Royale CIC where General Wexell was seated, arms folded, watching the battle shrivel on-screen before her beady eyes.

"I had kinda hoped for more of a challenge, you know?" She allowed to no one in particular then popped an olive into her mouth.

The lieutenant halted beside her and saluted. "Ma'am, there's been activity reported in the old tunnel system," he said, his voice quaking.

"Activity?" Wexell's eyes almost sparkled. "What sort of *activity*?"

"An explosion, ma'am. Two minutes ago."

"Well, well, Captain Jacques Bastille, I presume. This will certainly make things more interesting. Don't just stand there with your thumb up your ass! Send in the Manglers."

The lieutenant touched the earpiece he wore, and as he listened, his face went even whiter. "Ma'am, they've just breached the main corridors."

"That's impossible. Nobody can move that quickly," Wexell said, rising to her feet.

"General," Her quartermaster shouted. "You're gonna want to see this!"

Wexell looked over at the monitor, which zoomed in and focused on three unidentified objects headed straight through the Ion shield. They had no profile of any discernible ship programmed into the radar, but their heat signatures were off the charts. The tracking SATs just tagged them on-screen as "Bogey1," "Bogey2," and "Bogey3."

Wexell gasped incredulously. "What the hell is that?"

The quartermaster shook his head in disbelief. "It looks like… dragons?"

Wexell hit the comm, "Red Alert, this is not a drill, we have incoming… targets… I want them dead before they make landfall. Seal off the city!"

Wexell paced back and forth in the CIC. "Dammit!" She smashed her fist on the closest surface, spilling the bowl of olives and leaving a healthy sized dent in the metallic tabletop.

"Ma'am?" the quartermaster said.

"That infernal Draccario nuisance!" Wexell seethed. "They have to be out there somewhere. There are no *dragons* without the Draccarios." She pointed an angry finger at the outermost battle map on the monitor. "*WHAT ARE THOSE SHIPS DOING?*"

"They've all pulled in toward the fight," the quartermaster said. "I thought—"

"And not only have they left the hyper-gate wide open, they are clustering and making themselves easy targets. Tell them evasive maneuvers, *now*!" Wexell yelled, her calm composure long gone. "Spread the f*ck out!"

* * *

The crew aboard Tavi6's *Challenger* were frantically running out of options. "They've got a lock on us, sir!" reported the helmsman.

"How long til our missiles impact the lead carrier?" Tavi6 asked.

"Five seconds, four, three, two—" The helmsman replied, and then they watched as the missiles detonated harmlessly a hundred yards in front of the carrier.

"Well, that is just *bangin'*! Well done, us," Tavi6 said, clapping derisively. "That is one for the storybooks—"

He stopped as the lead carrier exploded in a chain reaction, ending in a huge fireball.

"What in the actual—" Tavi6 said after the shockwave had passed by, rattling the whole bridge.

"Sir," the helmsman interrupted, "Draccarios!"

Sure enough, the gigantic Draccario warship *Phaedra's Deliverance* materialized right in the middle of the carrier group and opened up hell's fury, firing in multiple directions at once. And all the Dominion carriers began evasive maneuvers and returning fire.

"Helm, that is disgusting and bigoted language," Tavi6 corrected him sternly. "Those are the *Croix*!"

"Yessir," the helmsman responded, and he blinked a couple of times before reluctantly continuing, "And whose side are they on, sir?"

Tavi6 opened his mouth to answer, but then caught himself. He wasn't sure whose side they'd be on. "Helm," he said, straightening his lapels, "put some distance between us and those damned Draccarios."

"Roger that," the helmsman said, punching co-ordinates into the system.

* * *

A small formation of New Dominion fighters rolled and twisted in the air, trying to lock targets on the dragons. This naïveté amused R'zar as he played with the enemy, luring them closer into range. The organic beasts were much more nimble, grabbing, biting, and clawing those ships in half one after the next—all the while continuing their rapid descent to the surface.

One fighter finally just opened fire. He shot at Tr'm, but the ammo ricocheted off his back. It did upset Tr'm, though, and he blew a fiery, acidic blast, melting three ships and severely crippling another two.

Ground fire intensified, which buffeted Ga'al around the sky. The flak also sent a few Dominion fighters down in flames. Whoever was coordinating this counter-strike on the ground had reached full panic.

R'zar was the first to land. He touched down right on the launch pad, his chest swelling with a massive orange glow. He sent the first wave of sorties scrambling from the hard deck, engulfed in flames. He didn't really concern himself with the rest of all the tiny humans running this way and that, scattering before him. Instead, he jumped forward, flapped his wings twice, and pounced upon the structure that would host the core of the Ion shield.

With ferocity, he attacked and scratched at the titanium metals and finally was able to peel off the roof. People inside screamed and leapt from the tower as R'zar's chest swelled again in that deep crimson, and then he blew a wall of molten liquid into the heart of the Ion shield generator. The flames fused the structure into a blazing inferno for thirty-two floors below ground.

Primary goal accomplished, R'zar, Tr'm, and Ga'al returned to destroying and eating everything else in their paths.

* * *

Aboard the *Libellule,* a cheer went up on the bridge. Captain Mizuke clapped Jeffries on the shoulder. He may have been a newly promoted captain but during this battle, he was acting as her quartermaster. He held the conn steady.

"Alright," Mizuke said. "Take us down to a 500-meter hover and target that headquarters.

"Aye, Captain," Jeffries replied.

"And watch the 6 o'clock high. Those carriers are starting to push into the atmosphere."

* * *

In the main corridor beneath the city, the lights flickered as the explosions of the battle continued rumbling up on the surface. Bastille and his team had carved through a lot of guards but met their strongest resistance now. The heard them before they saw them. Clang clang clanging their way down the hall.

"So much for the little worker drones," Bastille said. "Time for the Manglers. New Dominion's Elite Death Squad. The perfect Mech-warriors. With one small problem. They're driven by…"

"Skinbags. Just like you said," Dash smiled as he watched them form up down the hallway. "Professional meat-suits."

"I'm gonna draw some fire. That'll give you time to go to work," Bastille said to Dash.

Dash stood and holstered his weapon.

"Ready?" Bastille asked.

"It's a good day to knock on death's door," Dash said with a nod.

Bastille stepped out into the middle of the corridor, both guns blazing with supreme accuracy. Moose followed behind and also began tearing up the hallway. Dash jumped out, flipped past a small explosion, ran as fast he could, and then, at the last minute, slumped to the floor as if he'd passed out. Blue energy shot from his body, along the floor, mixed with the circuitry down there and then travelled up the leg of the closest Mangler. The entire Mech-machine stopped firing, then, much to its driver's horror, turned its weapons on his partner, blowing him away point blank. Then it started shooting up his other teammates. The other Manglers realized what was going on and fired back, blowing up the driver and scattering organic matter all over the walls.

Dash, escaped before the explosion. The blue energy tracked back along the floor to Gen's body, which rose up again, ran forward past that first flaming pair of Mech legs and then he slumped down again.

In the middle of the Mech unit, Dash possessed the rear Mangler who operated a powerful multichannel rail gun. Dash took control, turned it on three of the other Death Squad in front of himself. They didn't know what was happening as one after the other exploded helplessly. The remaining Manglers farther back turned on the saboteur and wasted him, but Dash had already leapt free. He repeated the grisly, but effective process again and again.

All the while, Bastille and Moose pressed steadily forward. Some troops, trying to be sneaky, came around behind, but Peanut was ready for them and opened fire, shouting, "Get you some, brats."

Bastille arrived at a precise point along the wall and triggered a side passageway. Peanut popped some smoke canisters and dropped them to the floor to add to the confusion. Dash returned to Gen's body, and they all dove through.

There were several moments of chaotic in-fighting between the Manglers and the other Dominion troops in the rear as they battled through the smoke and debris. They were just picking each other off before they realized their actual targets had vanished. They moved forward, checking around cautiously, but there was no trace.

* * *

"What do you mean, you've lost them?" Wexell yelled, her face a blotchy red. "They were right in front of you."

"Sir, they just vanished," the embarrassed captain of the Mangler Death Squad reported in an apologetic tone.

"Sir," the quartermaster cycled through some ancient maps, "it appears they are headed for this area here. Looks like an old throne room."

"But there's nothing down there," Wexell said, exasperated. "Unless..." she suddenly jumped to her feet. "Commander," she pointed to the nearest guard, " You and your men come with me."

"General," the quartermaster said before she could exit.

"What?!" Wexell yelled back.

"A dozen KACorps resistance ships have just cleared the hyper-gate."

Wexell gave him a look that would have shriveled a lesser man. "Deal with it," she commanded, then turned on her heels and left.

- 23 -
BAPTISM OF FIRE

"I repeat, we've been hit," Mizuke yelled into the comm.

"How bad is it?" Tavi6 responded back over headsets.

"We're bracing for impact. Jeffries, forty degrees starboard, take us straight into that depot." Captain Mizuke indicated a row of high rises near the center of Fort Royale, where a reserve fleet was preparing for liftoff. Explosions rocked the entire ship. It was coming apart at the seams, and the super-carrier in pursuit was relentlessly pounding them.

Mizuke continued dishing out as much as they could, fore and aft. Tavi6 swung alongside with his flagship, targeting the carrier. One of the larger Mandreen ships, low on ammo, accelerated straight into the supercarrier and broke her spine upon impact. Both ships exploded and careened off of the flight path, vectoring toward the ocean.

Mizuke had no time to celebrate. No time to mourn. The ground was rushing up at them quickly. With her ship's 360-degree visibility, she could see the dragons on the north side of town. But only two of them. One was missing. She scanned the city and found him. Ga'al collapsed onto a building, a gigantic wound on his left side exposing ribs and flesh.

She triggered the comm. "Bastille, this is Captain Strouthers. Do you read me?"

She paused and ducked as some of the ship's bridge exploded to her left, and some bedraggled seabees ran to put out the fire. She braced herself firmly against the console in front of her.

"Jacques, this is Mizuke. Do you read? Over."

* * *

Bastille had just broken radio-silence to give an update, when Mizuke's call came through.

"Jacques, this is Mizuke. Do you read? Over."

"Mizuke, I read you. Yes, I read you, Mizuke," he confirmed.

The comms cackled and hissed in return.

"We're going down, Jacques. I repeat, we have lost the *Libellule*."

"Mizuke, abandon ship. That is an order!" He growled into his comm, growing more and more concerned.

"We will get… collision… 10 seconds—heart of…" Her voice cut in and out.

"Mizuke?" Bastille listened helplessly to his comm, but there was no answer. Just a droning hiss. Up above, a thunderous explosion hit, and the entire fortress shook. Dust fell from the catwalks as the entire structure settled again, knocking them all to the ground.

"Bastille…" Dash winced in great pain.

Bastille looked behind, and Dash was doubled over, holding his stomach. He looked up at Bastille with a worried expression on his face.

"Genwa'ar is back," Dash warned him. "I'll fight her off for as long as I can. Run!"

"Ok," Bastille said, and he and Moose took off for the closest hatchway.

Moose ran through and was instantly besieged by enemy gun fire. His momentum carried him to the other side of the hall as he laid down suppressing fire, signaling to Bastille, but it was way too hot for him to enter.

Suddenly, the door between them slammed shut, and all was quiet around Bastille. Except for tiny footsteps padding down the hall. Bastille turned and knew that Gen was back.

"Welcome to the party, little dipper," Bastille said, casually slipping the Mauzer from its holster. "What took ya?"

"Been to hell and back, Bastille," she said, advancing rapidly forward.

"Awww, come give us a hug—" Bastille said, swinging the Mauzer up and squeezing off a couple rounds.

Gen was faster. She dodged, kicked off the wall, and threw a blue bolt of lightning through his arm, sending his gun flying. It stung, but only a little. Surprising both of them. Gen looked disappointed.

"Tsk, tsk, tsk. Was that meant to kill me?" Bastille laughed. "I think somebody needs to recharge their battery."

She looked down at her own hands. "Dash is putting up a bigger fight than last time. That's quite alright," she bit back at him. "You and I can do this the old-fashioned way."

She launched at him, and he fought back, but her lithe body moved so quickly that he blocked most of the blows but not all. He finally landed an upper cut, and she flipped back to recover, then sprang right back at him, so his break was short-lived.

Bastille feinted back to draw her in closer, and the moment she struck for him, he brought his arm around and extended the blade aimed right at the bridge of her nose. She dodged—barely in time—and the blade sliced across her cheek. That really pissed her off.

In a single motion, she grabbed his arm and wrenched it back. He heard snapping sounds as she brought her leg around over it and twisted with everything she had. Bastille cried out in pain, collapsing to his knees as she twisted the cybernetic arm right off his shoulder. Sparks flew out and small gears locked up as the bionic shoulder went into self-repair.

Gen approached him, throwing the arm onto the floor at his feet, the blade automatically retracting. Bastille just stared at it blankly as the physical shock twisted up his thoughts and clouded his brain.

"Just so you know, Bastille, everything has gone according to plan." Gen yanked his head back so they were eye to eye. "So I owe you one. And I'll settle this for you now. A gift for all your help. Your life. Every. Last. Memory. And the only thing I want in exchange is the Dragon-eye."

Her other hand glowed with that blue-ish power and she brought it down to touch his Relay box as she leaned in to kiss him. Blue energy zapped and swirled between them. He had imagined that feeling his own arm being ripped off would be the most painful thing he would ever experience, or that watching Kyra and her mother drown in front of him would have been the singularly most horrific thing he had ever felt. He was wrong. This was infinitely worse.

Fzzzzzzzht.

* * *

Dash sat at a dinner table in NeoTokyo.

The tiny dragon peered up from that table into Dash's eyes and forever imprinted on him with the Dragon-eye. Dash twitched and glitched and his face became Bastille's face, now old and bearded, then Gen's. The entire room glitched before disintegrating.

Fzzzzzzzht.

* * *

Bastille was back inside J'Annelie's head from Da'karh. She was naked, standing before the mirror with his Mauzer pointed at her own reflection. But her face twitched and glitched as if this memory were being re-coded before him. Or de-coded. Either way, J'Annelie now had her true face. Her true identity. Like a veil being lifted.

Mizuke.

No, not *the* Mizuke, but one of the Mizuke BLU units. BLU-132. She touched a finger to the back of her earlobe and said, "Shleev'n ven griz'a d'ahn!" And then let out some clicking sounds. Then she mouthed the words, "Bang."

Fzzzzzzzht.

* * *

NeoTokyo

Dash stood beside a very pregnant Mizuke. Dr. Vance was at work delivering the baby. Dr Vance's face glitched and snapped and became Bender's face. He quipped, "I hope you like mucous-colored hair, because that's what she's got, Captain Bastille."

Dash's young face glitched and snapped into Bastille's face. A very confused face.

"Mizuke Noelle, what are we calling this girl?" Bender asked between contractions.

Bastille said, "Don't you mean Mizuke Strouthers? Or Mizuke Blue? Who is Mizuke Noelle?"

They both ignored him.

Mizuke Noelle breathed in short lamaze bursts, *hee hee hee*, "Her name is Kyra!"

Fzzzzzzzht.

* * *

Bastille found himself in the Draccario bathhouse. All twelve of the blue-haired servants digitally scrambled for a brief second and then resolved as Mizuke BLU units. All of them.

Fzzzzzzzht.

* * *

Bastille stood at the bars in the Bravo Bay tunnel, separated from Kyra and her mother, as he pounded the edges with a rock that crumbled in his hands.

The mother's face glitched and became the face of a different Mizuke BLU unit. BLU-27. Every false memory that had been implanted and altered was being undone somehow by Genwa'ar.

Mizuke lifted Kyra up in her arms to hold her higher above the waterline. And Kyra glitched and disappeared from the scenario. As if she didn't belong there. As if she'd only been added to that heartbreaking scene to wreak emotional damage on Bastille. Why? To focus him? To bait him into this battle?

Suddenly he knew that Kyra had never been real. She wasn't a past memory at all. Somehow she was a vision into his future. Of Mizuke Noelle's future.

Mizuke BLU-27 reached through the bars and yelled to him, "Goodbye, Jacques Bastille. Go now! And find me again."

Bastille saw the wall of water behind them an instant before it pounded them.

"Noooooooooooo——!"

Fzzzzzzzht.

* * *

The mental link with Jacques Bastille was ripping R'zar apart. He reared up on his hind legs and twisted backward, roaring in pain. He tried to catch himself, but he didn't know which way was up and wound up crashing down off the roof he had been perching on into the streets below.

So many buildings were on fire. Half the city was sinking into the bay. The powerful beast lay there in the watery streets, writhing.

A band of Dominion guards saw this as their opportunity and jumped from building to building until they were street-side. They raised their Ion long-rifles and began point-blank shooting into the belly of the beast.

R'zar roared again in pain and could only barely make out the enemy forms surrounding him. He blew a protective arc, a wall of fire, and then braced an arm and a leg against one side of the street and arched his back against the other side, growling mightily as he pushed.

It worked. The couplings came undone, and the streets of the flotilla parted and began to collapse. The crumbling buildings in the immediate area fell atop the guards in the process as the dragon slowly slipped beneath the surface.

* * *

Jacques Bastille. 1-4-9-mark-5-2-mark-6-1-alpha-tango.

As Gen and Bastille stood there locked in that embrace, both their eyes white-hot and glowing, Moose and Peanut returned through the hatch, guns drawn. They didn't know who to shoot. Then Bastille pulled a knife from Gen's belt and stabbed her through the abdomen. Gen screamed as it pierced her belly.

Bastille withdrew the knife, and Gen inhaled sharply in surprise. He lowered her to the ground, where she gasped for breath, slowly bleeding out.

Peanut, breathing hard, asked, "What the hell? We're getting our asses handed to us and you're out here tongue wrestling a teenager."

"Change of plans." Bastille stood. "You two take Genwa'ar back to the MedUnit on the Mustang. Quickly or she may bleed out."

"I'm cool with her bleeding out," Peanut said as he turned to Moose. "You cool with that?"

Moose looked at Gen, cranked his head to the side like a confused dog, and then bent down and picked her up, carefully.

"Oh, thanks for the backup, buddy." Peanut wrinkled his brow in confusion, then turned back to Bastille. "So what are *you* going to do, boss?"

"Finish this," Bastille said, bending down to retrieve his own arm.

Peanut took a step in his direction. "Then we need to—"

"Alone." Bastille's eyes burned white hot. "Go."

Moose took a step back. Bastille turned and went back through the hatch, closing it behind him. Peanut watched him go and then waved a dismissive hand.

"Ugh, whatever. Come on, Moose, we've got our orders from Captain Cranky Panties. Let's move."

On the other side of the hatchway, Bastille grabbed his side in pain and fell to his knees. General Wexell's guardians rushed up, and before he could speak, one of them knocked him unconscious with the butt of a rifle.

* * *

Bastille slowly regained consciousness and realized his body was being dragged along the floor.

Jacques. 1-4-9-mark-5-2-mark-6-1-alpha-tango.

He was dropped unceremoniously on the floor. And he began to hear voices around the room. All his systems were slowly coming back online on his internal-HUD. With tremendous effort, he crawled up to his knees. Wexell stood over him, wielding his loose, cybernetic arm like a club.

"Well, this is, this is—can't say that I didn't see this coming. You should have stayed dead, my friend." She took a swing at him, connecting hard against the side of his face with his arm. Bastille sprawled to the side.

"I mean, before I kill you for real this time, what… what… were you even thinking coming back here? There is nothing here for you here in Fort Royale. Or Earth, for that matter. Except maybe a better coffin this time."

Bastille grunted painfully as he rose again to his knees, lips curling into a smile. "Everything has happened, Wexell, just as I have planned it," Bastille said, looking right at General Wexell, who looked surprised at his new tone.

She backed quickly away and waved the guards around. They all formed a tight circle, aiming weapons at Bastille.

Wexell stopped a safe distance away, regaining her composure. "Ah well. I was gonna give you the professional courtesy of some big Ma'kobi final words, but now I want you to know that—"

Wexell did not finish. At that moment, Bastille mentally triggered the loose arm the general was swinging about. The blade shot out—lightning fast—cutting through the general's mouth into her brain and out the back of her head.

The general was dead before the blade had fully retracted. Her body dropped to its knees and then collapsed to the ground.

"No speeches!" Bastille said to himself, relishing the delicious irony.

The guards spun around in shock. No one knew what to do without their dead dictator.

When the guards turned back around, Bastille had gotten back to his feet, and his eyes glowed white. They ran straight at him. Bur with blinding speed and deadly technique, he skillfully cut them down one by one. He was fast, efficient, and lethal. Just a tornado of death. All too soon, he was the only one standing.

Next, Bastille turned to the throne at the top of the stairs and said, "Jacques Bastille. 1-4-9-mark-5-2-mark-6-1-alpha-tango!"

The whole room shuddered alive as the floor shifted and monitors dropped down into place. In a matter of seconds, the derelict throne room was transformed back into a working bridge. Somewhere deep in the engine rooms, the turbines miraculously sparked to life.

"Hold on," the captain of the guard said from the ground. He pulled himself up to his feet, despite his bloodied shoulder, and leveled hi s weapon at Bastille. "That's far enough."

Bastille ignored him. He picked up the loose arm off the floor and held it in place on the socket. An army of NITs swarmed out and began stitching the arm back together at the seam. Bastille walked to the front of the bridge, then began keying a sequence into the helm. "Dash?" Bastille said, not even looking over at the guard.

A flash of blue light sparked out of the mainframe, and Dash instantly Re-cycled up into the body of the Captain of the Guard. He raised the weapon to his own head and pulled the trigger.

Blue light jumped from the falling body back into the master control panel beside at the conn.

"Dash," Bastille said. "Take us up."

* * *

On the surface of Miramar, the fighting had stopped. A single dragon patrolled the air, bellowing loudly. Searching. Some sea condors rose up to face this new challenger to their territory, but one fiery blast from Tr'm left half of their group dead and the others diving for the sea to extinguish their flaming appendages. And that's when the sharks began a frenzied retaliation of their own against the crippled birds of prey.

Topside, the New Dominion forces, who had been crawling out of the debris, suddenly felt a large earthquake. The ground of their huge flotilla city began splitting apart. Soldiers ran screaming everywhere and tried to jump across the chasm to the other side. Some made it; others did not. Fort Royale's epicenter began crumbling. Vibrations sent everything careening off the edges.

From his vantage point above, Tavi6 watched and smiled as he could detect an old, familiar form amid all that rubble below. When the buildings collapsed and slid into the sea, a ship began to emerge, water cascading from its decks like a baptism.

"Son of a bitch," Tavi6 said. "That's the *Bellevue!* Right under our noses. *Son of a bitch!*"

Indeed, it was the St. Croix Vessel B*ellevue.* Now, Ma'kobi Ship Bellevue. The *MKS Bellevue* rose from the deep waters where Bastille had carefully hidden it years and years ago. Water rained down from its belly and all over the port below. The ship rose higher and higher until it was completely airborne.

The mighty *Bellevue.* Arisen One.

The top bay doors slid to the sides, revealing a superclass rail gun. It rose into position, aiming into the heart of the on-going battle in space above.

* * *

When the KACorps ships had gotten close enough to the battle zone high above the planet's surface, *Phaedra's*

Deliverance had fired upon them too. Three forces at war. The KACorps army had intended to sail in and engage their New Dominion rivals. But the Draccario battleship attacked them. So they momentarily joined the Fugs and Ma'Kobi ships in repulsing the Croix.

Even banded together, they were still losing to the dreadnought, which had seemingly endless shields and energy weapons at its disposal. They'd barely even scratched it. All of that changed when a powerful blast from the planet below rippled through their ranks and scored a direct hit on the Draccario vessel. Their shields disintegrated as they absorbed one hell of a hit down the left side.

The remaining twelve vessels in the battle group opened fire, but the Draccario ship wouldn't surrender. In a gigantic volley, it retaliated with a huge counter-spread against the remaining warships, sending them careening this way and that. In the brief moment of respite before the remaining ships could return fire and before the *Bellevue* could recharge its own super-weapon, the *Phaedra* powered up their drives and dove back into hyperspace.

Gone.

"The Croix vessel has disengaged," Tavi6 reported to the rest of the fleet. "The Croix vessel has disengaged."

* * *

Beneath the Fort Royale destruction, the Mustang sat on the landing pad in the secret grotto. Inside, Moose and Peanut were pretty excited about the battle report. They stood below decks in front of a monitor in Bastille's quarters.

"I can't believe it. We won. We're gonna be so stinkin' filthy rich that we—"

The distinct sound of a weapon arming behind them interrupted Peanut's celebration. They turned, and Gen leaned there against the doorway—bleeding through her fresh bandages—with a Squawk box rifle aimed at them both. One move, and they would both be atomized easily. Especially in these confined quarters.

"You just don't know when to quit, do you, Lady?" Peanut growled, slowly reaching behind his back to the concealed pistol in his belt.

* * *

On the bridge of the *Bellevue*, Bastille opened a comm channel.

"This is Captain Jacques Bastille of the *MKS Bellevue*. Fort Royale has fallen. The Croix have been routed, and a new dawn rises. Everyone who lays down arms and accepts clemency, we will take into our new League of Nations moving forward. But continue fighting? And we will cut you down to the last man, woman, and child." Bastille paused to let that sink in before continuing. "Carrier group, prepare shuttle transports for the Fort Royale survivors. Attention all fighters! We will begin assembling in hangars two, three, and four aboard the *Bellevue*. We depart for NeoTokyo within the hour."

Unit leads responded on the comm as he looked over at the gigantic screen showing Fort Royale below.

At the center was the wreckage of the *Libellule*, burning stem to stern.

Bastille watched on-screen as Tavi6's *Challenger IV* hovered over top of it. He zoomed in twice to see what they were doing. A small Med-Unit emerged from a hole in the bridge with what appeared to be some very broken bodies inside Medvats.

"Tavi6," Bastille called over comms, "any survivors on the *Libellule*?"

"None," Tavi6 called back. "I'm sorry, brother."

"Okay," Bastille said, finally. "Bring her home."

"Roger that."

Another officer reported in, "Captain Bastille, all ships have reported en route into position. That just leaves hangar one, sir."

Bastille nodded. Then closed his eyes and called, '*R'zar!*'

* * *

The waters and debris swirled around on the surface of Fort Royale, and then a host of bubbles steamed to the top before R'zar burst forth back into the sky. Clutched in his paws was a half-eaten sea creature.

Tr'm roared and flipped backward excitedly. R'zar flapped his leathery wings mightily as he passed him on the way to the *Bellevue*. R'zar chuffed once, and Tr'm fell in with his Alpha.

R'zar dropped his sea snack on the flight deck. Tr'm landed beside him and took a huge victory bite from the squirming creature. As the *Bellevue* rose, the hangar door slowly closed, and the dragons watched the orange sun rays disappear behind them.

They collapsed, battle-weary, on the floor. R'zar let out a sigh, and then a giant dragon belch.

Conditions were perfect. It was good to be going home.

* * *

There were now five Dominion carriers and three KA-Corps ships left—all of them extensively damaged. A pyrrhic victory indeed. They just sat up there, slowly spinning in empty space across from each other. By now, there were hundreds of distress signals emanating from the wreckage of all the other ships.

The KACorps moved out to aid the wounded and bring them aboard. The Dominion ships moved to do the same. Each one rescuing, independent of whether the distress was KACorps or New Dominion or Ma'kobi. It looked like the new League of Nations was already working together.

* * *

Back in the Fort Royale grotto aboard the Mustang, there was a tense standoff between Moose, Peanut, and Genwa'ar. Gen had recovered enough from her injuries to fire up the Squawk Box and level it at them both. In such tight quarters, it'd make a mess of them both in short order.

"You've got some nerve, brat," Peanut scowled at her.

"Shut it, pocket monkey. What did I tell you both back on the *DayStar* when you first told us your suicidal Mandreen plan? If there was dying to be done, it would not be us," Gen said.

Or was it Gen at all? Peanut was confused. Gen de-activated the long-gun and tossed it to Moose, who caught it handily in one paw.

"What's going on?" Peanut asked, not quite ready to let go of the butt of his own gun. "Who's driving that skinbag?"

"Jacques Bastille." He smiled wearily. "Or... what's left of him."

Moose and Peanut stared at him, unblinking.

"Sorry, we've already got one of those," Peanut replied with a slight twinkle in his eye.

Bastille said evenly. "I doubt it, pocket monkey. But this I guarantee, you put me in a room with *that* Jacques Bastille and only one true Ma'kobi King emerges."

"Son of a bitch," Peanut smiled. He smacked Moose's leg and said, "You knew all along, didn't you?"

Moose grunted back at him with a nod.

"Holy sh*t. She traded places during the, the, the electric French kiss thingy," Peanut said, finally catching up.

Bastille nodded.

"We've gotta go find her. Kick her ass. Get you back in your own—"

"You know what?" Bastille inhaled deeply and pointed to the Viddix monitor where Gen masqueraded as Jacques Bastille. "She can have it."

"What?" Peanut asked.

"The whole Ma'kobi King thing. This'll be good for little dipper," Bastille lifted his shirt and checked the gauze expertly wrapped around his abdomen.

"Yeah, I don't follow, boss," Peanut said.

"The perfect Jacques Bastille skinbag with all Jacques Bastille's long-lost memories, by the way. She's got all of that. At the helm of Jacques Bastille's long-lost ship, leading Jacques Bastille's brand new League of Nations Dominion Kytos Alliance of Ma'Kobi squiffing brotherhood."

"You're just gonna… let her be *you*?" Peanut scratched at his head.

"It's not our fight," Bastille waggled a finger at him.

"Not our—" Peanut was deeply confused now.

"Our mission," Bastille counted out on his fingers, starting with the index finger, "was to crush General Wexell. Raise the *Bellevue*, route the Croix army, and end the slavers at Fort Royale. Done," he said, wiping his hands together and holding his palms out. "Now, if Gen wants the headaches of nation-building, interplanetary diplomacy, committees, unification talks, and political diaper changing, she can have it, boys."

"A-and—" Peanut shook his head to clear it out. "Whoa. Okay, but what do you get?"

Bastille sighed happily and then spread his arms wide. "Retirement."

"Gross!" The whole concept didn't sound right to Peanut.

"You asked me why I left the Ma'kobi brotherhood? Freedom. That's it. To live a single day without washing another man's blood off my hands. Freedom.

Anonymity. We can go anywhere and do anything. Start all over."

"We?"

"We," he motioned to all three of them, "and Mizuke, of course."

"Oh, boss," Peanut dropped his chin sadly, "how can I put this—Mizuke is gone. You didn't see what we saw in the topside footage. She is *gone,* gone."

Bastille nodded thoughtfully. "A temporary setback, I assure you. Nothing our good pal Bender can't fix, right? Besides, I've received good word from Savvy Tavi that arrangements have been made. He's got Mizuke's Relay. Bender's got the next-generation BLU units. But we've gotta move fast. So, are you in or out?"

Moose definitely looked like he was on board from the start. He nodded to Peanut, who nodded back with a shrug, saying, "Of course we're in! Hell, you think we're gonna go topside and—" he pointed to the monitor of Jacques Bastille commanding from the *Belle-vue,* "—spend the rest of our lives taking orders from some woman?" Peanut smirked at the irony of his own words. He straightened, planted a fist against his heart. "Our swords are yours, boss. Mizuke, too. To the end of the sky."

"Alright then, we best weigh anchor, boys," Bastille said, taking a shaky step forward.

Moose grunted something, and Peanut translated. "Moose questions whether you're in any condition to fly."

Bastille lifted his shirt and peeled off the bandages. Moose and Peanut objected but he waved them off. He yanked the last strip of it all the way off. With the exception of some dried blood, there was no sign of any knife damage.

"What the living hell?" Peanut scrunched up his face. "We saw you get cut up pretty bad, boss."

"Apparently, between Dash and Gen's modifications, this Byno-Core has some pretty cool upgrades." Bastille held his arms akimbo as Peanut and Moose surveyed the completely healed stomach.

"Cool, I guess, then should we rejoin the *Challenger* or the *Bellevue*?" Peanut asked.

"No, sir." Bastille pushed past them as he headed up to the cockpit. "We have pressing business on Ver-Dav'n."

Peanut looked up at Moose. "The Outlands?!"

"The Outlands." Bastille threw two thumbs up.

Peanut sighed heavily. "By Hera's cooch, you will be the death of me yet, Bastille."

"I want gear up in ten." Bastille climbed the ladder up into the pilot seat and triggered the latch, raising the seat into flight position. "And Peanut?"

"Sir?" The little man cranked his head up to see him better.

"Don't forget DUG."

"Aye, aye, Cap'n," Peanut saluted and then tapped Moose, and they both headed out to retrieve the underwater AI unit.

\- Epilogue -
AFTERMATH

VerDav'n Colony in the Outlands

Bender limped into his laboratory with a bionic cast around his left leg. Even though it was his own workmanship, he didn't wholly trust it, hence the cane. The lab was still in some disarray, walls were charred from the battle with Bastille almost a month ago. Everything was still pretty chewed up. So was he. But he had at least reclaimed a small corner and brought it back into operational order. So, technically, he was open for business.

Bender limped over to the clean corner of his laboratory and hit a button. The entire wall moved to the side and a giant Medvat stood before him. Inside the Medvat was a very pregnant Mizuke form. Bender walked up reverently and tenderly placed his arms around the blue glowing tube in an oversized hug.

"Good morning, my love! I am so sorry. I'm moving a little slow today. But you are looking as radiant as ever, Mizuke Null. And how is little Kyra today?" He checked some monitors and feeds, and everything was normal. Heart rates, temperatures, and overall development of the mother and baby were perfect. He tapped the glass lovingly, saying, "Right on schedule."

He paused as if he were hearing a second half of the conversation from the inert woman, then continued, "I know. I can't believe it either. They said it couldn't be done. A pregnant BLU unit. Impossible! Hahaha, those pignut—oh! Sorry!" He clapped his hand over his own mouth apologetically. "The baby. Yes, I promised to watch my language."

He placed two hands up to block out her pregnant belly from his sight and whispered, "Those pignut Draccario sh*tcorkers said it couldn't be done." He dropped his hands from the glass, giggling, and resumed his normal voice. "Yet here we are. A Fourth-Gen Mizuke unit. One of one. Version zero. Mizuke NULL. In her third trimester. And absolutely crushing it! No, you stop." Bender looked around coyly and said, "So can you tell me who the father is, I promise not to get mad or—"

He stopped when he heard a loud voice in the hallway. A human voice. How very odd. He shut the lights off, so the whole corner went dark. Out here, humans were a rare occurrence and always problematic. The fat man almost tripped over some floor rubble on his way to the door, but then kicked it angrily out of the way, cursing loudly. "Sorry, my love! Language." He shouted back over his shoulder towards the MedVats.

With great scraping and grinding sounds, the janky lab doors slid aside, and two Outworld Snakes stood there atop their hover-disc transports attached to their single-leg appendages. They each securely held the arm of Tavi6's lieutenant. His feet dangled a foot off the ground. The Snakes maneuvered their hover-discs forward.

"Lieutenant Meeks, you little squiffer." Bender beamed, waving him forward. "Come in, come in."

"Bender," Meeks pleaded, "they're trying to kill me."

The Snakes dropped him, and he fell to his knees and scurried through the rubble toward Bender, grabbing his leg as though he were some sort of home base.

"Ouch! Do you mind?!" Bender rapped him on the forehead with the cane.

"Sorry, Bender." He continued to grovel, but at a more respectful distance. He whimpered again, loudly, "They're trying to kill me."

"Nonsense, Meeks." Bender waved the preposterous idea off. "Now tell me. What did you bring me?"

Meeks pointed back to one of the Snakes, who unwrapped a cloth and handed over a pristine Relay box. Bender's eyes lit up. "Is that what I think it is?" He kicked Meeks aside and moved quickly to take the prized possession from the lead Snake.

"Meeks, what are the chances you were followed here?" He glared back at the young lieutenant.

Meeks's eyes grew wide. "No, no way. No way in hell, Bender, I copied her Relay just like you showed me with your special stick thingie, and *nobody* saw it, nobody knows it's missing, nobody even suspects a thing. Zero witnesses. Just like you said."

Bender was actually impressed. "Wow. Very good, Meeks." He nodded at the Snakes who stepped around to grab Meeks and drag him, kicking and protesting from the room.

"Wait, Bender! Wait! What are you doing? You promised!"

"No witnesses," Bender shrugged as the doors squealed and vibrated closed at a painstakingly slow pace.

Bender hobbled quickly back to the MedVats. "My love, oh, my sweet darling, finally after all these years, I have found you a soul. A healthy mind. I can bring you alive. I mean, as soon as I reprogram a few things, of course, add in a spicy fetish or two, maybe a few vices, but the point is, my precious, we can finally be a family together."

He stood on his tiptoes and kissed the "Mizuke NULL + Kyra RED" signs on the glass case and even slipped in a little tongue action before a gigantic monitor to his left beeped loudly.

"What?!" he yelled obnoxiously. He loathed these interruptions. He triggered the comm, and a highly decorated reptilian stood before him.

"Commandant. My apologies." Bender bowed as low as he could. "How may I serve you, your supreme excellency, sir?"

The Commandant answered in pure Outworld fashion as a series of clicks and pops.

"The countdown? Sir, are we ready? So soon?"

A few more bat-like sounds from the Lizard Commander.

"Very good, sir. Of course. Understood. I will—"

The monitor flashed off. He was gone. And Bender stood there, stricken. "My goddess, I've got so much work to do. Are they insane? I don't even—" He looked at the Relay box again in his hand. "Ah yes, coming, my dear."

Bender waddled back over to the terminal and began typing feverishly, humming an old, old wedding tune while he worked. "Dum dum de duuuuuum. Dum dum de duuuuuuum."

Another communication interrupted his happy dance. "This better be good," he growled at the screen.

It was the Port Authority, clicking and popping about an incoming bogey.

"A M-mustang, you say?" Bender began to turn pale. "Y-yes, don't touch them. Send an escort and bring the piker straight here."

The transmission ended. He hung his head dejectedly. Then he turned to regard his beloved Mizuke NULL again. Sadly this time. "Sh*t! So close this time. So squiffin' close." His eyes narrowed at her suspiciously. "You're gonna choose him over me again, aren't you?" He held his hand up, laughing derisively, "Hahaha, oh no, no, you don't have to defend him to me, you slutty little minx." He stopped and his smile faded with a heavy sigh. "I know. Language."

Bender flipped a switch on another MedVat to the left, and a light turned on. Growing inside was another Biosynth form. A male form. The NITs were far from finished with their dynamic reconstruction, but this Byno-Core could easily be recognized as a Jacques Bastille 2.0 model.

"Yes, you two were literally made for each other."

The End

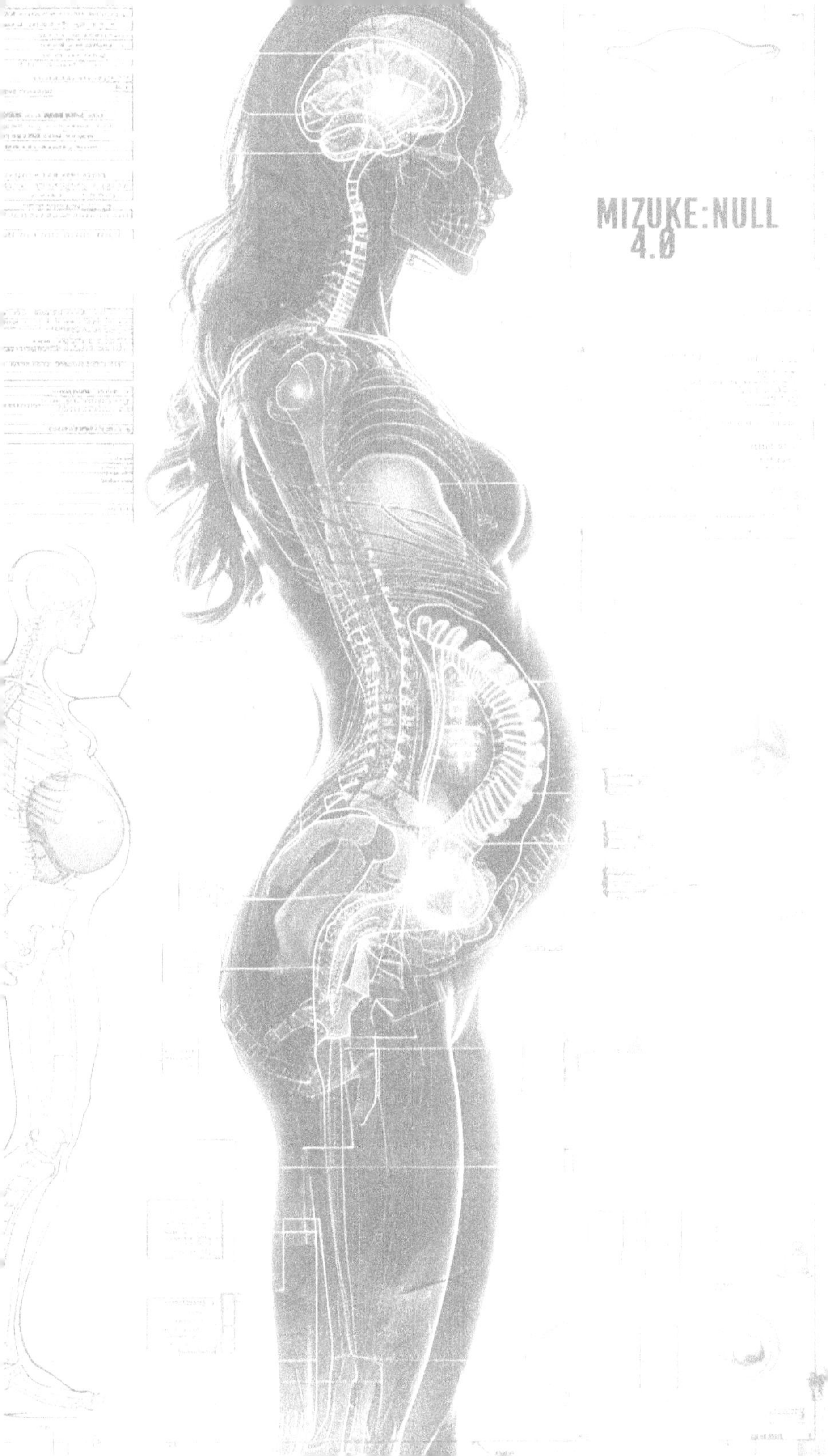

MIZUKE:NULL
4.0

CREDITS

BETA READERS	Joe Wilson
	Kenneth E. Niblock
	Melissa Nunnally
	Scott Davidson
	Stephen Pfann Jr.
EDITOR	Bryan Thomas Schmidt
COVER ART	Frank Capezzuto
CONCEPT ART	Midjourney AI

BRAVO BAY BOOKS

Bravo Bay is a fictional top secret test facility for fighter jockeys and experimental aircraft in Acuff's best-selling release *Battle Tides*.

BravoBay Books, on the other hand, is a top-secret test facility for word jockeys and experimental ideas.

Those who have read our books, *Historians Proper, High School Masquerade, The Wrestling Girl, Slay Bells Ring,* and *A Kingdom Without A King* know the high quality of our work and our commitment to first-rate story-telling.

Stay frosty and bleed the edge, my friends.

ABOUT THE AUTHOR

S. David Acuff grew up the son of an Air Force Colonel and lived all over the US and Taiwan.

Being the new kid every year in school bestowed on him a resilience and objectivity; to see through local prejudices, politics and predilections. It gave him the best vantage point to view all of these different lives and delicious stories and see how they intersected and collided with often unexpected results.

Since 2014, Acuff has lived in Los Angeles, CA. He was a Producer-Editor for Walt Disney for seven years. And he enjoys doing voiceover work for Audible book projects as well as animated characters.

He has three *amazing* daughters—Caitlyn, Alexis and Raegan. And his life-motto is very simply, "What doesn't kill you makes you funnier!"

Keep tabs on his book, film, and TV shenanigans at:

www.davidacuff.com

GLOSSARY

AlphaN1 Wormhole - The hyper-gate closest to Earth, just off Saturn; heavily guarded by the Kytos Alliance.

Atmospheric Drives - The range of engines which allow for flight maneuvering inside Earth-type environs

Aurora Band/Ring - Hyper-gate technology to cap and stabilize the wormholes; allows material transfers from hyper-space to neutral space; produces travel over great distances

BaseZero - Earthprime language a lot more like traditional English

Battle Dragon - A home-grown lab experiment by the St. Croix scientists to create a sentient, organic weapon

Bender - The only human living on VerDav'n. A mad scientist, who is shadyAF and dabbles in outlawed and forbidden tech and dark science

BLU - Biosynthetic Lifeform Utility. These particular models are generally romantic servants aka poppets

Bly'nette Olferr'n - Oldest and orneriest member of the St. Croix council; political enemy of Genwa'ar

Bounty hounds - Derogatory name for bounty hunters

Bounty Hunters - A working union class of the Masada people in the Outworlds like Veegr and Dak; otherwise known as Snakes for their lizard-like features and their single leg; originally human but so genetically modded up and mutated there's less of a person and more of a cold-blooded killer

Bravo Bay - This is the informal code name that the test pilots call the top-secret KACorps underwater testing facilities at Miramar Settlement in the Caribbean

Byno-Core - Binary cybernetic organism aka a meat-suit or wearable skin that can be Re-cycled into; Byno-Cores are fully assembled at the optimal human age of 16 instead of being developed from embryos like a clone

Byno-Nurse - Cybernetic medical staff on board the *Bellevue*

Captain Arkin - Ma'kobi ship captain who mutinied against Mizuke's command and was sent to the Dragon Council never to be heard from again

Caverns of Lycendale - Hunting grounds near the home world of Jacques and Tavi6 where they would get into trouble growing up; they both have wicked scars from there to remember it by

Challenger IV - Tavi6's massive Ma'kobi flagship vessel; A mish-mash of new tech and ancient ships including an old Space Shuttle

Cici-D - Renowned artist and painter from the Colonial Rise Period after WWIII circa 2264; brilliant and peaceful oil renderings eschewing man-made tech

Coda Force - VerDav'n special security forces in the Outworlds

Comms Relay Box- Information and memory nexus at the back of a Byno-Core's neck that allows humans to interface seamlessly with ships and computer systems both wirelessly and via cables and other attachments

Corrina's Delight - a Mandreen warship; it briefly materialized in the planet core where the *DayStar* attempted its escape through the wormhole and a deadly battle ensued

Cryo-tanks or Cryo-tubes - These medical vats contain technology to build out a fully organic Byno-Core or act as storage for organic materials before Re-cycling

Cybervision - Electronic enhancements that allows a pilot to see through their cockpits and into a 3D space around their entire ship

Cyrenium Shell - High tech composite material that the H2X shell is made from; 12x stronger than Titanium, yet pliable enough to cushion and absorb impacts from space junk or small arms fire

D'erik - Genwa'ars all-digital associate on the Shadow Moon; an elaborate AI program

D/U/G or DUG - Defensive Underwater Guardian; these mother drones are tethered in place and are equal parts science laboratories and weather stations and military defense; they contain up to 50 smaller attack drones

Da'karh - Desert planet off the shipping lanes to the Outworlds; this is where Bounty Hunters ambush Jacques Bastille and force him to crash land

Dav'n Jess - An important historic figure in space flight history. He manned the first interstellar expedition to the Outworlds and was responsible for introducing the Sea Condor firebirds to Earth

Dr. Morrisey - The KACorps surgeon responsible for Dash's neural enhancements

Dr. Vance - A 150-year-old genius doctor aboard the *Bellevue*; helped invent the Re-cycle process which is why he's so wary of it

Draccario Bath House - Communal bathing and social experience on the Shadow Moon of Phaedra that boosts healing and vitration in an open group nudist environ

DragonRider Rifle - A formidable St. Croix weapon; concussion blasts from a crossbow-like, long-barrel configuration

Dragon Council - A mock-trial system aboard the *Scarlet Libellule* conducted by R'zar, Tr'm, and Ga'al that always ended in the accused human being devoured

EMP - Illegal Electro-Magnetic Pulse weapon included in the latest Mustang H2X-Ø; kills everything electrical powered within a 3-mile radius

Enginion powered - Cyclone technologies embraced by the Mandreen and Ma'kobi engineers that are a more modern and dirtier cousin to the steam engine

Fists of Ma'kobi - Prophecy revealed to the St. Croix council concerning some massive weapon technology which they invented but would not be able to harness

Flight Control - The Combat Information Center (CIC) for testing operations at Bravo Bay

G9 Gate - On the other side of Tamora; one of the many hyper-gates used to navigate great distances and time; one of the quickest routes back into the Milky Way

General Wexell - a rogue KACorps warlord that grew to power during the Surface Wars; she split off her own group called the New Dominion which she headquartered in the Miramar ruins she renamed Fort Royale; hellbent on power and galactic subjugation

Genwa'ar - Fearless leader and visionary of the St. Croix people; 16-year-old petite blond on outside, devious 220

year old on the inside; hell bent on power and galactic peace

Ghorkin Ale - A very specific adult mead in the Ma'kobi colonies

"Good Scat!" - A military communication meaning "Hit confirmed. Good scatter"; generally used after a target is blown to smithereens with a one in a million shot

Gravitron - On board the *Libellule* this inertial regulator allowed you to dial the gravity of the ship from ZeroG to 10x; useful aboard freighters for loading ships easily

H2X-1 Mustang - This is Jacques Bastille's personal space craft; similar to a Millenium Falcon or a Firefly it can lead an attack, smuggle cargo or people, or act as a battering ram; it's predecessor the H2X-Ø was first test driven by KACorps pilot Dash Strouthers at Bravo Bay

Hover-discs - Travelling devices for the Outworld Snakes; fits on their single appendage so they can maneuver upright without crawling

HX-45f Marauder - Kytos AirCorps top fighter before the advent of the H2X-Ø Mustang; highly maneuverable

Hydro Drives - Engines and turbine assemblies utilized specifically for maneuvering ships like the HX-45 and the H2X-Ø underwater

Hyper-gates/JumpGate - This St. Croix technology caps off various wormholes to stabilize them allowing interstellar travel and exploration

Ion Drives - Engine systems designed for space travel up to Sub-light speeds

Iridium Core - What powered the Ion or sub-light drives aboard the *DayStar*

J'annelie - A rogue MizukeBLU unit that Bender conscripts to track down and land Jacques Bastille so he can acquire the huge bounty; she and Bastille are mates before her grisly demise in the Da'karh attack

Jacques Bastille, Captain - A retired Ma'kobi King; he was Re-cycled into Dash's old modded up Byno-Core and after an attack loses all his own memories; at the same time it triggers Dash's rebirth as latent storage and personality is shaken loose

Johnny "Walker" Sato, Captain - One of Dash and Step's Academy mates that got pinned to Captain even before they did; a helluva story teller

K-Gate - The hyper-gate for VerDav'n in the Outworlds

Kamo (aka Kam) - Messenger on Mandreen Colony carrying news of the approaching Shadow Moon to Tavi6

Kuraac - Coffee. It was a potent home brew that prisoner's made that could jolt an elephant

Kyra - Some mystery surrounds this young girl who appears at first to be a memory, but later is revealed to be a prophecy; she will be the daughter of the BLU 4.0 unit named Mizuke Noelle

Kytos Academy - The Kytos Alliance Naval Air Corps training university located under NeoTokyo

Kytos Alliance - A consortium of hundreds of nations and survivors of the Earth Singularity Event of 2264; when global top-side becomes unlivable they migrate underwater to NeoTokyo

Landing Pad III - Basically the driveway of Bender's place on VerDav'n; as the sole human, he doesn't reside in the city proper rather has his lab on the outskirts of town

Leviathon-Class super-carrier - The monster ships had been theorized for years but never materialized until the St. Croix unleashed their own version in the crazy Battle of Fort Royale

Liz T'arn - She is a wise and weathered old ship captain fighting under Tavi6's banner

Lunar Dale - This was a former military base and colony located on the surface of Earth's moon before it was destroyed in World War III along with 2/3 of the moon

Ma'kobi - a gypsy clan of scavengers and outcasts and roughnecks who settled in Miramar for a while before they were driven off-world to the garbage planet of Mandreen where they thrived

Mag-chocks, binders - Magnetic devices that create a seal around a ship's landing struts so it doesn't dance around the cargo bay during flight maneuvers and hyper-dives

Mandreen Catamaran - The type of ship Bastille commandeers from Mandreen when it is being destroyed; it's a smaller one-manned fighter with an outrigger that allow for interstellar travel

Manglers - Special ops mech-soldiers in stolen KACorps gear. They are New Dominion warriors with augmented exoskeletons and exist as part of General Wexell's death squad

Mauzer - Outlawed military dirty weapon that Jacques Bastille favors with two settings: Stun or Scatter

Mech-room - aboard the *Daystar* this space allows a single operator to harness all the external weapons systems on the ship to focus an attack or defend

MediPen - The vape device like Peanut uses for doses of a strong, weed-type medicine and pain reliever

Megasaur - See, *Battle Dragon*

Michael "Dash" Strouthers, Captain - A brilliant KACorps test pilot stationed at Bravo Bay. He's 6' 2" and aged between 18 to 24 in the flashbacks; currently more that 100 years old when he reanimates in Jacques Bastille's time

Miramar Settlement - Located in the Caribbean; a top secret military testing labs and facilities for research and development similar to a Skunk Works or Area 51; see, *Bravo Bay*

Mizuke Blue; (Mizuke BLU) - Originally a Biosynthetic Lifeform Utility invented by the St. Croix people; a limited edition Japanese servant class model with electric blue hair and blue eyes; the original Mizuke BLU never learns her origins until later in life which sets her on a path to emancipation and self-discovery alongside Jacques Bastille

MobileComm - An internally referenced heads-up-display technology that links to ships like the Mustang H2X-Ø and *Daystar*

Moose - Beast of a man; Peanut's partner-in-crime; lost his ability to talk after his tongue was removed during a brutal time at Tomar's Ranch in the Rangoor Nebula

Nanoids - Teeny tiny repair droids; see *NITs*

NavCOMM - Like an interstellar GPS guidance system

Neural Implants - Fabric and chip implants for the human brain; performance and communication enhancers

New Dominion - General Westerly's dark new off-shoot faction from the Kytos Alliance Corporation

New Thegas - An entire city based on gambling and vice; Bender's dream residence

NeoTokyo - The hub of the orient; a massive underwater city and home to KACorps headquarters

NITs - Nanobot Integration Technology - an electronic salve of AI bots that serve medical or military purposes

Othello's Ruin - A high-tech colony terraformed by the St. Croix before the bloody dragon schism drove them off-planet

Outveldt - the language of the Outworlders; not a Latin-based language, either. It is closest to Japanese kanji but with a braille influence. Spoken by a series of clicks and pops akin to a bat.

Outworld expeditions - Deep-space exploration in the year 2315s brought on by the advent of Hyper-dive technology in 2310; see *Dav'n Jess*

Outworlders or outlanders - The Masada people who have built up their colonies and civilization past the known edges of explored space. Derogatorily called Snakes due to the fact that these former humans have been so genetically modded up and mutated they resemble lizard people; their language is *Outveldt*

Peanut - A killer dwarf with a dark past and a quick trigger-finger; Moose's partner-in-crime

Perkweed - type of cigar sourced on Rangoor; some use for medicinal purposes but also a stimulant booster

Phaedra's Deliverance - a Draccario dreadnought class battleship; built inside the Shadow Moon is this White Chrysolyte super structure

Poppets - Derogatory term for Mizuke BLU sex dolls

Prairie Lizards - delicious cattle-like creatures that raise up on their hind legs sniffing the air for danger along the Synad River below Bender's headquarters; their main predator is the Sea Condor

Puerto Rico Trench - The deepest trench located on the boundary between the Caribbean Sea and the Atlantic Ocean; training ground for the BravoBay corps

Qubits - Form of digital currency like credits, dollars or woolongs

R'zar, Ga'al and Tr'm - The names of the remaining megasaurs of St. Croix; see *Battle Dragons*

Ranger Force or SkyCross Squadron - KACorps Elite Security forces for Bravo Bay

Ranger Skiffs - Ships of the SkyCross Squadron shaped like a "T"; high tech Tartan-Ballard engines allow them to hover securely in precise 3D airspace as lookouts or long-range sniper bunkers

Rangoor Nebula - The grisly, precarious system where the infamous Tomar's Ranch is located; even worse than Mandreen

Re-cycling - The now-outlawed process of injecting someone's essence or *Tchula* into a new Byno-Core; sometimes done for life-extension for the rich and notorious, sometimes as a witness protection solution

Reeks or Re-cycle Geeks - Dark science engineers who can perform the Re-cycling process successfully; see *Bender*

Retinal HUD or HUD-link - It's like a computer terminal in your eye; no one else can see because it's only in your own vision; can provide information, analysis, or assistance on any given task or subject

Ronin, Spectral Ronin - A leftover ghost line; one of the reasons Re-cycling was outlawed; it's a soul without a body to call home; a temporal gypsy

Rovers - Workers on the Mandreen Settlement who scoured the surface looking for usable garbage or supplies to upcycle

Salty Dawgs - Old school name for the KACorps Navy pukes who'd earned their wings

Sanji - The guardian left behind after Tavi6's forces abandon Mandreen; Bastille takes over his Byno-Core and uses it to commandeer a ship to escape

SATDrones - A military-based satellite drone swarm

Satellite Beacons - Twelve of these line an Aurora ring to cap a hyper-gate and allow ships to pass through upon activation

Scarlet Libellule - An old Croix transport ship and battle wagon designed to transport dragons into action

SCV Bellevue - The only other St. Croix dreadnought class battleship that could take on *Phaedra's Deliverance;* it changed ownership several times through the years and then was lost all together

Sea condors or firebirds - Large fire-breathing birds of prey imported from the Outworlds and now residing in Bravo Bay and terrorizing the local wildlife

Seabee - General crew members in the KACorps

Seedlines - The ghostline or soul of a person; a spirit that can move into a new Byno-Core

Señora Remoras - Like the little Remora fishies these impressionable club minions flock to the naval cadets to swim in their shadows and pick from their table crumbs

Seklas - Seed bricks; worth a fortune on the black market; can jump start an entire colony worth of food, vegetation and animal life from one brick's DNA

Shadow Moon/Phaedra - Draccario engineered/terraformed planet; surrounded by a water layer; it's a glorified bio-dome

"Shin'sey" - Means hello in St. Croix language of Croi'shu

Sig Cannon - Battle upgrades to freighter's and blockade runners to weaponize them; a dangerous plasma blaster on a gatling-type platform

Skinbag - A derogatory name for a person inhabiting a Byno-Core or meat-suit

SkySAT - The monitor and conducting station orbiting the earth that tracks all sky and space traffic patterns

Sonic Safety Pulse - An agitating soundwave that clears the flight path underwater in Bravo Bay of fish and other aquatic invaders

Sonic Wafers - Drug addicts akin to meth heads

Squawk Box Rifle Cannon - A specialized hand-operated artillery weapon akin to a bazooka; standard issue on KACorps ships

SS DayStar - A Sea Scout class ship with an iridium core and mech weapons and sig cannons; commanded by Captain Mizuke Strouthers

St. Croix - A once peaceful religious group of separatists; highly intelligent and evolved; they developed hyper-space travel, ion drives, dragon technology, etc; see, *Draccarios*

StarNET and D/S - Intergalactic internet and D/S (data streams); similar to wifi it has hotspots throughout the galaxy (generally along the Hyper-gate lanes) and not 100% available 100% of the time

Stephanie "Step" Phillips, Major - A Kytos Alliance colleague and best friend of Dash Strouthers since Kytos Academy

Stone Scorpion - A deadly gravedigger warship that hangs out in the dumps around Mandreen airspace picking off visitors

Tanner - Flight Engineer and pilot of the *DayStar*; brother of Zimmer

Tartan-Ballard Engines - VTOL Engines on the Ranger Skiffs

Tavi6 - The leader of the Ma'kobi clan on Mandreen; has the upper body of a man and the lower body of a bull; Jacques Bastille's brother

Tchula - A person's spirit or essence which is transplant-ed into another body in a process called Re-cycling

Thirium Relay Upgrade - What Genwa'ar gives Bastille to upgrade his Byno-Core functionality; she promises 'bigger stronger faster smarter and younger'

Tomar's Ranch - Makes Alcatraz look like Sesame Street; a horrible place to intern as a prisoner as Moose and Peanut can attest to first hand

Viktor Tomos - Philosopher and engineer during the KACorps hearings of 2522 when Re-cycling humans was outlawed; quoted frequently

Traci "Gigsby" Riggins, Ranger - Trusted and capable Ranger Lead of the SkyCross squadron

Triangulum Quadrant - Location of the Draccario Shad-ow Moon when it is anchored around ESB K-80 ice planet

Vancinex - A mind-enhancing and pain-relieving med-ication invented by the Croix; urban legend says it gives certain users the ability to see into the future

Vega System - Location of the Mandreen Settlement of the Ma'kobi people commanded by Tavi6

VerDav'n - The home colony and headquarters of the Masada people in the Outworlds; discovered by Dav'n Jess; current home of Bender the Reek

Viddix - More than just video these vidscans are 3D and holographic motion pictures, archives and communications

Vincent "Gator" Gordon, Lt. Colonel - One of Dash's best friends from their Kytos Academy days and a squadron commander at Bravo Bay

Vitration - Special powerful vitamin supplements with long-lasting boosts and enhancements at a cellular level

Zimmer - Flight Surgeon on the *SS Daystar*; degenerate brother of Tanner

Jacques Bastille and Mizuke BLU
will return.

www.ingramcontent.com/pod-product-compliance
Lightning Source LLC
Chambersburg PA
CBHW031334010826
48972CB00012B/133